Cruel Education

N. DENNIS

Cruel Education

Ravenwood Academy #1

Copyright © 2022 Nicole Dennis

ISBN: 9798839777156

For everyone that just wants a little time to escape from reality.

Trigger Warnings

Knife play
Needles
Murder
Hostages
Sexually explicit scenes
Torture
Drugs
Death
Blood
Gun violence

Playlist

Can't Help Falling In Love – **Elvis Presley**

You Don't Own Me – **SAYGRACE**

Don't Blame Me – **Taylor Swift**

Gangsta – **Kehlani**

Believer – **Imagine Dragons**

Never Tear Us Apart – **INXS**

Sweet Dreams – **Emily Browning**

Dangerous Woman – **Ariana Grande**

Sucker For Pain – **Lil Wayne, Wiz Khalifa, Imagine Dragons, X Ambassadors, Logic and Ty Dolla $ign**

Poison – **Alice Cooper**

Play With Fire – **Sam Tinnesz, Yacht Money**

We belong Together – **Ritchie Valens**

Bad things – **Machine Gun Kelly, Camila Cabell**

ACKNOWLEDGMENTS

I have so many people to thank that I don't really know where to start. I have such a massive support network that I'm afraid I will miss some out.

I want to start off with thanking my husband. Not only has he helped me when I needed it, but he has been my biggest fan from the start. He was my rock through the whole process of writing and publishing this book. He dealt with my tears, fears and tantrums and over excited moments. So, thank you and I love you.

Next, I want to thank my children who have been supporting me from the first word. I want to thank them for getting excited with me and for also telling anyone that will listen that their mum is writing a book. It makes me so proud that they are proud of me. I love you three so much. I want to thank my little brother, Olly, for helping me with my front cover. He put up with me changing my mind every five minutes and had such patience (especially when I deleted it all and he had to help me get it back).

Thank you to my mum too. She believed in me when others didn't think I would do it. She has always believed in me throughout my life, and I can't express how much I appreciate her. I love you mum.

I want to thank my friends for putting up with me telling them all the details of what I have been doing and for just showing an interest. You really are special to me.

And to my beta readers. Without you I wouldn't have had the confidence to actually release this book. So thank you for all your feedback and lovely comments

.

Chapter 1

I was five years old when I first intentionally killed. Little Susie from across the street and I were playing in the garden. A large spider had crawled on to one of the dolls we were having a tea party with. Susie had screamed and I knocked it off then squished it.

My mum had come running out to check on us after hearing the high-pitched squeal. After explaining to her what had happened, she sat me down and told me that I should not have killed the spider. I should have let it crawl away as it was one of god's creatures and was more scared of us than we were of it.

It was a spider. There were thousands more, if not millions in our small garden. But that was my mum. Caring of all creatures in the world.

I was thirteen years old when I first unintentionally killed. Drew Chapman was the most popular boy at school. He was three years older than me and had a reputation. Not a bad reputation as such, but everyone knew who he was. Drew was the best football player on the school team, straight A student and always had a different girl on his arm each week. He was also my older brother's best friend.

1

On a night where my parents had gone to attend a fund raiser, Antonio and Drew had decided to have a few beers in the garage of our house. It wasn't long before I joined them. I was bored being on my own, shut away in my room. And Drew always had a way of enticing me in, convincing Antonio to let me have a drink too. Drew had had a few too many when he tried to kiss me. I had pushed him off but with the alcohol swimming about in his veins, he lost his footing and fell back on to the rake that hung on the wall. The prongs pierced through the back of his neck, and I watched, speechless, as he choked on his own blood and the life drained from his eyes.

I was fifteen years old when I intentionally killed three men.

And that was the reason I was standing at the bottom of the stone steps that led to the most prestigious boarding academy in England, with my suitcase sitting beside me. The term after my eighteenth birthday. The first term of the academic school year at Ravenwood Academy.

The old gothic manor was something picked straight out of a horror movie. Against the backdrop of the setting sun the house looked darker with spiralling towers, black stone and vines that were slowly decaying in the ever-changing English autumn weather.

I couldn't count the number of windows from where I was standing, there were too many to see. Each one was panelled, and some were stained a deep red. Although the academy was not meant to be, it felt like I was walking into a prison. A prison marked by death. It seemed fitting.

Jefferson came to stand beside me. "Ms. Russo. Your father asked me to tell you that he apologises for not being able to say goodbye in person, but he will see you over the Christmas period."

I smiled sadly at the aging man knowing my dad wouldn't have come with us even if he wasn't in a meeting. The meeting was probably a lie. A cover story to stay away once again.

He hadn't been anywhere with me since the day my mum and brother had died. Since the day I had killed those three men. Not because he blamed me but because he couldn't forgive himself for not being there. Every time he looked into my green eyes; he saw my mother staring back. A reminder that he had failed to protect us all.

Jefferson let out a deep, heavy sigh, and pulled the keys to the black Mercedes out of his pocket. "You have my number, Isabella." His Oxford accent was now less formal. The tone that he adorned for me when it was just the two of us. "You need anything, anything at all, and I will come back for you."

"Thank you." I smiled a little brighter but even his promise didn't help with the nausea in my stomach.

Rocking back on the heels of his feet, he took one last look up at the building. Without another word, he returned to his car and the engine roared to life. I watched as he drove down the gravel drive and back out through the black iron gates we had arrived through.

Taking in a controlled slow breath, I closed my eyes and let it back out. It was time to face the punishment for the crimes I had committed. It was time to pay off the debt I had unwillingly gained while trying to protect myself and my family.

The main hall of the house was quite large with several doors leading to different areas. Paintings hung on the walls, all encased in black frames that hung on the surprisingly light walls. At the far end was a small desk that looked like it could have been easily set up for the day with every intention to be removed again. Seated behind it, looking less than pleased to be there, was an elderly lady. I shouldn't assume her age but with the creases on her face and the silver of her hair, there was no mistaking that she was well into her seventies at least. Or had a very rough life.

I wheeled my suitcase across the grey flagstone floor. Each time it hit the cracks, a clacking sound echoed around the room, alerting the lady to my presence and making her look up over her thick rimmed glasses.

"Name?" She screeched across the room. Picking up the pace, I stopped in front of the desk. She tapped her pen against the table impatiently and repeated herself, her voice gravelly. "Name?"

"Isabella Sofia Russo." I answered quickly, glancing at the name tag pinned to her periwinkle knitted cardigan.

"You're late." Ms. Crawly reprimanded as she pulled the last file from the tray in front of her. Opening it up she began handing me each paper inside. "Your class schedule. You will do well to not be tardy when it comes to your lessons. Punishment in this academy may not be the type you are used to."

I didn't expect anything less. Not that I was used to punishment at all. I was a diligent student who tried hard despite the crimes against me.

"A list of extracurricular activities." Another paper was thrust into my hands. I glanced at the first activity. Archery. Normal enough.

"Breakfast, lunch, and dinner menu. We rotate every four weeks. If you have an allergy, you will do well to keep it to yourself. It will be used against you." I blinked twice at her, but she ignored my apparent shock. Although I was lucky enough to have no allergies, how did other students' cope?

"A list of rules, a map to your classes and finally a map to your dorm." Looking down at the final sheet of paper she had given me, I saw a small box circled in the Gabrielle wing of the manor. Each wing was named after a different angel. I wanted to laugh. A school like this should have nothing to do with angels.

Reaching inside a brown envelope, she pulled out a key and placed it on the desk. Nudging it with her pen and raising a brow, I grasped at the hint and picked it up. "Your uniform and all the books that you need are already in your room. Anything that you may need for the extracurricular activities are available in the shop. You will find the location to that on your map. Classes start on Monday at 8.30am sharp." Ms. Crawly went back to tapping her pen on the table and arched a very thinning brow, expecting me to ask questions that she clearly had no patience for.

"Thank you." I muttered and she went back to whatever she was doing before I had disturbed her.

It took all of twenty-six minutes to find my dorm and I couldn't help but notice on the way that there were no other students filling the halls. Although it was past dinner time according to the menu, it was still too early for everyone to be in bed. Especially on a Friday night.

I pushed open my door and was straight away greeted by a squeal of shock. A small, blond-haired person jumped off one of the two beds, clutching a pocketknife in one of her hands.

My face must have shown the sudden fear that I felt because she lowered the knife and chuckled gleefully. "You must be my roomie." Flipping the blade back into its casing, she chucked it onto the bed then skipped across the room. "I'm Madeline but everyone calls me Maddy."

Thrusting her hand into mine she pulled me further into the room then shut the door. Her grey eyes studied me for a while, waiting for me to introduce myself.

"Umm, Isabella." I tried to smile, and her face lit up as if by telling her my name we had just become best friends.

"Isabella." She repeated, seeing how it felt on her tongue. "Can I call you Bella. I bet everyone already calls you Bella. It's a very pretty name. Oh, but if you prefer, I'll stick to Isabella, but it just seems like such a mouthful. Bella just rolls off the tongue."

Her enthusiasm was infectious, and I couldn't help the genuine smile that stretched across my face at her rambling.

"Bella is fine."

"Oh good. I have a feeling that we're going to be good

friends. That's your bed over there. Unless you would prefer this one." She pointed at the bed I had seen her jump up from. There were a few extra cushions thrown across it and a pink teddy blanket. "I don't mind either way. I just chose this one because it was further from the window. After the stories my brother told me what they do to new meat, I didn't want to risk sleeping under it." Her face dropped and she looked back at me, concerned by her own words. "Not that you will be in danger sleeping there. I'm sure he was only trying to scare me. Do you have a brother? Does he play mean tricks on you too?"

"I did have a brother and yeah, he used to play tricks on me too." I smiled thinking back to the fond memories I had with him.

"Oh, did? I'm sorry. Me and my big mouth sometimes. I don't really have any girl friends. My family is very male orientated and female company is hard to come by with what they get up to."

"You're fine," I chuckled then moved closer to the vacant bed. Maddy sat on hers, crossing her legs and placing a cushion on her lap. "I didn't really know what kind of people to expect when I came here so talking to you has definitely been helpful."

She smiled broadly at me and for a second, I wondered if she could have been younger than the eighteen-year-old requirement to attend this school. Her features were very pixie like, yet her eyes seemed beyond her years. Like she had seen stuff that would make your nightmares seem like little fluffy dreams.

"Your books are all set up on the desk. Are you taking AP poisons? I saw the book and thought first years couldn't take advanced placement classes."

I heaved my suitcase on the bed then flicked through the many papers I had been given until I came across my schedule. AP Poisons. Mondays, Tuesdays and Fridays.

"Yeah, I guess I am." I shrugged, feigning indifference when inside I was dying. Along with AP Poisons I had combat training, weaponry, Psychology and AP Art of Killing. The five lessons that were non-compulsory, my dad had told me after he had signed the contract and the cheque for my tuition fee.

"Were you smart in school?" Maddy asked, rocking backwards and forwards. "Callum said that smart people didn't go to a school like this and that they went to normal boring schools like Cambridge university or even Oxford."

"I did get good grades but nothing to brag about." That was the first lie I told her. All the grades I received would have been brag worthy if my mum were still alive. She would have arranged a huge party to celebrate my graduation with our little family of four and friends. Instead, when I got my results through the post, dad scanned through them with a sad smile.

No matter how well I did, my grades would not have saved me from the fate of having to come to this school.

For the night I had killed those three men, was the same night my father had been given a choice. I would either spend years of my life in prison for murder or attend a school of likeminded students to become a trained killer. With those skills I could either rid the world of vermin or add to it.

Professor Williams, the headmaster of Ravenwood Academy, had arrived at our door the same time as the police. He looked at the lifeless bodies of my mum and brother with their gunshot wounds then to the three mutilated bodies of the men that had killed them. Each of the men had slashes across his face and body, making them all completely unrecognisable for anyone to identify without DNA testing.

His eyes were next on me, on my knees, in-between them all with my bloody hands resting on my lap. I didn't make a sound as he crouched down before me and asked if I had done it all. I just shook my head, refusing to look at him.

Dad arrived home moments later. The scene in front of

him must have been brutal. Seeing his beloved wife and son, cold and dead on what used to be white tiles, in pools of blood. Then to look over to the little fifteen-year-old girl who he had always known was a killer, since the day he helped cover up the accidental murder of Drew Chapman.

I had always been a daddy's girl, but he looked at me like I was broken. And maybe I was because I felt no remorse for what I had done. I intentionally killed those fuckers for taking my mum and brother from me. I wanted to hear their screams and feel their fear.

Professor Williams saw that in me too and that was why he had given dad the choice. I spend years in prison, or I become a student at his school for the gifted in this type of art as he so nicely put it. Dad agreed, signing my fate without even a moment's thought. Anything to keep his little girl out of prison. So then everything was covered up. Statements and evidence of my crimes went missing and everything was kept out of the papers. Dad moved us to a new house, closer to the city of London and we started fresh. Nothing was mentioned again, and I was expected to finish my studies until it was time for me to attend the school for killers.

"You must have done something well." Maddy giggled. "Did you kill someone before coming here?"

"You have to kill someone to get into the advanced classes?" I frowned and she sucked in her bottom lip while she thought of an answer.

"No but it's a bonus I suppose. Is your family in the mafia?"

I laughed at her joke but the seriousness in her eyes made my mouth snap shut. "No, I'm not part of a mafia."

"Oh good, I was going to say I hadn't seen you at the civil gatherings. I would have hated for you to be in one of the rival families." She laughed again.

"You're part of the mafia?" I asked, giving her a look that I could only hope wasn't insulting as I tried to make sense of the fact in my mind. She just nodded with a big, sweet grin. "Going to be honest, I always thought that the mafia was a glamorised fiction written in erotic books."

"Yeh, they do seem to portray us in a rather amusing light. They are good reads though."

"Oh definitely. I love reading a good mafia romance." Placing my schedule on the bedside table, I started pulling out clothes from my suitcase to put away. "I'm intrigued now though. The reason you were sent here was because you are in the mafia?"

"Yep. Women from our family don't come here apart from a couple in the past but I begged and begged my father until he finally agreed to let me."

"Why would you willingly come here?" It never occurred to me that some people would want to kill for a living.

"I didn't want to be seen as a weak girl that only serves her husband. That's what the women of the mafia men do." She shrugged then hopped up from her position and skipped across the room to where I was sectioning out my clothes. Picking up the pile of tops, she neatly placed them in my assigned drawers.

"Sounds dated." I smiled at her appreciatively.

"Oh definitely." She agreed, taking another pile from my hands. "But that is the way it has always been. All the younger boys from my family are here. Callum, my brother, he is second in line to become Boss."

"Oh my god, there's a Boss?"

"Yes, there's a Boss." Maddy giggled again. "Ooh, I like these shoes." Placing the black heels at the bottom of the wardrobe, she went on with talking and distracting me from the fact I was in a school of future murderers. "My cousins are here too. They all stick together and are quite…" She paused, thinking of a word to use. "They're not that nice sometimes."

"Let me guess. Typical bad boys of the school, that rule the halls and beat anyone that disrespects them?"

"Oh, you've met them?" Maddy joked, giving me an exaggerated surprised look.

We both laughed and I pulled out the uniform I was expected to wear from the wardrobe. The black, pleated skirt, white shirt and black blazer with a red trim, were all pressed and ready in a cellophane wrapping, protecting it from any dust. There were two other matching sets beside it.

"The socks you are expected to wear are already in your drawers and I'm pretty sure your necktie and combat uniform are in there somewhere too."

"Combat uniform?" I hung the garments back up and saw her pull out a tiny pair of gym leggings and matching sports bra. "We're expected to wear that while fighting?"

"Of course, wouldn't want to fight in our uniform. Although I did question once what if the situation arose that we would have to fight in a dress and Callum told me to shut the fuck up."

"Your brother sounds amazing." I rolled my eyes and grabbed the sports bra off her then shoved it back into the drawer.

"He has his moments." She shrugged then went back to her bed and reached for her own welcome papers that were on her bedside table. "We must do some extracurricular activities together. They expect us to do it during our free periods and in the evenings too." I glanced over my schedule. There were several free periods between the mandatory lessons. Two of which were the first lessons of the day, I made a mental note to not choose any activities for that time. "I was thinking maybe cheerleading. Or ballet. Ballet is quite good. And then there is student council, but I don't think I would want to be part of that. Callum said they were the first ones to be poisoned."

"Poisoned?" I looked up from my extracurricular sheet. "Why would they poison the student council?"

"The student council try to have control, and that isn't how things are run in this school." She replied, running her finger down the page. "What about cooking? That coincides with poison class though and we are already different levels at that."

"None of these activities sound particularly deadly?"

Archery,

Baseball,

Acrobatics.

They were just some of the others on the list.

"Anything can be deadly if you want it to be Isabella." She smiled sweetly. "So, how did you come to be in this school? You're not mafia. Military daughter?" I shook my head. "Crazed murderers' child?" Another shake of the head. "No? What did you do then?"

"I- I killed someone." Bowing my head in shame, I went back to reading the next paper. The rules.

1. Lights out at 10pm
2. No leaving the grounds
3. Boys and Girls stay in their own dorms
4. No sex
5. No drugs or alcohol
6. Respect authority
7. No killing other students
8. Survive

I didn't know what scared me more. That there was a written rule to not kill other students or that the last rule was to survive.

"If you've already killed someone then you have done more than half of the students starting this year. After all, it's what we are here for isn't it. To learn to be the best killers in the world." Maddy's warming smile would have made me feel a lot better if it was under different circumstances but right now it was too much. Everything was too much.

Still, I smiled back at her and made a promise that we would choose at least two activities to do together over the next few days.

"What's the time?" As she reached for her phone to check, I grabbed mine from the front zip of my suitcase. 8.30pm. I stared at the screen for a second. No missed calls, no texts. Nothing from my dad at all. "We better get going if we want to actually have some fun. Shall we change into something dressier, or will that be too much? Actually, stick to jeans. We don't want to be the only ones to go all out and then look the odd ones out."

I laughed at how she had started rummaging through her clothes, chucking tops on her bed. "Where are we meant to be?"

"At the graveyard." She replied, completely unfazed but my eyebrow arched in doubt.

"I don't think I want to spend my first night here in a graveyard."

"You have too, everyone is going to be there. Ooh this will look cute." Pulling out a 'my little pony' cropped tee, she stripped off her top and replaced it. "You look fine in what you're wearing anyway."

I glanced down at my ripped black jeans and my oversized hoody I had stolen from my boyfriend... Ex-boyfriend.

"Am I not over dressed for a get together with the rest of the school?" I smirked at my new friend.

"Maybe let your hair down." She giggled. I pulled at the red scrunchie that had been holding my dark chocolate waves back from my face and let them fall down my back. "Perfect, now let's go!"

Chapter 2

The graveyard was in fact what it was called. A graveyard. Headstones stood dotted around the small clearing in the woodlands that surrounded the Academy. Each one had the name of a student that had died while training, Maddy had explained when I questioned whose they were. Late professors were buried in the very few stone crypts. What had taken me by surprise was that the doors to these crypts were open, allowing students to come and go as they pleased.

Several small fires were lit, providing heat and light. The place had been used as some type of dumping ground too. Littered between the graves were unusable household items such as armchairs, and old fridge freezer and even a washing machine.

Bottles of drinks were being passed around and poured into red Solo cups. No one seemed to care what substance was in the nameless bottles, just that it got you drunk. How they could be so trusting when one of their lessons was clearly named poisons was beyond me, but no one seemed to be as wary as I was.

Low music was provided by a black Cadillac, parked on the dirt road that led further into the trees. I wasn't an expert with cars, but it looked expensive. Maddy led me over to the blonde boy leaning against the hood.

"Bella, this is my brother. Callum."

Callum looked like his sister, the same grey eyes that reflected the flames of the fire and the same high cheek bones. His tight white shirt made his milky skin look tanned and showed off the sculpted muscles in his arms. And I was sure there were just as much underneath. Even leaning against the car, I could tell he was a lot taller than my 5foot 4inch frame. He could have easily been six feet, maybe taller.

"Nice to meet you." I quickly said, catching myself before he caught my wandering eyes.

"Is it though. Is it nice to meet me?" He smirked, letting his own eyes drift up and down my body with no shame at all.

"Don't be an arse, Callum." Maddy scolded. "Where are the others?" Her gaze wandered around the small clearing and mine followed, although I had no clue who I was meant to be looking out for in the crowd of students.

"Felix is over there somewhere." He nodded towards the small group of about four girls and three boys, standing by one of the fires. "Archie and Tommy will be here soon."

Callum reached over the hood of his car for two red cups. He handed one to each of us then reached in his pocket for a small, silver hip flask. "My personal preference. None of that cheap shit that is being passed around."

I let him pour some into my cup and thanked him with a smile that he didn't return. Instead, he took a swig strait from the source, not taking his eyes off me.

"So, what's your story newbie. Whose family do you belong to?"

Before I could answer, Maddy did. "She doesn't belong to anyone, she's here because she killed someone. She got in all by herself." There was a tiny bit of pride to her voice that made my chest warm.

Callum raised a brow, "How?"

"How did I kill him or how did I get into this school?"

I asked, tilting my head to the side. I wasn't ready to share how I had killed the three men, but I would share how I killed Drew because his death was an accident.

"How did you kill him?" His eyes narrowed, as his smirk grew to a lopsided grin.

"When he tried to kiss me, I pushed him away, and he fell against the spikes of a rake."

"Interesting." He took another swig of his drink, and I mimicked his actions. The brown liquid burned the back of my throat, but I kept my poker face impassive. "So, you got into this school for an accidental murder." He gave me a cynical smile; he knew there was more to my story, yet he looked away at the rest of the people around us. "Well, it's still more than some of these pussies have done so good on ya."

"Bella's already in AP Poisons too." Maddy bragged and even though I appreciated that my new friend was already proud to show me off, I wished she would stop. I wasn't the type to brag. I liked to keep to myself. I attracted less trouble that way.

"Is that so," Callum's eyes were on me again with his brows raised. "Well, if we share the same lesson, I'll look forward to seeing your skills."

I felt the blush go to my cheeks as I looked away and I really hoped that he didn't notice.

Before anything else could be said, another lad came to stand beside him, leaning against the car too. He was slightly taller than Callum but just as muscular. The golden tones of his brown skin reflected the flames of the fire, making his sculpted muscles appear larger. His tight curls were kept short with the sides shaven, and he had a dark stubble over a strong jaw.

Taking the hip flask from Callum, he took a large mouthful.

"See anyone interesting?"

"Found the ones we need. Looks like we got a good haul of newbies this year." The newcomer shrugged then ran his eyes over me before settling on Maddy. "You alright Madz?"

"Felix, this is Bella. She's my new roommate and my new best friend." She smiled fondly at me, and I smiled back. I was fast becoming to love this girl.

"More fresh meat. I didn't see you at the assembly." Felix took another mouthful before passing the hip flask back to Callum.

"I was running a little late."

"Shame, you missed an excellent speech."

"The last three years have been the same one. You would have thought the old fuck would think of something new by now." Callum complained, topping up mine and Maddy's cups even though neither of us needed it. "Every year a repeat of the rules that no one listens to."

"No killing. No drugs or alcohol. No mixing dorms and no sex." Felix scoffed, "He knows no one follows them. Half these fucked up cunts have already done it all."

"Yeah but everyone listens to some of the rules, right?" Sex, drugs, alcohol, even staying out past 10pm, didn't bother me. Those rules were made to be broken like they would have been at any other school. But no killing other students. Surely that was a rule that everyone could agree on. "Everyone sticks to the not killing each other rule, right?"

Both Felix and Callum exchange a look, grinning wickedly at each other.

"Depends whose bad side you get on."

I felt the deep voice vibrate through every part of my body and turned to see two men standing feet behind me. The first looked past me and at Maddy. Tall and muscular like his friends with long golden-brown hair that was tied back into a messy bun. There was a scar down his left cheek but that didn't affect the attractiveness of him. But even his good looks didn't subtract from the violent gleam in his brown eyes. He wasn't the one who had answered my question though.

The one who had spoken was looking down at me with a harsh smirk tilting his lips. Although, the cruel, unforgiving stare showed no amusement whatsoever and I had to look down, away from the intensity of it. Hands in the pockets of his jeans, he screamed power.

"Archie, Tommy!" Maddy squealed beside me. "This is Isabella. Bella."

"Isabella." The one in front of me repeated, the same way Maddy had done when I first introduced myself. Without saying another word, he walked past me, opened the door to the car and switched the music off.

"The fuck, Tommy." Callum cursed, glaring at him.

"You want to listen to that shit, do it in your own car." He simply replied.

Callum huffed something under his breath about his car being back home but didn't argue anymore. Maddy chuckled to herself then knocked the drink in her hand back.

"Well now you have met my brother and cousins, let's go have some real fun."

I drained the liquid in my own cup and graced the four of them with a small wave then followed Maddy through the crowd.

After what seemed like hours of drinking and dancing around the many fires, Maddy and I finally collapsed onto an old, beaten sofa, giggling at people as they fell about each other. Most were half dressed, fondling the person in front as they danced to the music that was amplified from someone's phone.

"So, tell me. When you graduate from this hell hole, who is the first person you're going to kill?" Maddy asked, flinging the almost empty bottle of Jack Daniels around that she had smuggled out of her cousin's car at some point.

"Hmm." I had never thought about it. There wasn't

really anyone I had planned to kill. I just wanted to get through my three years and then forget about the whole experience. "The person who invented the crocs."

"Noo," She screamed out. "I love crocs."

"Oh Maddy. I don't think we can be friends anymore." I teased and she pouted her perfectly plump lips and batted her eyelashes.

"But I love you already." With that, she pounced into a cuddle, pushing me sideways into the hard body beside me that I hadn't noticed was there before.

"Careful newbie." Callum chuckled, pushing me back up off him. I pushed Maddy back too and adjusted myself so I wasn't almost sitting on his lap. Mumbling sorry, I shot her a death glare.

"Why are you here?" Maddy asked rudely.

"Am I not allowed to keep an eye on my little sister on her first night of playing with the big kids." She shot him an incredulous glare and he chuckled darkly again. "I'm waiting for certain targets to go to bed so we can begin our game."

"Game?" I asked, curiosity getting the better of me.

"My cousins and I like to have fun with some of the new students. We go for the ones that look like they will be the most fun to break. If they can't handle what we have to offer, then they aren't going to handle what being a student at this school means."

Someone laughed across from us, and I had to squint through my hazed eyes to make out who was sitting on the log stools. Archie and Felix.

"You don't actually hurt them though, do you?"

"We hurt everyone eventually." Archie let out an evil laugh, making me shudder at the thought of them physically tormenting students just to weed out the strong from the weak.

"What do you actually do to them?"

"Inquisitive little one, aren't you?" Callum smirked down at me before throwing his arm over the back of the sofa and making a grab for the bottle still being swung about by Maddy. "If we told you, we would have to kill you." And I believed him.

Tommy stalked over next. He didn't acknowledge anyone as he leant against a tree and sparked up his cigarette. Placing the lighter back in his pocket, that's where his hand stayed.

While he wasn't looking at me, I took the opportunity to really take in his appearance. Tommy was ridiculously handsome. His dark, wavy hair was longer on the top, falling over his forehead but he had swept to the side at some point. He had the same shape jaw as Felix, strong and chiselled but he had a five o'clock shadow rather than the thick stubble.

His dark blue eyes met mine and I quickly turned away. Something told me that he was dangerous and to keep staring into the eyes of the devil wasn't going to be in my best interests.

"So Maddy tells me your second in line to be the Mafia king or something like that?" I asked Callum, trying to distract myself. He let out a dry laugh and the other two on the logs did the same.

"The Boss, sweetheart." He corrected, taking his arm from the back of the sofa and swigging from the bottle he had taken from Maddy. "And we don't like being called the mafia either. Too much taboo around that name. We prefer firm."

He tipped the bottle towards the boys in front of him and they did the same. Saluting their little family gang. All except Tommy who continued to puff away on his cigarette in silence.

"So how does it work for you to become first in line?"

"You wanting to work your way up in some other firm?" Callum smirked, raising a brow in amusement. I shrugged, not really knowing why I had asked. Curiosity or just trying to make conversation. "The boss man must die. Once he dies, I go to first in line."

"Oh, so who is first right now? Your father?"

He let out a low chuckle and his arm draped over the back of the sofa again. Leaning closer, he pointed with the arm around me. "He is."

Glancing at who he had indicated to, Tommy stared back. He removed the finished cigarette from his lips and flicked it to the ground, with a corrupt grin that made the rest of his handsome face appear sinful.

I swallowed against the urge to keep staring at him and took the bottle from Callum's hand for a reason to look away.

"So, Cal tells us that you're in AP Poisons. What other classes are you ahead in?" Felix asked, leaning forward on his elbows.

"Umm, AP Art of Killing, I think." I tried to think back to my schedule. That was the only other AP class I had.

"Interesting." Callum said again. He leaned across so his lips grazed my ear and kept his voice low so the others couldn't hear. "That accidental murder is sure getting you far, sweetheart."

I tried to pull my head away, but I felt the gentle tug of his finger twirling a lock of hair.

"AP Art of Killing." Archie repeated, running his thumb and finger over his jaw as if considering what I had said.

Felix shot him a look with a wide grin before turning back to me. "Well, you will be in our class for that then. Williams only teaches in the mornings and the other two days are for the thick shits."

"I resent that." Maddy pouted, throwing her finger up to him. "You lot have been here for two full years already. It's not my fault I came here not knowing anything."

"You don't count Madz. You weren't meant to be here in the first place." Felix stood, took the drink from my hands and sat back down.

"Again, I resent that." Maddy grumbled and crossed her arms in protest.

I let out a laugh and wrapped my arms around her

pulling her too my chest. "I'm glad you're here Maddy. You've made my first night here bearable."

She nuzzled against me, giggling and pushing me further against her brother. He didn't seem to mind as much this time and placed his hand on my leg. Maddy lifted her head, glowering at his movement. Climbing over me, she wedged her body between mine and Callum's.

"Nope," She wiggled her bum down and Callum sighed in aggravation. "You are not ruining my friendship with this one. Go find another girl to be a man whore with."

Felix and Archie barked out a laugh and even Tommy smiled before walking back through the trees.

"What extracurricular activities are you going to try out Madz" Felix asked, lighting a cigarette. He offered Archie one then tossed the pack to Callum.

"I'm not sure. Me and Bella are gunna go through them tomorrow. I was thinking cheerleading or ballet."

"Good classes." He nodded his approval. "Those skills can come in useful. What about you? Any skills?"

I shook my head staying silent. It wasn't entirely true. I was a good aim. In the three years that I had been waiting to come here, Jefferson had taught me certain things. I could shoot. Only a handgun and a rifle but I had excellent aim and very rarely missed my mark. I was relatively good with throwing knifes too. Slashing and stabbing didn't take much skill but that I could do. That was as far as it went though. Apart from being academically smart, I had no other skills.

He huffed in amusement, looking at me like I was easily breakable and weak.

Don't let them see your strengths until you are ready. That's what Jefferson had said. Then give them what they least expect.

"They like to think they are more skilled than everyone." Maddy whispered to me, rolling her eyes, but by the glare she received from her cousin, I was pretty sure he heard. "Felix likes to think he is the best with a gun. Archie with knifes."

"What about you?" I looked past her to Callum.

"I'm good with my hands sweetheart." He winked then went back to smoking. I raised my brows, pondering what he had said. I hadn't missed the inuendo, but I guessed he was talking about close combat fighting.

"We are all good at everything but some of us are just a little better at certain things." Felix smiled and it was the first smile I had seen that felt like there wasn't some kind of hidden meaning behind it.

"So if you all have a certain skill that you are better at, then what's Tommy's?"

"If you manage to find that out, it means you are already close to death." Archie grinned as his eyes darkened in a threat. I looked away quickly and he laughed at my unease.

"I've had enough of this, let's go dance." Maddy shot up and dragged me with her. Not saying goodbye to the others, I let her lead me to some others that were moving their bodies to the beat of the music. A few of them were sticking to their own groups, trying not to mix with anyone else.

"They are new students like you and me." Maddy shouted over the music as she noticed me looking. "They don't know anyone else yet, so they stick to their own kind." She nodded to a group of boys. "Military kids." Next, she pointed towards a group of designer looking kids that she looked down her nose at. "New money kids. They never survive here. Their parents just send them like it's a new trend, but Williams accepts them for the mullah." She rubbed her finger and thumb together and I nodded in understanding. "There are also the kids of complete psychos here. There's a bit of everyone here really."

I glanced around, searching for the psycho kids but couldn't really tell the difference. I suppose everyone was a psycho.

"If they survive the first night, they will start mixing with others to learn who they can trust, that's what Callum told me anyway. Forming alliances is what will see you through the next three years but choose wisely. You already have me though."

I nodded like I understood when really, I didn't. I had no interest in any of it. I was just happy with having her as my only friend. So I danced and drank, laughing with the girl who had given me no choice but to be her friend.

Chapter 3

A small creak sounded from beside me, making me stir awake. I didn't open my eyes, but I laid with the blanket pulled up to my chin and listened. It was an old building. There was bound to be noises throughout the night from the old floorboards. Probably the piping in the walls too. No other sound was heard, and I wiggled down further into my bed blaming my skittishness on being in a school for killers.

I couldn't get back to sleep though. My throat was scratchy, and my head was already starting to pound from all the alcohol I had consumed. I really shouldn't have continued drinking with Maddy's family.

Another noise.

I was certain it came from the foot of my bed. Maddy. It had to be Maddy getting up for a drink or something.

Another creak.

My eyes shot open.

"Maddy?" I whispered, squinting into the darkness as my eyes tried to adjust to it. But I didn't dare move.

No reply. "Maddy?"

A cloth was thrust over my mouth and muffled out the scream that wanted to escape. I breathed in the sweet, chemically smelling liquid that the cloth was saturated in. The same person that was holding the cloth to me, dragged me up into their arms. I tried to kick out, but my legs were already starting to feel weak against his strong grip. Not one sound was being made as I struggled against him, but my weak efforts were futile against the hand across my mouth. The man lifted me in his arms with ease as he took the cloth away. My body sagged into him, not putting up the fight I wanted it to. My vision blurred the more I tried to focus on who was holding me. All I could see was the outline of my kidnapper.

My first night here and I was being taken. But as terrified as I was, I couldn't find the strength to get free.

"Please, don't."

A whimper was all I could muster as my eyes fluttered closed again and I fell into a deep unconscious state.

My head was pounding when I came to. Like someone was repeatedly whacking a blunt object directly over my temple. Even lifting it was extremely painful. I tried to swallow but my throat was too dry. I couldn't make any saliva. There was something between my teeth. My tongue ran along the fine silk that was tied through my parted lips. The placement was perfect to muffle my speech and screams and I bit down on the fabric in frustration.

I leant forward in the seat that I had been placed in. I couldn't move. My hands were bound behind me and by the feel of the pinch as I moved them, it was by duct tape.

Finally, I dared to open my eyes. I was in a small room. There was little light, only from the moon that seeped in through the windows. I could just make out the layout before me. A sofa, two chairs, small table and log burner was one side, the other was a small kitchenette. There were doors leading off to other rooms but the one I had my eyes fixed on was the door in front of me. The exit. I hoped.

Muffled sounds came from beside me and my head whipped round to find the source. Cursing under my breath as the sudden movement caused the pain in my head to throb, I saw the bobbing head of a boy. I had seen him earlier that evening, standing with the rest of the boys that came from military backgrounds. He was gagged too and just coming round.

Whimpering came from my other side and there sat a blonde-haired girl in the exact same situation. Once again, I had seen her before. She had been with the rest of the posh bunch that came from new money, as Maddy had said.

This was fucked up.

I was aware of my whole body trembling. Fear was consuming every part of me as memories of the night my mum and brother had died flashed in front of my eyes. Them both tied to the kitchen chairs of our family home. My mum begging for them not to hurt her children. Silencing her with one shot to the head. Then my brother's promise to kill every one of them. And everything that happened after.

I had escaped from the duct tape bindings then, and I would do it again now.

I blinked back tears and took in a deep breath, willing for my fingers to stop shaking enough to feel around the back of the chair. Wooden. Meaning no screws like the chairs back home. But there might be a nail.

Running my fingers across the smooth surface, I let out a breath at the touch of the cold metal biting into my skin. It was already slightly sticking out of the wood, and I silently praised the craftsman's shoddy work. This was a happy coincidence for me and a severe lack of attention to detail from my kidnappers.

Both other captives were thrashing about, trying to free themselves from their bindings. Muffled screams were coming from them both, both begging to be released, that they were sorry for whatever they had done. The girl even went on to say something like she will give away all her father's secrets if they let her go. Although I could have been mistaken. It was hard to tell with the gag and her crying.

I closed my eyes, trying to concentrate on wriggling the nail free. It was stuck in there good but with each jiggle there was a little more give. The sharp head cut into the tips of my fingers as I squeezed, pulling harder.

A crash rang through my ears from the left and I quickly turned to see the boy on the floor surrounded by splintered wood. I had to give it to him, he had used his head. By jumping up and using his full body weight to smash the chair, he had freed himself. It was just a shame about the racket he had caused.

My heart banged painfully against my ribs as the door in front of me swung open. A flashlight shone straight to the boy on the floor, followed by two shadows of our kidnappers. They were moving to keep out of the way of the light so we couldn't see their identity but the third that was now by the door made the mistake that cost him my fear.

"He said she's last,"

I knew the voice, but I couldn't place which one of the four boys it belonged to. Callum, Felix, Archie or Tommy. The torch shone in my face, and I blinked away from the brightness. Anger fuelled the heat rushing through my body while I glared at the silhouette of one of the bastards in front of me. If I didn't have the gag in my mouth, I would have spat in his face.

He gave a low chuckle as he followed the two others, dragging the kicking and screaming boy out. The door slammed shut behind them and I breathed again.

"Oh gog- Oh gog." The girl cried out, thrashing about on her seat once more.

They wouldn't hurt him. They wouldn't hurt any of us. It was a scare tactic. Like they had said earlier. This was a game, and they were seeing what we were made off.

A blood curdling scream filled the darkness and it felt

as though my heart dropped through my stomach in fear of what I had just heard. My eyes squeezed shut, wanting to shut out the cries of pain and torture. But nothing could block out that sound.

Archie had said they hurt everyone eventually, but it never occurred to me they were being serious. The severity of the situation I was in began to sink in. I was in a school that taught kids to kill. No one abided by the rules and at this moment it was about survival because it didn't matter who you were. Rich, military or friend of the enemy. In this school, anyone was a target and a threat.

This wasn't a game.

Digging my fingers around it, I pulled at the nail again, ignoring the burning sensation of my own nails being slowly ripped from the beds. Pain was a part of survival and if ruined nails were a part of what needed to be done to escape then I was willing to pay that price.

The iron nail finally slipped free from the hole and without wasting anymore time, I started running the sharp point up and down the duct tape.

"Ey oing oo ill us." The girl sobbed beside me, and I refrained from rolling my eyes. I had no time to reassure her that once I was free, I would free her too. She wouldn't have been able to make sense of what I would be trying to say anyway.

The nail ripped through the tape, slicing it to near the edge. The screaming stopped and I froze before I could tear it apart completely. Was he dead? Had they actually killed him? I held my breath, trying to calm the thumping of my pulse in my ear and listened for any sign of life. Nothing. I couldn't hear anything but the faint sobs of the girl beside me and the footsteps of boots hitting wood outside.

The door opened and once again, three shadows stalked into the small room, flashlights glaring over to us.

I glanced at the frightened girl beside me. The black tear tracks down her face made me wonder if she was grabbed straight from the graveyard or if she had just not bothered to remove her makeup before bed.

None of the boys said anything this time round. Two headed straight for the girl and sliced the binding around her wrists, then grabbed her from the chair and out of the door.

Once it slammed shut again, I made quick work of the rest of the tape. Tearing my hands apart, I allowed myself a breath of triumph then stood up only to fall forward. Cursing, I looked at the loose ropes tied around my ankles and to the legs of the chair.

The screams started. High pitched shrieks of terror that made me wince. I could save her. I had killed three men with one knife. I could save her if I had a weapon.

With shaking hands, I freed myself from the knots and ran to the kitchenette. The drawers rattled as I rapidly opened them, searching for any type of weapon to use against the four psychos. The screams thankfully drowned out the sounds of my search.

Opening the last drawer, I found what I needed. An array of kitchen knives. Plucking the chef's knife from the mix, I ran across the room for the door. It was too late though; the screaming had stopped, and the footsteps had started.

Running to the chair, I sat back down with my hands behind my back, hiding the knife from view. The gag remained in place, and everything was as it was when they had last left me alone.

The door opened but instead of three shadows walking in, there were four. I had all four of the cousins in the room with me. There weren't any flashlights this time, so I just glared at them in the darkness, not knowing who was who.

"I'm disappointed. I really thought she would put up a fight." Felix. That one was Felix. Though with the pounding in my head, I couldn't concentrate on what shadow the voice had come from.

"Or at least cry. I like it when they cry." Archie. "I like tasting the fear as it runs down their cheeks." The sick fuck.

I wanted to cry. I wanted to cry and scream at all of them, but I wasn't going to break. They didn't deserve that satisfaction. Plus I had my best chance to escape hidden behind my back and even if I couldn't beat them, I was going to cause as much damage as I could before they killed me.

Because I had come to terms with it now. They had killed the other two and I was next. I wasn't sure why they had chosen me. Not after spending the night laughing and joking with me and Maddy. How was Maddy going to feel about this. My heart clenched for the sadness that she might feel. But then again, we had only known each other for a few hours. She would probably get over the loss then never introduce her friends to her brother and cousins again.

I weighed up my chances once more, my eyes darting around the room. I had killed three men because I knew my surroundings. I knew where to hide and reappear, using my home to my advantage. Here, I didn't know anything. I could run into another room and potentially trap myself. I could run outside and not have a clue where I was or where to go.

There was also the fact that I would be fighting against four men who towered over me and had been training for two years to be the world's best killers. The men I had killed could have been trained for all I knew but I was certain they weren't as skilled as the ones staring back at me.

I wouldn't go down without fighting though. I would give Felix his wish and kick, slash, bite and scream until the very end.

"For someone who only accidently killed a boy, she seems calmer than most." That was Callum. His voice was nearly as smooth as Tommy's but not deep enough. There was a hint of amusement behind it too, like he never believed that was all I had done. "Who tied her feet?"

Shit!

The ropes lay on the floor, forgotten.

"Looks like she has tried a little." Felix chuckled. One

of the shadows stalked forward and I saw the blade in his hand reflect the moonlight from the window behind him. Before he could touch me, I swung my own knife round, slicing across his outstretched arm.

"Ahh fuck."

He backed away, but the one beside him advanced, taking his place. I stood up, bracing myself for another attack but the sound of the chair being flung across the room distracted me. Someone grabbed me from behind, squeezing my forearms to my sides. His fingers dug into my pressure points, making my hands spasm so the knife dropped to the floor with a clang. I kicked back, hitting his shin. With my bare feet, it probably felt like a fly had landed there and he let out a low chuckle in my ear. Callum. One of the others grabbed at my legs but I kicked out again, making sure he couldn't get the grip he needed. The gag slipped from my mouth in the struggle, and I took the chance to yell obscenities.

"Cunts! Fucking Cunts! Murdering Pricks!"

"Such a dirty mouth." Cullum hummed, holding me against him tight. Biting back my tongue, I refused to give him the satisfaction of more words. Instead, I used all my weight and kicked myself back off the floor, making the top of my head collide with his jaw.

Grunting in shocked pain, Callum dropped me, and I fell to my knees. Scrambling for the knife, my fingers grabbed the handle. One of them made to grab me again and I took the opportunity I needed. Stabbing the knife into his leg, he fell back roaring in pain. I couldn't tell who it was that I just struck but I grinned, happy I had hurt three out of the four already. Even if the first two weren't as bad.

Leaping on to his body, I brought the knife up over my head in the most sacrificial way I could, ready to plunge down into his chest. I just wished that my eyes weren't blurry with rage, and it wasn't so dark so I could see the light of life drain from his eyes as I got revenge for what they had planned to do to me.

"Fuck, she's gone feral."

A body slammed into mine, knocking me off my target and the knife slid across the floor to under the sofa. Swearing, I started to rise slowly, glaring at my attackers. None made any attempt to come at me again. It was like they were all contemplating what to do with me. This wasn't a part their plan. They hadn't expected me to fight back.

But without that knife, I was defenceless. There was only one other option and that was to run out of the door that they had left open. The only issue with that, was the man standing in front of it. With his hands in his pockets, I could sense the condescending smirk on his lips. Tommy.

He saw me looking, he knew what I wanted to do. He also knew that I now had no weapon to fight against him if he tried to stop me. But he stepped to the side, leaving the path clear.

I didn't hesitate. I ran from the room I had been trapped in, straight onto a raised porch. Without stopping, I ran down the wooden steps and was hit by the chilly, early autumn air.

I was in the forest; the only light was the tiniest glow of dawn peaking between the tree branches. There was no telling what way to run. The obvious way would be down the dirt road that I assumed was the way we had got here. But then they would just follow and possibly bring me back if they didn't just kill me there and then.

I ran round the side of the small cabin and hid between two cars. Tommy's car and a black Range Rover. Voices could be heard from the doorway, and I threw my hand over my mouth to stop the sound of my heavy panting coming out as my heart raced in anticipation of being caught.

"We need to go after her." Callum spoke.

"No, there is nowhere for her to run. See if she can survive on her own out there." Felix replied. Prick. Leaning against the car, I closed my eyes to concentrate on their movements, wondering if they would come round the corner to check for me or just assume that I had headed straight for the trees.

"You shouldn't have let her just run out Tommy." Callum huffed and I was betting there was a glare that went with that tone.

"You didn't even help." Archie groaned in pain, and I wondered if it was him that I had stabbed in the leg.

"You all seemed to be fucking up just fine on your own." There he was. Tommys deep voice sounded, and I shivered at the sheer darkness of it.

"The girl is running around the trees, half naked and covered in my blood. What's your plan now?" Archie demanded and I looked down at my small grey shorts and white tank top. Both were smeared with his blood, possibly the one who's arm I had slashed too, and more was wiped across my thigh. I dreaded to think what a stranger would think if they came across me.

"There is nothing for ten miles. If she makes it back to Ravenwood still alive, I will be shocked." With that, Tommy must have gone back inside because there were a few mumbles under the boys' breaths then the door shut.

Ten miles? Ten miles of nothing but trees. He was right, I wouldn't make it back to the school alive. I wouldn't even know what direction to head in.

Sliding up the door of the Range Rover, I peered through the window but could see nothing on the driver's side that I needed. Part of me had hoped the keys had been left in the ignition but they weren't that stupid. Although, they had been stupid enough to think I wouldn't fight back.

I tested the handle without really thinking of a plan. The door opened and my breath caught in my throat. Sliding into the seat, I looked across, through the window on the other side. I could see the boys through the gap in the curtains of the cabin window. They were passing back and forth, probably cleaning the mess we had created.

Looking away again, I saw what I needed on the passenger seat. The keys. I didn't have a licence; I had failed the three tests I had taken. But I did know how to drive.

Turning the key, the engine roared. That was sure to grab the boy's attention.

Three ran around the corner, Archie limping and I smiled to myself. Callum ran straight to my door, but I locked it before he could reach for the handle. Banging on the window, he yelled at me to get out.

"What? I can't hear you?" I frowned, pointing to ear then holding my hand up in mock confusion. His face creased in anger, and he pulled at the handle again. Felix came to stand in front of the car, pulling a Glock from the back of his jeans and aimed it at my face.

I could taste the fear at the back of my throat but swallowed it down as I revved the engine.

"Get out now." I couldn't hear the words but, in my mind, I could hear Felix's voice loud and clear. His eyes were alight with fury, and I glanced down at the slash on his arm. My face split into a wicked smile, knowing that I did that.

He fired the gun, and my head flew down as the bullet came through the front screen then embedded into the head rest behind me.

"The fuck you doing, shooting at my car?" Archie roared from the other side. Callum had stopped trying to rip the door open and had stepped away. I sat back up straight looking at the small hole in the screen then over to Felix who surprisingly looked shocked at what had just happened.

"I thought you had bullet proof glass." He yelled back, shaking his head in disbelief. "Shit, Bella, I'm sorry." Holding up the gun, he started to back away from the car.

My eyes narrowed as I zeroed in on him, baring my teeth like a rabid animal. That fucker was sorry. He was sorry. Not only had he kidnapped me, tied me up and planned to do God knows what else, he had just shot at me with perfect fucking aim. Sorry did not cut it. Revving the engine again, I lifted my foot of the brake and the car shot forward. Felix swore and leapt out of the way.

I glanced at the wing mirror. Callum was helping Felix

back up. Archie was staring between them and his car that was now leaving. Tommy was standing by the door, watching me leave, hands in his pockets as if he didn't give any shits over what had just happened with a mischievous smirk tipping up one side of his mouth.

Lowering the window, I did the only thing I could think off and stuck my hand out, giving them my middle finger.

Chapter 4

The car kept going, down the long winding country road and past all the trees. The same road that I had been down on my way to the school. Although I had no intentions on going back there. I was going to drive past them gates and keep going on for as long as the tank of fuel lasted.

I didn't care what the deal was to keep me out of prison. Or that I would be hunted every single day for the rest of my life until they found me. Anything was better than living in a building where anyone would try to kill you at any given time. Even people who you had been laughing with hours before.

They had won. They had weeded out the weak, because that is what I was for not going back. I was weak and I was fine with that. Better be weak and survive than strong and dead. One sounded more stupid than the other.

I passed the iron gates, not even giving the academy a second glance. I didn't belong in a place like that. I wasn't like them. I couldn't be like them. I couldn't purposely torture people without a good enough reason. I couldn't become the type of killer they all wanted me to be.

Stomping my foot on the brake, several miles later, the Range Rover came to an abrupt stop. I was like them. I was a killer like them and not even a couple of hours ago I had proved that I could do it. Because I would have done it. I would have killed Archie and I wanted to until one of them stopped me.

I cursed as I made a U-turn. My body went into auto pilot as my conflicting thoughts fought against each other. Two voices were arguing in my mind. One thinking of all the excuses to not go back and the other thinking of ways to get through the next few years. But one had clearly won because I found myself down the same gravel drive as the day before. Slowly coming to a stop outside the stone steps of the academy, I looked straight ahead at the steering wheel, not quite registering what I was actually doing.

My hands trembled as I gripped on to the leather, my knuckles turning white. My throat tightened as tears burned my eyes. I opened my mouth and screamed at nothing. Screaming and punching the wheel was the only thing I could do to release the pent-up frustration and anger from everything. Hot tears fell down my face, but I let them flow, screaming words that were incoherent to anyone who wasn't even about to listen.

My father told me that revenge would never help resolve hidden feelings but right now I disagreed with him. They were going to pay for what they did to me. Callum, Archie, Felix and Tommy were all going to pay.

Taking a deep breath to calm myself, I took the keys out of the ignition and chucked them back where I had found them. As I stepped out the car, I looked up at the large building. In the early morning light, it didn't look as sinister as it had the night before, but that didn't hide the fact that inside were four, pure evil spawns of Satan. One of which was grinning down at me from the above window.

I glared back at Callum, making his grin wider. That's it, you horrid fuck. I'm staying. You haven't got rid of me. Instead, you have just made me a challenge.

Ignoring every stare I got, I walked straight to my room with my head held high and a permanent look of 'speak to me and I will kill you' etched across my face. I was aware of what state I was in and if anyone wanted to know why, they had the sense to not ask.

Opening my door, I saw Maddy frantically tapping away on her phone while sitting on my bed. As soon as she saw me, she leapt up and crossed the room to wrap me in her arms.

"What happened?" She rushed out, holding me at arm's length. "I'm so sorry. I thought if they knew you were my roommate, my friend, that they wouldn't touch you. I've been trying to get hold of them all morning for answers, but no one is replying to my messages. There isn't even anything in the school chat or our chat group. Everything has gone silent." She took a deep breath, looking over my body. "What happened? Did they do this to you?" Her eyes focused on all the blood, looking for the wound that could have caused it all but when she could find none her grey panicked eyes met mine again. "Whose blood is that?"

I pushed past her, thankful for her concern but my whole body ached as the adrenaline faded and I was met with exhaustion. "How would you feel if I told you I had stabbed one of your family members?" I asked, taking out a clean top and pair of leggings from my drawers.

"Depends, are they dead?"

"No, not dead." I chuckled dryly as I turned back round.

"Depends on what one then." She ran a finger over her lips as she considered which one I could have injured. "If it was Tommy, you would be dead already. If it was Callum, he would be in here going mental. So it was one of the others. I'm fine with that." She shrugged at the end and sat down on her bed.

"It was Archie."

"Noo, you didn't." She laughed, "Well I'll applaud you for that. That's the first time he has ever been hurt by a target. Not the first time for being stabbed. They've all been stabbed at least once. Callum and Tommy have actually been shot before but that was an accident. Well not really an accident, they were playing Russian roulette and-"

"Maddy," I interrupted. "I have many questions about this Russian roulette game and a thousand other things, but right now I really want to get showered and wash Archies' blood off me."

"Oh sorry." She apologised and picked up her phone again. "See, I rabbit on when I'm nervous."

"And excited." I reminded her, smiling.

"And excited." She smiled back brightly, flashing me her teeth.

After letting the scolding water run over my body for near on an hour, burning away the sins from the night before, I stepped out the shower and changed into the clothes that I had prepared.

Maddy was on her phone still when I walked back into the bedroom after brushing my teeth. Her brows were pinched together as she stared at the little screen.

"You ok?" I asked, chucking the blood-stained clothes into the bin. There was no getting those stains out so there was no point in trying.

"You definitely made an impression last night."

"Oh god, what now?" I rolled my eyes, dreading to think what the boys had been messaging her.

"It's all over the student chat page."

"Chat page?"

"It's an encrypted site that was set up for the students at the school. No one knows who done it, but everyone uses it. We can book our extracurricular activities on there and there is also a chat page. You can also order stuff from there too, like weapons, clothes, anything really. The teachers know about it, but they don't bother monitoring it. They just let it flow how we like it too."

"Sounds interesting." My brows rose in curiosity as I reached for my phone. There was a text from Jefferson that I would reply to later but still nothing from my dad. "What's the website?"

"It's encrypted silly. Here, pass me your phone and I'll

sort it out." She held out her hand and I placed my phone into it.

By the time I had finished blow drying my hair and sticking it up in a messy high pony, she had finished.

"I've added my number too." She smiled sympathetically as she handed it back and I thanked her. "Now brace yourself for the recent chat."

She already had me on the page she wanted me to see, and my mouth dropped.

Tommy Kray
Isabella Russo has been claimed.

"Claimed?" I managed to whisper. The comments that followed made my stomach turn.

Courtney Jones
Who's Isabella?

Hayden Adams
Int she that hot first year who was with Callum's lil sis?

Simon Smith
The one that was covered in blood in the hall. That one.

Darren Biggs
#Hotasfuckkkkk

Chloe Thornton
Tommy claimed her though, Tommy actually claimed her
#WTF

Sandra Morgan
I heard she fucked all four of the Kray cousins last night
just to get in with them.

Penny Morgan

And the reason she was covered in blood is because she likes knife play and wanted to show everyone who she belonged too. #SLAG

Hayden Adams
Shame the Krays don't like to share #fuckyoubetter #Kinkybitch

Chloe Thornton
Eww #Kraywhore

Rik Dennis
Careful how you speak about the claimed. #Remembertherules

I couldn't read any more and locked my phone. My nostrils flared and my teeth ground together as I stared at the now black screen. Every part of me wanted to launch it at the wall but that wouldn't solve anything.

"What does claimed mean?" I asked Maddy and she swallowed before going to our mini fridge and taking out two bottles of water.

"Claimed means you are part of our group now. Not really part of the firm but Tommy has marked you as one of us. You're his." It was the first time I had heard such a wariness in her voice, and I knew that she didn't agree with what he had just done. "It's going to be hard to make friends now or even find a boyfriend actually."

The boyfriend bit I wasn't worried about. I didn't have time for that type of complication. And friends, I was fine with just Maddy. I had learnt that friends could come and go, lack of them wasn't an issue. What did bother me was the fact I was now branded as someone's property, not just one someone but four someone's. And those certain someone's had made my first night here hell.

"I'm going to kill him." I snarled at the blank screen.

"It'll die down soon." Maddy tried to reassure me,

offering me a bottle of water but I waved it off. "It's because Tommy claimed you. Tommy doesn't claim anyone, especially a girl, so you must have done something spectacular to impress him."

"Who is usually claimed?"

"Boys who have impressed them all. They all discuss who they think is best suited for certain jobs and then one of the others claim them. It's seen as an honour. "

My head snapped up to glare at her and she cowered back a little.

"You obviously won't see it that way because of what happened last night." She quickly added. "Most just do little run around jobs like drug runs and that sort of shit."

I was not about to become a drug mule.

"What's his room number?"

"Bella, I don't think that is a good idea." She chewed her bottom lip nervously, but I wasn't about to back down.

"You either tell me or I'll knock on every single door in the boys wing until I find him." I shrugged, pulling on my trainers. I wasn't sure what I was going to say once I found him, but I was too livid to let it lie.

"48." She mumbled. I gave her a brief nod and headed for the door.

It didn't take long to find the room I needed but it did take a long time to figure out what I was going to say. I stood on the wrong side of the door for what seem like forever before I built up enough courage to knock.

As I had walked here, nerves took over the anger and the closer I got, the sicker I felt in the pit of my stomach. I was about to walk willingly into the lions den.

I knocked lightly and he didn't answer so I knocked again a little harder. Still no answer.

The door up the hall opened and a girl with curly post box red hair walked out, giggling as a boy grabbed her hips. I shuffled on the spot, suddenly feeling awkward that I was standing here.

"Isn't that the girl that Tommy claimed." I heard the girl

sneer.

"Probably, looks like her but less bloody." The boy replied, yet his voice was muffled as his face buried into her neck.

"Can't believe she's slutty enough to go to his room at this time of day."

"Say's the slag now coming out of a boy's room." The words slipped out before I could stop them, and I had to catch myself before I recoiled from the death glare she threw me.

"You may be protected by the Krays at the moment darling, but they will drop you as soon as they get bored."

I held my chin up, refusing to back away. "Do you know why I had blood on me this morning?" She crossed her arms and raised her perfectly pruned but oddly matched to her hair, brows. "I stabbed one of them, so I don't think it is me that needs protecting, do you, darling?"

The door opened beside me and without looking, I pushed the person back inside and shut the door behind me before the red head could say anything else.

After scanning the room for anyone else, I glared at the topless boy in front of me.

Holy shit, it was like he had been sculpted by a god. His arms had been covered by his jacket the night before but now I could see everything. Water droplets glistened off his toned, muscular arms and chest and my eyes followed as they ran down to his stomach, past the deep V and into the white fluffy towel that was wrapped around his hips. Clearly having just got out the shower, water continued to drip from his dark hair onto his body.

Tattoos worked their way up his right arm and down the same side on his chest. Each piece of art was dark and shaded, just like his soul. There were a couple more on his left arm but room for more that he probably had planned. A shaded skull against a rose with a snake coming out its mouth was drawn on the left side over his ribs. The light reflecting off the water made the tattoo's come to life. I could have stared at them for hours if the owner wasn't such a dick.

I quickly looked at his face, hoping he hadn't noticed that I was staring at every other part of him. I hadn't noticed in the dark just how blue his eyes really were. The midnight colour was ringed with black, making them appear cold and unyielding.

"Are you here for a reason?" He drawled, arching a brow.

"Err, yes." Fumbling to unlock the screen on my phone, I brought up the post on the chat page and thrust it in his face. "Take it back."

"Take what back?" He moved his head away, trying to see what was on the screen.

"This claimed shit. Retract it." I thrust the phone forward again and his mouth tipped up at the side.

"Can't do that." Turning his back to me, I was blessed with another tattoo. A dragon. His wings spread across from one shoulder blade to the other while the body went halfway down his back. Why does someone who looks that fucking good always have to be a cunt?

He disappeared into the bathroom, and I took the opportunity to glance round the room. It was the same size as mine and Maddy's and the same layout with the ensuite off to the left. But there was only one bed. Tommy didn't share with anyone, but something told me that no one would want to volunteer anyway.

Tommy walked back out, now with grey joggers on but still no top. "You're still here." He sighed, bored.

"I'm waiting for you to put up a post to say there was a mistake and I haven't been claimed." I pouted, crossing my arms and tapping my foot impatiently.

He picked up his phone and started typing away. He was doing it. He was actually doing the right thing and taking back the claim. Maybe there was hope for him yet.

His phone pinged and he let out an amused sound before tapping away again. My own phone pinged, and I looked at the screen. A text from a group chat.

Maddy
Sorry Bella, Tommy made me.

Ping after ping as message after message came through.

Callum
She looked pissed when she got out of Archies car

Felix
At least she brought it back in one piece, he will be pleased.

Maddy
You are all arseholes for putting her through that.

Callum
Her face when she nearly ran you over lmao

Tommy
You should see her face now.

Felix
Where is she??

Callum
Are you with her??

Felix
Just seen. She's in his room lmao!!

Maddy
WTF have you done Tommy! Bella don't look at the chat page.

I tapped off the group chat and back on to the school chat.

Sandra Morgan
OMG! The #Kraywhore has only gone to Tommy's room. Spouting that she stabbed one of them. The girl is delusional. Probably why they claimed her #Easyfuck

Felix Kray
@SandraMorgan Only easy fuck was you love. Seem to remember every hole is a goal right bucket?

Maddy Kray
I'm only going to say this once. Isabella Russo may have been claimed by my cousin but that is only because she impressed him where the rest of you skanks couldn't. And she done it without opening her legs which is more than all of you can say. How many of you have been claimed even after having sex with all four of them? #sluts #remembertherules #shecankillyou

I let out a feral growl as I looked back up at his perfectly smug face. Something snapped inside of me like a little switch that flicked off my common sense. Dropping my phone to the floor, I launched myself at him. I would scratch his eyes out, bite his flesh until I made him bleed. Anything to hurt him in anyway.

But he was too quick, too strong. Grabbing hold of me, he spun around and flung me onto the bed like I was a ragdoll. Before I could get back up, he was on top of me, pinning both of my arms up beside my head. I thrashed about, screaming for him to get off but he remained where he was, glaring down at me with menacing eyes.

After a few minutes I stopped wasting what little energy I had. My chest rose and fell rapidly as my body tensed beneath him. His breathing matched my own after using some of his strength to subdue my attack.

"You fucking done?" That hint of a smirk made me want to start up again, but I refused to fall for the bait and continued to stare hard at him. "Do you want to know why I claimed you as one of ours?" He kept his voice low and slow, making sure I understood every single word. Again, I didn't answer. "It's because you did impress me. You were the only one not to cry. Even the boy shed some tears in the end." In the end? End being his death? "But you found a way out. You found a weapon and you fought back. Not only that but you came back. You could have taken Archie's car and kept going but you didn't. You came back here to prove to us that you weren't weak."

He read me like a book. His smirk disappeared. His jaw was set, and he leaned down to speak in my ear like it wasn't enough to just say it from the position he was in. I jerked my head to the side, but I could still feel his warm breath on my neck. "That makes you a threat. And I don't like threats."

A minor chill ran through the entirety of my body, and I prayed that he didn't feel the shudder. Sitting back up on me, I glared up at him again. His one-sided smirk was back, and it now occurred to me how truly wicked it was.

"Now we have claimed you, you won't be able to get close to anyone else. You are now ours and we are all you are going to have."

Carefully, he released my arms and climbed back off. I remained laying there for a few more seconds, still breathing in and out rapidly as my anger and now fear surged through my body. He moved away and I slowly stood up, testing the strength in my legs that I was almost certain had turned to jelly.

I picked up my phone from the floor, refusing to look at him and stepped across the room. Pausing at the door, I fisted my hands down at my sides. He wasn't going to win. And I sure as hell wasn't going to let him get the last say either. Turning back, I watched him slip on a plain black tee, covering the art that I probably did secretly admire.

"Tommy?" He turned to regard me. "When I first came here, I didn't come to make friends or enemies. I came to do my three years then leave. Having your cousin as my roommate was a bonus but I still had no interest in getting to know her family. I wouldn't have been a threat to you."

My words were so soft and innocent that he just lowered his gaze.

"You have now made me a threat, whether I am in your little group or not."

He looked at me again, eyes gleaming at the challenge I had just made to him. I wasn't stupid enough to go against the mafia, but I wasn't about to sit or roll over like a good doggy either. He wanted me to be seen as claimed by everyone. Fine. But I wasn't going to make it easy for him.

Turning on my heel, I opened the door and walked out without closing it.

"Archie's leg is fine by the way." Tommy called after me. I didn't need to turn back to know he was standing in the hall too; I could already feel his eyes burning into my back.

"I didn't ask."

A low deep chuckle followed me, making the fine hairs on the back of my neck stand up. I wouldn't admit it to him, but he had a certain effect over me already and it didn't feel at all good.

Chapter 5

I sat at my assigned seat in the classroom full of twenty-year-olds, on the Monday morning. I was the only first year that had been given a place in AP Art of Killing and I was already resenting whoever's job it was to sort out placements.

After managing to avoid the Krays for the rest of the weekend, I was now stuck in a room with all four for the next hour. Callum had taken it upon himself to completely ignore the seating plan and sat beside me. Tommy was seated at the other desk next to me, flicking his pencil against the wood and impatiently glaring at the white board. Felix and Archie had thankfully stayed in their assigned seats.

Although I hated the four pricks, they sure looked good in their uniform. Black trousers, white shirt, black tie and the same black blazer with the red trim. If they weren't such arseholes, I might have thought them highly attractive.

I however, looked extremely uncomfortable in my uniform. The skirt wasn't as short as it looked on the hanger thankfully and came to halfway down my thighs. The shirt was fitted, along with the black knitted jumper I had decided to wear after waking with a chill. My necktie was suffocating but it did look cute. The tails were tucked into my jumper, out of the way. The blazer was shaped for a woman but was a little big with only my fingers poking out of the sleeves. But none of that was really the problem.

The problem was the shoes on my feet. The comfy, inviting, black pumps that I had bought to wear were, according to Maddy, social suicide, and she had insisted that I wear her wedged black heels instead. It was true that no other girl was wearing flats but right now I wished I had stuck to comfort over looks.

After approving my hair style, (I had let my loose waves fall naturally down my back, with a simple red silk headband.) and my subtle makeup, Maddy had let me leave the room while she enjoyed the relaxation of her first free period.

The door swung open behind me, but no one turned to see who had entered. I didn't dare look back either, the nerves of my first lesson finally kicking in.

"Put your books away and hands flat on the table." I recognised the voice before I saw his face. Professor Williams.

He hadn't changed one bit from when I had first seen him three years ago. He was in the same dark grey suit that he had worn the day he had turned up at my house. The top two buttons of his shirt were undone and no tie. His thick grey hair was swept to the side, a timeless style. Greying stubble shaded his strong jaw.

Taking off his suit jacket, he slung it over the back of his chair and rolled up the sleeves of his white shirt. Tattoos covered both arms and the fabric of the shirt stretched around his biceps. Daniel Craig. That was who he reminded me of.

The ice blue eyes scanned the room, taking in every student as they done what he had instructed then turned to pick up a long wooden ruler.

"Anderson." He bowed his head, studying the ruler in his hands but didn't turn to who he was speaking too.

"Yes sir?" The boy I assumed was Anderson replied. He was a couple of desks in front of Tommy.

"Can you please explain to me why I took the time to sit down and write out a seating plan for you to completely ignore it and choose your own seat?" Professor Williams voice was smooth and silky, sending unnerving shivers through my body.

"Umm, Callum Kray is in my seat sir."

Williams's eyes shot to Callum and then to Anderson. "So someone took something that was yours and you are going to let them." Anderson swallowed hard, looking down at his hands still splayed out in front of him. "Go get your seat back." Williams snarled.

Anderson looked up at the professor and when he glanced back at Callum, I saw unfiltered terror. The chair scraped across the stone flooring as he stood up and I quickly glanced at Callum to see his reaction.

Callum watched as Anderson moved across the room to stand in front of him. His face was impassive when he looked up at the young lad.

"You need to move out of my seat." There was a tremble to his voice and if he had said it any quieter, I wouldn't have heard him.

Callum looked down, hiding a mildly amused smile. He rose slowly from his seat, pushing himself up by his hands on the desk. "Can you repeat that. I didn't quite hear you."

I silently begged for him not to say it again. I felt like it wouldn't be worth whatever Callum had planned. My eyes widened in horror though as the boy swallowed and repeated himself, a little louder.

Callum's hand shot out, hitting Anderson in the throat. My hand flew over my mouth as the boy fell back, clutching his neck and gasping for air. No one else moved or tried to help him. He continued to make rasping noises and flailed about on the floor like a fish out of water.

"Anderson, if you are going to continue making them pathetic sounds, you can remove yourself from my classroom." Williams sighed in a bored tone.

He didn't need telling again. Scrambling to his feet, he ran from the room. Callum slid back down into his seat beside me, not saying a word and set his hands back down on the desk. I glanced at every face I could see. No one was fazed by what had just happened. I couldn't see Felix, but Archie was grinning like a psycho. Tommy looked positively bored and when I turned back to Callum, it was like nothing had happened.

"Question of the day. You have a four-body count in the room and two police officers enter. What do you have now?" Williams asked, continuing with his lesson. "Dennis?" He pointed the end of the ruler at a boy with curly, black hair.

"A sore arse hole."

Whack!

The ruler came down across his knuckles. Each one split open from the force, spraying the students in near vicinity with blood.

No one flinched but I did, much to Callum's amusement as his shoulders bounced with silent laughter beside me. His answer had been rude and that was the punishment. Common sense had already told me that this wasn't the kind of school you could joke with the teachers but after being here for two years, it seemed the Dennis boy hadn't learnt that yet.

Walking up between the desks, Williams pointed the ruler at a small, ginger girl. "Thornton"

"About five seconds to come up with an alibi."

Whack!

I flinched again as the ruler came down and blood sprayed my cheek as he whipped it back through the air. Tommy tsked in disgust as some landed on his shirt.

Williams continued down the walkway and back again, coming to a halt beside me. "Russo?" It was like he enjoyed the way my name sounded on his tongue; I could hear the ecstasy in his voice. Every set of eyes turned to gaze at me as they waited for my answer. Waiting for me to get it wrong. My shirt all of a sudden felt constricting as my chest rose and fell rapidly under it. The palms of my hands started to feel clammy against the wooden desk.

"We don't have forever, Russo."

"Six dead bodies."

The ruler came down and my body tensed as my eyes closed, waiting for the pain. But nothing came. All I had felt was the rush of air. I dared to peek at what had happened and saw the wooden ruler centimetres from my quivering fingers.

"Next time, don't take so long to answer. We have an hour, and the rest of the class doesn't want to wait on you." Walking back to the front of the class, Williams set the blood smeared ruler on his desk then turned back round to lean against it. "Russo was the one to get it right. Why would there be six bodies now?"

A few hands rose in the air, but I noticed the ones that had been hit remained on the tables.

Williams pointed to a boy with glasses and freckles. "Leave no witnesses sir."

"Leave no witnesses." He repeated, grinning at me. "And how would we kill them two witnesses, Russo?"

My knee started bouncing under the table as nausea churned my stomach. Chewing on my bottom lip, my eyes pleaded with him to ask anyone else, but Williams' hard gaze remained emotionless and on me.

"Today, Isabella." He drawled out my name, picking up the book beside him and flicking through the pages.

Something warm landed on my bare thigh, just above the ridiculous long socks the girls were required to wear. I glanced down to see Callum's hand pressing gently but firmly down, forcing my leg still. There was something weirdly comforting about it. Looking back up to him, his attention was still facing the front of the class, completely jaded.

Letting out a breath, I spoke. "Depends on what you

had around you sir. And depends on the situation. If you had used a gun to kill the four men, then you could easily shoot the officers on entry."

"And what if you used, say, a knife."

A knife like I had used on them three men and like I had used on Archie.

"Then you best hope you are quicker with the knife then what they are with whatever weapon they have."

He let out a low chuckle and placed the book back down. "Turn to page 47 of your handbooks. There you will find a list of torture methods. Get into teams and plan how you are going to use one of those methods on your victim. You have forty minutes."

Chairs scraped across the floor around me as everyone got into their groups. Being the only new one in the class, I wouldn't be welcomed with any of them, and I was fine with that. I went to stand, if only to move to the back of the room, out of the way, but Callum's hand stayed put. Archie and Felix pulled up a chair each in front of me while Tommy sat at the side.

"You've got to be kidding me." I exhaled, looking down at my clenched fists.

"Are you going to apologise for stabbing me?" Archie asked and I looked back up to the condescending smile on his face.

Giving him a sweet as honey smile, I gritted my teeth together. "Shame I didn't hit anything of importance."

His laugh was low and wicked as he leant back in his chair and ran his fingers through the strands of hair that had fallen from the messy bun, pushing them back from his face.

"Don't be like that sweetheart." Callum said from beside me and I glared at him. "We only wanted to see what you were capable of."

"What about the other two?" I hissed trying to keep my voice low, but I was surprised with the amount of venom that came spitting out. "What happened to them once you found out what they were capable of?"

"They're dead." Callum nodded proudly while Felix ran a finger across his throat, tilted his head to the side and let his tongue hang out. Archie roared with laughter, making the professor clear his throat in annoyance.

I stared blankly at him, blinking rapidly as I let what he said sink in. I knew at heart, they had killed them, but I didn't want to believe it. "If I didn't escape, would I now be dead?" I wasn't sure I wanted to know the answer.

"We never intended to kill you." Tommy was the one to answer while the others glanced at him. I twisted in my seat to face him. He was staring down at the book, tapping his pen against it.

"Then what were your intentions?" I seethed.

A crooked smirk played on his lips as his cold eyes flicked up to meet mine. But he didn't answer me.

"Our intentions were just to play with you. We were going to let you go after we scared you a little. You just kinda fucked up our plan a bit." Callum answered for him, relaxing his arm over the back of my chair.

"Oh, I am so sorry. Next time I will be more considerate." I snapped, picking up the book and turning to the page I had been told to.

The three boys continued talking amongst themselves with Tommy just sitting back, tapping his pen repeatedly against his book, deep in thought. The sound was grating on me. All I wanted to do was snatch it from his hand and stab him in the eye with it but instead I tuned them all out. I was done talking to them or even acknowledging them. Callum's arm remained where it was and occasionally, I would feel a gentle tug on my loose waves as he twisted them around his finger, bringing me back to reality. Other than that, they left me alone to my own thoughts.

"Times up." Williams clapped his hands together and I looked up from my book to see him leaning against his desk again. Shit, none of us had discussed any forms of torture at all. I wasn't even sure if the boys had been coming up with ideas while I wasn't listening.

"Russo." Why me? Why single me out. "What form of torture have you decided on using?"

"I- I don't know sir."

"You don't know?" His eyebrow raised as his fingers twitched towards the ruler.

"She's being shy sir." Callum piped up. "She was just telling us how she would go old school."

Felix grinned at me, joining in. "Yeh, what was you saying Bella? Rat torture?"

"Please elaborate and explain to the rest of the class what rat torture is, Russo?" Williams smiled at me wickedly. He knew I hadn't come up with any idea at all and I had no idea what rat torture was. My eyes darted between his and Felix's as I wondered how I was going to explain myself.

"She's still being shy sir." Callum chuckled.

"The victim is tied down. A small cage with an opening on one side would be strapped to their body." Tommy started, not bothering to look up. "It would be filled with rats and a heating element would be placed on the other end. Because the rodents would want to escape the heat, they would burrow through the victim's body. Resulting in a slow but extremely painful death."

"That's barbaric." I hissed under my breath.

"You came up with that all by yourself, did you?" Williams smirked but didn't wait for my answer before turning to another group to give theirs.

"Is that really a thing people do?" I whispered to Tommy and his lip twitched before he shrugged.

"Can you think of a better torture?"

"Sitting here with you morons has got to be on the list." I muttered and he actually laughed lightly with a genuine smile on his face, but it was gone again before I could really take it in.

Ripping a piece of paper out of his exercise book, he scribbled something down then slid it across the table towards me. I lifted it curiously.

8.30pm
Friday
Graveyard

Frowning at the note, I looked up at him. His hand rested on his chin as his finger ran over his bottom lip. There was a sparkle of mischievousness in his midnight blue eyes. Something different from the cold harshness I was usually met with.

I opened my mouth to question what the note meant but he moved one finger to his lips, telling me to be quiet then flicked it towards the Professor.

"Your assignment this week is to find someone who has wronged you and torture them. I don't really give a toss what method you use, just get it done." Williams eyes wondered to me. "And I want pictures of proof."

I felt the blood drain from my face. How was I meant to do that? I was a first year in a third-year class. Surely that wouldn't be assigned to Maddy's class.

"You have until next Monday to complete the assignment, or you have failed my class and this school."

Tommy tapped the note in my hand and without saying a word, he stood and walked out of the room. I stared after him, not sure what to make of any of this. Had he known what the assignment was going to be? What was going to happen on Friday? Shoving my books into my bag, I made to follow everyone else who had started to leave but Callum wrapped an arm around my shoulder.

"You're in AP Poisons with me and Archie. We'll walk you there."

"Err, I was meant to meet your sister."

"Then we will come there with you too." There was no point arguing as he led me from the room. I looked behind us to see if Archie was coming too. He was limping slightly and when I turned back round, I couldn't stop smiling at the fact that I had been the one to do that. Small victories.

Chapter 6

For the full half hour that I had between AP Art of Killing and AP Poisons, I had Callum and Archie up my arse. Even when Maddy had dragged me into the girls toilets to discuss my first lesson away from them, they waited outside.

"Do they do this to all the ones they claim?" I complained.

Maddy merely shrugged, padding some balm on her lips with her finger. "Told you, they don't invite girls to the group, it's mainly boys."

"It wasn't exactly an invite was it."

"They probably wanted you because if not, I would have been the only girl. Company for me." Tightening the scrunchy in her hair, she turned to face me. Even she knew what she said wasn't true. "But this, the following you and the teasing you, is their way of fucking with you. You can either retaliate or let them have their fun until they get bored."

"Or I end up dead?" I scoffed and she chuckled like I was joking while linking her arm with mine.

We walked back out of the bathroom. Archie was leaning against the wall, chatting to some girl while Callum was looking down at his phone.

"Ready?" I snapped at them both. The girl glared at me for interrupting her, but Archie pushed himself from his resting position and bent down to pick up his backpack, wincing at the pain in his leg.

"Are you gunna have an attitude all day?" Callum asked, slinging his arm around my shoulders but not taking his eyes of his phone.

"Depends, are you going to be near me all day." I smiled sweetly at him and Maddy stifled her laughter with her hand.

"Retaliate it is then." She muttered under her breath, and I shot her a smirk.

After saying our goodbyes and making a promise to meet for lunch, I walked into AP Posions. There didn't seem to be a seating plan for this class but once again, Callum sat beside me. Archie took a seat next to the red head I had seen coming out of that boy's room the other day. Thanks to the school chat page, I could put a name to the face. Sandra.

The teacher was already at the front of the class, making notes on the white board. She was wearing a white lab coat and her auburn hair was tied back into a simple pony. When she turned around, I was surprised by how young she was. And absolutely stunning. I had a feeling many of the boys here had a fantasy or two about her when alone.

Looking over the top of her thick, black glasses, she surveyed all her students. "Great, you're all here. Let's begin." Setting her marker down on the desk before her, she picked up a small pretty flower. "Can anyone tell me what this is?"

I knew what it was, but I wasn't about to give myself up for unwanted attention, so my hand remained down on my desk. Sandra had her hand raised, waving it in the air like she thought she couldn't be seen.

"Miss Morgan." The teacher smiled, welcoming the answer.

"Sorry Dr Bane but I was just wondering why a first

year was in another AP class. I know she is fucking the Krays but surely that shouldn't give her special treatment."

The pure audacity this girl had. I turned in my seat to gawp at her, but she just smiled back across at me smugly. I felt my cheeks burn as every other set of eyes in the room fixed onto me.

"Miss Russo," I turned back to the teacher, Dr Bane, nervously as she placed the flower back down on the desk and stepped towards me. The only comfort I had was the warm smile on her face. "Name me two household chemicals that you could use to make chloroform."

"Umm," I hesitated for a second and glanced around the room. Everyone was still staring at me. "Bleach and Acetone."

"Good," She smiled. "Now can you tell me a poison that is odourless, tasteless and colourless?"

"Thallium." I answered straight away. Dr Bane nodded and turned her attention to Sandra.

"Miss Morgan, can you please tell me what household items a certain poison used to be found in before it was banned."

"Err" Sandra's face nearly went as red as her hair as she looked down at her hands.

"No? How disappointing. Can you tell me Miss Russo?"

"Rat poison and Ant poison, Dr Bane."

Once again, she smiled warmly at me and gave me a small wink. "And that is why Miss Russo is in AP Poisons." Moving back to her desk, she picked up the flower again. "Now can anyone tell me what this flower is or will Miss Russo be answering questions for the whole class for the rest of our time here."

This time a few more hands rose in the air, not wanting to be outshone by a first year. I didn't raise my hand though; I had had enough attention.

"Oleander," Someone answered. "It can cause vomiting, erratic pulse, seizures and death. It's very bitter tasting though, so many people can taste it before consuming enough to cause death, but it can put you in a coma still."

"Correct, Miss Jones." Dr Bane smiled brightly and walked behind her desk. "Now, I want each of you to put your gloves on and come down here to collect a petal. Just one single petal, for we are going to create a single dose to put someone in a coma."

Everyone started moving to the front, but I stayed put and looked at Callum. "Are we really going to make that poison?"

"This is poisons class." He smirked, arching a brow.

"But everyone will try to use it on each other." Glancing around the room, none of the students strike me as having any morals. In fact, half of them seemed positively exhilarated at the thought of having a new deadly weapon at their disposal.

"Williams wouldn't give a shit, but Bane does make sure that all poisons that are made are handed in." He sighed as if explaining this to me was a burden. But I nodded and followed the rest of the students to the front of class.

After an hour of creating a potent poison and Sandra trying to kill me with her glare, Dr Bane worked her way round the room, collecting the small vials we had been given. I placed mine in the tray, then looked up at her and smiled.

"Good work today, Miss Russo." Instead of moving on, she waited for the others to place their vials in themselves. Once everyone else was distracted with placing their books in their bags, she spoke in a hushed voice. "Don't let the others here make you feel less than you are. I read what you did in your report and why. You are stronger than a lot here will give you credit for, so don't let them break you."

I gulped back the lump that had formed in my throat and nodded, refusing to look her in the eyes. Because I was almost certain that if I did, if I looked up to see her warm smile, I would do exactly what she told me not to do. Break.

Grabbing my bag and books, I ran from the room,

disappearing through the crowd of students heading to the lunch hall before Callum and Archie could get hold of me. I know I had promised to meet Maddy for lunch, but I couldn't face them all. Not right now.

Running to my room, I locked the door and dived under my quilt. That is where I stayed, crying silently to myself until I fell asleep through my two free periods.

I woke up to the sound of rummaging from across the room. Sitting up abruptly, I reached for the knife that I now kept under my pillow.

"Sorry, I didn't mean to wake you." Maddy whispered, looking at the knife then to me. She knew I kept one close now, so she seemed unfazed that I had just pulled it out on her. She sat down on the edge of her bed, giving me a kind smile. I was well aware of the state I must have looked. Crying yourself to sleep with makeup on was never a good idea.

"First day a bit too much for you?" I nodded, bringing my knees to my chest and wrapping my arms around them. "The first week is always the hardest. Coming to terms with the fact you are now being trained to take people's lives is something that most people can't comprehend. I suppose it's easier for me. Being brought up in a family that kills for pleasure as well as a job kinda prepared me for life at this school. And having family in here already helped. But I can completely understand how someone who killed by accident is feeling out of place and vulnerable."

"I didn't just kill one person, Maddy." I sniffed. Looking over at her, she had tilted her head to the side, frowning. "I'm not ready to talk about it yet but I didn't just kill someone by accident. Well, I mean I did kill him by accident but there were others."

"If you're not ready to talk about it, that's fine. But I'm here for when you are." She shifted herself off her bed and came to sit beside me. Placing her arm around me, her head lolled on to my shoulder. "I think you should get yourself sorted and come down to dinner though. Food will make everything better. Maybe don't look at your phone just yet. Callum isn't best pleased that you ran from him. Archie and Felix are finding it hilarious though."

"What about Tommy?" I found myself wondering what he felt about me running from them. Not that I should have cared. I didn't care.

"Tommy's Tommy. He probably hasn't even looked at the group chat yet." She shrugged then stood back up, dragging me with her. "Go sort your face, I'm hungry."

Laughing lightly, I walked past her to get sorted for dinner. Maddy was still in her uniform, so I didn't feel the need to get changed but I did clean off my mascara-stained face and applied a fresh coating.

I really needed to toughen up. I was in a school for killers for fuck's sake. It was either toughen up or let them break me.

As we walked into the hall I had a big smile on my face. Maddy's bubbly personality really was contagious, and I found myself laughing at the stories she was telling me about what happened in her first poisons class. About a lad that fainted as Dr Bane extracted poison from a venomous snake and how she had showed them how it worked against a rabbit, then he fainted again.

The hall was full of students sitting at rectangle tables with a mixture of benches and chairs circling them. At the far end was where the food was being served. The same food that had been there over the weekend plus the daily specials. Helping myself to a small burger and chips, I grabbed a bottle of coke then followed Maddy. She headed straight for the boys table, but I quickly tugged on her arm.

"Can we sit at another table?"

She frowned as she looked over at them then back to me but nodded anyway and made her way to an empty one. I sat down beside her and dared to look up at the table from which I could feel the eyes burning into me. Archie and Felix were paying no attention, talking to each other about unimportant shit but Callum and Tommy were both watching.

Callum leaning across, whispered something to which Tommy's lips tipped up into a malicious smirk and he nodded slowly. Callum then slapped Felix's arm, grabbing his attention. Muttering something again, Felix turned around to look over at us. Giving me a wolfish grin, he stood up.

"We should have just sat with them and saved the agro." Maddy sighed, placing her fork back on her tray.

Before I could even question her, Callum was at my side. "Yes, we would love for you to join us. Let me help you over there." Grabbing my arm, he heaved me up.

"What the fuck do you think you're doing?" I snarled as he dragged me from my seat. Felix had already got hold of my tray and taken it back with him. Maddy followed, turning her head to give me an apologetic look like it was her fault.

"Your place is with us at that table sweetheart." Callum snarled low in my ear.

Not wanting to cause a scene by having him drag me there, I ripped my arm out of his grip. "Fine!" Storming over to where my tray was placed, I sat down in my new seat. Right between Tommy and Callum.

Gracing me with a triumphant smile, Callum sat down and started eating his food again.

"Nice of you to join us, Isabella." Tommy drawled, not looking up from the phone in his hand. "Eat."

I was starving but as soon as he commanded it, I didn't want to take a bite. Instead, I took my own phone out of my blazer pocket and finally read the last few messages on the group chat.

Callum
Anyone seen her?

Felix
Who?

Callum
Who do you fucking think!

Felix
Lost her already lmao

Archie
She ran away

Callum
Maddy?

Maddy
Just leave her alone for a bit.

Callum
MADDY! TELL ME WHERE THE FUCK SHE IS!

Maddy
JESUS! She's asleep ok. I checked the room for her at lunch and she's asleep

.

Maddy
Just let her sleep.

Wow, just wow! I don't think I've ever had a boy act so possessive over me. I glanced over at him to find him on his phone. They all were. I quickly typed out a message.

Isabella
You're all dickheads. I hope you get explosive diarrhoea and all the toilets are out of order.

Isabella

Except Maddy. I like Maddy. I hate you all

Everyone's phone beeped and I sat back in my seat, waiting for their reaction. Nothing.

I took the opportunity to change the group name that had previously been family chat. A family that I had no interest of belonging to.

2beauts and 4fucktards

Apart from them all grinning down at the screen, none of them said anything. The only one that made a sound to my surprise was Tommy. Breathing out his amusement, he gazed over at me. "I see you are making good use of the group chat."

Growling in frustration, I started picking at the bun of my burger. I ate in silence as the others talked amongst themselves about family business. Maddy startled me though when she slammed her phone down on the table. I looked up at her concerned, but she shook her head.

"What's wrong?"

"That fucking Sandra is getting on my last nerve."

I arched my brow, and she lifted her phone, showing me the student chat page.

Sandra Morgan:
#Kraywhore alert. She's wormed her way into their beds and now their hearts. Poor Callum Kray was so upset, looking for her earlier. Is her cock sucking really that good or has she bewitched them all?

There were a handful of comments under the post, but I didn't bother reading them. Callum gripped his knife beside me until his knuckles turned white. He turned his head to look past me and at Tommy.

"I'm gunna kill her."

"We've let it go too long now." Archie cut in, agreeing

with Callum that it was something that should be done. Tommy simply nodded, still looking at his phone, giving permission for them to go ahead. Callum started to rise but I quickly placed a hand on his arm. Pausing, he looked down at me.

"Let me sort this one out?"

Callum looked at Tommy once again and I did too.

He was gazing down at me, frowning. "And what do you intend to do, Isabella?" The way he says my name, like it sounds good rolling off his tongue. I had only heard it from his mouth a few times but each time goosebumps would scatter down my body.

"I'll need your help." I said, quickly turning away from his intense stare and towards Maddy. She nodded quickly and we both stood up.

I explained my plan to her as I took what I needed from the food counter. Maddy laughed at the absurdity of it but agreed that it was better than having her blood all over the floor where we ate.

Maddy was the first to pull up a chair next to the flaming red head. I sat on the table beside Sandra, concealing her and her salad from her friend.

"Hi Sandra."

"Maddy." Sandra nodded curtly then glared up at me. I gave her a sweet smile as Maddy continued.

"We've come over here for a little reminder. You see, my brother wanted to come over and he isn't really in the best of moods." The three of us looked over to where the boys were seated. All four of them were watching us and Callum looked absolutely murderous. "He wants you dead to put it simple, so think of this as a small mercy." It was so blunt coming from her mouth and completely different from the sweet Maddy she was with me that I had to look away to stop myself from laughing.

Sandra's face was ashen, and I felt the tiniest bit of pity as I thought about the effect the words had had on her. Was this truly what it was like to fear the Krays?

"You know the rules, Sandra. Bella is one of ours now. Tommy claimed her himself. The rules are that you are not allowed to touch her, insult her, threaten her. Fuck me, you shouldn't even be looking at her in the wrong way if you valued your life."

My head tilted to the side as I looked back at the boys, all still watching. So that's what the rules were. I was protected by them. I've never needed protection before. I've proved I can look after myself. Yet there was something weirdly comforting about it. Maybe they would protect me from the students at this school but only I could protect myself from them.

"Is it because when you fucked Tommy, he dropped you like a worthless whore? But then again, you did go through my cousins, didn't you? Oh and my brother. One after the other." I grimaced at the thought. Not out of jealousy but because... Eww. "Is that why you assume that Bella is doing the same?"

I dropped what I needed to into the salad bowl and mixed it a little with her fork. Sandra was too busy listening to every word that left Maddy's mouth to realise what I was doing. She even started shaking. I wasn't sure if it was from fear or from anger that Maddy was saying such things to her, and she couldn't do anything about it with our boys watching.

Our boys.

The thought made me chuckle and I gave Maddy a nod to say I was done. She obviously wasn't though.

"Did you know what they told each other about you. How desperate you were. That they found you that repulsive they actually had to fake finishing just to get you to leave. All four of them Sandra, could not even come over you."

I stifled another laugh as I leapt off the table and Maddy got up too. Plastering a huge sweet as pie smile on her face, Maddy gave her one last look. "Bye, nice talking to you." She skipped beside me, like she hadn't just been a vengeful bitch with me.

"Oh and Sandra?" The red head looked at me with a piecing glare. "My cock sucking skills are on point, just for future reference."

A couple of boys from the table choked on air but soon dropped their heads when they caught the fiery glare of Callum. I smiled sweetly at him, and he rolled his eyes as he patted my empty seat. I shook my head though. My plan wouldn't work if I couldn't see Sandra.

Maddy sat down in the seat I was originally in, and I sat opposite, now between Felix and Archie. I didn't smile as I watched Sandra, and she stared back. Both of us were glaring, waiting to see who would back down first. She brought the first fork full of salad up to her mouth and as she started to chew, I let the smile creep up. Frowning, she went for another bite and my smile grew wider.

She chewed her food but then slowed down, tasting it. I could see her little mind working as her tongue was probably feeling out for what the new taste was. Her eyes bulged in realisation, and I gave her one slow nod, indicating that she was right.

Poor Sandra jumped out of her seat. "She's poisoned me! The psycho's poisoned me!" Her screams filled the hall, and everyone went quiet, watching the girl ram her fingers down her throat to try and make herself sick.

"How?" Felix asked and I merely shrugged while Maddy clutched her sides through laughter. Every student had their phones out, recording the girl retching on to the floor.

"I'm going to die." Fingers down her throat again. "She's fucking killed me!" That time, sick came up and I nearly retched myself. Tommy swore as he looked at her in disgust then shot out of the chair as she fell to the floor before him. More sick protruded from her mouth.

My hand flew over my mouth. I wanted to laugh but the smell made me want to heave. Both Callum and Tommy came to stand behind me, but Maddy was in hysterics as she clambered from her own seat and sat on the table.

"What is going on?" Williams stormed into the hall, silencing everyone immediately. He took one look at Sandra on her hands and knees, surrounded by the undigested remains of her dinner then around the room, looking for the culprit. "What happened?" He demanded through gritted teeth.

"She- She's poisoned me." Sandra slurred, pointing an accusing finger in my direction. Williams' eyes darted to me, and I instantly felt the flutter of panic, fearing what punishment he was going to give me for creating this.

"And how has Russo done that?" His voice was disturbingly quieter.

"The salad, she put something in the salad." Sandra's friend shot out, holding the bowl. Williams snatched it from her loose grip and sniffed at it. He frowned for a second then observed the green leafage.

"And what poison do you assume Russo has used?" He asked, cocking his grey brow.

"Oleander. She would have gotten it from poisons class today sir." Sandra retched again. Callum's hand came to my shoulder, and he gave it a soft squeeze. He knew I hadn't taken anything. He had seen me place the vial in the tray.

"What makes you think it was that?" Williams looked positively tired with this shit now.

"The bitter taste sir." She rasped and I had to turn to hide my smile. The taste wouldn't have been bitter at all. It would have been sour. But thanks to Poisons and the subtle smiles, I had got in her head. She tasted bitterness because that was the only logical explanation to what I had done.

Williams' fingers dug into the salad, and he pulled them out again, licking the tips. "That 'bitterness' you tasted was lemon Morgan." He sighed in frustration. "What Russo here has given you is an extra dose of vitamin C."

Her jaw dropped to the floor as she looked up at me and I smirked down at her. Everything had worked out better than I could have hoped. I had only wanted to worry her a bit but forcing herself to be sick was an added bonus.

The real icing on the cake though was seeing her face right now. I had won through sheer humiliation. Without killing her or hurting her at all, I had won.

"You will stay behind and clean the whole of this hall, Morgan." Williams reprimanded then turned on his heel to leave. A slow clap came from beside me and I twisted my neck to see Archie grinning and nodding his head in approval.

Tommy stepped up closer behind and I felt his chest press against my back as he leaned forward. His breath warmed my neck as his lips got closer to my ear, making the hairs on the nape of my neck lift. "Again, you've impressed me."

He walked away, following Professor Williams out of the room then everyone else started filing out too. I looked over at Maddy who was still giddy with laughter. Without saying a word, she took my hand and pulled me away from the boys so we could spend the rest of the night in our room, laughing about what had happened.

Chapter 7

I stood at one end of the gymnasium, watching Felix and Callum sparring in the ring at the other end. I wasn't ashamed to admit that I was admiring their bodies. Who wouldn't? Both were glistening with sweat on their rippling muscles. Their hard chests rising and falling with every pant.

Tommy and Archie were standing at the side, leaning against the ropes, encouraging the others to get in some hits. Both were in the same state after finishing their time in the ring. They may all be arseholes but even I could appreciate a good looking male.

Maddy was rabbiting on beside me about her first Art of Killing lesson, going into detail about how good Professor Williams looked in his tight suit trousers but it was a shame he had a big cock or something like that.

"Are you listening?" She accused, narrowing her eyes at me.

"Yeh, he's got a big cock." I answered, tearing my eyes away.

"No, he is a big cock." She pouted then pulled at the baggy jumper I had given her. "Just like Mr Letch for making us wear what's under here."

Mr Letch wasn't his real name, it was Petch, but the

73

older girls had all given him that nickname for his apparent lewd ways. I hadn't met the bloke yet, but I agreed with them. The tight leggings were already riding up my arse and the sports bra that was compulsory to wear without any cover up, left very little to the imagination. Especially when you were rather well endowed in that department.

"You would think this was classed as sexist, but I heard the boys have to be topless throughout the lessons too." Another first year girl smiled as she came to stand next to us. She too was looking in the direction of the Kray cousins and I smirked at her knowingly. Our combat class was girls only on a Tuesday and mixed on a Wednesday and Thursday. So other than the older ones using the gym, we didn't know if that statement was true or not.

The girl who had just joined us was quite petite, probably the same height as me but slimmer. Her bobbed, ebony hair was tied back as best as it could be with a single band and the strands that didn't quite reach, framed her face.

The doors to the gym opened and a man who I guessed was in his early thirties strolled in, duffle bag in hand.

"What do you think that's for?" I asked both girls.

"Probably a bag of thongs because our leggings aren't revealing enough." Maddy shrugged and I pressed my lips together to stop myself from laughing.

Mr Petch set his bag down on the floor and opened it up. Pulling out a length of rope, my mouth fell open.

"Morning ladies." The man drawled, snapping the rope between both hands. "I thought I would make our first lesson interesting with some rope play."

"How is that fighting sir?" One of the girls asked, sneering at the piece of material.

"You will be surprised what you can do with a rope in the middle of a fight." He answered with a bright smile.

"But sir, shouldn't we be learning the basics first. I mean, some of us don't know how to fight." I asked, looking at the others and wasn't too shocked when they nodded in agreement.

"And where is the fun in that." He winked and I internally recoiled. "First, you two. Jumpers off." A finger wiggled between Maddy and me.

Rolling my eyes, I started to lift the jumper over my head. Once I had removed it, I chucked it over to where Maddy had put hers then looked back at the teacher. Petch's eyes bulged as he looked between us all and I found myself glaring, hoping he would just drop down dead at any given moment.

"Lovely, now come retrieve a rope."

"Perfect." Maddy muttered under her breath. "He's going to be the first person I kill when I graduate."

Stifling another laugh, I made my way to the duffle with the other girls and grabbed two ropes to give one to her.

"Who would like to be my lovely volunteer?" No one, absolutely no one put their hand up. "Come on now, don't be shy. We all must start somewhere. You."

His thin finger pointed to the girl who had spoken to us. Her eyes widened with terror but then was quickly replaced with disgust and annoyance. He wiggled his finger, telling her to get closer to him.

"Name?"

"Daisy, Sir. Daisy Upton."

"Well Miss Upton. Drop your rope and run at me." Petch lowered his body as a sick, perverted grin ruined his youthful face.

"I'd rather not sir. I wouldn't want to hurt a teacher." Daisy's grip on her rope tightened and I couldn't have felt sorrier for her if I wanted to. I was just glad he hadn't selected me.

He gave a gruff chuckle and held out his hands. "I very much doubt you will do much damage. Now run at me."

"No, but I'd like too." Daisy muttered but ran at him anyway. In a flurry of limbs flying through the air, Daisy was slammed to the floor, the rope around her neck.

I was definitely glad I wasn't selected because what the

fuck! Daisy groaned; her eyes scrunching shut from the pain I imagined she was in. Petch was straddling her stomach, holding either end of the rope and the only thing she could be thankful for was that he wasn't pulling it tight. Although, in that situation, death was probably preferred.

"Now who would like to learn to do that?" He grinned down at her before facing the rest of us. Although my hand remained down just out of pure shock of what happened, everyone else raised theirs. "Lovely. Just lovely." He smiled brightly and stood back up, pulling Daisy with him.

She staggered back over to us, and I tried to reach out to support her, but she shook her head. Pity was a sign of weakness. I forgot.

"I agree with Maddy. He's going to be the first to die." She grumbled, rubbing her lower back and turning to face him.

"What we need is some others to practice with." Petch looked round the gym. Oh fuck no. This wasn't happening. "You four." Callum and Felix had already stopped sparring and were currently unwrapping the bindings on their hands. Archie lifted his head to show he was listening but couldn't look less bored if he tried. "If you have finished your training, I need you over here for a little one on one with the girls. The five of us together can take on these ladies, I'm sure."

Callum's eyes shot to me, and he grinned devilishly. "Of course, sir. It would be our pleasure."

He exited the ring with Felix close behind him then walked over. Tommy pushed off from where he was leaning and followed Archie.

"Daisy, you will be with me." Petch instructed. Muttering under her breath, she went to stand beside him. "Archie, that one there." He pointed at one of the others and Archie sauntered to her side. Felix didn't need instructions as he came to stand beside a girl who was slightly taller than me. She looked up at him, terrified and took a step away but he just grinned down at her like it was a game.

Callum came to stand next to me because why wouldn't he. I was always next to him. But Maddy had different ideas.

Grabbing his arm, she pulled him to her side. "I am not missing this opportunity to kick your arse." She sneered. He chuckled before looking over to me and giving an apologetic shrug. Not that he needed to. I liked the thought of watching Maddy beat him even if she probably couldn't.

But that left Tommy. His cold eyes glared down at me as he took his place. His lips were in a straight line as he crossed his arms, like this was the last thing he wanted to be doing. And I realised, playing with ropes with him was the last thing I wanted to do too.

"Sir, can I be partnered with you instead?" I called out, aware of how much of a coward I looked but I didn't mind, I had more chance of survival with the pervert.

Tommy's lips tipped up like what I had said amused him on some level. "Never took you for someone who backs down, Isabella."

"Depends what the level of survival is, and something tells me you're not going to go easy on me."

"Care to find out?" The mischievous glint in his eyes melted the coldness but it unnerved me and yet I was still intrigued enough to hold out the rope.

"Do I get to keep this or do you?"

"You're meant to be using it on me. I think that means you keep it." Placing his hands in the pockets of his shorts, he waited for me to make a move. Everyone had already started around us, and I noticed that the Krays weren't going easy at all on the girls. Callum currently had his sister in a headlock while she was trying to punch him in the face and the rope was left forgotten on the floor.

"I haven't got all day, Isabella." My attention went back to Tommy, just in time to see him roll his eyes with impatience. Placing both ends of the rope in either hand, I leapt at his throat with it. I didn't know what I was doing but it seemed like the best option. Wrap the rope around his neck like Letch had done to Daisy. He stepped out the way and I stumbled past him. Letting out a frustrated growl, I tried to ram into him again. Again, he avoided my advances with his hands still in his pockets like I was a joke to him.

"Fight back." I gritted out.

"If you actually manage to touch me, I will fight back." He flashed me the most handsome yet sinful grin. "You need to take me by surprise and everything that you are doing right now is predictable."

"How am I meant to be more unpredictable when you know that I'm meant to be trying to attack you with a length of rope that I have no idea how to use." I held up the rope again. "What am I meant to do with it. Whip ya?"

He arched his brow suggestively making me scowl.

"If you can't get inventive then you may as well pack your bags and leave."

"Fine." God, he irritated me so much. Fisting the rope in my hand, my nails bit into my skin. My eyes narrowed onto the exit behind him and that's where I started walking. Tommy bowed his head in what was probably disappointment. I didn't care. Let him think I had given up.

As soon as I walked past him, I quickly turned back around and jumped for his back. The bastard knew though. He knew I wasn't going to give up and turned just in time to grab me by the waist. Twisting me round in one swift movement, my arms were behind my back, secured by his hand and the rope that was twisted round my wrists. His other hand was around my throat, pulling my head back and making sure I couldn't escape.

Every breath was heavy as I panted out. My body was stiff against his, but fire burned through me as the anger grew.

"Having you at my mercy is my new favourite look on you." He breathed against my ear, making my stomach flip and not in a bad way.

"Don't get used to it." I managed to snarl back. Letting out a dark chuckle, his warm breath hit the most sensitive part of my neck, making me press my lips together tightly to stop any sound that I didn't want to make from coming out. Tommy's thumb started moving in circles over my wrist, soothing the pinching of the rope. Probably the nicest thing he had done for me and very un-Tommy like.

"You need to go to the gym."

"Excuse me?" I snapped, being brought back to what a prick he was. I was curvy yes, but I didn't need to lose weight. And I especially didn't need some arrogant narcissist to tell me I did either.

"Not for weight loss," I could hear the exasperation in his voice. "You need to build muscle."

"Oh." I suppose with having to learn to fight, muscle would come in handy.

"If you were stronger, you would have been able to fight me off by now." His thumb continued to rub gentle circles.

"Maybe I'm just impressed that you managed to see an attack coming from behind." I grinned.

The hand on my throat rose higher, craning my neck back. I gasped for the air that he was restricting but he seemed unbothered.

"So I've impressed you?" Another whisper to my ear.

"I'd be more impressed if you actually tied the rope."

The hand around my throat dropped as he glided his hand downwards. Passing through the cleavage of the sports bra, his fingers ghosted my heated skin until they stopped just above my navel. Every nerve in my body felt his touch just on that one spot of exposed skin.

Breathing in as controlled as I could manage, I focused on his other hand that had now stopped comforting me. Tommy tugged on the ropes around my wrists and let out a deep low growl of satisfaction. He let go and I tried to pull my arms, but they were stuck. His thumb hadn't been comforting me at all. He had been distracting me while tying the ropes securely.

Letting out a huff of frustration, I forced myself to turn around and face him. We were so close that I had to lean my head back even further just to look at his cocky grin.

"So I guess your thing is ropes?"

His eyes darkened menacingly but the grin stuck. "I'm good at many things, Isabella. Ropes just happen to be one of them 'things'."

Before I had the chance to reply, he left the gym without looking back. I stood, hands tied behind my back, speechless.

"Do you want to have a go with me, Bella?" Callum chirped as he walked over to me with Maddy.

"Err, yeh, sure." I looked at the door Tommy had just walked out off then back to Callum. I guess that was my training with him done. "Um, you might need to untie me first."

He glanced down at my wrists then burst into laughter. "Could have been worse, you could have ended up like them." He nodded towards the other girls. Felix currently had one pinned, face first, to the floor while he sat on her arse, texting on his phone. Archie had his partner on all fours, with the rope wrapped around her neck like a dog on a leash. What the fuck was wrong with these boys?

Chapter 8

With my music up loud and phone in hand, I was ready to select what extracurricular activities I wanted to do. That was how I was spending my evening after Weapons class being cancelled (Apparently the teacher had an unfortunate accident with a grenade, and they were still looking for a replacement.), AP Poisons going uneventfully well and dining at the table with the people I hated bar one. Maddy. She sat on her own bed, scrolling through to see what ones she wanted to do too.

My phone pinged in my hand, but I ignored the chat group and carried on reading through the description of the firearms class.

Want perfect aim to avoid missing your enemy or just to get the best shot at the neighbour's cat that keeps you awake at 3am. Then firearms is the best lesson for you. Learn all about the different varieties of guns while practicing with each one. Shooting at your friends has never been so fun.

"Shall we do firearms? There's one on Tuesday at 3 but I have AP Poisons then, but can do the Thursday one at 10?"

"I have poisons then. I think that's the one the boys take though." She replied, looking at her schedule then back at her phone.

"Not doing that class then." I deadpanned.

She let out a little chuckle then shook her head. "I think they do paintball for practice. Are you really going to let up the chance to shoot my brother in the face?"

That was tempting. Not only shooting Callum but also getting to shoot the others too. They wouldn't be expecting my good aim and the look on their faces would be all the satisfaction I needed. Well maybe not all, but a huge part of it.

"Ok, you've convinced me." I sighed dramatically at her.

"Didn't take a lot to do that." She offered a bemused smile and I shrugged.

"What can I say. The thought of shooting your brother just pleases me in ways it probably shouldn't."

Her head flew back as she cackled her amusement. Both our phones pinged again and once again, I ignored it. Maddy started tapping away as I looked at the next activities.

Archery, football, extreme driving, martial arts and computer hacking.

Martial arts would come in handy but with combat training, that would kill my body. I'd wait until next term for that one. Archery and football I had no interest in at all. Or computer hacking. But I suppose those skills were also good to have. Archery and computer hacking I mean. I had no idea how football was a good skill for killing people.

Extreme driving caught my attention though. I wondered if they would let me do that without a license. A part of me doubted it but the whole school worked without law so there was a possibility.

"Cheerleading is on Fridays at 1. I think we both have a free period then, so we have to do that." Maddy said happily, interrupting my thoughts.

"Cheerleading? I thought you was joking about that one?" Frowning at her, I swiped off another notification for the chat group.

"No, just think of the skills we could learn from it. And who would expect innocent cheerleaders to be trained killers."

"True. Let's do it then." I shrugged casually and submitted my name to cheerleading and firearms. I would do some of the others next term. Laying back on my pillow, I closed my eyes while listening to 'You Don't Own Me' by SayGrace.

My phone pinged again and Maddy groaned. "Can you please just look at the messages because they are actually pissing me off now."

"Fine, but I'm not replying." I grumbled. For the past thirty minutes, we had been messaged nonstop and although Maddy was happy to entertain her cousins and brother with replies, I had refused.

Picking up my phone, I tapped on the group chat.

2beauts and 4fucktards

Tommy
ISABELLA!

Callum
What the fuck is she doing?

Maddy
Listening to music

Tommy
Get her to reply now!

"Bella?" She looked at me hopeful and I almost felt guilty for my answer.

Almost.

"No." I went back to looking at the chat and smiled at Maddy's next reply.

Maddy
She said no

Tommy
Get to the common room now

Maddy
I'm now leaving but I doubt she's coming

Callum
Come on sweetheart

Yes Callum, because you asking me is going to make all the difference.

Maddy stood up and put on her trainers then crossed the room to the door.

"You sure you're not coming? He's going to be pretty mad." She asked, looking back at me with concern etching over her face.

"No, not after the little stunt he pulled in combat class. He can apologise first." I gave her my best sweet as honey smile and she shook her head in disbelief. My betting was Tommy wasn't told no very often. "Besides, I'm not exactly dressed for the occasion."

As soon as I got back from dinner, I had showered and slung on a pair of tiny shorts and a little tank top, ready for an early night.

"I'll see you in a bit." She smiled, rolling her eyes and then walked out the door, locking it behind her.

After a few more minutes of listening to music, the song was interrupted by my ring tone. Groaning I looked at the caller ID. Unknown. Narrowing my eyes at the numbers on the screen, I knew exactly who it was. I really should have saved their individual numbers. Cancelling it off, I resumed my relaxation.

Not even a second later, I was disturbed again by the same caller. Cancelling it off, I pulled up the group chat and finally started typing.

2beauts and 4fucktards

Bella

Can you please refrain from calling me, you are disturbing my quiet time and I am starting to question your aggressiveness.

Tommy

Isabella, I'm not a very patient man.

Bella

Are any other 'Claimed ones' at this 'meeting'?

Tommy

No

Callum

It's just us sweetheart

Bella

Then I don't need to be there either.

Felix

She got you there

I chuckled to myself at the small victory, but it was short lived.

Tommy

Get your arse down here now

Bella

Can't. Busy.

Tommy

Doing what?

Bella
Painting my nails.

Tommy
Isabella, so fucking help me, if you're not down here in 5minutes, I'm not going to be so nice anymore.

Bella
This is you being nice?

Tommy
Last chance

Bella
Make me.

Three little dots appeared, showing me that one of them was typing, then disappeared and no message. Shrugging, I placed the phone down beside me but as soon as I did, it pinged again. I would have ignored it but curiosity to how Tommy would react got the better off me.

Callum
Oh shit

Maddy
You may want to hide

Archie
See you soon love

I suddenly felt sick. I hadn't known Tommy long enough to know how far I could push him and although, according to the rules Maddy had told Sandra, I was protected by the Krays, it didn't tell me anything of what they might do to me. Maybe I should have listened to Maddy and hid.

A loud bang made me sit up and the door swung open, colliding hard with the wall.

I hadn't seen Tommy get angry. He was usually quite calm. Calm but extremely dangerous. The man that stood in the doorway though, was something else. I winced as his lethal glare sliced through me. His jaw was clenched, and nostrils flared as he just stood for a few seconds, staring. I didn't want to show fear and give him the satisfaction, but I was certain he could probably see it already.

Without saying a word, he crossed the room and ruthlessly grabbed my waist. Flinging me over his shoulder, he stalked back out, slamming the door shut again behind him. A useless gesture as he had already broken the lock. Not a single word came out of my mouth as he carried me down the hall. I was too stunned. Astonished even that I had got him angry enough to forcibly take me from my room.

Realisation kicked in and so did I against his chest. Screaming at him to put me down, I hit at his back with my tiny fists. Nothing penetrated the hard exterior of the animal. People were staring and whispering as we passed. Not one of them dared to get in the way of his path or wrath, leaving me a kicking and screaming mess.

Tommy's hand came up and slapped down against my arse hard in an attempt to silence me. It worked. I instantly tensed and shut my mouth, shocked again by his actions. The place he had struck stung like fuck, and I was certain there was already a massive handprint there.

Pushing myself up so I wasn't just hanging, I tried to twist my body to get him to release me but instead his fingers dug in tighter on my thighs.

"If I promise to come quietly, will you put me down?" I asked through gritted teeth as calmly as I could. He didn't answer, instead I heard a low, deep growl, telling me to keep my mouth shut.

Walking into the student common room, Tommy dropped me on the sofa beside Callum. Straightaway, the blondes' arm was round my shoulders, pulling me into his side possessively.

"Nice of you to join us."

"I don't get much choice these days." I grumbled, pursing my lips at him.

He laughed softly, brushing my hair behind my ear. "The best thing to do is just accept it now, sweetheart. You're a part of us. You're ours." His hand wondered to the back of my neck, and he pulled my head closer to his. "But that doesn't mean I won't try to make you just mine."

My mouth went dry, but I still gave him a sweet smile. "Oh Callum, you know exactly what to say to make me melt in your arms." He knew I was being sarcastic, but his lips still inched closer to mine. I didn't move, I waited to see how close he would get before he would stop. Our mouths were almost touching. I took a sharp intake of breath, shocked that he had got so close.

Tommy cleared his throat from across the small table and I pulled away quickly. Was I really about to let Callum kiss me? I think I was. I pulled a face in confusion and wiggled myself away from him and further up the sofa. He didn't protest, probably just as confused at what was about to happen.

I threw him a quick glance. He wasn't confused at all. He was looking down at his lap, running his hand over the smirk he was trying to hide.

Prick.

Rolling my eyes, I turned my attention back to Tommy and the reason I was here. He glowered back at me, and I cocked a brow. Why were they both such arseholes?

"So why are we here Tommy?" Maddy asked, interrupting our death glare match.

"The Italians are in town." Archie snarled at this, but Tommy ignored him and continued. "My father wants to know why. Carlo and Lorenzo have stayed behind, it's

Lorenzo's son and a few of his friends that have come to visit. They will be at the charity games night on Saturday."

Callum and Felix nodded while Archie looked ready to tear someone another arsehole. I glanced over at Maddy, and she looked as confused as I did as to why we had to be here for this conversation.

"We'll all be attending and yes Madeline, I also mean you two." Tommy sighed in aggravation as Maddy rose her hand into the air. I choked back my laughter when she pulled a face and put her hand back down. "While he won't share anything with us, his sister is rather friendly and that is where you two come in. Find out what they want."

That was our orders. Befriend a girl just to use her for information. I exchanged a look with Maddy, and she shrugged like it was something normal for her to be used for. Being claimed by them, I guess I had to get used to it too if I wanted an easy life.

"When is the games night?" I quickly asked, without putting my hand up like Maddy had.

Tommy glared at me again before repeating. "Saturday."

"Oh but Saturday, I-"

"Don't." He growled through his teeth. "Do not tell me you have plans just to piss me off and if you actually do. Cancel them."

"But-"

His cold gaze dared me to disobey. And I wanted to. Oh, how I wanted to. But I shut my mouth. I had to pick my battles wisely and this was not a wise time to test his patience any more than I already had.

When he was certain I wasn't going to utter another word, he continued. "The following week, our friends from up north will be visiting for a night. My father has already arranged for them to stay in the family home-" (He did not look pleased at all by this.) "- and he wants all of us there."

Archie looked over to him, frowning in confusion. "Why are they coming down?"

Tommy took a cigarette from the packet on the small

table in front of him. Sparking it up, he leant back in his seat and took a long drag.

"Probably because Thomas tried to sell on their turf." Felix replied as Tommy let the smoke leave his lungs. Thomas? Turf? None of it made any sense to me but that was because I wasn't meant to be a part of any of it.

Resting his arms on the side of the chair, Tommy finally answered Archie. "They want to visit on friendly terms. Pay their respects for Charlie's passing. Nothing to do with my father's little transgression apparently. But that's why he wants us all there. And I want us all together." His eyes wondered over me and Maddy briefly.

I opened my mouth to say something again, but he quickly rounded on me.

"Isabella, if you are going to open that smart mouth of yours again, I will find a way to fill it." His expression remained hard and cold, but Felix's lips tipped up at the innuendo that none of us missed. I pressed my lips together to stop myself from biting back.

"I think, what she was going to ask is what we are all probably wondering." Maddy quickly addressed. "Does she have to be there too?" That was exactly what I wanted to know.

"I wasn't wondering that. I assumed she would be." Callum shrugged and Felix nodded in agreement.

"I was just wondering if I could get away with killing one of them this time." Archie grinned like a wolf spotting his prey.

Tommy ignored his comment and scowled at Maddy. "Isabella will be there too."

"Because Isabella doesn't have a choice." I grumbled under my breath. Callum huffed out a chuckle beside me but thankfully Tommy didn't hear my little attitude.

"That's everything for now." Finishing his cigarette, he flicked the butt into a glass on the table and went quiet. The others started talking amongst themselves and Maddy plonked herself next to me. Lifting my bare legs on to her lap, I leant against Callum.

"So how are you feeling about meeting the rest of my family?" She asked trying to be nonchalant, but I could hear the wariness in her voice.

"I see it as meeting my best friend's parents and look forward to it." I tried to reassure her with a smile but in actual fact, I was scared. It wasn't like meeting a friend's family at all. It was walking into a den of vipers and hoping that you came out alive. Maddy smiled a little brighter though, so I didn't regret my answer.

"Nana will love you. She loves anyone who pisses her grandsons off."

"Then I promise to try extra hard while I am around her." I giggled.

Maddy started tracing her fingers over my shin. "You can stay in my room there and we can watch films and eat so much crap."

"Like a normal night then?"

"Yeah, pretty much but my room is a lot more luxurious than ours here." She chuckled. "I'm nana's favourite so I got what I wanted when it came to designing it."

"She kicked off till nan gave in." Callum corrected and she stuck her tongue out before giving him an eye roll. "You can stay in my room, the bed's big enough."

Before I could refuse, Tommy interrupted. "Isabella will have her own room."

Knowing there was no point arguing, Callum shrugged and started running his hand down my arm. His fingers jerked away as quickly as they touched me, "You're freezing."

I hadn't been aware that I was before he said but as soon as he did, I felt the chill around my body. I had been so annoyed with Tommy that I hadn't realised how cold it actually was.

"I didn't exactly have chance to grab something warm." I smiled up at him shyly. Something soft hit me in the face, making me jolt my head back and it fell to the floor. Picking it back up, I saw it was a hoodie. I looked over to where it had come from. Tommy sat, leaning back in his chair, ankle on his knee and with just his soft grey crew neck top on. His navy hoodie was removed and now in my hands.

There had been a very small number of times that Tommy had left me surprised but this was the first time through doing something nice. As he gazed over at me, his eyes seemed somewhat warmer.

"Thank you."

He gave me one nod then went back to looking at his phone. I slipped the hoodie over my body, letting the sleeves fall past my fingers and the hem skim my lower thighs. Inside was still warm from his body and the smell of his cologne filled my nose. A blend of rich woods and a mix of warm spices. Something I never knew I liked until that moment.

Chapter 9

I grabbed the last croissant of the counter and a bottle of orange juice. Maddy had already filled her bowl with a fresh fruit salad, but I had no interest in being healthy. I wanted that flaky, buttery pastry. Adding a small pot of jam and a knife to my tray, I followed her to our usual spot.

"Why you up so early? Haven't you got a free period?" Callum asked his sister as I sat down beside him.

"Woke up with Bella so decided to come for breakfast at the same time." She shrugged and shoved a piece of apple in her mouth.

The food hall was pretty empty for a Friday, but we were running slightly late. My first lesson was AP Art of Killing but I still had 10minutes to get to it and all four boys were in the same class so if they hadn't left yet then I wasn't too worried.

The only other classes I had today were AP Poisons and Weaponry. Cheerleading would have been between the two, but extracurricular activities didn't start until the following week.

Slicing the croissant, I started adding the strawberry jam. Felix watched me, frowning slightly.

"What?" I asked, setting the knife back down.

"I've never had one with jam?"

"Then you have never lived. Open up."

"What? No, I didn't wan-" Too late, I had already ripped off the end and shoved it in his mouth. "I idn't ant… Mmm"

"Good?" I asked, laughing as his eyes lit up when he swallowed.

"Yeh." He reached across the table and tried to grab the rest, but I held out the small butter knife.

"Oi, no! This one's mine." Slashing the knife around jokingly, Felix snorted before backing down. Callum shook his head in amusement. Gripping hold of my chair he slid it across the floor until it nudged into his then placed his arm over my shoulder. Leaning against him, I ate the remainder of my breakfast. It was something that we did now. Every mealtime, I would be at his side, and he would pull me closer. I didn't grumble or fight against it anymore. I had already come to accept it.

Picking up his coffee, he brought it to his lips. The smell wafted my way and I hummed in delight.

"Want me to get you some?" He asked, looking down at me.

"No thanks." I couldn't stop my nose from scrunching in disgust. He looked at me puzzled so I felt the need to explain. "It's the smell. I hate the taste of coffee, like in chocolate, cake, normal coffee. I even hate the artificial smells that you get in candles. But I love the smell of fresh coffee."

"You're a weirdo Bella." He chuckled then went back to drinking.

I smiled softly to myself but stopped when I felt Tommy's midnight blue eyes on me from across the table. They were unreadable as usual but as soon as mine met his, he stood and walked away from us all.

"Time to go." Archie informed and we followed him out the room.

"What makes a killer?" Williams was in his usual grey suit, jacket off, sleeves rolled up to the elbows. His typical look. "What motivates someone to become a killer. You," His favourite wooden ruler whipped round, stopping inches from Anderson's head. "Give me a reason?"

"Revenge."

"Good."

Anderson let out a heavy sigh, thankful for not being hit. Was there really a wrong answer to this question though.

"You." Williams pointed at Archie.

"Because you like the feel of their blood between your fingers."

"That's psychotic and a brilliant answer that we will look into more." The professor grinned at him, and I wondered if both of them had to go to meetings together for the same issues. "You." The ruler rounded on to a girl I recognised to be Courtney.

"Umm, infidelity."

"Yes. If you catch another woman in your bed with the love of your life, are you going to slit that girl's throat?"

"I'd stab any bitch who touched my man." She nodded enthusiastically.

"And him?"

"I would stay with him and slowly poison him. Each day that he suffers will be a treat before he dies." She smiled sweetly and I had a fleeting thought that we could easily get along as long as she wasn't one of Sandra's friends.

"Very good." He grinned at her. Turning round, he walked up the aisle between the desks. "What else can make a killer." Standing next to Tommy, Williams placed the ruler over the pen he had been tapping on the desk, making him stop. "Thomas Kray?"

"A birth right."

"Explain."

"Being born into a family that already kill for a living, you tend to grow up doing the same." Tommy started flicking his pen against his desk again, obviously finished with his contribution to the lesson. Williams nodded in satisfaction and continued to move down the aisle.

Coming to a standstill beside me, his hand rested on my shoulder. "And what about you, Russo. What was the reason for you to kill someone?"

I swallowed hard. He knew what I had done but I still wasn't ready for the others to know. Not yet. I know that killing was a big deal in this school but reliving the reasons why would be a torture that I wasn't ready to face.

"Unwanted attention." I answered quickly.

"Hmm unwanted attention." He nodded slowly, taking what I said into consideration. "So if you were to receive unwanted attention from, say Mr Kray here," His ruler landed on Callum's shoulder softly. "You would kill him."

"Callum? No. I wouldn't kill him for giving me unwanted attention. I've got used to that now." Callum gave me a sneaky smirk, complete with a wink.

"But you would kill for other reasons." He was trying to get me to talk about it in front of everyone. No one else would care but Callum would ask questions. He would make me talk.

"I would kill to keep someone's mouth shut." I threatened and he barked out a dry laugh. He could probably kill me with that ruler, so I understood the joke. Tommy was eyeing me suspiciously though. Whether it was his intentions or not, Williams had made Tommy interested, and I just had to hope that he would forget about it. Unlikely.

Moving on, Williams stood at the front of the class, and leaned against his desk. "We all have our reasons for killing people. May that be for a job, revenge, or to keep someone's mouth shut, everyone can find an excuse. What you need to figure out is, are you using that reason as an excuse, or did they really deserve it?" His gaze wondered over every student. "But I don't care if you kill for a fucking good reason or just for pleasure when you leave this school, I still get paid either way."

I snorted a laugh but quickly disguised it with a cough. Williams gave me a rare wink of his eye though, shocking me enough to shut up.

"Now open your books to page 75. Read the passage and get into your groups to discuss your reasons."

Ping

Callum
Hi sweetheart

I gazed down at the message on my phone, contemplating if I should reply or not. Callum hadn't messaged through the group chat. It was a personal text, just for me. I wasn't stupid enough to not save their individual numbers now. After Tommy had phoned, I thought it might have been for the best.

Bella
Who's this?

I smiled at my response. He didn't know I had his number saved.

Callum
The better looking one out of your four favourite boys

Bella
Felix?

Callum
Try again

Bella

Archie?

Callum

Now you're just trying to wound me

Chuckling to myself, Maddy looked up from her Poisons book. "What are you laughing at?"

"You're brother." I grinned at her and she playfully rolled her eyes before dropping the book and leaping up from her bed.

"Budge up." I shimmied to the side, and she dived down beside me. "Did you want to do a film night tonight?"

"I can't. Tommy wants me to meet him at 8.30. Not sure how long I will be though so maybe after?" I quickly glanced at the time at the top of my phone. 7.45pm. Whatever Tommy had planned tonight; I was going to find out pretty soon. The fact that he wanted to meet at the graveyard though didn't seem at all appeasing. I typed out a reply to Callum before he felt the need to message me again.

Bella

What do you want Callum?

"Oh really? Didn't realise you were getting closer to Tommy." She nudged me tauntingly and I tsked.

"He probably wants to use a new form of torture on me." I joked, then I remembered, he had given me the note during the lesson about different methods of torture. "Actually, it might be to do with our AP Art of Killing assignment."

"Could be." She shrugged. "What film do you want to watch?"

"Something funny, I feel I'm going to need it by the time your cousin is finished with me." My phone pinged again, and two messages appeared on the screen.

Callum

Am I not allowed to check in on my favourite girl. I have a little surprise for you.

The second message was a picture, and I didn't dare open it.

Bella

If that's a picture of your cock Callum, I swear I will cut it off.

Callum

Lmao. When I want you to see that, I won't be showing you it through a picture.

Bella

What makes you think I would even want to see it?

Callum

Don't you?

"What about Ace Ventura?" Maddy asked, flicking through Netflix and distracting me from her brother's flirty messages.

"I love Jim Carrey." I smiled at her.

"Me too and I'll make sure to have popcorn and cookies ready. Just text me when you are done with him."

Callum

Your silence is all the answer I need sweetheart

"Your brother is relentless." Sighing, I quickly finger punched a message back.

Bella

Don't get ahead of yourself, I was talking to Maddy. I

don't want to see any part of your body unless it is clothed.

Maddy sighed but nodded her head. "Yeh, he doesn't give up on things that he wants but I wouldn't worry about it too much. He knows the rules."

"Are a part of the rules that you can't touch someone who has been claimed?"

"Sort of. Ask Tommy to explain it to you because I'm sure if I do, I will just get it all wrong and then you will be more confused and you will end up hating them all more."

"I don't think it's possible to hate them more." I chuckled softly then clicked on the picture that Callum had sent. The most stunning diamond choker sat on a plush black holder. Each stone gleamed in the light of the flash, making the picture almost blinding.

Callum

It's to wear tomorrow night. It's outside your door so hurry and get it before I have to kill the person that attempts to steal it.

Gaping at the message then back at the picture, I sat frozen for a good thirty seconds. Jumping off the bed, Maddy grunted as I accidently kicked her then ran to the door. The velvet box lay closed on the floor with a single blue rose placed on top. Picking them both up, I shut the door and walked over to my desk. The rose was in full bloom and unmarred by any imperfections. The bold colour struck me as unusual. I had only seen blue roses before on Pinterest and other media platforms but never in real life, let alone received one. I placed it down on the wooden surface and opened the velvet box.

The choker was even more luxurious in person. The picture really did not do the jewels justice. Each single diamond was cut with the upmost care and the value of it had me already feeling like an imposter before it even touched me.

Bella
I can't wear that. It looks really expensive

Callum
£114,500

My mouth fell open again as my eyes bulged at his message. There was no way I could wear such a costly item.

Callum
It's a family piece. Think of it as borrowing if you don't want to keep it.

I tried to swallow but my throat was too tight. "Maddy, do you recognise this?" I handed her the box and she studied it for a few seconds.

She looked back up to me, her brows creasing together. "Yeh, that was my nana's. She gave it to Tommy a couple of years ago to give to someone special."

"How special?" I all but whispered.

"Like a wedding gift or something." She handed me back the box.

"Oh." I managed to breathe out and Maddy looked at me concerned. Showing her the messages quickly from her brother she shook her head.

"Either Tommy gave him it to lend to you or Callum has a death wish." She tried to smile then shook her head again. "Either way, I can see why they want you to wear it to the charity games night. It's a glamourous event and if you're with us then you will need to look the part."

I had never actually thought about what an evening out with this group of people may be like. "I didn't even take that into consideration. What shall I wear?"

"Umm, that blue dress will be ok. It'll match the rose that I assume was from my brother too?"

I didn't reply as I looked back down at it. Callum had

been the one to message, but the jewellery was Tommy's. That really didn't help with who the rose was from.

"Roses are a big thing to give the women of our family. The men will always give a rose. They come in a range of different colours and each one has a different meaning. Uncle Thomas, Tommy's father, often gives a black rose to his enemies. Black signifies death."

Placing the velvet box and phone down on my desk, I picked up the rose, twirling it in my fingers. "What about a blue rose?"

"Hmm," She considered it for a moment, probably trying to remember the meaning behind it. "I'm almost certain that blue means unattainable."

"Unattainable?" I repeated, less than impressed by that meaning.

"And mysterious." She frowned.

"Suppose unattainable makes sense in some ways, seeing as they claimed me and I'm now unable to make other allies." How fucking romantic.

"Could be worse." I raised my brow at her and she chuckled softly. "Ok, so I can't compare it to anything yet but give me more time and I'm sure I'll be able too. But really, that blue dress will look lovely for tomorrow night."

I walked over to the wardrobe and pulled out the dress she had been speaking about. I gave it a good once over. The sheer fabric would come down to just past my knees while the underskirt stopped just above. The sweetheart neckline was quite high. The overall dress was rather modest and plain. It wasn't fancy enough to compliment the choker, but it was all I had.

"What are you wearing?"

"My mum would have bought me something to wear. She's quite particular with that sort of thing. Always wants us to look our best because God forbid we embarrass the family name." Maddy rolled her eyes in annoyance then shifted off the bed and to her feet. "The boys will all be in suits."

"Will your parents be there?" My stomach twisted slightly at the thought. Not that they had given me any reason to be worried but mainly because of how tolerant Tommy was of me, it made me wonder at what kind of people the rest of the family were.

"No." She smiled reassuringly, like she knew of my concerns. "We are representing the family tomorrow so best behaviour for us all."

"Still don't get why I have to come." I grumbled under my breath, and she shook her head laughing then walked into the bathroom.

I hung the dress back up then placed the velvet box with the choker into the top draw of my bedside table, nestled on top of my underwear. My phone pinged from its spot on the desk, and I launched myself at it, ready to reply to whatever Callum had messaged now. Only it wasn't from him.

Tommy
Change of plan. Meet me out the front in 15.

I started to message back but before I had finished, another came through.

Tommy
Don't even think about asking who this is. I'm not in the mood for your brattiness.

Well that completely ruined my reply. Although it did put a smile on my lips that he knew exactly what I was about to do, and that Callum would have told him I did the same to him. I placed the phone in the pocket of my dark denim jacket and then threw it on over my white summer dress. I wasn't sure what we were doing or where we were going so wasn't too sure what to wear but the autumn heat was high this evening and I didn't want to get too hot. Paired with white canvas shoes though, the dress looked casual enough.

"I'll see you later Maddy. Don't eat all the popcorn before I get back."

"I won't. Text me when you're on your way." She called back and then I heard the sound of the shower running.

Making sure I shoved my keys into my pocket too, I left the room, ready for Tommy's surprise evening.

Chapter 10

There he was, leaning casually against his black car, arms crossed with a cigarette between his fingers. He wore dark jeans with a black top and black leather jacket. Nothing about him gave an aura of innocence. He looked like your typical bad boy but when his eyes glided up to meet mine, they were full of something so much worse.

Pure maliciousness.

I stepped down the stone steps, careful not to trip as his cruel glare bore into me and made my legs feeble. Stopping a few feet in front of him, his gaze dragged over my body. Bringing the cigarette to his lips, he took a deep intake of nicotine then exhaled, blowing it away from me.

"A white dress?"

"Should I have worn something else?" I asked, looking down at the thin cotton fabric then back up to him.

"What you wear is of little concern to me but white probably wasn't the best decision you have ever made." The indecent smirk sent a ripple of anger through me, and I scowled at him. "Get in the car."

He chucked the finished cigarette end to the gravel, opened the door behind him then rounded the car to the other side, expecting me to just obey his command. And of course, I did.

I sat down, the cool leather biting into my bare thighs as my dress lifted slightly. The interior of his car was exactly what I had expected. Pristine and organised. Not a speck of dust or an empty crisp packet in sight. Unlike his cousin's Range Rover, that had empty beer cans littering the back seats.

"You know, maybe I would have worn something different if you had told me what we were doing exactly." I retorted to his statement at last.

He remained stoic as he turned on the ignition and the car roared to life. Taking it out of park, we started moving forward, the gravel crunching under the tires.

"You never asked." He responded finally.

I opened my mouth to answer back but closed it again, pouting and frowning. He was right. I had never asked. Would it really have been that simple to find out? Merely asking? I looked across and even though his eyes remained on the road, his lips tipped up into a smug smirk.

"Would you have answered truthfully if I had asked?"

"No." My mouth gaped open, and he breathed out a laugh. "But I would have told you not to wear white."

"But a dress is fine?"

His eyes left the road to graze over my unclothed legs. My fingers pulled at the hem of my dress, suddenly feeling more exposed than I had wished. The heat of his stare made my skin prick with goosebumps and my body shivered involuntarily.

The movement didn't go unnoticed, and Tommy moved his hand from the gear stick to turn on the heater. That was the last thing I needed with my body already on fire from just one of his looks, but I also couldn't really explain why I had shivered.

"Can I put some music on?" I asked, hoping to distract myself from the sudden nausea I was feeling in my stomach.

Tommy nodded, handing me his phone. "Spotify is already linked to the sound system. Put on what you want."

There were two unread messages on his screen, but I had no right in snooping and found the app I wanted. He had a couple of playlists, but I ignored them both and searched for the songs that I wanted. Angry Too by Lola Blanc. As the tune filled the car, Tommy subtly shook his head.

We remained quiet for the duration of the song and when it played the next, I looked over at him. "Where are we going?"

His focus remained on the road. "The cabin."

My stomach lurched and I shifted in my seat to angle myself towards him. "Why? Please don't take me back there." Memories of my first night at the school came into view and even though I came out unscathed, I still didn't want to go back and relive it. Especially if he had similar plans for tonight.

"You won't be the one tied up tonight, don't worry." His mischievous smirk threw me a bit, but it didn't stop the sick feeling.

I opened the window by a few inches, letting the cool air hit my face. Tommy reached for the heating again and switched it off. Both made the nausea ebb away slowly.

"Why are we going there?" I asked again, probably a little too quietly.

"I'll tell you after you answer one of my questions." The car turned off the road and on to the dirt track that I recognised led to the location we were going. I stayed silent, waiting for him to ask what he wanted. He drove for a little while longer then slowed down to a stop. Turning off the engine, Tommy took the keys from the ignition and spun them around his index finger. We sat there stationed in silence for a moment before his body turned to me.

"Who did you kill?"

I swallowed at the hard stare of his midnight eyes. "I told Callum already, I accidently killed that boy who tried to kiss me when I was 13."

"I believe that. But that wasn't the reason Williams

requested you come to this school. You would not be here for an accidental murder." He studied me for a moment, taking note of my fingers that were currently picking at the cuticles of my nails. "I'll only ask one more time."

"Or what?" I dared to ask.

His hand came up in one swift movement, seizing my jaw and pulling me closer to him. "I won't be as nice as what I am being right now." Releasing me, we both faced the window in front. My heart raced while he looked impatient. "So, who did you kill?"

I crossed my arms, almost as an act of protest but I knew it was to protect myself from what I was about to tell him. I wouldn't be leaving this car without giving him the answers he wanted. I could lie but that wouldn't benefit me in the future if he found out the truth.

Taking in a deep breath, I unfurled my arms and placed my hands idly onto my lap. "I killed three men."

I hesitated to continue for a second and his head turned to look at me. His eyes wondered down my tiny five foot four inch frame then up to my face. There was an incredulous look in them that made me not want to even bother to explain but he kept his mouth shut, not saying what he was thinking and prompting me to go on.

"When I was fifteen, I was at home with my mum and my brother. Antonio always used to go out with his friends but that night my father had to stay at work late so Antonio stayed home because I begged him to. I wanted to have a games night because we didn't do it as often as we used to. Dad and Antonio didn't have the best of relationships. If dad was there, then Antonio would go to his friends or shut himself away. As soon as I found out that he was working late, I pleaded with Antonio to stay home and play monopoly with me and mum."

"Monopoly?" Tommy asked, amusement lacing his voice at my choice of game.

"I'm old school. I love games like that. Cludo, game of life." I shrugged before continuing. "It was getting late, and we had finished playing. I had won of course."

Antonio would always let me win. If I was low on money, he would slip a few hundreds into my pile or if I owed him anything, he would write little IOU notes that meant I would have to do one of his chores or make him drinks all of the following day. He would never pull me up on the IOUs though. I smiled sadly at the bittersweet memory.

Tommy watched me, patiently waiting for me to get to the part of how and why I had killed three men. I kind of appreciated his patience now that I was finally admitting it all to him.

"Antonio packed up the game while mum and I took any cups and bowls we had used to the kitchen. There was a knock at the back door, and I ran to answer it. It really didn't occur to me that it was late at night and there wasn't any need for someone to be there. I just thought it may have been dad and he had forgotten his keys.

"When I opened the door, there was a man on the other side. He seemed nice enough, smiling at me the whole time.. He asked if my parents were home, so I called mum over. As soon as she came to the door, she tried to shut it again, but he stuck his foot in the way. Mum screamed at me to run so I did. I left her to fight off this massive man on her own, but I didn't know what else to do. I heard the door smash into the side as he forced his way into our home. Mum was screaming and Antonio was at the kitchen door within seconds. As soon as I saw him, I was relieved. Antonio was big and stocky. Archie reminds me of him a bit. He flew past me and into the man that had hold of mum. But then two other men stormed through the door. I didn't know what to do. Mum was screaming at me to run but I couldn't leave them. The first man hit mum round the face, knocking her to the floor while the other two had grabbed Antonio. I tried to run for the knife on the side but one of them grabbed my hair and as he pulled me back, my feet slipped under me, and I managed to knock myself out on the cabinet."

Tommy was still watching me, his face a blank canvas as he held back what he was thinking.

"When I came to again, I was tied to a chair and gagged." I stopped again, thinking about how all three of us were side by side. Mum had semi dried blood at the corner of her mouth where she had been struck and Antonio's head was hunched over, not a sound coming from him.

"But you managed to get out. You managed to get free." Tommy wasn't asking a question, he was prompting me to keep going, so I did.

"I did but it came with a cost. The men were in the kitchen with us. All three of them. They all spoke in a different language and at first, I didn't know what it was until I later heard it again. They were Russian."

That caught Tommy off guard slightly. His eyebrows knotted together, and his head tilted to the side, but he remained silent.

"My hands were bound with duct tape and while they were distracted with talking to each other, I found a loose screw in the chair that dad kept saying he was going to tighten but never got around to it. The men kept talking and glancing over at us like they didn't really know what to do next. Mum had managed to get the gag free from her mouth and she started pleading with them to let us go. Not her, just me and my brother. They shouted at her to be quiet, but she wouldn't, she just kept going."

I sniffed as tears filled my eyes. If I blinked, they would fall, and I didn't want that to happen. So I forced myself to stare hard at the dashboard, even avoiding his gaze.

"One of them said in broken English that they didn't need her. He shot her. Just once in the head." I could still hear the ringing in my ears now when I closed my eyes and pictured her there. Slumped in the chair. Blood pooling on her lap as it dripped from the bullet hole.

Tommy had leaned forward slightly, and it was only then that I realised my voice was so quiet he could hardly hear me.

"My brother was shouting against his own gag, yelling that he was going to kill them all but there was no way he could. He wouldn't have been able to get out of the bindings. I had become distracted though and the screw was still in the chair."

"Two of the men seemed distracted now too. They were rounding on the other one and even though I can't speak Russian, I knew they were angry with him for shooting my mum. They kept pacing, talking amongst themselves and eventually they left the room, leaving the killer to keep an eye on us."

"Antonio was still throwing muffled curses at the guy while I went back to loosening the screw more. Once it was completely free, I started scraping it against the tape, slowly freeing myself."

"That's how you escaped your first night here."

I gave him a soft, cheerless smile. "Yeh. And whoever tied those ropes that night, was pretty useless too." I managed a gentle chuckle, and he breathed a sound of light amusement as he nodded in agreement. "As soon as the tape was cut, I kept my hands behind my back, waiting for an opportunity to show itself. It didn't take too long. The man had been drinking the cans of coke from our fridge like they had been going out of fashion. He left us to go to the toilet and as soon as he was out of the room, I stood up.

"I tried my hardest to free Antonio but there wasn't enough time. We heard the footsteps of him coming back and I wanted to stay, sit back on my chair and pretend I was still bound but Antonio shook his head. He begged me with his eyes to run. Kept looking from me to the door and nodding his head." I will never forget the look. Fear, anger, sadness. All of those emotions were flooding out any happiness we once shared hours before.

"I didn't leave the house though –"

"Of course you didn't." There was a roll to his eyes but also a sense of pride in his voice.

" - I grabbed a knife from the block on the side and ran into the pantry. Our pantry was concealed. I can't really explain but the door to it looked like any other cupboard door in our kitchen so from the outside it looked like somewhere we would keep our plates or cups. Does that make sense?"

Tommy nodded. "Ours is the same at my family home."

"So obviously when I went in there, they didn't know where I had gone. Especially because there had been no sound of the back door at all. The man hit my brother and questioned him to find out where I was, but Antonio kept his mouth shut. Even when he taunted him to get a response, he didn't retaliate.

I watched from a gap in the door, wondering how I could get us both out of there, but I didn't know what I was doing. I didn't know how to defend myself. The only weapon I had to fight with was a kitchen knife. And I was 15. I didn't know what I was doing with it. Not really.

Two of the men left the room again, searching the house for me. The one left, the one who had killed my mum, stood a few feet from where I was hidden. He had his back towards me, and I thought that that was my chance. I pushed the door open and before he could even turn to see what was going on behind him, I jumped on his back and ran the knife across his throat."

Tommy's brows rose as I looked at him . A proud smile tilted his lips before he realised what was happening and his mouth went to a straight line.

I breathed out a heavy sigh and started speaking again. "The man fell to the floor, gargling on blood that was coming from his mouth. Antonio was begging me to run again but I didn't. I ran to him, but the commotion must have alerted the others because I heard them coming back. I hid in the pantry again, trying to think of a quick plan to kill them both.

"When they walked through the door, they- they saw their friend on the floor, dead. I thought they would just come looking for me again but instead they shot my brother. They shot him in the chest." My gaze was back on my hands resting on my lap and I started picking at my nails.

Tommy didn't press for me to continue but I did. "I had to cover my mouth with my hand to stop any sound coming out. I could feel the blood of the man I had killed on my cheeks, smell the metallic tang of it. I wasn't sure if it was that that made me want to be sick or the sight in front of me. Antonio's body fell forward, falling off the seat, and I realised that he too had managed to get out of the duct tape, but had stayed where he was to give me a chance to run. But I hadn't. The two men started calling for me. Telling me to come out and they would make my death quick. I contemplated it. I really contemplated leaving the tiny safe room and facing them. What was the point of staying there? I was only delaying the inevitable, right? I wouldn't be able to take on two more of them."

The silence between us was deafening as he waited and I stalled, reliving the memories, the fear, all over again.

"I don't believe in good or bad luck. I believe we make our own, but something seemed to help me that night. A noise came from outside. It could have been a cat or anything, but it had caught their attention. The man who had first knocked sent the other one out to look around. Leaving me alone with him. While he was distracted, looking out the window, I ran from the pantry. I wasn't quiet about it, and he fired some shots at me, all missing their target.

I ran upstairs to my bedroom where I purposely shut the door loudly, so he knew where I was. I wasn't sure if the other guy had come back or not but the man who had followed me banged on my door. My brother and I shared an ensuite. Both our rooms had a door that led into it. I ran to the bathroom and slammed that door shut. Just as the man had got into my room, I slammed my brother's door to the bathroom shut too, making as much noise as I could, then silently hid in the small cupboard where we kept our towels.

The man kicked the door in. I assume he heard the other door slam because he went straight for the next one. His gun was in the back pocket of his jeans, and I should have grabbed it, but I wasn't thinking straight. Instead, I ran from the cupboard and stabbed the knife into his spine, slicing it down. He wasn't dead when he fell to the floor, but he also couldn't move. I stood back up and left him there to bleed out. Then I left to hide from the other man."

Taking a deep breath, I peeked over to Tommy. He observed me intently, but I noticed a softness in his eyes. Definitely something I wasn't used to, but it felt almost calming.

"I could hear him coming up the stairs, each footstep was slow and quiet. I was surprised I could even hear it over the cries of the man in the other room. I hid under Antonio's bed. He was in the bathroom; I could hear his voice. He was talking to the other man in Russian. The dying man must have told him where I had gone because he walked into the bedroom. I could see his white trainers walking from one side of the room to the other. Each step making a new footprint of blood until he came to a standstill right in front of me.

I was about to put the knife through his foot, but he shot at the bed. Three shots. Each one missed me but only just. I rolled out and he grabbed me and chucked me against the wall. The force winded me and I had dropped the knife. I was certain I was going to die. All he had to do was lift the gun and shoot me. But he didn't. He wasn't going to let me die so easily for what I had done to his friends. " Tommy notably tensed but I went on. "He grabbed my arm and kicked my legs apart. I stood frozen to the cold wall as he ran the gun down my front and in-between my legs. He didn't care about the tears streaming down my face or the blood of his friends covering my body. He wanted me to suffer for what I had done.

He shot once. It didn't hit me, but it was enough to

nearly make me piss myself. I was so scared. It hit the wall and he laughed at my pathetic cries. But I didn't beg for him to let me go. I knew that was what he wanted, and I didn't give it to him.

He said something in broken English but it didn't really make sense. Something about he was meant to bring me and my brother back alive, but he wanted fun now. I couldn't really understand him so probably got that completely wrong. He grabbed my face and kissed me. No," I shook my head. "It wasn't a kiss. A kiss isn't meant to be like that. He violated me with his lips, and I bit him. I bit him as hard as I could until I tasted blood. When I let go, he hit me round the face with the gun."

I still remembered the sharp pain to my cheek where the gun had left a small slice. I was lucky in some sense that it hadn't left a major scar. Only a thin white line that was barely noticeable.

Tommy's jaw twitched as his eyes burned holes through the window screen. His hands clenched on to the steering wheel even though we were still sitting stationary in the middle of the road. His knuckles turned white through the force of his grip, and I felt the need to reach across and place my hand on his.

So I did.

I placed my hand on his so delicately and his fingers instantly loosened. He turned his head slowly, his eyes meeting mine. The rage that burned in them made me flinch and I tore my hand away. His fingers stretched out then left the steering wheel. One hand settled on his thigh while the other made a gesture to me to keep going before resting on his chin.

"The hit made me fall to the floor. He kicked me in the stomach, but it wasn't as hard as it could have been, and I managed to reach for the knife as he bent down to grab hold of my hair and pull me back up. I managed to stab him in the side, and I must have hit something of importance because once I ripped the knife back, he bled out in seconds."

Tommy nodded. "If he died quickly, you would have angled it up into his ribs and either punctured at lung or pierced his heart."

"Either way, he died." I shrugged. "The only one still alive was the man in the bathroom. I left him there while I dragged the man who I had just killed down the stairs and into the kitchen. I wanted all the bodies together. I don't know why; I just didn't want them in my brothers room. When I went back upstairs, the man in the bathroom was barely conscious and I knew he wouldn't last much longer. Still, I dragged him down the stairs and into the kitchen with the others. He begged me to end his life quickly. To end his suffering. I sat him against the cupboards and started pressing the knife into parts of his body. Each time I would ask if he could feel it. His cries told me that he could, yet he couldn't move. It confused me a bit, but I was glad that he could feel every painful incision I made.

I didn't stop until I had pierced his flesh in at least a dozen places. Once I had got to his heart, he was too weak to even beg. I slowly forced the knife in, watching his eyes widen as he finally died.

After, I looked at the body of my mum, still slumped in the chair and my brother, sprawled out on the cold tiles. Both lifeless. I snapped, screamed at the already dead intruders and sliced at their bodies more out of pure hatred and rage. After probably a few minutes, I sat on the floor, covered in blood, crying silently to myself.

That was how the police found me. How Professor Williams had found me. How, soon after, my dad found me."

Another long pause.

"Williams wanted you here and convinced your dad it would be the best decision?" Tommy asked but he already knew the answer.

"It was either here or prison," I shrugged. "So dad signed the papers and wrote the cheque. Everything was cleaned up, there had been no mention of what had happened, and everything just disappeared. I wasn't sure how all the evidence went missing or even how the police turned up. I guess a neighbour would have heard the gun shots and phoned them."

He gazed at me for a few minutes, his brows slowly creasing together then relaxing again. I wanted to ask what he was thinking but I kept quiet. Did he think I was a monster for what I did? I protected myself but there came a point where I went too far. I didn't know if I could handle being judged, not by him anyway.

"You're the first person I know not to brag about who or how they killed to get into the school. And now I know why." I tilted my head, wanting him to explain. "You didn't kill because you wanted to. You killed because you had to. You killed to survive. And talking about it brings back memories you want kept buried."

"But no one really wants to kill, do they?"

"You will meet a lot of people at this school Isabella and none of them kill because they have to. They kill because they want to. They just have different motivations. But everyone kills to survive. It's how we are programmed as a human. It's what makes us human." He placed the key in the ignition again, twisted it, bringing the car back to life.

"What about you?"

"What about me?" He turned the wheel, setting us straight on the road again.

"Do you kill because you want to or because you have to?" I wasn't sure I wanted to know the answer but whatever it was, I was part of it all now.

"I kill for many reasons and I'm pretty sure you won't agree with any of them so there is no point going through it with you. I won't lie and say that I don't get any pleasure from it because I do." An immoral grin formed across his devilishly handsome face, making my cheeks heat.

I quickly looked away and at the road ahead. I could just make out the soft lights of the cabin in the distance as we drove closer, and my heart lurched. "Why are we going to the cabin?" I asked, hoping this time for an answer.

"We have an assignment to complete, and I have a feeling you wouldn't have been able to complete it on your own." His face was a blank canvas again as he stared ahead.

"I may have had a plan to do it at some point this weekend." I pouted, crossing my arms like a petulant child.

He let out a dry laugh and reached across towards my lap. I immediately stiffened as his fingers grazed my thighs through the thin fabric and as I glanced down, I let out a small breath. He grabbed his phone that I had forgotten was there and placed it back in his pocket.

"You had two texts by the way." I quickly said, remembering them when I had been looking for music.

"Felix." Answering a question I hadn't asked, he shifted in his seat slightly. "Reminding me that although your attitude makes it so tempting, I shouldn't hurt you."

My mouth fell open as I glared at him in shock. "You need reminding to not hurt me?"

"I need reminding to not do a lot of things to you... daily." His lips twitched into a smirk, and I rolled my eyes. "Oh, and I didn't need that long description of why you killed. Just saying you killed three men would have sufficed."

I could hear the amusement in his voice and straightaway, my mood went to pissed off. By the way I grumbled "Prick", he knew it too and his dark laugh sent shivers through my whole body.

Chapter 11

Tommy pushed the door of the cabin open then stepped aside for me to enter before him. As soon as I did, I wished I hadn't. Archie was sat in a high-backed chair, his ankle resting on his knee as he casually nodded a greeting to me. Felix was sat at the table in the kitchenette, on one of the chairs I had been tied to, reassembling his gun and Callum…

Callum was standing behind a metal chair. It was a different style to the one I had been tied to. This one had arms. On it sat a man. Each of the man's wrists were zip tied to the arms and his ankles to the chair legs. There was a burlap sack over his head, but you could hear muffled whimpering from under it, giving away that he had also been gagged. Callum's sin filled eyes settled on me as soon as I entered, and a naughty grin lit up his face.

What was on the table in front of him though, was what made my mouth go dry and my heart race ten to the dozen. An array of different instruments was placed in a line. Pliers, bolt croppers, a hunter's knife and a blow torch was just to name a few. Beneath it all, covering the wooden floor was a plastic sheet, protecting it from any spillage.

My stomach plummeted as I quickly realised what they were intending to do. I looked between the three then turned to face Tommy, a silent plea in my eyes to not make me watch this but he simply crossed his arms and blocked the only exit I knew.

I looked back at the man. His nails were scratching at the metal of the chair then flexing out and trying to pull free from the restraints. Callum glanced behind me at Tommy, and he must have given an unspoken command because he ripped off the sack, revealing a man that was in his late thirties, possibly early forties. But I didn't know who he was and that brought me some kind of relief.

"Did you know, a woman can withstand more torture than what a man can." Felix lifted his head, throwing the unnecessary fact around the room. I could have come back with a witty reply like of course we can, we withstand the torture of men daily, but I couldn't quite get the words out as I stared at the bloke. "They can withstand a lot more pain. But they also cause the most too."

"Trust you to know something that useless." Archie grumbled from his seat but then stood up and moved across to the kitchen. He opened the fridge door and pulled out four bottles of beer then held one up to me, asking if I wanted one. I shook my head and he pulled out a bottle of water instead.

Popping of the tops with a bottle opener magnet from the fridge door, he started handing them out. Reaching over me, he handed the last beer to Tommy and then passed me the water. "Sit down, we're not going anywhere until this is over so may as well get comfy."

"Until what is over?"

"Our assignment, of course." He grinned viciously.

Daring another glance at Tommy, he took a swig of his drink, but his eyes didn't leave me. I had two choices. Cause a scene and probably be tied down and forced to watch or be a good girl and do as I was told and complete the assignment.

I chose the latter.

Sitting in the chair that had hosted Archie, I pulled my legs up to the side. The man was starting to become more frantic now, looking around the room at all of us and moving his body in the seat. Callum placed a firm hand on his shoulder, making him stop but tears started to stain his face.

Tommy stepped over to him and picked up the pliers from the table. Not wasting any time or any words, he placed it under his nail and painfully slowly ripped it up. The gag couldn't even silence the man's cries and I winced. He moved on to the next nail and I was thankful that I was sitting down already because I had to look away. It was going to be a slow and severely agonising process for the man.

"How long do you think he will last?" Felix asked.

Callum answered first. "Fifteen minutes."

"Twenty." Archie smirked, taking another swig of his beer.

"Pass me the knife and I will make it five." Tommy's smile was terrifying. This was undoubtedly the happiest I had seen him and yet I should have probably feared him the most at that point.

Callum did as he asked though and passed Tommy the hunter's knife, taking the pliers and placing them back on the table. Tommy sliced across his fingers, and they dropped to the floor, one by one. I hated to admit that watching Tommy work was oddly enjoyable but horrifying at the same time. He went on to making deep lacerations along his exposed arms, not seeming to be too concerned by the amount of blood that was starting to cover him.

Sure enough, five minutes later the man had passed out.

"Make sure he doesn't bleed out; I'm not done with him yet." Tommy instructed, placing the knife down and wiped his hands with a cloth. Callum nodded and reached for the blow torch.

"Who is he?" I asked.

"Does it matter?" Tommy replied, arching his brow as he sat down opposite me.

"What did he do to deserve this?"

"He beat his pregnant girlfriend to an inch of her life, ending the life of her baby." Callum answered, his eyes dark and penetrating as he looked up at me. "Is that a good enough reason to deserve it?"

I didn't speak because yes. Yes, it was a good enough reason. How someone could do that was beyond me. I couldn't fathom their reasons to harm any woman who was pregnant. Even babies. Or children. People who hurt them were pathetic, worthless and deserved everything bad that happened to them.

Callum probably knew what I was thinking because he didn't ask again and went back to what he was doing. Igniting the torch, he ran it across the bloody wounds, cauterising them. As soon as the flame touched his arm, the man came back around, his eyes still rolling through the pain. His cries were louder but was still muffled enough to not disturb the conversation between Felix and Archie.

"Have we still got them noodle packs in the cupboard."

"Get up and look." Archie was still in the kitchen with the cupboard behind him, leaning against the counter as he drank from his bottle.

"You're already there, just open the door and look." Felix snarled at him, and Archie just carried on drinking.

"I'm not your slave."

"Just open the fucking door and look."

I looked between them. Felix was glowering at his cousin while Archie just took another swig of his beer, grinning at the confrontation.

"How can you eat while that is going on anyway?" I asked Felix, pointing at the body and at Callum having nearly as much fun as Tommy had been having. The smell of burning flesh was starting to circulate, making me feel ill.

He shrugged casually and stood up. "When you're hungry, you're hungry." Moving to the cupboard, he pulled the door open then groaned at the emptiness.

"I ate the last packet." Archie grinned wolfishly at him.

Felix punched him in the arm roughly before walking back to his seat and muttering bastard under his breath.

The room went quiet for a while. Just the muffled screams breaking the silence. I didn't dare look to see how far Callum had got with his job. I didn't want to think about it, but it was also hard not to. He finally finished and set the blow torch back down before coming to sit on the arm of my chair.

Moving a loose curl behind my ear, he continued to move his fingers down the curve of my neck and carried on down my arm. "You look nice tonight."

"Thanks." I muttered, managing to include a tiny smile with it.

"Maybe don't get too close if you don't want to ruin that pretty little dress of yours." His gaze grazed over the white dress and then to my naked legs.

"I don't intend on getting close to that." I peered over at the man and my stomach instantly took a turn. His skin was blackened and burnt from the flames while blood covered every inch of his arms and hands. I wasn't sure how deep the cuts had been, but I guessed they were deep enough to know there was going to be no surviving without Callum's help.

"I did tell her white probably wasn't the best idea." Tommy cut in but didn't look up from his phone.

"You didn't even tell me what we were doing. If I had known, I would have worn disposable coveralls."

"Or you would have found any excuse to not come, and I would have dragged you kicking and screaming again." He finally looked up, giving me a crooked smirk.

"Something tells me you would enjoy that." I glared at him, and he breathed out a sound of amusement as something dark and twisted flashed through his eyes.

"We have coveralls in the back room if you still want to wear them?" Felix offered, breaking the unusual tension between Tommy and me.

"Why do you have — you know what, I don't want to know." I shook my hand in the air and stood up.

Bracing myself, I walked over to the man. I could feel the eyes of all four boys on me, wondering how I was going to react most probably. But I kept my chin up high as my gaze lowered to the marks that had been created. He wasn't screaming anymore, only whimpering softly.

"Is he dying?"

Tommy stood up, coming to stand beside me. He was careful not to get too close so the blood on his clothes didn't transfer to mine. "No, probably exhausted from the pain. He will be dead very soon though."

"What will you do to him next?"

"Scalp him. Cut out his eyes. I haven't yet decided."

"Oh." My fingers glided over the handle of the bloodied knife then the bolt croppers. "When will you let him die?"

"When we have had enough." He stepped to my front and picked up the knife then offered it to me. "Want a go?"

I looked down at it. Maybe I should. It was part of the assignment after all. But I really wasn't ready for that side of things. I couldn't bring myself to take it from him.

Tommy placed a finger under my chin, bringing my head back up to meet his unusually soft gaze. "You don't have to."

Looking past him at the man, I saw Felix bringing a needle to his arm. I wasn't scared of a lot of things. Clowns and spiders were definitely on the list and Tommy had found his way on there too when I wasn't feeling brave. But needles were right at the top. I could watch him torture this man and get through it with only feeling a little sick and disgusted. The sight of blood and gore didn't affect me as much as the sight of needles did. Needles were a big no. I couldn't explain why, and I had no reason to be, but they terrified me.

"What's he doing?" I whispered and Tommy turned to see what I was talking about.

"Giving him something to keep him alert. We don't want him passing out again."

I watched as the needle went in and felt all colour drain from my cheeks.

"I need some fresh air." I didn't wait for a response. I just turned and rushed out of the front door.

The fresh evening air hit me with a welcoming breeze. If I had stayed in there much longer, I would have been sick. Closing my eyes, I could still see the needle going in. It wasn't just that thought. It was the sight of the blood and the smell of burning flesh. My stomach turned again but I held it in.

As I sat down on the edge of the small porch, I stared out into the trees that surrounded us. Inside was an assignment. An assignment set by the school that I now attended. I could barely handle it. How was I going to feel when the time came to do so much worse? What the hell was graduation going to be like? And exams?

Maybe I wasn't cut out for this. Maybe I wasn't strong enough to stay at this school. Because I sure as hell didn't think I was going to survive watching something like this again.

The door creaked open behind me, but I didn't turn to see who it was. Whoever it was shut it softly behind them then stepped up beside me. I peered up at Callum and he smiled kindly with a steaming mug in his hand.

"Here." He crouched down and handed me the hot drink.

I smiled back appreciatively and took the mug, but it didn't stop my teasing jibe at him. "Aww, you can be nice."

"I'm very nice to you all the time." He chuckled and moved his legs, so he was sitting too. "But I can't take credit for this." He tapped the mug of tea in my hands. "Tommy said you will need the sugar. You look pale and sick."

"Cheers for that." I rolled my eyes as I looked back towards the trees. My fingers hugged the mug, thankful for the warmth against the autumn chill. "And can you blame me for feeling sick." He didn't know about my fear of needles, and I wasn't going to share it but the scene in the cabin was enough to churn anyone's insides.

"No," He leaned back on his hands and looked up at the sky. "But you get used to it."

"I don't think I could ever get used to that." I grumbled, then blew into the mug like it would actually help speed up the cool down process so I could take a sip.

"Give it time." He leaned forward again, clasping his hands together and resting his forearms on his knees. He was hesitating before saying something. "Tommy told us what you spoke about in the car. Not every detail but we got the gist of it all."

My chest tightened. Why would he tell them? Well, why wouldn't he? I would have had to tell them eventually, so he basically saved me a job of having to go through it all again but still. Shouldn't it have been my choice.

"Are you mad?" My eyes met his for a second. "That he told us?"

I swallowed. "Yes – I mean no." I shook my head. "I don't think I am. I suppose I knew he would have told you anyway. I guess I just didn't anticipate how soon he would."

"Or that you would be about when he did?"

"Yeah." I took the first sip of tea. Sweet but not overly.

"I was fourteen when I first shot someone." Callum began and I turned my gaze to him. His head was down as he thought for a minute then he looked towards the trees. "My dad and Tommy's thought it would be a good idea to let us make our first kill early. The other two didn't until a year before attending this school."

"Who did you kill?"

"Some local perv who had been stalking the girls outside a primary school. It was an easy kill. Straight to the bonce and he was gone. A quick death, but he deserved a more painful one in my opinion." I found myself nodding in agreement but kept my mouth shut. "My kill was easy. Set up for me."

He was quiet again for a few seconds. "I guess what I'm trying to say is, yours wasn't easy. You fought for survival and came out the other side. When pushed into a corner you are a lot stronger than you probably give yourself credit for. I think you would even give us four a good run for our money if we pissed you off enough."

"Don't tempt me." I grinned.

"There she is. That wicked attitude." He nudged his shoulder into mine and I chuckled lightly. "Why do you think Tommy claimed you as one of us?"

"He told me. It's because I'm a threat and it's better to keep me close rather than making allies to take you all down."

Callum blinked at this but then smiled. "You are smart. But no, that wasn't the only reason. And if you repeat this to him, I will deny telling you because I don't fancy an arse whooping." Shifting in his spot, he faced his body towards mine. "He claimed you because you didn't run from him. You came back. We were all certain that you would take Archie's car and disappear, but you didn't. That showed guts. He saw something in you then that he needs. A challenge. You're the only girl apart from my sister obviously, that won't submit to him."

"But he makes it so much fun to disobey." I smiled as sweetly as I could, and he let out a small laugh.

"Just don't push him too far. I've grown quite attached to you sweetheart. I wouldn't want him to completely destroy you."

I bit on to my bottom lip as little flutters formed inside. Destroy me?

Callum stood back up and headed towards the door.

"Callum?" He waited as his hand reached for the handle. "Who did Tommy kill that day?"

For a second, I thought he wasn't going to answer. "That's his story to tell."

Without another word he opened the door then closed it behind him again. Tommy's story to tell. The words played back in my head as I continued to drink my tea. Was it that bad or was it merely out of respect that he wasn't telling me?

Roughly five minutes later, Tommy walked out. He walked down the steps and came to stand in front of me. For maybe a little too long we just gazed at each other. He didn't say anything and neither did I. The only sound was the cries and laughter from the others inside.

Holding out his hand, I let him pull me to my feet. "I'm taking you home with me."

"Are you finished in there now?"

"The others are still having their fun, but I think you've had enough. We're going back to the school." He walked over to his car and opened the door on my side. I followed, neither of us saying a word as I slipped into my seat.

When he got into the car, he handed me his phone to put the music on again.

"I'm sorry." I muttered. He looked at me confused. "That I didn't do it. Hurt that guy I mean."

"I'm not going to force you to do it before you're ready Isabella. But whether you like it or not, you have it in you."

I didn't answer but curled up on the seat as he drove off, leaving the cabin and what was inside behind.

When we got back to the school, he dropped me off outside the main building then drove back away, leaving me on the gravel. I stared after the car, watching the headlights get smaller and smaller as he disappeared back through the gates. What a weird, fucked up night.

Chapter 12

Saturday. The day of the charity event that I was being forced to attend. Could I refuse to go? Sure. Would it be worth it if I did? No, probably not. So instead, Maddy and I curled our hair then set it in pins ready to release before we left. Well, I set my natural waves in pins to make them more prominent. She was adamant that our nails should be perfectly neat, so painted mine a blood red that didn't match my dress at all, but she seemed unfazed by that.

Our makeup was done to excellence but the rest of us left little to be desired. Sitting in the library in our oversized floofs, as Maddy liked to call them, (An over fluffy poncho with a fur trimmed hood. Unflattering but oh so comfy.) and shorts, we decided to finish our homework before we got dressed for the evening events.

"I honestly hate psychology." Maddy slammed her book shut and smacked her head against the cover. "We haven't even had our first lesson yet and already have homework."

"Careful, you might smudge your contour." I teased and she stuck her tongue out.

"Why would we need to know about killers of the past and why they did what they did." She waved the book in front of my face then dropped it to the table. "No one cares as long as we do a good job ourselves."

I couldn't help but agree. Psychology was a goreified history lesson. "Maybe it's to get more ideas on how to kill people."

"We should just watch films for that. At least they are more inventive than these unimaginative fucks." She sneered down at the book then threw herself back in her chair, sighing with exasperation.

"I don't think it's possible to do a Freddy Krueger and kill people in their dreams."

Her eyes widened as her mouth split into a massive grin. "Imagine if we could. How much easier would that be to just get rid of people. Hey, dreaming of a unicorn? Pow. Just got impaled by the horn."

"Fuck sake Maddy." I laughed quietly. "Please say that in one of your essays."

"I can't wait to not pass that class."

I let out a light chuckle just as a shadow cast over me.

"The lesson is to teach us about the mistakes that they made so we don't make the same ones." I turned round to see one of my classmates from AP Art of Killing. "Ricky." He held out his hand for me to take and then kissed my knuckles.

Rolling my eyes at his cheeky, crooked grin, I pulled my hand back. "Isabella."

"I know. And Maddy." He smiled warmly at her then sat on the table beside my books. She smiled her greeting back.

"You're in her brother's year, aren't you?" I asked.

"I am." He smiled broadly, like he was impressed that I had recognised him. "Sorry to just interrupt but I was curious to know who the hell looked like the mad cat ladies from across the room."

Maddy laughed, resulting in a scowl from Ms. Crawley, who I had recently found out was actually the school's librarian not receptionist.

"Yeah, I can see how we look strange from a distance." I agreed, regretting coming in our white floofs and pinned curls for the first time. "But I would say more adorable abominable snowmen than crazy cat ladies."

"I said mad, not crazy."

"What's the difference?"

"How far you push them." The boyish gleam to his eyes made me smile.

"I like you." Picking my book up from the table, I started reading again. This time about a man who had murdered his wife and stuck her body in a water tank so no one could find her. Brutal. But stupid when the town's people started noticing a weird taste to their water supply.

"So what's the special occasion?" Ricky asked and I tilted my head up to look at him. He wasn't bad looking. Black, curly hair and big brown eyes. He had a strong jaw and was clean shaven.

"Family gathering." Maddy answered quickly making Ricky raise a brow at our made-up faces. Bit extravagant for just a family gathering. "I mean it's the charity event, but we are going with my family."

"Ahh, I forgot about that." His attention slipped back to me. "Well your hair looks…" His eyes flicked up to the massive, pinned curls and he tried to keep his mouth in a straight line, but I could see the struggle. "Interesting."

"Obviously we aren't completely ready yet." I sneered playfully and he laughed. "And before you feel the need to add, we won't be wearing this either."

"And there was me thinking there was some sort of marshmallow man theme going on."

"You just keep coming with them compliments, don't you?" I didn't mind his playful teasing. It made a change for another boy to talk to us other than the four that I had been unwillingly subjected to.

Although, that did make me wonder if he had waited for us to be alone before talking to us. No one would usually dare with our guard dogs around, but they were off playing elsewhere. Or they just didn't know that we had wondered from the safety of our room.

"Kidding. It's unusual to see you both without your usual entourage." Ricky did a quick scan of the room before resting his eyes on Maddy. "Was surprised to see you here this year."

Maddy merely shrugged. "Thought it was about time someone other than the men held power in my family."

"What will your fiancé say." He chuckled then picked up the book beside him and flicked through the pages. "Is he going to be happy that his little English rose is going to have some thorns?"

"Fiancé?" I spluttered out, looking to Maddy in shock.

She smiled across at me, somewhat apologetic of keeping that information a secret. "The women in our world are married off to the men of other families. Basically to keep peace treaties between us all." The look I must have given off was disgust because Maddy felt the need to explain to me further. "Yes, it's archaic and completely unreasonable but it's what's normal for us." Us being her family. The firm. And other families like hers.

"Do you love him?" I dared to ask.

Something bordering pity flashed through her eyes then was gone in a blink. "He seems nice enough. I've only met him twice. Once last summer when the marriage was promised and again this summer. Jullian. That's his name. He's kind and gentle from what I have heard. One of the Parisian firm's nephews."

"He's French?"

"Yeh. Uncle Thomas needed a way in with them and being the only girl old enough in our family to marry… the job was mine."

Again, my face displayed all the disgust I was feeling. Maddy just laughed. "Honestly Bella, when you have grown up in a family like mine, this is what is normal. Plus do you really think my brother would let me marry someone who would treat me badly."

I shook my head and looked away, finally relaxing my features. "No I suppose not."

"Even with the order coming from the boss, Callum would argue it and Tommy would have done something about it too."

"What about the others? Are they set to marry anyone?"

"My brother and the other three?" I simply nodded. "No, different rules for men. Callum, Archie and Felix can marry whoever they want."

"Tommy's engaged though." Ricky interrupted, still flicking through the book.

"Really?" My gaze darted from him to Maddy.

"No, he called that off a few nights ago." She shook her head at Ricky.

"Is that so? I wasn't told about that." This had piqued his interest and he closed the book to give her all his attention. "Why'd he do that?"

She just shrugged again and studied her nails.

"So you can just call these things off then?"

"Not usually. There has to be some sort of broken agreement to nullify a contract." Ricky answered me but kept his eyes on Maddy, wanting to fish for more information.

"What sort of broken agreement?" My interest in their traditions was definitely taking a turn. Before I didn't care but now... now I wanted to know, just in case there came a time where I might have to use this information to get my friend out of a marriage she didn't truly want.

"Mainly between the parents or the main bosses. Could be over territory or money. Drugs. Anything really that could be exchanged to benefit both parties. If one party went back on one of the agreements, the contract would be void and the marriage would cease to exist."

"The whole marriage? Not just the promise of it?"

"Even after the vows." Ricky confirmed. "But it really isn't worth it. A civil war would break out between both families and there would be a lot of death."

"So how did Tommy get away with it?" Surely if he had made the contract void, there would be a lot of trouble coming his way.

"I'm guessing he used the old virgin clause?" He smirked slyly at Maddy, and she just nodded to verify his suspicions.

"Virgin clause?"

"Every contract is made redundant if the woman is not a virgin – seriously, you need to stop looking so repulsed every time I shock you." I quickly adjusted my face to fake a smile at her and she laughed before continuing. "It's to make sure that the woman isn't pregnant before she is married. That their offspring had to be their own to keep the family blood pure. But no one actually cares about that rule anymore. None of the men are bothered about that and never use that reason to nullify a contract."

"But I'm guessing Tommy did?"

"Yeh. He said that by being next in line he couldn't take any risks. Her father was pretty pissed according to Callum, but it was in the contract. There was nothing he could do about it. So Tommy walked away from the marriage agreement."

Wow. That easy for a man.

"I'll expect a phone call soon then if it all kicks off eventually." Ricky sighed. "Surprised I wasn't told about this sooner."

I looked up at him confused. Who was he to them for him to feel the need to know about a personal family matter?

Maddy noted my confusion. "Bella, meet one of the other claimed ones."

My mouth dropped open. I hadn't met one of the others yet and was surprised to have only just been introduced to this one after already sharing classes together.

"Don't look so shocked." He chuckled. "I wasn't claimed as quickly as you, but I was claimed for certain skills I have."

I tilted my head, waiting for him to explain but it was Maddy that answered. "Ricky is a sniper."

"I'm the best this school has." He flashed me a smug toothy grin, eyes shining. "Not that I like to brag."

"So they have you there because?"

"Because if all goes tits up, I'm in the distance with my AWM ready to clear up."

"Why not just use you to begin with?" I frowned at him.

"It's all about bargaining. Everyone wants something and yeah Tommy and the others could just take by force but that would leave unnecessary mess. Tommy will bargain with the others and come up with deals but then sometimes it doesn't work out and there's a fight. Or a threat of one anyway." He gave me a little wink. "I'm there, in the distance with my little red light shining on the man in front of Tommy. Once they see that, they either yield or Tommy gives the signal and I shoot."

"Does Tommy actually do any dirty work himself?" It seemed like certain jobs fell on everyone else.

"Oh Tommy does the dirty work. He's just smart about it and knows when to use others to get a job done... cleaner I suppose." He flashed me that cheeky grin again and I shook my head. What Tommy did last night was definitely not the cleaner option.

"Also if they can't get close to someone, Ricky will be called in. Like someone who is highly guarded." Maddy added and I nodded.

"What about you though? Why were you claimed?"

"I didn't run." I simply replied with a shrug. Ricky frowned, looking slightly bemused then exchanged a look with Maddy that I missed as when I turned to face her, she was smiling broadly at me.

"Where are your wonderful cousins and brother anyway?" Ricky asked, changing the subject quickly.

"Getting ready still I should think. They are worse than girls, you should know that by now."

Ricky let out a light breath of laughter while I felt the

need to add. "They will be here soon anyway." He graced me with another puzzled glance, and I shrugged. "They don't want me making friends so catching wind that I am talking to someone else will summon them like the demon spawn they are. Don't think it will matter much that you are part of the claimed crew or not."

Maddy snorted but nodded in agreement and Ricky just tilted his head making his black curls flop to the side. "No one else is in here. They won't know that you're speaking to me."

"You've known them a lot longer than me and even I know not to underestimate their skills. They're like a fly to shit."

"I'm not sure if I should feel insulted right now or poor Ricky here, being referred to as shit."

All three of our heads snapped to the person walking over to us.

Ricky jumped out of his seat on the table as soon as Felix approached. "Just seeing if the girls wanted help with their psychology homework."

"I'm sure you were." Felix rolled his eyes, grinning then clapped hands with him and brought him in for a hug. "And we don't really care about you making friends"

That was meant for me, and my brows creased as I smiled, happy but confused.

"You can be friends with whoever you want as long as we approve them."

My smile faded. "You were my favourite for almost thirty seconds."

Laughing, Felix turned back to Ricky. "We have a job tonight and Tommy has messaged you to meet him for a briefing about something else."

Ricky removed his phone from his pocket and looked at the screen. "Shit!" He didn't even say goodbye before fleeing from the library and no doubt to Tommy's room.

Felix fell into the seat beside me, swinging his legs onto the table. I tsked, moving the book his shiny black shoes had hit. He was already in his black suit trousers, dress shirt and bow tie. The jacket that I was sure he would have to wear at some point was nowhere to be seen. His dark eyes flicked from Maddy to me then back again.

"You haven't replied to any of our messages." It wasn't just a statement but a question.

"I left my phone in my room with Bella's." She smiled sweetly at him, and I smiled too knowing that one of Tommy and Callum's triggers was not replying to messages.

"She's a bad influence on you." Felix smirked, pointing his finger at me. "We leave in thirty minutes."

"What? Why?" Maddy demanded, shooting up from her seat and I did the same. "We're not even ready."

"If you had your phones, you would know that Tommy wants to make a quick stop off first."

"Arghhh! He could have told us this earlier." She stalked towards the door. Felix and I followed silently whilst listening to her grumble that her cousin was a dick.

We parted ways, Felix heading back towards the boys dorms while Maddy and I made our way to our own room.

Waiting outside was a large black box, with a black satin ribbon tied into a bow around it. Beside the bow lay another rose. Orange this time.

"For you?" I nudged Maddy, smiling softly at the gift.

She picked up the small card that rested on top of the rose stem. "For you."

I took the card as she passed it to me.

Isabella

Chapter 13

Maddy picked up the box as I unlocked our bedroom door. We both walked into the room, and she placed it down on my bed then sat beside it, waiting for me to open up the gift.

I slung the keys on to my desk and picked out the rose from the satin ribbon. "Another gift from your brother? What does orange mean?"

"Fascination." She frowned, thinking about it for a second. "But it can also mean desire." A smirk played on her lips then and I rolled my eyes before turning my back to her, grinning to myself.

Adding the rose to the thin vase that held the blue one, I studied them both.

Unattainable, mysterious, fascination and desire.

"If Callum keeps sending me roses, I'll end up with a rainbow of them soon."

"If he sends you a red one then we best start looking at wedding dresses." I snorted out a laugh but as I turned to face her again, her expression was stern. "I'm serious, I told you that roses are a big thing in my family. I'm actually surprised that Callum is going this far though." She fiddled with the satin ribbon of the box, and I walked over to her.

"Maybe he isn't meaning the more intimate meanings."

"Maybe. But I still don't think… If he gets too much, I'll have a word."

I smiled my thanks and pulled at the bow, loosening it. Lifting the lid off, my eyes widened at the item that was in the box.

I carefully picked up the black dress from the tissue paper bed it was neatly folded on. The material was a soft satin, slipping over itself as the skirt of the dress fell to the floor.

"Oh my god." Maddy breathed out but all I could do was gape at it. It was stunning. "You need to try it on."

"This is really too much." I shook my head in disbelief. "First the choker and now this."

"You have to wear it." She quickly said, tearing her eyes away from the dress to gawp at me.

Part of me wanted to say no. This was just another thing to control me with. Telling me what I had to wear. But at the same time, the dress was beautiful and had been selected to match the choker perfectly. It was better than the blue dress that I was going to wear.

"If it fits me, I will." I whispered, fingering the delicate material.

Maddy nodded but didn't say anything as she pulled her outfit off the hanger and disappeared into the bathroom.

I placed the dress back into the box, careful not to make any creases and walked across the room. Standing before the floor length mirror, I started to remove the pins from my curls then carefully brushed them out. The big, bouncy waves hung down my back, not needing anything else to be done to them. By the time I was finished, Maddy walked back into the room.

Her blonde hair was now styled similar to mine but pushed to the side by a big diamond clip. She wore a red satin dress that her mum had someone deliver that morning. The material pooled around her ankles, a little too long without the six-inch heels she was to wear with it.

"You look amazing." I gushed and she smiled brightly, adjusting her bracelet on her wrist.

"Why, thank you bestie. Now go try that dress on. I want to see it and be jealous that you have a boy sending you gifts even if it is just my stupid brother."

I chuckled, lifting my dress from its box. "Does Jullian send you gifts?"

"No, but if he wants a happy wife he best start." She sassed but the grin on her face told me she was joking.

I left her strapping her silver heels to her feet and walked into the bathroom, pulling the door shut behind me.

Stripping out of the floof and shorts, I removed my bra too. There was no way I would be able to wear one with the new dress. Stepping into it, I shimmied it up my body. The lavish material kissed my skin delicately. Slipping my arms into the capped, off the shoulder sleeves, I pulled it further up my body. A deep slit at the side of the skirt showcased my thigh and part of me feared that at some point during the evening if I wasn't careful, someone would get quite an eyeful of something they shouldn't.

I adjusted my breasts against the sweetheart bodice and slid the zip at the back of the dress up as far as I could without help. It fit perfectly. I didn't know how he had done it, but Callum had chosen the perfect dress that was also the perfect size.

"Maddy!"

No reply.

"Maddyyy." I stretched out her name, hoping my whiney voice would bring her to the bathroom so she could finish pulling up the zip. Still no reply. I walked out the door, picking up the skirt a little to stop myself from tripping over it. "Can you finish doing the zip please?"

Looking up, I stopped. Callum was sitting on my bed, playing with the orange rose that he had taken from my desk.

"Beautiful." He smiled, gazing at the rose. His eyes

wandered up and fixated on me. "But it's nothing compared to you."

Heat rose to my cheeks as I looked down. "Can you do me up please?"

He stood from his seat, placing the rose down and took slow steps up to me. I turned around, my back facing him and moved my hair to the side.

His knuckles brushed my skin as he slid the zip fully up. I looked across into the mirror at my reflection. The size of the dress was definitely precise. The curves I had inherited from my mum were flaunted by the soft material clinging to them.

Callum's fingers glided across the bare skin of my back then down towards the zip again. "It's a shame I had to do this up and not take it off." I watched his reflection while his head dipped, close enough to my neck to feel the warmth of his breath.

My heart thumped against my ribs as his touch lowered even more to my hips and his nose pressed against small space behind my ear. Breathing in, his fingers pinched my side. "You smell delicious."

"Callum." I warned but it came out breathy, almost a plea to continue.

His chuckle vibrated against me, sending a shiver through my body. "Where's the choker?" He stepped back and I focused again on his reflection in the mirror. A playful but knowing smirk graced his lips and I rolled my eyes to look away from him, hating that he had probably won whatever game he was playing.

"Top drawer." I pointed to the set beside my bed, and he walked over to them. I didn't bother waiting for him to retrieve it. Instead I walked over to my jewellery box that was on top of my chest of drawers and took out a thin diamond bracelet and a ring. The ring had been my mothers. Her engagement ring. Dad had kept her wedding band, but the engagement ring was mine.

I slipped it on my finger on the opposite hand to which

it should be placed and turned back round to Callum. He had taken the box out of the drawer, along with something else.

"Seeing these makes me want to know what you have on right now." He held up my pink lacy thong.

"Put it back." I launched myself across to grab it, but he caught me and held it out of my reach while laughing. I glared up at him making his laughter stop but there was still amusement across his face.

"Can I keep it for later?" His voice was so innocent in contrast to the question that I wanted to laugh but instead I grinned and stepped out of his grip.

"I don't think it will fit you."

"I don't need it to fit me with what I plan to do." He responded and my head tilted for him to explain. "I'm going to wrap it around my cock while I fuck my hand thinking of you."

I almost choked as my eyes went wide.

Laughing again, he chucked my underwear back in the drawer. "No witty comeback for that sweetheart?"

I had hesitated so whatever comment I would make now wouldn't have a great impact, but it didn't stop me from saying "You wanted to know what I'm wearing right now?"

His grin told me he was listening as he walked behind me. Taking the choker from the box, he slid it round my neck and fastened the clasp.

I licked my lips as I twisted round, his hands coming to rest on my hips again. I stood on my tiptoes so I could lean into his ear. My breasts pressed against his chest, and I heard his sharp intake of breath. "I'm not wearing anything."

I was, but he wouldn't be able to tell if I was lying or not. They were of the thinnest material, meaning there would be no visible lines through the dress. And I definitely wouldn't give him the opportunity to find out.

Callum's fingers gripped the fabric of the dress, scrunching it in his fist. A deep growl came from his throat, and I pushed myself away from him. His eyes had darkened as his pupils dilated and his breath was ragged.

A smile crept on my face. I could handle the harmless flirting between us in front of the others, but with no one else around, just how far would he go?

"If Tommy hadn't bought this dress, and we didn't have somewhere to be, I would be ripping it off your body."

I stepped back further, creasing my brows together. "Tommy –" Cutting myself off, I looked towards the roses. They were from him?

"Get your shoes on, we've got to go." Callum instructed, walking away towards the door.

I swallowed before sitting on the bed and putting my shoes on. Before Callum had told me the dress was from Tommy, I had started to believe Maddy that the roses meant something but now, knowing they were probably from him, they meant nothing. Callum may like to play with me, keeping me close to him, caring in his own fucked up way but Tommy didn't feel anything for me and that ruined the allure of any romance.

Following him out the door, I locked up and chucked the keys into my little black clutch along with my phone and red lipstick.

"Where's Tommy got to go first?"

Callum looked back at me then took my hand, pulling me to his side. "He's got to pick some bits up for something that's happening in a few weeks."

"What's happening?" I nearly stumbled in my heels at the pace he was going but caught my balance once he slowed down at the stairs.

"You'll like it, don't worry." His Cheshire grin made my stomach tense. Something told me I wouldn't like it at all. "All first years are involved, and we'll have fun."

"Your definition of fun is very different to mine." I deadpanned and he laughed while leading me through the corridor and across the entrance hall.

Tommy's car was parked at the bottom of the stone

steps and once again, he was leaning against it with a cigarette in one hand and his other in his pocket. Like Callum and Felix, he was dressed in a suit. I had seen him in a blazer and tie before but seeing him in the black fitted suit with a bow tie screamed something else. Power. Authority. He claimed both like it was meant for him.

My bottom lip became trapped between my teeth, and I let go of Callum's hand. It didn't seem to bother him as he continued down the steps and headed for Archie's Range Rover.

Tommy's head rose from looking at the ground and those midnight blue eyes fell on me. They ran over my body with such deliberateness that every nerve ignited inside, heating every inch of my skin. My stomach clenched as my breasts rose and fell, suffocating against the dress that had fit so perfectly just seconds ago. The dress that he had bought me in the exact size I needed. How he knew was a mystery. Much like this foreign feeling that was creeping up.

A small grin tipped his lips as he looked back down, and he pushed off the car. Opening the back door, he waited patiently.

Maddy stuck her head out, her bright smile calming the strange feelings a little. "You look hot!" She half screamed and I let out a nervous chuckle.

Taking a step down, I wished that Callum was still beside me because my legs felt like they were unwilling to cooperate. Tommy seemed to notice though and walked towards me, rolling his eyes.

Climbing the first few steps, he stopped two below and held out his hand for me to take. Without a word I placed mine in his. His fingers curled round my own and I almost stole my hand away again at the electricity that sparked between us. His eyes flicked up to mine with a look so fleeting, I most likely imagined it. If he had felt it too, he was doing an excellent job at concealing it. Helping me down the last few steps he led me across the gravel. Heels were not made for this sort of thing.

Carefully, I climbed into the seat beside Maddy, and Tommy shut the door before getting into the driver's seat.

"I'm actually really looking forward to tonight. We can drink and gamble and have fun without the rules of school. Not that it stops anyone anyway." Maddy shot me a sneaky grin then carried on talking, distracting me from my own thoughts about Tommy, the roses and the dress. "Have you ever played poker before? Oh it might not be poker tonight. It might be blackjack. I'm not as good at that."

The engine roared to life and Tommy sounded the horn, grabbing Callum's attention.

"Obviously we will have to dance too and before you say anything Tommy –" He raised a brow, not even opening his mouth to say anything. "- I know we have to see if we can get any information about why the Italians are here."

Tommy smirked just as Callum slid into the seat beside him and then we were off, Archie's Range Rover following us with Felix.

Maddy carried on talking about poker explaining to me how to play after I told her I wasn't really any good at it. I was better at 21. Callum interjected a few times to correct her if she got any of the rules mixed up.

My phone pinged in my bag, and I got it out to see three messages. One was from Maddy and the other two were from Jefferson, checking in again but I swiped those two away. I would reply to him later.

Maddy
I love the dress. My brother has good taste. Don't tell him I said that though.

Bella
It wasn't your brother who got it, it was Tommy.

"What!?" Her outburst made Callum spin round and Tommy even swore in shock. I pressed my red lips together as a breath of laughter escaped. "Sorry, I just saw that someone is getting married who I thought didn't want too."

I arched a brow at her. What an excuse. She started tapping rapidly on her phone again and I quickly put mine on silent before it went off and the boys could get suspicious.

Maddy
Were the roses from him too?

Bella
Not sure. Callum didn't mention them. Just that Tommy had bought the dress so he couldn't rip it off me. But I think they were.

Maddy snorted but then started tapping away again.

Maddy
Firstly, Eww!! Do not need to know what my brother wants to do with you. And secondly, Tommy is never this nice to his other claimed ones, but I don't think Ricky would look as good in a dress. Just thought you should know that.

Maddy
That Tommy is never nice, not how Ricky looks in a dress.

I breathed out a quiet chuckle as my eyes rose from the screen to look into the rear view mirror at Tommy's reflection. He was already staring at me though. His eyes were cold and fierce as they peered back at mine. Any doubt I had of his intentions were put to rest. If the roses had been from him, there was absolutely no other reason than just to play with me. He hadn't given me the dress for any other reason than for me to look the part tonight because all I was to him was another claimed one that could be used whenever he needed.

Part of me wanted to scold him and tell him to keep his

eyes on the road but the other part wanted him to keep watching me. I wanted him to see that I wasn't going to back down or be the submissive he obviously wanted.

My phone vibrated in my hand, making me tear my eyes away though.

Maddy

Then again, Tommy has never claimed a girl before, so I don't have much to go on. Good luck with that.

I rolled my eyes but smiled and put the phone back in my clutch. The rest of the journey, I listened to Maddy go on more about the games at this charity event. The only time she was quiet was when Tommy stopped to go into a building and emerged again with a gym bag that he slung into the boot and returned to driving.

Chapter 14

The car came to a standstill just alongside a wide path. Tommy turned off the engine and without saying a word, he stepped out into the night. Callum followed suit and I exchanged a look with Maddy who just shrugged then moved to the middle seat to get ready to follow me out.

I reached out my hand to unlock the door, but it was already being opened. Callum held out his hand, helping me from the car then turned back for his sister. Archie and Felix were already by my side but not a single bit of my attention was on them. It was on the sight in front of me. A red carpet led towards a set of glass double doors. The whole building was glass and on the other side, through the sheer drapes, you could already see many people mingling and drinking champagne. Paparazzi were snapping pictures, trying to get the attention of certain guests that were entering the building, but I didn't know who they were.

There was no privacy in the building but there were bouncers circling the premises. Two were standing at the main doors, deep in conversation with Tommy.

The car started up behind me and I spun my head around to see a valet pulling away from the curb, Archie's Range Rover following it.

I looked back over to Tommy, still talking to the bouncers. Both seemed to be filling him in with information and he was nodding, taking it all in. The bald one shifted his black blazer to the side, showing off his gun. Both had one and I guessed all the others did too. Tommy just nodded again then held up his hand for us to come over.

"Tommy owns this place." Maddy informed me as if I had asked. "Well he doesn't but he will once his dad dies. It's the place where we always host public parties or things like this. And the men of the family do legitimate business here instead of the shady shit that makes the real money."

"Jesus Madz. It's a good thing Bella is one of ours or you would have just got her killed for feeding her that information." Felix gave her a frustrated glare but then sighed and carried on with her explanation. "Every year we hold a charity games night here. It's invite only and quite high profile. Nothing is shady about it and all the money does go to charity."

"What charity does it go to?" I asked, stopping just before we got to Tommy.

"It's different every year. This year it's for children who have become orphaned or lost just one parent." I looked up at him and Felix gave me a soft smile. I smiled back but didn't say anything else. I had been one of those children.

Tommy stepped up to us all, looking from one to the other and then his eyes focused on Maddy and me. "You understand what to do?"

"Have a few drinks with the sister while you four distract the men at the table." Maddy answered, "Don't worry Tommy, we've got this." She nudged me and I nodded quickly, looking from her to him. His eyes burned into me, not trusting me to not fuck up. It was my first time working a job with them, but the task was simple. Befriend someone to get information. How hard could it be?

"No surprises. No attitude. No arguments." He turned to Archie at the last command and Archie rolled his eyes. "This is still a charity event."

He walked through the glass door first with Archie and Felix close behind. Callum angled his elbows for me and his sister to take then led us into the glass building too.

As soon as the doors were shut behind us, a lady in a burgundy skirt and white shirt, was at our side. She held out a tray with champagne flutes and Callum took two, passing them over to Maddy and me. He nodded his thanks to her and she scuttled away to serve someone else.

I scanned the room I had just walked into. Rich, privileged people were laughing, nattering and throwing back drinks. All the men had black suits on while the women wore evening gowns in an array of different colours. Many were standing, while some were at the bar over on the far side of the room and others were already sitting at games tables at the opposite end.

There was a small clearing in the centre that I assumed was going to be the dance floor once people had more to drink, but it was currently empty. Music played softly, creating background noise while everyone spoke.

As I looked at everyone, trying to see where the other three had gone, someone caught my eye.

"Oh my god, is that –"

"Tom Hardy? Yeh." Callum confirmed. Felix was right when he said high profile. "You're not going to start fan girling are you? I don't think my jealousy will be able to handle that."

"No. I'm too mature for that." I scoffed, creasing my brows at the fact he would even insinuate it but then turned to Maddy, wide eyed, mouthing 'What the fuck'. She snorted into her champagne, dribbling some down her chin.

Callum rolled his eyes at us both then led us further into the room. Archie was already at the bar, scotch in hand and scanning the near vicinity. A couple of people had tried going over to speak but he glared them down, making them change their direction and disappear. Once he had noticed us, he pushed off the bar and walked over.

"Felix is already at the poker table." Sure enough,

looking across the room, Felix was at an empty table talking to the man who was to dish out the cards. "He's keeping it open for us."

Callum nodded then looked over to Tommy who was talking to three men and a girl who was probably my age. All three men wore matching suits while the girl had on an elegant forest green evening dress. All had the same dark hair with dark eyes and flawless olive skin.

Once again, Tommy signalled for us to come over and like the good, trained dogs that we were, we did. I stood beside him, looking up at the man at the front of the new group.

"Matteo, you remember my cousins." Tommy gestured to Archie, Callum and Maddy.

"Of course." His Italian accent was thick as he grinned at the three of them then took Maddy's hand to kiss it. "Always a pleasure mia cara Madeline."

"Matteo." She nodded curtly.

"Archibald, Callum, I believe you have not met my friends. Enzo," Matteo pointed at the stockier one of the two. "And Nico."

The four men nodded and grunted a very impolite greeting then Matteo's attention went to me. "And is this a new cousin we are just meeting?"

"This is Isabella." Tommy's hand came up to rest on the small of my back, warming me through the fabric of the dress. "My wife."

My eyes instantly flew up to Tommy in shock. He wasn't looking at me, just at the man in front of us and there was no emotion on that lying face of his.

No surprises my arse!

He had just put me on the spot, and I had seconds to react without making a scene or dropping him in the shit too. A test. That's what this was.

I turned quickly back to Matteo smiling as brightly as I could while slowly moving my hands behind my back.

"I thought your engagement was cancelled?" He asked,

looking from Tommy to me.

"And she is the reason why it was cancelled. I wanted her instead." Tommy responded like it was true and no big deal. I quickly slipped my mother's ring from my finger and slid it on to the left hand. All while my hands were trembling and trying to keep a grip of my clutch.

"Ahh, well, congratulations then." Matteo held out his hand for me to place mine in and I felt Tommy's fingers twitch on my back, but I was ready. Placing my hand in his, his eyes went to the rock on my finger. Small and romantically simple. Perfectly me. "I see no wedding band."

"Tommy likes to get ahead of himself. He proposed only a few days ago but loves to tell everyone that I am already his wife." I side glanced at my 'fiancé', expecting him to want to say something but he just bowed his head so I couldn't see his expression. Callum couldn't conceal his though. Anger burned in those grey eyes of his and I was almost certain he was fighting to keep his mouth shut. I wasn't the only one who Tommy's announcement had caught by surprise.

"How did he propose?" The girl quipped in, all starry eyed at the chance of hearing a truly loving story. Matteo rolled his eyes but still smiled as he released my hand.

"Oh he did it in the most romantic way." Tommy huffed out a heavy sigh beside me but didn't make any attempt to stop what I was going to say. He was just as interested with how I was going to play this, and I had no plans of letting him down or letting him get away with springing this on me. "He turned up at my father's house with one of those old fashion boom boxes. Think the breakfast club kind of vibes. Marry You by Bruno Mars was playing, waking up our whole street but he didn't care, did you, pumpkin?" I glanced up at him, expecting to see anger or frustration in those blue eyes but instead they gleamed with amusement. I looked back at Matteo and the girl. "After the song had finished, he got down on one knee and held out the ring. I still remember the words as if it was yesterday. He said, 'My love, there's only you in my life. The only thing that's right. My first love, you're every breath that I take. You're every step I make.'"

Maddy snorted beside me, but the girl was staring, doe eyed, clinging on to every word. I wasn't finished yet, Luther Vandross had good song lyrics.

" 'And I, I want to share all my love with you. No one else will do. Will you marry me?'"

"Oh that is so romantic. Isn't that romantic Matt." She looked up at him, but his eyes were squinting slightly at me.

"And you said yes I see."

"Oh, I said no."

Maddy had to walk away. I couldn't watch her, or I would break too.

"You said no?"

"Well I didn't want to make it easy for him did I."

Tommy's hand slipped from my back around to my side and pulled me tighter to him. The move tickling me just enough to send a flutter through to my centre. I gazed up and he was already looking down at me. The amusement in his eyes was gone, replaced with a dark desire that I was positive would mean I was in deep shit if I carried on. "She made me grovel and behaved like a complete brat but if she hadn't then she wouldn't have been the girl I fell in love with."

I swallowed then my lips parted to say something, but the words became stuck. His words felt so real as he stared down at me, but I knew this was all pretend.

"Anyway." I manage to tear myself from him and turn to face the girl. "Why don't we leave the men to their games, and we can go grab a drink."

"I'd like that." She looked at Matteo, asking if that was ok.

"Vai ma stai attento. Non mi fido di loro." He answered thinking that we wouldn't be able to understand them.

But I did.

Translation was that he didn't trust us.

"La fiducia va in entrambe le direzioni. Lei e perfettamente al sicuro con me."

Matteo studied me for a second and Tommy's fingers dug into my waist, unsure whether I had just insulted the man in front of us or if he was going to need to jump in. Callum even stepped to the other side of me, taking the spot that Maddy was once in.

I dared to glance over at Archie who was eyeing the other two men behind Matteo, judging the best one to take out first.

I had simply said that trust goes both ways, and she will be perfectly safe. I wasn't stupid enough to cause an argument with people when I didn't know what they were capable off. I may not have been particularly fond of the company I kept but I didn't want to put them in danger either.

"Yes well, we can never be too sure." The Italian finally responded. He nodded at the girl, giving his permission and her face split into a wide smile before he turned back to me. "What did you say your last name was?"

"I didn't." I smiled at him sweetly then linked my arm through the girls and escorted her away.

"You're going to have your hands full with her." I looked over my shoulder at Matteo, waiting for Tommy's response but he merely shook his head, chuckling. Callum still didn't look too impressed and knocked back the rest of his champagne then turned abruptly on his heel to storm towards the table where Felix was waiting patiently for them all to start the game. Tommy and the others followed, talking amongst themselves.

Chapter 15

"I need to use the toilet." The girl announced just as we got to the bar where Maddy was already waiting with three brightly coloured cocktails.

"Um, I'm not sure where they are." I said, looking round the room.

"Don't worry, I'll ask one of the staff and meet you back here in a minute." She waved as she walked away smiling to herself. She seemed so sweet. I felt bad that all I had to do was strike up a fake friendship with her to get information. Actually I didn't feel bad. I felt utterly shitty. I hadn't even learnt her name yet.

"So how much trouble are you in?" Maddy asked, grabbing my attention.

"Huh?"

"That engagement story." She chuckled then took a sip from the straw in her cocktail. "I'm sorry, I had to walk away. I couldn't hold it in anymore. That was brilliant."

"Serves him right for putting me on the spot like that." I huffed, taking my own drink and taking a sip. I wasn't sure what it was called but it was fruity and refreshing. Just what I needed.

"I'll ask again. How much trouble are you in?"

I swallowed and looked back over to where all the men were now surrounding the games table that Felix had procured. All seven were sitting down, getting dealt cards. None were looking our way; all their concentration was on the game in front of them. Tommy actually looked relaxed as he smiled then nodded at something Felix said.

"I guess we'll find out when we leave here. Hopefully he'll have a drink and let me off the hook."

"Oh no, he isn't going to let that one go." She cackled and I glared at her. I had a feeling that Tommy wasn't going to make my punishment enjoyable. But fuck him. He put me on the spot, he was lucky I didn't go into more embarrassing details.

"Hopefully if we get the information that he wants, he'll go easy on me."

"She's coming back now." Maddy quickly turned on her bar stool to pick up the girl's drink.

"What's her name? I didn't ask." I quickly muttered but it was too late to get Maddy's answer as the girl stepped in front of us.

"La signore." She smiled brightly.

"Elena." Maddy smiled back and passed over her cocktail. "Now that we have got rid of the men we can really talk."

"Si, when they start talking, you can't usually get a word in."

"I feel lucky to have told a whole story then." I chuckled and Elena nodded, still grinning.

"When was the last time I saw you. Three years ago?" Maddy asked, taking another sip of her drink. Elena sucked on the straw, bobbing her head in reply. "You've changed so much. I love your dress."

Elena grinned, "Both of your dresses are bellissima too."

"That's the last time you were in England? Three years ago?" I asked, stirring the straw around my own drink.

"Si, my godfather was ill, and we had to come to England to find his son and bring him home ready to take over."

My eyebrows rose as I side glanced at Maddy. She seemed to be as shocked as I was at how loose lipped Elena already was. This information finding might just be easier than I thought. We still had to be careful though.

"I'm guessing you found him then?"

"Si, he wasn't in a very good way though. Was in the ospedale with a gunshot wound." Her smile faded slightly, and I winced at the thought.

"I'm so sorry. That must have been an awful way to find him."

"It was but he recovered fully after a few months." Elena smiled again. "My godfather died a couple of months ago, so Tony took over –"

"Carlo is dead?" Maddy spewed out, narrowing her eyes at Elena.

"Umm." She looked over her shoulder at the boys table then back to us, nibbling her lip nervously. "Si. I thought you would have been informed."

Maddy shrugged, placing her almost empty glass on the bar. "I guess even if they had been told, I wouldn't have found out." I could hear the resentment in her voice, but she quickly recovered and put on a sympathetic smile. "I'm sorry for your loss though. I understand how close family is and losing your godfather must have been hard?"

"We knew it was going to happen. He was on borrowed time, and we were lucky to get the extended years with him still. It was nice to see him finally get to know his son."

I nodded, agreeing with her. But I also felt for this Tony. To be found, taken to your father and then to find out he was dying. That must have been terrible. "What was his illness?"

"Cancer." A one worded answer that could hurt more than a thousand knives.

"I'm sorry." I said again because I didn't know what else

to say.

I had hundreds of people say they were sorry to me over the years for the death of my mum and brother. It wasn't their fault though and I never understood why they would say sorry. I promised that if someone ever told me that someone close to them had died, I wouldn't apologise but here I was, saying the exact thing I didn't want to because I didn't know what else to say.

"Basta, enough." Elena waved her hand that held her glass, sloshing the liquid over the edge. "I came here for a good time. Not to speak of sad memories. Bere, drink! Let's have fun."

I laughed, clinking my glass against hers and Maddy ordered us a shot each.

"Is that why you're back in England then, for this charity event." I asked as Maddy passed me a tiny glass with florescent green liquid. Just looking at it made me feel queasy.

Elena gave a light chuckle, taking her own shot from Maddy. "No, this is just good timing. We're actually here looking for someone. Tony had a sibling that he left behind and he wants them found and back in Italy with us."

"Oh, so that's the reason for this visit, just to find someone?" Maddy asked, glancing at me.

"Si."

"Well here's to found family, blood or not." I grinned, dipping my head to Maddy and she grinned back. We had found out what we needed, and it was a lot easier than I could have hoped.

We knocked the shots back and all grimaced at the horrid taste. My whole body shuddered even though the liquid warmed my throat all the way down to my stomach.

"What do you think?" Maddy asked, still scrunching her nose in disgust.

"Tastes like paint thinner and bad decisions."

"Perfect." She turned to the man behind the bar. "We'll have three more please and probably the rest of the bottle too so just leave it out."

Elena and I laughed and after a few more shots and two more cocktails, we decided it was time to see how the boys were doing with winning or losing. I hoped the former so Tommy would be in a good mood.

The seven of them were concentrating on the game as we sauntered over. Each one side-glancing at the other to look out for the subtle tell that they were bluffing.

Gently, I placed my hand on Tommy's shoulder and he looked away from his cards up to me.

"Hi lover." I winked and he placed his cards face down on the table to put his arm around my waist and pulled me on to his lap. My body instantly stiffened against his as he adjusted my position to be sitting sideways.

His fingers glided through the slit of the dress, resting on my naked thigh. "Relax." He breathed, circling his thumb against my skin. "You're meant to be in love with me, remember."

This was his fault that I was so nervous. He should have given me the heads up with saying something like that because how the hell was I meant to pretend I was in love with him. I swallowed and took in a deep breath, letting myself melt further into his lap. I looked around the table. Matteo and his entourage weren't paying us any attention, but Archie had a shit eating grin on his face as he glanced over at me then back at his cards. It took all my power not to give him my middle finger.

"Are you sober?" Tommy asked, not caring about the others listening in.

Maddy pressed her lips together, coming to stand beside us. She was worse than me, the drink had gone straight to her head, and I remembered she hadn't actually eaten anything before we had left.

"I'm moderately functional." I giggled softly.

A small smirk came to his lips. "I'll take that as a no."

"I can handle my drink, Mr Kray." Leaning forward, I glided my hand up the lapel of his suit jacket and to the back of his neck. Brushing his ear with my lips, I whispered, "I know why they are here."

His grip on my thigh tightened. "Dance with me." He started to move, and I stood back up, running my hands over my dress to straighten it out again. Tommy stood up too. "I'm out of this one boys but keep my spot warm."

Felix picked up his cards and looked at them before passing them back to the dealer. "You had a good hand too."

Tommy winked at him and took my hand, leading me to the dance floor, completely ignoring Matteo muttering "Whipped".

Circling back around to face me, his hand went to my waist as he pulled me closer. His other hand stayed squeezing mine gently. Running my fingers up his chest to his shoulder, I took a quick look over at the table again. Matteo was staring at us, and I remembered it was him we had to pretend to be in love for.

My eyes wandered to Callum who hadn't said a word to me since the whole wife/fiancé fiasco. He was watching us too. His cold grey eyes maddened as he caught my gaze and he looked back down at his cards.

"What's wrong with Callum?"

"He's sulking because he thought I wasn't serious about something."

Tommy's smirk was mean as he looked over at his cousin and it confused me a little but then it softened to something warmer.

"What did you find out?" He asked, lowering his head to my ear. Even with six-inch heels on, I was still smaller than him. The music was slow enough for us to be close to speak but also loud enough to not be overheard.

"They are looking for someone. Carlo is dead?" I think that was the name of Elena's godfather. Maddy was probably the best one to tell Tommy everything because she already knew the names of everyone.

"Carlo's dead?" He repeated, shocked but didn't stop

moving.

"Uh-huh."

"We didn't know about that." His fingers dug into my side in frustration but not enough to hurt.

"I figured you didn't when Maddy didn't know either."

"So who are they looking for?"

"I'm getting to that." I frowned at him as I pulled my head back and he rolled his eyes. The doting fiancé act had disappeared, replaced with the cold, dark emptiness that I was now used to glaring down at me. "Someone called Tony took over. He was Carlo's son. I assume he was staying in England but they didn't know where abouts and he was found three years ago."

His brows creased together.

"Tony has a sibling though and they are here searching for them. That's all. There is nothing else in it."

"She didn't say anything about this sibling? Girl? Boy?"

"No, we didn't want to pry too much and make her suspicious."

He nodded at that and looked back at the Italians. "Well if that's all they want and not to cause trouble then we'll leave them be." His gaze wondered back down to me. "Well done, you did good."

"A compliment." I smirked at him, "Shall I get used to them now that you are my future husband."

"Only when you have been a good girl. Be bad and you'll be punished." A dark desire swirled around his eyes, and I grinned at the thought of him wanting to hurt me. There was something exciting about it when there probably shouldn't be.

"What was that wife crap about anyway? How could you trust that I would go along with it?"

His lips thinned as he studied me for a second before answering. "I didn't trust that you would go along with it, but I was glad that you did, even with your theatrical description of my proposal." I chuckled lightly and his stare warmed. "And as for why I did it. I didn't want to just introduce you as Madeline's friend. That would indicate that you were nothing to the rest of us. By saying you were my wife or fiancée as you corrected, they now know that you are protected by me personally."

"So you will always protect me?"

"While you are claimed by us, yes."

Maybe there were some perks to being claimed.

"Well it's a good job we aren't really getting married. I'd make a terrible wife." I said casually.

"And why's that?" A small smirk played on his lips.

"I can only cook one meal and that's lasagne." I shrugged.

"I like lasagne."

"Good because that would be all you are getting." His body shook softly against mine as he chuckled. I smiled at the feeling and nuzzled my face against his chest.

"So while I'm working you would be cooking lasagne every day." He muttered, bowing his head and I lifted mine again.

"Oh no, I'll still be in bed. Who said anything about getting out of it?" I frowned playfully but grinned at the mischievous look on his face.

"So I would come home to find you right where I left you. Doesn't sound too bad." His grin widened, flashing me his straight, white teeth.

I rolled my eyes and he laughed again. The sound was fascinating. It was like seeing him in a whole new light and I could see us getting along as friends at some point in the future. Well until he pisses me off again.

We had discussed what we needed to and there was no reason for us to be so close anymore or still be dancing but we did. We danced in silence through another two songs. All to keep up the appearance of being in love.

"Thank you for my dress." I sighed as his fingers gently teased the fabric at my lower back. The song had changed to Can't Help Falling In Love by Elvis Presley and even though we were dancing slowly before, we had slowed down more, just swaying even closer to each other.

His hand, that had been resting on mine touching his chest, glided up and down my arm. I watched the movement, not expecting him to reply but he did. "If I told you that you look beautiful, would you believe me?."

Lifting my head away from him again, I looked into the midnight blue eyes that were already fixed onto me. I couldn't be certain what it was but there was something else other than the artic glare I was usually met with. Something different from the mischievous glint that sometimes played in them too. But I had left him waiting for my answer too long and he blinked back whatever he had dared to reveal.

"Have we finished dancing now?" I asked and he stopped moving.

"You did really well, pretending to love me."

My throat bobbed as I swallowed. "Part of the job, right?" I smiled, but it was fake. Just like the feelings that we had to pretend to have for each other.

He released me from his embrace, and I stepped back. My heart thudded against my chest as his emotionless eyes stared at me. The bite it gave made me look down.

What the hell was going on?

Tommy's fingers cupped my chin, lifting my gaze to meet his again. He lowered his eyes to my lips then back up and his mouth parted but he didn't say anything.

"Are you going to kiss me?"

A kiss was how couples would end a dance. We were meant to be a couple, but I didn't anticipate that we would have to go that far.

"Do you want me to?"

His lips were now so close to mine, exchanging breath, that if either of us was to move in the slightest, they would be touching.

"I –"

"Tommy," I jumped back out of Tommy's hand, wide eyed and flustered. Felix looked between me and him, completely unfazed about our closeness but then why wouldn't he be. It was part of the act Tommy had forced me to take part in. "Callum is out the back. He's fighting."

"What!" Icy rage filled those blue eyes as he gave me his back and stormed across the room.

I watched him go then turned to Felix. "What happened?"

"No idea. We were all still playing poker and that Italian bastard said something to him."

"Matteo?"

"No, the other one. Nico?" We started walking across the floor, following where Tommy had disappeared to. "Callum grabbed his head and smashed it into the table."

We reached the door that led to the kitchen, but it opened just before I could do it myself.

Maddy walked through sighing heavily. "Well our night has come to an end." I tried to look behind her, through the small panel of glass but could only see the caterers getting rid of their empty trays. Maddy focused on Felix. "Tommy said to get the car and make sure me, and Bella get in it and stay there."

"Fuck sake. Babysitting duties!" Felix grumbled but turned back around and walked away.

Maddy tsked before linking her arm through mine then led us in the same direction. "Babysitting duties." She repeated, mumbling. "Like we can't take care of ourselves."

"And yet we are still following him." I smirked at her, letting her drag me.

"My brother's pissed off and I have a feeling Tommy is going to be soon too so I would rather not get on their bad side." She side-glanced to me, matching my smirk with her own. "Unless you want to chance it."

"Well apparently I've been a good girl tonight, so I think I'm going to end it that way." I smiled in a childish way, and she laughed.

When we got out of the building, Felix was already standing outside Tommy's car. We both slipped in the back wordlessly as he tapped away on his phone.

Fifteen minutes later the door opened beside me.

"Get out and get in the front." Tommy growled and I shuddered before moving. Maddy grabbed my arm though and pulled me back.

"I'll go in the front. I'm not staying in the back with that mess." She nodded towards her brother who I hadn't clocked until then.

Blood was dribbling from a cut above his eye but that was the only injury I could see. He was swaying a little and I wasn't sure if that was because of the hit to the head or the amount of alcohol he had consumed.

Tommy growled in aggravation, but Maddy had already climbed over the centre console and into the front passenger seat. I moved across and Tommy pushed Callum into the seat next to me. He slumped forward, smacking his head on the front head rest and I pulled him back.

"How much have you had to drink?"

He just grumbled, falling sideways onto my lap. I left him there. Even though we were driving, he was probably safer in this position.

Tommy said something to Felix then climbed into the driver's seat. He didn't say anything about the position that Callum was in before speeding off, back to the school.

"Mm sorry."

"Huh?" I looked down at the man's head on my lap.

"I'm sorry." His arm came around my back, pulling himself closer to nuzzle his face into my stomach. "You still smell delicious."

"And you're still insufferable." I chuckled softly.

His grin touched my belly. "But you still like me, right?"

I didn't answer but even if I had, he wouldn't have heard it. His eyes were closed, and his breathing became heavier. A sure way of telling me he had now passed into a drunken coma. I stroked my fingers through his hair, comforting him while he slept.

Out the corner of my eye, Tommy moved his hand off the gear stick and to the rear-view mirror, angling it so he could see into the back seat.

Our eyes met and for a second, I thought I saw a multitude of so many emotions. But only one focus on me now and even I knew that so many words were being left unsaid between us.

Chapter 16

I sat in class, waiting for Professor Williams to arrive. Tommy's and Callum's seats remained empty allowing Anderson to take his rightful place beside me. Archie had glared at him but thankfully let it go and didn't say a word. Felix just ignored everyone completely, staring out the window.

I hadn't bothered asking where Tommy and Callum were. I hadn't seen them since Saturday night. All of Sunday, Maddy and I had stayed in our room, watching Friends and when I asked why we weren't getting harassed by the boys, Maddy just said that Callum was nursing a sore head and Tommy and the others were on damage control.

Damage control meaning preventing an all-out war between their firm and the Italian mafia.

I had also asked what had caused the outburst from Callum, but she shrugged, saying Callum had a tendency of getting drunk and acting out before he thinks. Good to know.

The door swung open behind us, and Williams strode in, followed by my two missing boys. Tommy looked his usual stoic self as he sat at the table across from me and

N.DENNIS

Callum came to a standstill behind poor Anderson. He didn't even have to say anything before Anderson picked up his book and scraped his chair across the floor to move seats.

"How's the head?" I smirked across at Callum and he threw his arm over the back of my chair.

"Better." Leaning himself closer to me, he moved my hair behind my ear. "You should have come to my room; I wouldn't have minded you nursing me back to health."

"I'm not the most sympathetic type when it comes to self-inflicted injuries." I tapped the cut above his eye with my pen, giving him a sweet as pie smile. He had obviously tended to it himself or gone to the infirmary because there were two small butterfly stitches over the small wound.

"It wouldn't have been sympathy that I wanted." He grinned deviously and I rolled my eyes, looking forward again.

"Mr Kray, is there something you would like to share with the rest of the class or is your discussion for Miss Russo's ears only?"

Williams didn't even look up from the laptop on his desk as he reprimanded Callum. I smirked back at the boy in question waiting for his response but instead he gave me a wink then leant back in his seat.

"Hands on desks." Here we go. Everyone put their hands palm down in front of them. Williams walked round his desk and picked up his favourite wooden ruler. "Many of you completed the assignment I set last Monday. But a few of you didn't." Walking up the aisle, he stopped in front of a girl with olive skin and black hair, sitting beside Sandra. "Where was your proof?"

"I - I couldn't get any?"

"No? So out of all the pictures you took of your tits to send to Archie Kray, you couldn't take one picture of the person you tortured as proof." A wicked grin spread across his face and her eyes widened in shock. She quickly shot Archie a look of disbelief, but he just smiled arrogantly to

168

himself. "Next time you want to send sordid pictures to someone, make sure you enter in their email and not reply to mine."

Her cheeks turned an aggressive shade of red and she quickly bowed her head. The ruler came down across her knuckles and she winced at the pain and the blood.

"Russo." Shit. "Where is your proof?"

"I – I…" I didn't have the proof. I had been there with the boys that night, but I didn't get any proof that I was there. I didn't even get involved.

Tommy's seat slowly dragged along the floor and Callum straightened his back next to me.

"Well that is a disappointment." He brought the ruler up and I closed my eyes, fingers trembling, waiting for the impact. The air blew against my face from the speed that he brought it down with and the sound of it cracking against flesh made my heart skip a beat.

Only there was no pain. There was no collision with any part of my hand.

I opened my eyes, to see Callum's hand above my own. He had taken the full force against his palm, preventing me from being hurt. I glanced warily over to him. Animalistic rage filled his eyes as he snarled at the professor.

"Isabella was standing in front of the body in the picture that Felix sent you." Tommy's voice was eerily calm, but he was on his feet, taking a slow step to stand behind my chair.

"Ahh, I must have missed that." Williams grinned down darkly as he stared at me. "Apologies Miss Russo." Turning back round, he walked back to the front of the classroom. "Get into your groups again. I want you to come up with an original way to kill someone. Use your imagination."

"Do we have to actually do what we come up with sir?" Sandra asked.

"Excellent idea Morgan." He turned back to face his students and sneered over at Tommy who was still standing beside me. "Whatever idea you come up with has to be completed."

Tommy didn't say anything but pulled his chair across the aisle to the end of my table. Felix and Archie took their places in front of me while the rest of the pupils moved to their groups.

"Is your hand ok?" I asked, facing Callum.

He flexed his fingers before curling them back into a fist. "I've had a lot worse done to me sweetheart. That was nothing."

"Williams shouldn't have done it. He knew you were with us that night." Felix growled, looking back at the aging man who was once again looking at his laptop. "He's just pissed at Tommy and taking it out on you."

"Why is he angry with you?" I puzzled at Tommy. He had completed our assignment and I didn't think they had done anything else over the weekend to cause trouble. Tommy ignored me though, flicking his pen against the wooden desk.

"He requested we used a different man to torture but Tommy chose against it." Felix answered for him.

"So he wanted to use you for his own dirty work instead of doing it himself?"

"Got it in one sweetheart." Callum smirked then threw his arm over the back of my chair again. "So, original kill. Any ideas?"

"We've done a lot of shit already." Archie grumbled, flicking through the book in front of him.

"Any ideas Russo?"

I looked at Felix for a second trying to think of any new way of killing someone that they wouldn't have tried. "Umm, you know them windmill things that generate power." He cocked a brow, lips tipping up in amusement. "What if someone was strapped to one of them. Could that kill them?"

"They would probably pass out, but it wouldn't kill them."

"What if you tried shooting at them at the same time?"

"I'm a good shot Bella but that would be difficult." He

rubbed his chin with his hand, contemplating it. "It could work though."

"It's a difficult shot. Not very original." Archie said, putting a damper on it.

"Do you have any ideas then?" I answered back in aggravation.

"Like I said, we've done a lot of shit already." He smiled proudly. "Coming up with a new way is going to be hard."

"Who's Jefferson?"

My head whipped round to Tommy. He was glaring at the spot his pen repeatedly hit. "What?"

"Who's Jefferson?" He repeated slowly, making sure I heard the words perfectly this time. His head slowly turned, and his emotionless, dark eyes unsettled me.

"Umm, he works for my dad. Why?"

"Madeline said that you text him occasionally?" A nasty smirk tilted his lips. "Why?"

"Because he is also my friend."

"Are you fucking him?"

My heart lurched in my chest, but I was suddenly angry. "He's old enough to be my dad. What's it got to do with you who I text. And why would you be asking Maddy anyway?"

"I actually asked." I twisted myself around to scowl at Callum. "I wanted to know if there was a boyfriend on the outside. Needed to eliminate the competition you see."

"And what would you have done if I did have a boyfriend?"

"Made it clear that you weren't his girlfriend anymore." He grinned.

"Are you kidding me." I seethed through my teeth. "You know what, just as I start to actually like all of you, you just seem to do something to fuck it up again."

"You like us?" Felix asked in an innocent voice, but his conceited face made my blood boil.

"I did." I stood up from my seat, nearly nocking it back from the force but Callum caught it with his injured hand, making him wince but I didn't care. I didn't want to be near them anymore. Even if Jefferson was something romantic to me, they had no right in prying. And they had no right in telling me who I could and couldn't date outside of the school.

Tommy's hand shot out, grabbing my wrist. "Sit. Down." He growled pulling me back into my seat. I hit against the chair and crossed my arms.

"Think of it as looking out for you." Callum smiled, pulling my chair closer to him and away from Tommy. I refused to acknowledge him, pouting in frustration.

"Or think of it as it is, and you are not allowed to date anyone beyond these walls."

I scoffed at Tommy, not quite believing he had said it. He didn't say anything else as he stared back down at the table but there was a satisfied smirk on his face and a sinful glint to his eyes.

"Go swim with sharks." I muttered and he breathed out a chuckle.

That also wasn't a bad idea. "Ooh."

"Already done that love."

"Honestly Maddy, how have you gone eighteen years with not killing one of them." I ranted again for the hundredth time since sitting down for lunch with her.

We had opted to sit outside to eat. Although it was autumn and probably the coldest day it had been since being at school, it was still better than sitting in the lunch hall with them.

Maddy chuckled again, taking a bite out of her burger. She hadn't said a word apart from apologising at the start for telling Callum that I had been texting another man. She said it was either she tells him, or they would have got it out of me another way. I didn't argue with that because I knew they would have, and I dread to think of how extreme

Tommy would have gotten to get his answers.

"And what the fuck does Tommy mean I'm not allowed to date anyone beyond these walls?" I still went on, ignoring my own food. "Is this about that shit with not finding allies to work against them or whatever he said. Surely dating someone outside the school would be more beneficial than dating someone in the school. At least they wouldn't know how to fucking kill them. Actually no, I want to date someone who can kill them."

Maddy laughed. "You don't really want to kill them all."

"No you're right I don't." I sighed, finally taking a bite out of my cold pizza slice. "Archie and Felix can stay alive but your brother and Tommy. They can die."

"So you like Archie and Felix?"

"No. I'm still pissed at them for the whole kidnap bollocks and the fact that Felix shot at me but right now I'm more pissed at the other two." I smiled sweetly at her. She rolled her eyes, but it still made her laugh.

"You're on one today?" Ricky chuckled, coming to sit down between us both.

"You weren't in classes this morning?" Now that I knew who he was, I found myself looking out for him in both AP Art of Killing and AP Poisons.

"Aww was you worried?" He cooed, nudging me with his shoulder.

"No, but I would have rather spoken to you than the others." I grumbled.

"Trouble in paradise?" He arched a brow, looking from me to Maddy when I didn't immediately answer.

"She's angry at Tommy and Callum for acting possessive." She grinned at him, and I rolled my eyes.

"They feel they have the right to dictate my life and I've had enough. If they thought I was difficult before, I'm about to get a lot worse." I promised.

"What are you going to do?" Maddy asked, finishing her food and wiping her fingers on a napkin.

"Become lesbian. If they are so worried about me

getting with a boy, I'll get with a girl."

Ricky burst out laughing and Maddy glanced at me pressing her lips together to stop her own laughter.

"Maddyyy?"

"Oh no, I have nothing against lesbians at all but I'm not willing to become one so you can prove a point."

I pouted out my bottom lip to her.

"What did they say exactly? That you couldn't have a boyfriend?" Ricky asked once he had stopped laughing.

"Tommy's exact words were I can't date anyone outside these walls."

"So get with someone on the inside." He shrugged.

"I can't can I. I've been 'claimed'." I made little quotation marks with my fingers, making Maddy snort. "Boys are too scared to fucking talk to me apart from you."

My eyes widened and a scheming smile stretched across my face.

His face went completely deadpan, knowing exactly what was running through my mind. "No."

"Rickyyy." I said as sweetly as I had said Maddy's name.

"In fairness, you are a claimed one too so they might not have a problem with it." She added, liking my idea too.

"So you are going to use me just to piss Tommy and Callum off."

"When you put it like that, it doesn't sound good." I sighed. "I'll just be single for the rest of my life."

"You're being dramatic. You only have three years here then you can date again." Maddy chuckled.

"I'll be a self-proclaimed nun by then with a killer instinct." I joked. I hadn't actually thought about getting a boyfriend. I didn't want one but the more you are told you can't do something the more you want to do it.

"How good are you at sucking cock?" My mouth dropped at Ricky's question. "You're gunna have to open wider than that to fit mine in."

I instantly shut it again, grinning at his boldness and shaking my head.

He laughed playfully but carried on. "I'll admit, I did come over here for a reason but knowing you now want to use and abuse me, I don't think I want to ask."

I frowned at him and Maddy pulled on his arm as he went to stand up.

"You can't leave after saying that. We're invested now." She cried, nodding towards me.

"Yeah, what were you going to ask?"

He let out an exaggerated sigh before leaning back on his hand and resting his other arm on his raised knee. I waited patiently, curious of his reason.

"There's a Halloween dance coming up soon and I wanted to ask if you would like to go with me?" Although he said it with confidence, there was a little nervousness in his voice that was almost adorable.

"Wait, really?" Excitement ran through me.

"I mean, yeah. If you want to." He looked down and ripped a blade of grass from the ground.

"Yeah, ok."

His genuine bright grin made me smile even more. "Great." He stood back up, ready to leave us alone again.

"Wait." Something occurred to me. "If you were coming over to ask me that, then what was that about using you and aren't you worried about pissing Tommy and Callum off?"

He shrugged. "There are no rules about two claimed one's going to a dance together." He paused then wiggled his brows. "As friends."

He turned and carried on walking back to the old building.

"I've really got to look at these rules about claimed ones."

"Trust me, if you knew what half of them were you would be even more pissed off with the boys. It's best you don't know and be thankful that Tommy hasn't enforced a lot of them." Maddy raised her brows then picked up her rubbish and stood back up. "But the rules are probably different for girls."

I did the same, pocketing my apple for later. "That just makes me more intrigued."

"Let's just say, I'm surprised Callum is still so close to you."

I walked her to her class begging for her to give me more information, but she refused, just laughing at my needy whines.

I would just have to get Tommy on his own and ask him.

Chapter 11

It was that time of week again. Combat training with Mr Letch. And of course, as it was a Tuesday, it was without the boys in our year.

The previous Wednesday and Thursday combat lesson had been mixed and while working with the boys, we had learned the basics of martial arts. We had also confirmed that they did in fact have to train topless. Today we were back to being just us girls.

Daisy stood next to Maddy and me, while the other two girls spoke to each other. I only found out that morning from Maddy that one of the other two was Sandra's sister, Penny. Should have figured it out really, she had the same sour face.

"Is it weird that I'm standing here watching my brother and cousins fight while you two perv over them?" Maddy asked, cocking her head to the side.

Once again, we were watching the four boys spar against each other. This time it was Tommy and Felix in the ring.

"I can promise you right now I'm not perving. I'm hoping one knocks the other out." I confirmed, smiling at the thought. "I'm not fussed which."

"I'm perving. Your cousins are hot. And your brother."
I snorted as Daisy uncaringly said it. They were hot but they
were also dicks.

Tommy hit Felix in the ribs, making him lurch forward
but he managed to block the second hit.

"So what one are you with?" Daisy asked, trying to keep
her curiosity casual.

"None of them." I shot at her in disgust and Maddy
laughed beside me making me glare at her.

"She hates them all." She finally said after finishing
laughing.

"Really?" Daisy frowned. "I really thought you were
shagging at least one of them."

"What gave you that idea?" Once again, I was disgusted,
and my lips curled at the accusation.

"Callum is always all over you. Tommy looks at you like
he wants to either fuck you or kill you –"

"It's kill me, trust me."

"- and the other two pay you more attention than any
other girl at this school. So unless it's just for sex, what is
the reason?" She finished.

"It's the joys of being a claimed one." I said, unsmiling.
Tearing my eyes from the muscled men still scrapping in the
ring, I studied Daisy's expression. There was a longing in
those dark eyes of hers as she watched them. She would
have probably suited the position I was in a lot better. "If I
could trade places with you I would." A thought come to
my head, and I quickly turned to Maddy. "Hey, do you think
they would swap me for Daisy?"

"I'm not sure if you're joking or not." She chuckled and
even Daisy rolled her eyes before turning her back to the
boys and towards the biggest pervert now walking into the
gymnasium.

"Ladies," Letch greeted us, striding over with a warped
grin across his face. Long wooden staffs were cradled under
his arm and as soon as he got to us, he dropped them to the

floor. They started to roll away, but he used his foot to stop them.

"Gentlemen," He called out, grabbing the four's attention. I swore under my breath. Not again. "You know how to use a staff. Come and join us again for a little one on one." He turned back. "Girl's, grab two staffs and a partner."

I reluctantly stepped forward, behind Maddy in the small queue. Once I had my long wooden stick, I went back to my position, away from anyone I could accidently hurt with it. Because that was what was going to happen. Five girls with no training with this kind of thing, fighting against men that knew what they were doing. Disaster.

"Daisy, you can be with me again." Letch called over and Daisy looked at Maddy and me in horror. I felt for the girl and couldn't help the look of pity on my face as the colour seemed to drain from hers and she started walking back to him.

"Actually, I think Daisy should practice with me this time Sir." Felix spoke out and took the second staff off her as he went to walk past. He gave her a little wink and she blushed as she looked down, a small smile now on her lips. I couldn't tell if she was going to be better off with him or not.

Letch cleared his throat, clearly not too happy with the change of plan but pointed his finger at Penny and beckoned her to him. She swallowed hard and her expression suddenly matched what Daisy's had been, but she still walked over to him without any protest.

"Isabella," Tommy said from behind me, and I spun round to see him holding out his hand for the second staff. "You're mine."

Rolling my eyes and sighing heavily, I thrust the stick towards him, and he grinned in his sexy, tormenting way.

"Right ladies, the boys obviously have a lot more experience than you do, so take note of everything they do." Letch's hands went to Penny's hips and she instantly stiffened. "Watch the way their body moves." He started swaying her body, caressing her bare sides with his slimy fingers.

"Surely that's illegal to touch her like that." I murmured more to myself than anyone else, but Tommy heard.

"The whole school does illegal shit; you really think they worry about that."

I shuddered at the thought of at some point I would have to be partnered with him. His hands on my body during physical combat. I would probably be sick, or at least fake it to get out of the lesson completely. Breaking my own wrist sounded like a good option too.

For ten more minutes, the gym teacher continued molesting Penny whilst demonstrating ways to defend ourselves with the staffs when the boys would attack us. I wasn't sure if any of the girls were taking notice or not, but I knew I wasn't. It was hard to watch without wanting to scream at him to stop.

Once he had finished, the pairs backed away to their own areas of the gym. Tommy and I stayed where we were, happy with how far the others had distanced themselves.

"Is this going to be the same as last time when you don't even try." I asked moodily.

"Depends how much effort you put in this time."

I swung the staff, but he blocked it with ease. I swung it back round to the other side and he spun out of its way.

"Can you keep still?"

"So you can hit me?"

"Yeah."

He breathed out a laugh through his nose, shaking his head. The next time I jabbed the staff at him though, he didn't move. Instead he grabbed the end before it hit him and roughly pulled on it, making me stumble forward. Catching me, he spun me around with both mine and his staff across my chest, trapping me against his.

"This position feels familiar." He breathed against my ear.

"Only difference is you can't tie me up this time." I huffed out, rolling my eyes. "While I've got you though –"

"Got me?" The laughter in his voice made me smile.

"While you've got me so close," I corrected myself. "Could you explain this rule thing to me?"

"Rule thing?"

"The rules of being a claimed one. Maddy had mentioned a couple. Like no one can hurt me without receiving the wrath of you four but what are the others? Also how many other claimed ones are there?"

He lowered the staffs, and I took mine as I stepped away and faced him again. "If you can beat me, I'll tell you."

"We both know that's not going to happen." I scoffed but prepared myself to run at him again.

"Every time you get me on the ground, I'll answer one of your questions." He readied himself, grinning mischievously.

All I needed to do was get him to the floor. He was a lot taller than me, and his broad shoulders and muscular thighs made him a lot sturdier too. This might just be an impossible task, but I wasn't about to give up with him offering to give me answers.

Swinging the staff around my head, I aimed to hit his side, but he grabbed it. This time I let go before he could use it to pull me to him again but that was a mistake. Now I was without a weapon. He twirled both round his hands, making the air breezy, grinning still. I wanted to slap the smug look off his wickedly handsome face.

Running towards him, Tommy somehow managed to spin me back around so quickly and push me away from him again that I didn't even know how it happened. I stood there in shock for a second until one of the sticks whipped across my arse.

I yelped, jumping further away from him. Spinning back round, I glared and rubbed my sore bum cheek. "The fuck Tommy?"

"You're not trying." He growled, clearly getting as

frustrated as me.

I threw my hand up and pointed at what was meant to be my weapon. "You have my stick thing."

"Get it back."

"Arghh." Letting out a noise of pure irritation, I ran at him once more. Quickly whipping the staff out across my calves, I flew backwards and landed hard on the floor. My teeth gritted together as I winced from the pain in my lower back and propped myself up on to my elbows.

"Was that really necessary?"

"Take the staff." He held it out, just out of my reach.

I scrambled forward to my knees, and he took a step towards me. Looking up through my lashes, he was grinning savagely.

"What?"

"I always wondered what you would look like on your knees."

"Prick." I grumbled, snatching the staff from his hand. Before I could stand again, he crouched down, taking my chin in his hand.

"You brought down three grown men Isabella. Yet you haven't even come close to leaving a mark on me."

I pounced, catching him off guard. He lost his footing, falling back and I swiftly brought my staff across his chest, pinning him to the floor. "Did you wonder what it would be like to have me on top of you too?" I panted out, the quick movement elevating my heartbeat. The gym, I really needed to go to the gym.

Expecting him to be even the slightest bit angry that I was currently straddling him, I was shocked to see that his eyes were lit up playfully. Something I hadn't seen before. Heat flushed to my cheeks as his gaze lowered from my face to my rapidly rising and falling chest. Fuck Letch for making us wear these ridiculous sports bras.

As if he had been summoned by my thought, the pervert called from across the room. "That's it, Miss Russo. Get stuck right into him. Use your hips. Grind down to keep him in that position."

"He has just made this feel so wrong." I mumbled and adjusted myself, so I was hovering above him instead. Tommy moved slightly under me too but didn't make any attempt to throw me off, even though we both knew he easily could.

"What would you do now, in a different situation?"

"Different situation?" I tilted my head.

"If we were on our own, not in the gym." He smirked suggestively and the midnight blue of his eyes sparkled.

"Stab you." I answered simply and he barked out a laugh, taking me by surprise once again.

"Where would you get the knife from Isabella?" His hands went to my hips, forcing them back down and closing the small gap between us.

"Who said anything about using a knife." I pressed down harder on the staff across his bare chest. If I snapped one in half, that would make a good enough weapon to stab him.

"Now you're thinking like a killer." He grinned wickedly. His fingers dug into my flesh, gripping me tighter as he forced me to the side. I hit the floor with him now on top of me, kneeling between my legs. I watched as both our staffs rolled away, out of my reach and I groaned inwardly. "Don't let yourself get distracted."

"Obviously in a real situation I wouldn't have been." I argued back.

"Then maybe I should put you in a terrifying situation again." Tommy leaned forward, balancing himself on his forearms either side of my head. His eyes darkened as he moved inches away from my face. "Maybe I should take you home with me and chain you to my basement wall. Punish you for every little thing you have done to piss me off. See how your body reacts to danger then."

The muscles around my stomach tensed at just the thought of what he could do to me, and my mouth went dry. I knew that he had meant it as a threat, but it sounded oddly erotic, and my body was already wanting it in a way I didn't appreciate.

I slowly licked my lips, trying to get some moisture back to them. "You owe me an answer."

His dark eyes contemplated me for a moment before giving me what I had earned. "We have seven claimed ones at this school. Ricky who is a skilled sniper, but you already knew that didn't you?"

"We've met." I confirmed, not telling him we were somewhat friends and actually intended on going to this Halloween dance together.

"Darren is ours because his father is head of our security at the glass palace. But he has his own set of skills that makes him useful if we want to hack certain security feeds. The other four boys are in various year groups. Used to run errands that we don't feel the need to do."

"That's six, you said seven?"

"You are the seventh."

"I really am the only girl then?" I frowned and he nodded. "Have you truly never claimed a girl before?"

"No."

My eyes narrowed in annoyance. "So whatever rules you say there are, you are making them up as you go along."

He grinned wickedly again, not confirming that I was right or wrong. "Oh, there are rules Isabella and most of those rules were set by my father when he attended this school and claimed a girl."

"What are the rules?" I fumed, getting more agitated by his vague answers.

His dark chuckle rumbled through me. "You've got me to the floor once and I've answered one of your questions. You haven't earned another yet."

Growling in aggravation, I wrapped my legs around his waist and tried to use my body weight to push him to the side. All I managed to do was thrust myself into him hard. He simply looked down at me, amused at my weak effort. Releasing my legs and smacking my fists against his chest, I let out another exasperated cry. He glared down at me, unmoving and unaffected.

"At least tell me what happened to the girl your father claimed? Did she kill herself to get away from him like I'm now tempted to do?"

"She married him." My face must have said exactly what I was thinking because he rolled his eyes before adding, "I have no intentions of marrying you, Isabella."

"Oh thank fuck for that." I breathed out a sigh of relief. "So if you don't want me then I can date others."

Fury flashed through his eyes as my words instantly changed his mood. "I may not want you," He snarled venomously. "But no one else is touching you either."

I opened my mouth to snap back at him, but my words were drowned out by a shrill cry from across the gymnasium.

"TOMMY!"

The high pitch squeal ripped through me in the most irritating way. Tommy looked up in the girl's direction and his expression instantly reverted back to cold and emotionless.

I tilted my head back, arching myself into him to get a better look at the upside-down girl storming towards us. Her face was flushed with anger as her eyes switched between me and him.

"Friend of yours?" I asked, looking back at him and almost laughing.

He shot me a look, warning me to keep my mouth shut then pushed himself off me and stood up. I rolled over and stood to face the banshee.

She reminded me of the Barbie doll I used to play with when I was younger but the budget version that was ripping off the real one. What was her name? Sindy or something like that.

Her large breasts bounced in the little pink tight-fitting dress that she wore, threatening to escape with every rage filled step she took. The overly bleached hair was pinned back into a neat bun and as she got closer, I noticed her makeup was probably professionally applied. She was pretty but in a 'I've used my daddy's credit card, but I still look cheap' kind of way.

Not that I could judge. I used daddy's credit card all the time. I felt a tiny pang of guilt for passing judgement too quickly.

Her Jimmy Choos came to a halt a few feet in front of us. "Daddy said there was no one else but looking at this slut beside you, I see that was a lie." I take it back; I didn't feel guilty at all for judging too soon.

Tommy didn't respond to the insult towards me but roughly grabbed her arm, dragging her away. She let out a light whimper, but he pushed her in front of him, making her stumble. The girl looked back over her shoulder at him and then over to me. I raised my hand and wiggled my fingers in farewell, giving her my best sweet as pie smile to go along with it.

"Baby –" She whined loudly but Tommy pushed her again through the door and they both disappeared.

I stood still for a second, now partnerless and unsure of what to do. Maddy was soon at my side with Callum close behind.

"Who was that?"

"His ex-fiancée." Maddy answered, a grin twisting on her face.

"No," My mouth opened in shock. "Really?"

She giggled. "Yep."

"What's her name?"

"Sindy."

I snorted. That's perfect. "What was she doing here?"

"Probably came to talk him into marrying her again." Callum shrugged, crossing his arms and still staring at the door.

"Fair enough. Is she part of another firm? Like the ones from up north?" I remembered Tommy saying that they would be visiting this weekend and that we all had to be there when it happened.

"No, the only reason for the marriage was because her dad is the police commissioner, and it was to keep him sweet."

"Oh, does that mean the police won't cover up any of your crimes now?" I smiled slyly at him, and he grinned over to me.

"We are that good sweetheart that we don't need the police to cover anything up. There's not usually anything to cover up if there's no evidence."

I rolled my eyes at his big headedness. "What is he going to do with her now?"

"Probably give her an angry goodbye fuck then send her on her way." Callum shrugged then turned around again to return to his spot.

I puckered my brow as I looked at Maddy. "Will he really have sex with her after that little outburst?"

"Fuck knows. Tommy does what he wants and he's also a man. Any chance to get your dick wet I suppose." She shrugged too then followed her brother.

I glared at the door, unsure how I felt about that. He really was a complete arse. He was allowed to have fun with whoever he wanted while I was expected to be celibate until he was finished with me and would release me from this claimed bollocks. That's if he ever did. And I still didn't know the fucking rules because the last girl that was claimed was his poor mother. Hopefully his father treated her better than how his son treated me.

But there was also a feeling there that I didn't like even more. Bitterness for a completely different reason that I wasn't ready to look in to.

Chapter 18

I leant against Callum on the sofa, flicking through the school's social website on my phone. It was early evening and even though Maddy and I were planning on watching more Friends, we had found ourselves in the common room with Callum and Archie.

Both were working on the AP Poisons homework that we had been set but I had already completed it during dinner.

"What else has cyanide in it?" Archie asked looking up from his book and over to me. "I've put down pesticides and tobacco smoke."

"House fire would do it too and it's in plastics." Callum answered, looking at his own answers.

"Got them down too."

"Apple seeds and apricot pits." I added.

"Fuck off." Archie scoffed and I looked over to see him frowning in doubt. I shrugged, not caring if he believed me or not. "So we've been eating poison for years without knowing? How are we still alive?"

"Well assuming you actually eat the seeds from an apple and not a pit from an apricot, my guess is you are not consuming enough to have any effect and they are being digested before you eat a fatal amount."

Archie looked a little confused and I twisted myself round, still leaning against Callum but facing the clueless boy face on. "A seed contains roughly 0.49mg of cyanogenic compounds. It takes 1 milligram of cyanide per kilogram of body weight to actually kill a person. What are you?" I eyed his physique, judging his weight that was probably completely wrong due to all of them muscles that stretched his black top. "180 kilograms? Give or take?" He grunted in response. "If my maths is correct then it would take probably 367 seeds to kill you.

Given there are roughly 8 seeds in an apple, you would need about 46 apples. Plus you would have to consume all of those apples within an hour. And even then, it wouldn't have the full effect because the seeds would be whole, and your body is already working to detoxify the cyanide. You would need to blend all the seeds into a smoothie and drink it quickly to actually succeed."

"Well fuck me." He breathed out, leaning back in his seat and running his hand through his long hair that was loose for once. "I'll just stick to a knife 'cause that all seems like a fucking ball-ache."

"Not just a pretty face, are you sweetheart?" Callum joked, giving my hip a squeeze where his hand rested.

"You should be wary of what this pretty face actually knows. And sleep with one eye open." I smirked, tilting my head back to look up at him. He gave me a little wink then went back to looking at his textbook.

"Can we get back to our game now?" Maddy complained from the floor, in front of me. "Hit or miss?"

She showed me the picture of another student who was the year above us. Good looking but not my type.

"Miss."

"Same." She swiped across to a picture of a busty, auburn-haired girl.

"Hit."

"So has half the school." She jibed.

"Means she has experience. I'll stick to my answer."

She snorted out a laugh then showed me the next picture before calling out her answer. "Miss."

I looked at the picture of her brother. "Hmm…"

"I believe the word you are looking for is hit." Callum grinned and I managed to elbow him in the arm.

"Concentrate on your work." Smiling back at the picture, I muttered "Hit."

I could sense his smug smile as his fingers gently glided up and down my arm. Maddy pulled up a picture of Anderson. Definitely not my type.

Just as I was about to answer, Tommy and Felix walked over. Felix lightly hit my feet out of the way and I sat up, crossing my legs under me. Tommy sat in the seat opposite the sofa, fresh clothed while the rest of us were still in uniform. His hair was still damp from having a shower after giving Sindy a good time.

That feeling of bitterness balled in my stomach again and my nostrils flared as I glared at him. He wasn't paying me the slightest bit of attention though and I was glad because the resentment I had was hard to conceal.

"Bella," Maddy interrupted my thoughts. "This one."

She showed me the picture of Anderson again and I answered with complete confidence, "Hit."

She twisted her body round in shock. "Really?"

"Yep."

Raising her brows, she turned back again. "Ok. This one?" Another one from the boy's year group.

"What are you doing?" Felix asked, craning his neck to look at Maddy's phone too.

"Playing hit or miss with fellow students. Hit." I answered both and she swiped across to the next one. "Hit." Swipe. "Hit." Swipe. "Hit." Swipe. "Hit."

"Oh, hit as in kill?" Felix guessed and I stopped looking at Maddy's phone to smile at him.

"No, as in I would let them hit me." Giving him a wink,

I went back to our game. Every picture she showed me was an instant hit without hesitation.

"You've said hit to them all." Tommy growled, finally giving me his attention and I looked across at him. His face was hard and cold as he glared back at me.

I shrugged. "What can I say, haven't had it in a while." Then looked back down to avoid the look of death he threw at me.

The picture on Maddy's phone now was Ricky and I swallowed before I could give my answer. "Hit."

"You sound like a whore." He spat venomously, obviously not liking what I was saying.

I smiled sweetly. "Whores get paid for it, Tommy." Taking Maddy's phone from her, I showed him who was on the screen. "I'd let him hit it for free."

Wrong thing to say.

Tommy was on his feet before I could blink. His jaw clenched as he looked violently down at me from across the small coffee table. Callum had grabbed my arms, pulling me protectively to him but I elbowed my way out of his grip and leapt over Maddy, onto the table.

With it giving me some height, I was now at eye level with the devil in front of me. "What are you going to do to stop me, Tommy?" My voice was so light and sweet that it almost seemed like I was taunting him on purpose. And maybe I was. Maybe I wanted him to suffer for sleeping with another girl when I wasn't allowed anyone. The only one he seemed to be ok with me getting closer to was Callum.

"You don't want to push me, Isabella." His growl rumbled through me, making every nerve in my body shiver but it wasn't unpleasant.

"What are you going to do, *baby*?" I goaded, using the nickname Sindy had given him.

His little brain worked fast, realising what I had said. A vicious grin spread across his face and his hand shot up, grabbing my throat. Spinning me round, I flew through the air and landed hard in the seat that seconds ago he was sitting in.

With his hand still grasping my throat, Tommy bowed over me. "Jealousy really isn't a good look on you."

"I could say the same." I smirked but his fingers dug in, making me gasp for the air he was taking away.

Both our breathing was evenly matched. Erratic and fast. His eyes bounced furiously between mine as his lips fell into a hard line.

"You are meant to be…" He didn't finish so I kept going for him.

"What? Unattainable. Under control. What am I meant to be Tommy?"

He groaned deep in his throat, keeping what he wanted to say to himself and pushed away. I didn't even look at him as he stormed out the room. My eyes stayed fixed to the small table in front of me, refusing to acknowledge any of them. My fingers slowly went to my neck, gently touching where his hand had been moments ago.

"Are you ok?" Callum asked, getting to his feet first and crossing the short distance to get to me.

"I'm fine." I replied weakly as he kneeled down on the floor.

"Isabella?" He tried to take my free hand in his, but I pulled away.

"I said I'm fine." My answer was more abrupt that time. Ripping myself out of the chair, I stormed from the room. Not to go after Tommy but to be on my own and stew in my own fury.

Chapter 11

I was sat down in the food hall, tray of food in front of me and laughing at something Felix had just said.

Callum was in his usual spot beside me, trying to convince me to try his latte. He promised that it didn't really taste like coffee and was milkier but I still turned my nose up at it. It was Felix's response that had made me laugh.

"You can decorate shit with flowers but it's still going to be shit."

"This don't taste like shit though."

"I'm not trying it." I finalised and he rolled his eyes. According to him, refusing to try it made me overly stubborn and uncultured. I pointed out that it would probably be more uncultured for me to hate tea.

Tommy was sitting across from me, glaring at his phone. We hadn't spoken since our spat the night before and we hadn't even tried. Part of me felt a little wounded by that but I was also glad. The less we spoke, the less we were at each other's throats. Literally.

"Our first Psychology class today. I wonder what the teacher will be like?" Maddy asked, placing her spoon back into her bowl then pushing it away from her.

Archie exchanged a look with Felix and Callum, all three grinning at their shared thought.

"Who is it?" I asked Callum.

"Surprise."

Rolling my eyes I looked back at Maddy. "At least we finished our homework, so we won't be on their bad side already." Callum snorted. "What?"

"Nothing sweetheart. But if you have any trouble with them, just let me know and I'll come save you again."

"Again?"

He lifted my hand off the table and brought it to his lips. "Wouldn't want these delicate hands coming to near harm for a second time."

"Aww, my knight in shining armour." I sighed sarcastically, ripping my hand back. He grinned and rested his arm on the back of my chair.

Maddy started going on about our lesson once more, but I noticed Ricky across the hall, just finishing up selecting his breakfast.

Sticking up my hand, I called him over. He was a claimed one after all, he should be allowed to sit with us. He turned to see who had called him and when his eyes fell on me, I frowned in confusion.

Not at him shaking his head. Or at the fact he was rushing towards the door of the hall with his food. But at the bruised eye and split lip he was sporting.

"What happened to Ricky?"

Maddy quickly stretched out her neck to look behind me and just caught a glimpse as he vanished but not before he glanced back over his shoulder. "What happened to his face?"

I looked at Callum who slowly shook his head at me, pinning me with a look to not go on. Archie and Felix had occupied themselves with their phones. And Tommy...

Tommy took a bite out of his apple, smirking like he had got one over on me. A violent bliss in his eyes returned my stare and it took a few seconds for me to realise what had happened.

"You absolute cunt." My tame insult made no effect as he took another bite of his apple, still watching me. "He is one of you, he's a claimed one. How can you do that to him?"

He didn't reply.

"Why hit him? He hasn't done anything wrong. I was the one who said I would have sex with him, not the other way round."

Still silence. Callum's fingers slid on to my shoulder, giving it a firm squeeze and warning me to stop but I couldn't.

"Answer me for fucks sake!" I shouted, making the few others still in the hall turn their attention to our table.

"Ricky needed a reminder of the rules?" Finally. Not what I was expecting but he finally answered.

"What fucking rules Tommy because this is getting fucking old now. Everyone else seems to know them apart from me and no one else will tell me them because you make them up as you go."

The wicked grin didn't fade, pissing me off even more. He was relishing in my anger.

"Has anyone else made a move on you?"

"No, you've marked your property so well, every other fucking boy is too scared to even say hello." My answer only fed his ego. "So the rules are that no boy is allowed to ask me out, talk to me and what else? Is Callum exempt from these rules because you have no issue with him being all over me, or flirting, or picking out my underwear when he comes to my room."

Tommy's face darkened as his grin completely vanished.

"Fuck." Callum murmured, removing his hand from my shoulder. He lowered his gaze like he was guilty of a crime and Tommy's fury filled eyes rounded on him.

"We're going to be late for class." Maddy hastily said and got to her feet even though she had a free period. Tommy pushed himself back from the table and rose too.

He didn't say a word but marched from the room to our AP Art of Killing lesson.

I slowly stood up, not saying a word to the others. They did the same though and we followed Tommy out of the hall.

Maddy shadowed us for a while until we came to the classroom door and as the boys went in to take their seats, Maddy muttered, "This is going to sound controversial, but I think that went well."

I snorted out a laugh then closed the door behind me.

Psychology.

Getting into the minds of criminals.

Finding out what makes a murderer.

That's the lesson that Maddy and I now sat in, waiting for our teacher to arrive. We both had our textbook, notebook and pen ready on the desk. Not one to be a teacher's pet but first impressions were definitely important.

Daisy spun around in her seat in front of us. "Did you two do your homework?"

"Yeah, did you?" Maddy answered.

She nodded. "A lot of them didn't though. Probably thinking that the new teacher won't even be bothered."

"If he lets them get away with it, I'll be annoyed that I even did it." Maddy frowned, looking annoyed by everyone else.

"Is it bad I want him to punish them all." Daisy's malicious smile made us both chuckle.

"It might be a female teacher." The boy sitting beside her butted in then turned to face us. I recognised him from combat training the previous week but had never spoken to him.

Daisy rolled her eyes at him. "Maddy, Bella. This is Jack, my twin."

That took me by surprise a little. They looked nothing

alike. Where Daisy was short with dark hair and matching dark eyes, Jack seemed taller, even sitting down. His tight blonde curls were short, and he had the most striking blue eyes and full lips.

"Nice to meet you." Maddy smiled at him.

"We've met before." He grinned. "We just never spoke."

She withdrew herself a bit at that, blushing slightly. "Oh, sorry."

"Don't worry. I may be a first year, but I understand the rules. No touching or talking to the Kray girls." He laughed heartedly.

"Ooh, so the rules apply to you too." I smirked at her and Maddy scowled back.

"They don't have to worry about me breaking the rules anyway. I'm more interested in the Kray boys than the Kray girls." He winked at us, and it took a few seconds for realisation to hit.

"Ohh."

"Fair enough."

"They are hot, so can't really blame you." I nodded then fired Maddy a look. "That was said under confidence."

She laughed, holding up her hands. "I promise not to tell them what they already know and feed their egos."

"Felix is the hottest." My mouth gaped open a little as my brows rose at Daisy. "What can I say, we got closer while fighting."

"Must admit, fighting so close to them without feeling some form of excitement is impossible." I agreed.

"You are so lucky to get to do that. I wonder if they would give me a bit of one on one." Jack pondered, looking away from us and rubbing his chin.

"I have something to say to all of you. Firstly, Daisy." Maddy turned to her. "He's single. Go for it."

Daisy grinned mischievously.

"You," She pointed her finger at me. "What the fuck? You hate Tommy but you feel excitement when fighting with him?"

"I said some form of excitement Maddy. Mine is the thought of hurting him." I reassured her but she hummed back and nodded her head suspiciously.

If I thought back to all the times that Tommy and I had argued or fought and really thought about what I was feeling, then I would have to start questioning myself. So it was easier to ignore it all.

"What about me?" Jack shot in.

"I don't actually know." Maddy chuckled, distracted from thinking about me and her cousin.

"I'll ask them if they'll give you a private session." I winked at him, and he laughed again.

"Thanks chick. You are now my new best friend."

"Hey, that position has already been filled." Maddy flung her arms around my neck, pulling me to her for a possessive hug making us all laugh until the door swung open and revealed our new teacher.

"The next person that speaks will be punished in whatever way I see fit."

Williams strode down the aisle between the desks, trusty wooden ruler in one hand and his laptop in the other. I let out an audible groan before I could stop myself.

"Russo!" His ruler cracked across his new desk, making me jump and he turned to face me with a hideously crooked grin. "I don't usually give warnings but seeing as you volunteered to clean my office tonight, consider this your one and only."

"I didn't off —"

"And I definitely don't give second warnings Isabella."

Shutting my mouth, I leaned in my seat and glanced at Maddy. She chewed her bottom lip nervously then faced the front of the room too.

"For those who didn't complete the homework that was set, meet me after class."

I swallowed, suddenly feeling bad for them who didn't complete it and glad that the four of us had. Williams was a jerk at the best of times, but I dread to think what it would have been like if Maddy and I hadn't done it.

"Today we are going to discuss what…" His voice trailed off in my mind and I went into auto pilot. Opening the book when he instructed, writing down notes when he told us to. All the time thinking how I managed to get myself in a situation where I had to clean his poxy office.

I followed Maddy into the food hall, rubbing my arm that felt completely bruised from being pinned down by Letch and still in our gym wear because both of us were hungry and didn't give a shit. I had finally had my chance of a one on one with him and it was something I wished never to experience again. I was almost certain he had purposely swiped his fingers between my legs because every time he apologised, he would have a warped grin on his face like he would gladly do it again. And he did. Multiple times.

The only good thing about the last two lessons that we had was the first weaponry class. Learning about how to dismantle and reassemble a gun was rather therapeutic. That was until one student, Olly I think his name was, forgot to put the safety on once he had finished and shot himself in the foot.

I walked a few steps behind Maddy, grabbing a bowl of pasta salad from the counter and a bottle of water. We made our way to our usual spot, sitting between the three boys that were already occupying some of the seats.

"Where's Tommy?" Maddy asked as she opened her can of drink.

"Someone decided to make another surprise visit." Archie grinned like Tommy's unfortunate visitor amused him somewhat. Assuming it was Sindy, fire burned in my stomach, and I didn't like this new feeling of jealousy that kept creeping up on me at times.

I adjusted myself in the plastic chair, wincing at the pain

in my left bum cheek from being repeatedly dropped on it.

"What's wrong with you?"

"Letch." Was all I said, and Callum actually gave me a look of understanding.

"Your turn, was it?" Felix asked through his mouth full of sausage.

I nodded but Maddy gave a verbal response. "He had her on the floor several times. I thought he was using the karma sutra for inspiration at one point."

I grimaced at the reminder and Archie snorted out a laugh.

"Ooh, that's rough." Felix gave me the same sympathetic look as Callum.

"I think it was the one where you were upside down and your ankles were wrapped around his neck that really made me question what the fuck you were both doing."

I scowled at her. "I was trying and failing to snap his neck."

"I think he would have died happily after all the other positions he had you in. May have to try some of them with Jullian."

Callum shot his sister a look of disgust, making me chuckle.

"If it was my usual partner, it wouldn't have been so bad."

Felix raised a brow and the side of his mouth tilted up. "Oh really?"

"Yeh, at least Tommy has no interest in touching certain places like Letch does…" Although I wasn't sure I would stop him if he did.

My stomach fluttered, obviously excited by the thought and I mentally cursed it for betraying my hatred for him.

"What are you two doing tonight anyway?" Felix asked and Maddy shrugged, taking a bite from her own salad. "You both wanna come play target practice with us?"

"Who's the target?" He grinned devilishly at her, making her eyes roll. "Ok, but I need to shower first."

"I can't. I've somehow managed to get a detention with Williams."

Callum twisted my chair around to face him. "How?"

"I made a noise in class and now I'm cleaning his office." I shrugged then turned back around to carry on eating.

Callum didn't bother asking for any more information, but he didn't look too pleased either.

Archie looked past me, watching someone get closer to the table. "How did it go?"

I turned round just in time to see Tommy shaking his head. His stoic face gave nothing away of what he had just been doing with budget Barbie. The only thing that gave me some kind of relief, was that he was still in his uniform, and nothing looked out of place.

He took his place opposite me, not bothering to grab any food first and loosened the tie around his neck. Something was frustrating him, but I wasn't about to ask if he was ok and give the impression that I actually cared. Because I didn't.

"You doing target practice with us tonight?" Felix asked him.

Tommy let go of a heavy sigh and ran his fingers through his hair. "Maybe. I have a few other things to see to first."

Once again, I didn't want to ask. I didn't care.

But was it a few things or someone to see to?

"Ooh there's Daisy." Maddy smiled brightly as she looked across the hall. I followed her gaze and saw our friend filling up her tray, her brother beside her. "You two budge up so she can sit with us." She instructed Felix and Archie.

"There isn't enough room." Felix mumbled but still moved to the end of the table surprisingly.

Archie stayed in his seat. "She's not sitting here."

"Why not?"

"Because she's a nobody."

"She's our friend."

"She isn't claimed so she can't sit with us."

My head volleyed between their bickering.

"Well I'm part of this family too so I claim her."

My eyes widened in surprise. I didn't even think about the fact Maddy could possibly claim someone too.

"Can you do that?" I asked then flicked my gaze to Tommy with hope. "Can she do that?"

"No, she can't." He answered but a smile played on his lips. Looked like he was slowly cheering up.

"Why not?" Maddy argued back, glaring at him but he only grinned in response.

"Ohh, if she can claim someone does that mean I can too?"

"You are a claimed one so no. Neither of you can."

"Seems a bit unfair." Maddy carried on and I nodded, agreeing with her.

"There are —"

"Rules, we know. But I'm allowed friends so fuck it." Before Tommy could say anything else, Maddy stood up and called Daisy over to us. Jack confidently followed.

Tommy rolled his eyes, picking up my water and unscrewed the lid.

"Help yourself."

He flashed me a sarcastic smirk and took a massive gulp just as Daisy reached the table.

"Hey, do you want to join us?" Maddy asked her and she looked around the table nervously. None of the boys were very welcoming. Tommy was staring at me with a mixture of hatred and heat in his dark eyes. Callum was completely ignoring them. Archie was glaring between her and her brother while Felix… Felix was pushing the food around his plate with his fork.

"No, that's ok. We've got a table over there but thought we would come to say hi."

"You've said hi. Now go."

I shot a look of death to Archie, and he glared back like

we had invited some sort of plague to our table.

Jack completely disregarded his rudeness though and smiled over to me. "Did you want to go over notes from psychology tonight or tomorrow?"

"Tomorrow would be better." I nodded to him.

"Remember what happened to the last boy, Isabella." Tommy purred, smirking like he was enjoying the threat.

"Oh reel your domineering control issues in. I'm pretty sure he would rather you suck his cock than me." I quickly faced Jack, adding. "Sorry."

He laughed heartedly. "It's fine. I'm not shy."

Tommy regarded what I said for a second and it seemed like the rest were doing the same, staring at poor Jack. After a few silent breaths Tommy leaned back in his chair, grinning again.

"Ok, you can have him as your friend."

My brow rose as Callum snorted beside me but then attempted to conceal it with a cough when I elbowed him.

"Thank you for giving me permission to have a friend Sir. Now if I may be excused, I need to shower. My new friend will be coming with me because he is gay and won't try it on."

I expected some sort of response from Tommy but not the one he gave me. For his amused grin didn't fade and a playful glint lit up his eyes.

"You're welcome."

My eyes narrowed at him. "Come on Jack, you can help me out of these clothes." The poor bloke looked nervously between us both. But he had nothing to worry about. For this wasn't like a normal argument between Tommy and me. This was different. This was like he wanted me to push him.

Rising from my seat, Tommy's eyes followed me. "Jack, isn't it?" He glanced over at Jack, and he tilted his head to confirm. "Take that empty seat there," He flicked his fingers to the seat that had Felix in minutes before, right next to Archie. "You'll find you and Archie have similar interests that may… Excite you a bit more than watching Miss Russo shower."

Jack looked from me to Archie who at that point looked generally thrilled. A definite change to the previous attitude of not wanting them here at all. I had so many questions that I needed to ask but right now I just wanted to leap across the table and wrap my hands around the smug arsehole's throat. Not because he had done anything wrong. Fuck me, he probably just made Jack's night, but because he had won.

Pushing my chair away, I stormed out of the hall. And even though it did look like I had given up, I really did need that shower before I had to go to Williams' office.

Chapter 20

I knocked on the wooden door of the professor's office. I wasn't sure what time he wanted me there but seeing as he hadn't specified, I made sure to quickly wash, change into a white shirt dress and brown worker boots then bung my hair up into a messy pony.

The door jerked open, with the aging man standing just beyond it, holding on to the handle. Giving me a once over, he frowned as his eyes landed on my face.

"I'm sorry, you didn't tell me what time to come." I muttered, shuffling from one foot to another as my fingers nervously grabbed the opposite elbows, curling my arms around myself.

He didn't respond but moved to the side, allowing me to enter.

His office wasn't small but there was so much junk that it made it appear that way. The large desk was cluttered with paperwork and open files. Bookcases, all full, covered the wall to my left while filing cabinets filled the other side. Behind the desk were floor to ceiling windows that overlooked the small field before the forest. If the room was tidier, it would have been spectacular.

"What would you like me to do?" I asked, turning back around to look at him.

"I want you to clear away the files on the desk then organise the books on the shelves in alphabetical order."

I glanced around the room again. The desk wouldn't take too long but the bookcases would take me a good couple of hours, if not more.

Williams moved to his desk and picked up his phone and laptop that were hidden under the masses of paper. "Any loose documents can be placed in the tray." He strolled back around and passed me. "You won't leave until you are finished."

Slamming the door behind him, I jumped slightly. I was being punished for a tiny noise. The only thing that brought me some clarity was that it wasn't a physical punishment like the ones who hadn't handed in their homework, had received.

My fingers clenched into fists at just thinking about their knuckles receiving the lashings from the ruler.

Making a start on the bookcases first, I started piling up the works of old fiction and the encyclopaedias of useful information.

Three hours later, I placed the last book on to the shelf. Alphabetically perfect and I even tidied up the various ornaments that were strewn about.

Glancing dismally at the desk, I wished that I could just come back and finish it tomorrow but to walk out now really wouldn't be the best decision I had ever made.

I pulled out Williams' large leather chair and sat down ready to clear up his mess. The files could have easily been closed. Leaving them open was just pure laziness. After I had stacked them all up ready to put back into the cabinets, I moved on to the loose papers.

Nothing seemed too important. Some CVs to fill the

psychology position that Williams was currently substituting and a couple of admission forms. But I didn't want to chuck anything just in case and just neatly moved them to the tray like he had instructed then tidied up the rest of the desk.

The student's files that I was putting away were all from the last year group and I assumed it was to do with their progress. Opening up the filing cabinet, I started to slide the files into their allotted places.

After all the brown sleeves were neatly put away, my eyes searched the other two cabinets that had the files of the other year groups in. Curiosity was itching at my fingers, and I slid open the drawer for my own year group. It didn't take long to find my own file and I slid it out. It was thinner that the last year's ones but I hadn't been at the school long so there wasn't anything of importance to put in there yet.

Flicking through the papers inside I came across the crimes I had committed. One was the police reports, evidence documents that had been 'lost', and pictures of the men that I had killed. The images that had been permanently set into my memories had become less severe over time because the images in my hand were something out of a horror movie. I had done that. I had made those three men unrecognisable. The next image was of me kneeling, hands resting on my lap with my head down, staring at my palms. There wasn't any part of me that didn't have their blood smeared on. That was me. The little 15 year old psycho.

It was done now. There was no changing what had happened. Giving myself a little shake, I looked at the other papers. Writing had been scrawled over one of the sheets. A couple of words smudged by a coffee stain and then PETROV under that.

Under them papers were a missing person's report for Drew Chapmen and an email that had been printed off from my dad, explaining everything that had happened. Where he had hid the body, how he had kept it quiet from everyone and went out on the searches for the local lad to not raise suspicions. He had written everything in the email that he had sent to Williams.

All my crimes had been covered up but all the evidence of them sat in my hands.

A cough from outside the door made me jump, making the papers fall to the floor. Panicking, I scrambled to my knees to pick them back up. They weren't in the order I had found them, but I didn't have time to sort that out. Something did catch my eye though. My birth certificate. Isabella Sofia Russo. My mothers and father's names. Nothing unusual.

But what was unusual was the second birth certificate.

Isabella Sofia Moretti.

The handle of the door started to creak, and I shoved both documents back into the file then into the cabinet.

Just as I slammed it shut, the door opened.

"Have you finished sweetheart."

I released my breath, letting my shoulders relax as Callum closed the door behind him.

"Yeah, I think I'm done now." I smiled at him. "What're you doing here?"

"I messaged you to see how you were getting on and when you didn't reply and weren't in your room still, I thought I best check to make sure that old fuck hadn't tortured you."

"You care way too much about me." I teased, smirking over at him.

Callum shrugged then walked over to the desk and rounded it. "I've been in here way too many times to count, and this is the only time I have come willingly."

"Why does that not surprise me." I sighed rolling my eyes. "How many times have you been hit with the ruler of castigation?"

"Only once. But that was by the old one."

"The old one?" My brows knitted together, and I walked over to where he was now sitting in the chair with his feet resting on the just cleaned desk.

"Tommy snapped it." Both my brows rose asking why?

"Across Williams' back."

"You're kidding?" I shoved his feet off the desk again, not wanting him to mess up my hard work.

"It was just after the old Prof cracked it against my knuckles for not knowing the answer to a question. I think it was our first week at school."

"What a prick. Did Tommy get in big trouble?"

"You'd assume so wouldn't you." He grinned. "No, I think Williams was in shock at first and then respected him a bit. That's when all the others started respecting him too. No one had ever dared to fight back with a teacher before, especially Williams."

"Oh, I thought it was because you're this big mafia gang thing, so it gave you power straight away. And Tommy mentioned his dad went here so thought that had something to do with it too."

"Of course it does but just because we are part of the firm, –" He corrected "- doesn't mean we were automatically bigshots here. The teachers knew who we were and a few of the other kids too. But to others, we were just like them. Either we had killed to get in here, daddy's money had paid for it, or we were the kids of the corrupt government." He leaned forward, resting his elbows on his knees and I leaned against the desk. "You didn't know anything about us when you first came here did you"

It wasn't a question, more of a conformation that I was really clueless, so I shook my head. "I didn't even know this school existed, let alone anything about the four psychos that kidnapped me the first night."

His wicked grin made me roll my eyes, but I still grinned back. "Exactly. We had to prove that we were the best, that we weren't to be messed with. When Tommy snapped the ruler that Williams used for his form of punishment across his own back, word quickly got around. More people started to realise who we were. Tommy was already next in line in our family anyway, but because of that little performance, he soon became top dog here too. Soon after, my other cousins and I proved that we were just as strong, fearsome."

I snorted lightly and he scowled playfully. "Are we not scary?"

"Now that I've got to know you all more, not so much."

"Then I feel we should stop being so nice to you."

"I'm still a little scared of Tommy if that helps." I chuckled.

"And yet you purposely piss him off the most?"

"I know, ironic isn't it?"

He rolled his eyes at my sweet smile but then continued with what he had been saying. "Over time, we rose to the top. If anyone opposed us, we would fight and now no one in this school would dare question us or stop us."

"Is that why Williams didn't say anything else when you stopped him from hitting me?"

His eyes darkened, making his face resemble the scary he had just mentioned. "He won't get away with that. I might even add this unnecessary detention to my list of things that have pissed me off recently."

What else had Williams done to piss him off. Was it personal to him or the others too? More questions I wanted to ask but didn't.

"Thank you, Cal." I smiled softly at him. "For stopping him from hurting me."

He smiled back then got to his feet. "You know, that's the first time you've called me Cal."

Stepping in front of me, I looked up into his grey eyes. "I've called you different names before." I frowned.

"Yes." He grinned, the creases by his eyes deepening. "Prick, twat and my personal favourite, fucktard."

I giggled lightly as he placed his hands either side of the desk, caging me in. "Umm how were the others when I left earlier?" I asked, trying to distract him from whatever he intended to do.

He frowned, tilting his head, but then smiled, knowing I was trying to divert. "Tommy was unsurprisingly cheerful at getting one up on you. Maddy and Daisy spoke endlessly about shit and Archie, Felix and that other boy seemed happy enough too."

That reminded me, "Is Archie into boys?"

"He enjoys both."

"Oh, that'll make Jack happy."

"I have a feeling Jack will be extremely happy." His cheeky smirk made my eyes narrow.

"Why?"

"Archie went to find him after our game."

"Dirty fuckers." I laughed but was happy that they hadn't scared Daisy and Jack away. I really liked them.

Callum chuckled lightly. "I love that sound."

"What sound?"

"Your laughter. I don't get to hear it often but when I do…" His eyes closed, breathing in deeply through his nose, then when they opened again there was a look of hunger.

He leaned in closer, his chest grazing my breasts. My heart raced as nerves started to take over. This could go either of two ways. I could push him away and tell him to stop. Or I could let him do whatever he intended to do in Williams' office.

The latter sounding more appealing considering Williams was a dick and to do something lewd in his office was like a small victory. But I didn't want Callum.

"Callum." I whispered before he could get any closer and I placed my hand on his chest to keep some distance between us.

He sighed heavily and looked down to my hand. "Even if you wanted to, I couldn't."

My brows pinched together, and I pushed him away further. "What do you mean?"

"Why did he have to be the one to claim you?" It was a rhetorical question but had hit its mark.

"What does that matter?" I could feel the anger rising in my veins. Everything always came back around to being claimed.

Callum shook his head, smiling but it was anything but

happy. Moving his hand to my face, he slowly tucked the loose strands behind my ear then cupped my chin. "You still don't get it do you? He claimed you. No one else can have you. Not any other claimed ones. Not Archie or Felix." He broke the intense eye contact to glance down to my lips. "Not even me. You're his."

I twisted my head away from his grip then pushed him completely out of my way. Striding the other side of the desk, I glared over to him. He hadn't made any attempt to move but he was watching me.

"He doesn't want me Callum. He told me he doesn't. And I sure as fuck don't want him."

"It doesn't work like that."

"It doesn't work at all." My voice was louder, and I realised that I was now shouting. "He can't dictate who or what I do. My life is my own and I've had enough of him trying to control every little part of it."

I had the urge to fling myself over the desk and pounce on Callum. Let him take me over the desk just to prove a fucking point but there was someone else who I wanted to have it out with more.

Turning on my heel, I stormed for the door.

"Where are you going?"

I didn't answer him and kept raging down the hall to the boys' dorms, leaving Callum in the office calling my name.

"Isabella!"

Chapter 21

When I got to the corridor that led to Tommy's room, my anger had escalated. Every thought that raced through my mind was against him. His possessive attitude. Controlling my life by saying who I could be friends with, who I can see, who I can date.

I knew by coming to this school, my life wasn't going to be my own until I graduated but having it controlled by another student, no matter who or what his status was, was wearing pretty thin on my patience.

The door to my left opened just as I walked past, and the red head strode out of the same boy's room I had first seen her in.

"Little whore is looking for her next fix." Sandra sneered and I shot her a terrifying glare.

"Fuck off Clifford."

She scoffed, looking confused but leant against the doorframe, watching whatever I was doing in the hope of some gossip.

Sandra didn't need to wait that long. Before I reached Tommy's door, it opened. Budget Barbie strolled out with the biggest grin on her face and my rage finally went to boiling point. She turned towards me and as soon as her eyes met mine, she gave me a self-satisfied smirk. I wanted to rip out her eyes with my nails and slice her trout pout off.

Sindy turned back to the door just as Tommy came out, dressing in grey sweats and a black top. She muttered something, but I was still too far away to hear anything but a murmur. Tommy's head whipped round to look at me and his eyes widened in shock momentarily before darkening like my presence had inconvenienced his impending make out session.

Sindy kissed his cheek then flounced towards me. No words were exchanged between us, but the looks were enough. Her grinning smugly, like a cat who had just got the cream and my glare that I hoped showed her that murder was an option I was willing to use if she dared speak to me.

Tommy walked back into his room but left the door open, knowing there would be no point in closing it. I slammed it shut then stared at him. He was now standing in the centre of the floor, arms crossed, chin up and a cold glare that he probably thought would disarm me.

But I was ready for it. "So it's ok for you to fuck whoever you want but I'm not allowed." I snapped but as he opened his mouth to retaliate, I cut him off. "Callum told me. He told me what the fucking rule was."

Tommy's brow rose as his lips tipped up in amusement, making my veins burn with fury.

"You find this funny? You find controlling women, telling them who they can and can't see funny? Actually no. You find telling me that I can't see anyone at all funny. Because that's what you said wasn't it. You don't want me but that doesn't mean that anyone else can have me."

"So you've come here because your pussy cries for attention?" His smirk had faded but there was still a heat in his gaze.

"Oh my god, listen to yourself. No, it's about you trying to control me. Callum told me that I'm yours. That's what being claimed means. You claimed me so you get to control my life."

"Yes."

"No!" I fumed, throwing my hands in the air. "This is going to stop now. You don't own me. If I want to do something, I'm going to do it. If I want to have a relationship with someone, I will. You don't get to tell me if I can go with other boys or not. If I want to fuck Callum, I will."

Tommy's eyes filled with about as much rage as I was feeling. I couldn't even explain the sudden whiplash of emotion I got from him in not even a second because there wasn't an ounce of amusement in his midnight blue eyes anymore.

"Is that what you want?" His voice was low and sinister. "You want Callum?"

I swallowed, faltering slightly as fear tried to overtake my anger. "Yes." Lies.

"Were you going to fuck him?" He took a step towards me.

"You fucked Sindy, so why can't I?"

I stood my ground as he took another step but my heart banging against my chest was a dead giveaway of how I was feeling. Angry yet nervous and the betrayal of flutters in my stomach that was the subtle hint of excitement.

"Were you going to fuck him Isabella?"

"Yes," I grinned maliciously, "I was going to let him screw me over Williams' desk."

His hand flew up, grabbing my throat and spinning me around to chuck me onto his bed. I hit the soft mattress but before I could scramble up again, he was between my legs, his arms caging me in.

"You always say things to antagonise me. You want a reaction." He growled low, leaning even closer. I started to lift my head, to attempt to move from under him but his fingers tangled through my hair at the scalp, ripping it back down to the bed. A frustrated noise escaped from me, and he released a dark chuckle that matched the dark desire in his eyes.

"I want you to leave me alone and get the fuck out of my life." I seethed through gritted teeth.

Completely ignoring what I had said, his grip tightened through my hair as he used his forearm to balance himself. "I'm going to tell you exactly what the rules are."

"I'm done with your rules." I hissed and he grinned wickedly.

"But I'm not done with you."

Fuck. Heat rushed through my veins, igniting something it shouldn't have, and I would have given anything to close my legs and stop the pulsing between them.

"You belong to me. Every part of you belongs to me until I say so. No other man is going to touch you without my permission. And even then it will only be if it is convenient to me." His hand lowered to my leg, feeling the bare skin. My dress had risen in the struggle, revealing my thigh and making it so much easier for him. "But now I know how much you crave someone's touch; I'm going to make it so much harder for you to get it from anyone else."

His hand glided higher, skimming the hem of the cotton material. "No one is going to touch you unless it is me."

I could hear the blood rushing through me and feel myself quivering beneath him. His touch was something my body was screaming to taste more of.

"No one is going to make you feel the way I will make you feel."

My eyes closed, hating to admit that I was enjoying the feeling of his hands caressing my skin. Each little touch left a lasting imprint while his words set my body on fire. It was like a volcano, desperate to erupt. My breaths were uneven and ragged whilst his were controlled. Just like everything else he was doing.

He was so close now that even as his mouth moved to speak, our lips nearly touched. "No one will give you the pleasure that you want so badly, only me. You're not even allowed to pleasure yourself without my permission." His fingers dug into my flesh, making me bend at the knee as he lifted my thigh. A tiny gasp escaped my lips and he breathed it in, satisfied with the effect he was having on my body.

I hated myself for wanting it. I wanted the pleasure he was denying me, but he was wrong about something because I didn't want it from anyone else. I only wanted it from him. But I wouldn't give him the satisfaction of me begging for it.

His head lowered to the back of my jaw and his lips ghosted my ear. "I own that pleasure. I own you. You are mine Isabella."

My eyes snapped open, the feminist breaking through the illusion of having anything with the devil on top of me.

"I would rather kill myself than let you touch me."

"Then I will follow you to hell because not even death will keep you away from me."

Fuck me. I hated him so much but his words…

Raking my fingers through his hair, I snapped his head back, away from me. Catching him off guard, he released my own hair and was momentarily distracted enough to allow me to roll off the bed and on to the floor. Once I had scrambled to my feet though, he was already on his, blocking the only exit.

"Move."

"That was vicious." His voice was as dangerous as his gaze as he rubbed the back of his head.

"Think of it as a warning. Now. Move."

He took a cynical step towards me, and I did the only thing that come to mind. I ran for the door on my left, slamming it behind me. I turned the lock then silently cursed my stupid irrational behaviour for now being trapped in the bathroom with a covetous prick on the other side.

I glanced in the mirror opposite. My cheeks were flushed. My ponytail was looser from having his fingers gripping on to it and my pupils were overly dilated. I looked like I had just had sex. What annoyed me the most was my mind fighting against my body because one wished I had

had sex more than the other.

The handle moved behind me. "Open the door, Isabella."

I didn't reply, nor did I make any attempt to unlock it. Instead, I walked over to the sink and ran the cold tap. Splashing the cold water over my face in the hopes of cooling down, I stared back at my reflection.

What now?

I could walk out this room and face the inevitable anger of Tommy or I could stay in here and piss him off more.

Who was I kidding? It wasn't even a choice.

Patting my face dry, I walked back over to the door and sat down on the cold tiles, leaning against it. Tommy tried the handle again to no avail.

"You're a fool if you think I won't kick this door open."

"I'm on the other side and not moving so if you want to hurt me that much then go ahead."

His growl of aggravation was heard through the door, making my stomach twist anxiously. "Come out now." He gritted through his teeth.

"I'm busy."

"Get. Out. Here. Now." Each word was eerily calm but even though I couldn't see him, I could tell that a major storm was brewing, and I was ready to be the tornado that made it worse.

"I'm touching myself." I smiled, making it come out as breathy as I could.

A fist pounded on the door, making me jump and I had to throw my hand over my mouth to stop the laughter that was creeping up because of his reaction.

"Isabella!" This time he wasn't so calm. My name was a lot louder, and it was the first time I actually felt fear at hearing it. But that didn't stop me.

"Oh my –" I cut my self off, once again trying not to laugh as he pounded against the door for the second time.

He shouted again and I started going to town with the fake moans and groans while all the time looking around the room.

"Get the fuck out!"

"Ohh god, that feels good."

Dior Savage aftershave. Explains why he smells fucking delicious all the time.

"Your arse is going to be fifty shades of red for this fucking stunt."

"Fuck, I'm so close."

Bang.

"Isabella!"

I really needed to repaint my nails. The red was chipping badly, and it really wasn't a good look. Maddy might have some pink polish.

"When I get my fucking hands on you –"

"Oh my god! I'm going to come."

This outfit would look really cute with frilly socks too.

"Oh fuck, Tommy."

My mouth snapped shut and my eyes bulged at my mistake. Tommy had realised it too for his yelling and pounding on the door had stopped. I had said his name. Not Callum's, not anyone else's. His.

It didn't mean anything. Just a slip of the tongue while I was faking it.

I sat there for a few minutes, waiting for him to start up again but he didn't and neither did I.

Slowly rising to my feet, I clicked the lock and pushed down the handle. Not really knowing what to expect on the other side, I pulled the door open slowly.

Tommy was blocking my exit. Both his hands gripped the frame tightly, the veins pulsing in his arms as he leaned against it looking down at the floor. Slowly, his head lifted. Dark strands of his unruly hair fell over his eyes. And fuck did he pin me with a gaze I had never seen before. I've seen blue fire and I know that the flame burns the hottest. That was how passion had transformed his midnight eyes. A new desire had been ignited in them, making my own body ache with the same sensation.

Rushing under his arm to escape, my arm brushed against his side and even through the thin cloth of our clothes, the simple touch made my heart pound against my chest.

I reached the door and opened it. He hadn't even attempted to stop me or even yell anymore. I glanced back over my shoulder to find him still in the same position.

I turned round fully. "Tommy."

He slowly faced me; his jaw clenched but the same raw need in his eyes. I showed him my middle finger and brought it to my mouth. Running my tongue from the base to the tip, I grinned suggestively.

"I used that one."

Before I could see or hear his reaction, I ran. I ran all the way back to my room and ignored my phone that was going wild and promised Maddy I would tell her everything tomorrow.

Chapter 22

Laying on the bed, I finally looked at the messages on my phone while Maddy finished getting ready for her first lesson. Callum had texted telling me not to do anything stupid. Too late for that. And I had been tagged in a post on the school chat group. Nothing from Tommy but then again, he hardly texted me anyway.

Clicking on the post notification, I saw a picture of me and budget Barbie crossing paths the night before. Sandra had been kind enough to include a little description of what was apparently happening.

Sandra Morgan

Looks like the wannabe mafia princess is happy to take Tommy's cock after it was stirring someone else's pot.

Daisy Upton

You're disgusting Sandra.

Sandra Morgan

Fuck off shrimp, everyone can see you trying to worm your way into their group.

Daisy Upton
Are you really becoming that irrelevant that you have to make up shit to find some form of entertainment.

Sandra Morgan
Remember your place, first year.

Daisy Upton
Remember who you are trying to insult because from what I saw yesterday, while sitting at their table that you have never been invited to, all four cousins are protective over their girls.

Sandra Morgan
She's a freak and I will tell them that too. Called me Clifford like it was an insult.

Simon Smith
LMAO CLIFFORD #bigreddog #burn

Sandra Morgan
Fuck off Smithy, No one even likes you

There were so many more messages between them but nothing that concerned me now and I had lost interest. Sandra had made out that I was one of Tommy's harem of girls but that wasn't ever going to be the case. I had no interest in becoming one and never would.

But she was proving to be a problem that kept resurfacing.

"Maddy?"

"Hmm?" She walked back into the room from the bathroom, completely ready.

"Has anyone ever really got expelled for killing another student?"

"Not sure. You should ask the others. They've been

here longer so might know things like that."

"Have they ever killed students?" Stupid question. I knew they had. They killed those two that they had taken with me.

"Of course, they just covered their tracks." Picking up her bag, she walked over to the door. "You sure you don't want to come to breakfast?"

"No, I'll meet you at lunch though." I wasn't avoiding Tommy, but I also didn't want to willingly be near him. Lessons were going to be bad enough.

"Ooh and you can tell me all about your first firearms class." She opened the door and walked out. Before shutting it again, she stuck her head around and added, "Try not to kill anyone until your second lesson at least."

I smirked at her and she laughed, shutting the door.

I turned up at the old warehouse that was situated at the far end of the school grounds. Walking through, I sighted three rooms. The first was a small storeroom. Not that I could see inside but the plaque on the door told me so. The second was a shooting range. According to the girl who was a year above me, students could practice in there whenever they wanted but the faculty locks it up around 10pm.

The last room was the one I was currently in. It was also probably the biggest. False brick walls were strategically placed throughout, creating obstacles for us to work around but also hide-aways. Fake trees and foliage were dotted about too, making it harder to find your target. The high ceilings allowed for higher walls and stairs, adding levels to overcome too.

Because for our first firearms lesson, we were getting stuck straight in. That was what Alfie, our instructor and ex-marine, had said when I walked in. We were playing paintball.

The four Kray boys were already set, with their guns in

hand and checking out their ammo count. Each one was in the mandatory uniform that was required for the extracurricular activity. Army cargo pants and black tops. I wasn't ashamed to admit that it looked bloody good on them.

I glanced down at my own clothes. The same camouflage cargo pants that didn't look too bad, and a khaki tank that I had tucked into the waist band. I had tied my hair into a messy high pony and added a bow, just to sweeten it up a little. I hadn't put any protective gear on, but I hadn't assumed I would need it.

There was a handful of students behind them too, sorting through their own equipment. I recognised some of them from my AP classes and there were a couple from my year group, but the rest were new faces. None were wearing protective gear.

"Bella!" Callum called, flicking his head for me to come over to them. Tommy looked up from adjusting the fingerless leather gloves on his hands. I could have sworn I had seen shock before his expression completely blanked again.

Taking a deep breath, I strode over to them with my chin held high.

"Didn't know you were taking this class?" Felix stepped up beside me, giving me a once over.

"Thought I would give it a go." I smiled sweetly at him. *And show you all that I can also shoot a gun perfectly.*

That part I didn't say out loud.

"Careful you don't break a nail." he joked, grinning at me.

"Careful I don't break your neck." This sweet smile was going to start hurting my jaw.

"Ouch." He raised his hand to his chest, acting like my comeback had hurt, but then laughed when I rolled my eyes and nudged me playfully.

"Are we all here?" Alfie asked, walking up behind me. He did a quick head count, sixteen all together. "Tommy,

Callum. Pick your teams."

Both boys walked a little away from each other. Archie straight away went to Tommy's team and Felix to Callum's without exchanging any words.

"Would you like to do the honours?" Callum asked Tommy, a sly smirk on his lips.

"No, please go ahead." He matched Callum's smirk with his own.

He didn't need telling twice. "Russo!"

Tommy's eyes darkened, but his smirk twisted into a sinful grin. Shit. He was without a doubt going to try to hurt me. I just had to get him out first.

I made my way over to Callum, taking the gun that he held out for me. It was larger than I was used to and a bit lighter than a sniper rifle, but I would be able to get a good hit out of it. I looked at what Callum was carrying. He had the same as what he had given me plus a smaller one that was in its holster strapped to him. Felix had the same.

Tommy was next to pick and called out Ricky's name. I was surprised to see them both grinning at each other after the beating Tommy had clearly given him a few days prior. Ricky's eye still had a yellow colour of a fading bruise, but his lip seemed a lot better.

"Fuck." Felix grumbled beside me. "That's two snipers on his side."

"Archie? I thought he was good with knifes."

"I'm talking about Tommy. He never picks Rik to keep it fair between both sides, but I'm guessing with Callum picking you, he made it fair game."

"You're good with a gun though, aren't you?" I frowned, looking up at him.

"Yeah, but I'm not as good a sniper as Rik, and Tommy's the best." The fact he was honest about this apparent flaw of his was quite heart-warming. "I'll still be able to kill him of course, but not before he's able to take out a few of our own."

Callum and Tommy were still taking it in turns to pick

their other team players, taking their time, taunting each other.

"Who else do we need to look out for?"

"Apart from the obvious, the one with green hair. Darren Biggs. He's a wild card. You never know what to truly expect with him and if he's backed into a corner, he will use whatever weapon necessary."

I eyed the boy in the same clothing as the rest, but his green mohawk made him stand out. That and the three black tattoos across his face. He caught me staring and grinned like a maniac, displaying his missing tooth from the front top set.

"Felix, he looks like he is going to find me, brutally murder me then feast on my flesh."

Felix barked out a laugh just as Darren looked away. "You know, that really wouldn't surprise me."

"Thanks for the reassurance." I deadpanned then went back to watching Callum and Tommy tactically choose their teams.

Once everyone had their places, Alfie stepped forward again. "You both have your flags to guard. Tommy, take the red side." Tommy nodded, taking several red sweat bands and chucking them to the others on his team. Callum took the blue bands and did the same. "You have two chances to win. Either get your opponent's flag first or shoot them all. Kill shots are to the torso and head. Anywhere else on the body is just an injury and you are still in the game."

"Don't we need protective gear?" One of the first years from Tommy's team asked and he shot her a repulsed glare.

"Don't ever use offensive words like that in my lesson again or you won't be welcome back." Alfie threatened her then turned to the address the others. "I'll be watching from the window." He nodded up towards the other side of the warehouse and I followed his gaze to see a glass panel that was probably 6foot length ways. There was already a teacher watching from there, glaring down at us all. Williams.

"Get to your flags and when the horn sounds, the game

begins."

As soon as he exited the door, the others around me started moving. Tommy stared at me for a few seconds with a devious smile that made my mouth go dry and my pulse race. He was either really looking forward to hurting me or he had something else planned and neither I wanted to find out.

Turning on the heel of my black boots, I followed the rest of my team to the location of our flag. Crouching down with the others, Callum started going over the plan. He instructed a first year boy and a girl from the year above me to guard the flag, then he gave everyone else a plan on how to work the field.

"Smithy, Adams, guard that door over there." He pointed over the ledge and both boys craned their necks to get a good look. "Make it look like you are guarding something and shoot whoever gets close."

Both nodded but I frowned. "Do they not know the location of our flag?"

"Yeh but only half of them will be after the flag." My brows creased further in confusion, and he grinned mischievously. "I saw the way Tommy was looking at you. It was like a feral predator eyeing his prey. He's going to come for you and he's now thinking that I'll keep you this end, away from harm and trouble. If we make him believe you're in there that will distract him enough for the rest of us to get the flag."

I rolled my eyes. "And this is assuming he isn't just going to pick you all off one by one and leave me until last. Just to torment me that bit more."

"That's a possibility too." He shrugged after considering it for a second. "Felix, take out Ricky. He's going to be a problem."

"Tommy will have him nearer to his side, ready to take out anyone who gets close. I'll be able to get closer with someone covering me, but I'll also have to stay hidden. Riks fucking good."

"Girl who's name I can't remember. Tail Felix."

"I'm in all your classes Callum."

He blinked twice at her, like he didn't give a fuck then turned to speak to the others. I stifled a laugh. Even I knew her name, Chloe. She was one of Sandra's friends.

"Kid, you're with them too." He said to a boy from my own year. He nodded silently then shuffled slightly closer to Felix and Chloe. "Bella, you're with me. We're getting that fucking flag."

Perfectly timed, the horn blasted through the sound system and the game began. Everyone rushed away to follow the orders they had been given and I followed Callum.

Everything was unnervingly quiet as we edged closer to the other side of the warehouse. Felix was a little ahead of us with his two distractions, cautiously looking around corners and signalling for each other when it was clear.

"We need to get higher, see if we can see anyone else. Tommy has usually attacked by now." Callum muttered beside me.

"Do you usually go against each other?"

"All the time." He grinned, "It's how we learn each other's weaknesses so then in the real world we can defend them."

"What are Tommy's weaknesses?"

"I feel like I shouldn't tell you." He frowned but smirked like he also wanted to.

We came to three wooden shacks; each had some distance between them and beyond it was a wall of fake trees. Callum pressed a finger to his lips and then mouthed the words stay here. He snuck over to the first shack, peering inside, making sure that no one was in there.

I had lost sight of Felix and the other two. They had gone to the side and pressed on, avoiding the fake foliage.

Callum slowly moved to the next shack. Swinging the door open, he grabbed whoever was on the other side. Callum's hand went over his mouth, blocking out any sound threatening to escape and alert the others of our location. The boy looked over at me, but Callum shot him in the chest at close range. His eyes scrunched together in pain and a few seconds later, Callum released him.

"You're out."

"Fuck sake." The boy hissed but stalked broodingly away from us and off the playing field.

Walking back over to me, he had the biggest smile on his face. "One down."

"Seven more to go." I smiled back.

"Let's get some higher ground." He nodded towards the last shack. This one was on stilts with a thin wooden ladder leading up to it.

"How do you know someone isn't already in there?"

"They would have shot you by now."

Fair enough. I swung my gun over my shoulder by the strap and started the climb, Callum following close behind. "You better not be staring at my arse."

"But it looks so good in them trousers." He joked and I chuckled lightly. These trousers could make no arse look good.

Once I reached the top, I crawled into the small space, careful to avoid being seen through the glassless window. Callum slid over to the opposite wall.

"What now?"

"We'll wait for Felix to message that he's taken down Ricky then we'll start moving again. If we get past them trees, we're more exposed and will be waiting targets."

I leaned up slightly, looking out the window. "What if Tommy and Archie get to us first."

"Doubt it, Tommy will be working the outer edge, avoiding wasting pellets until he got to you and same with Archie, but my betting is that he will be the one going to the flag."

"Umm, well they may just surprise you then and change tactic." Standing between the trees where the two boys with Darren.

Callum scrambled to my side and peered out. "Shit. Of course he's trying to be unpredictable."

"I can take him out."

"Who?"

"Which ever one you want me to." I took my gun of my shoulder and rested the barrel on the thin wooden ledge.

"You can shoot?" The doubt and amusement in his voice was insulting.

"I can but I'm soon going to miss my chance." The three of them were getting closer.

"Assuming you can, and you are actually a good shot, you would need to shoot Archie."

"Why not Tommy? He's the better shooter, isn't he?" I asked, looking back at Callum in confusion and a tiny bit disappointed. Shooting Tommy would have made my day.

"He is but I would want to see his face if you actually made the shot. And then it would throw him off his game and the victory would be so much more satisfying." Callum flashed me a conniving grin and I smiled back.

"Archie it is then." I took aim, following him as they got close enough for the pellet to hit.

"If you miss, they will know there is someone here and I'm good but three against one isn't good odds."

"Trust me." I smirked. Firing the shot, the pellet hit it's intended target, splattering across Archie's chest. His hand flew up to the paint as he let out a feral cry of anger.

"Fuck." Tommy instantly flew behind the tree beside him, and Darren lurched into the fake foliage. Archie stomped away, grumbling to himself before he was completely out of view.

"Jesus Bella, you've been holding out on us." Callum whispered, eyes sparkling with excitement.

"I have many skills." I grinned then looked back out the window to see what the other two were doing.

"That was quite a shot Callum. You've been practicing more." Tommy called out from his hiding spot. I could take another shot but the most it would hit would be his arm and that would probably anger him more than anything.

"It wasn't me that fired it." Callum shouted back.

"Felix with you too? Bit of a bad move, keeping the best together while others are unguarded."

"It wasn't Felix. He's after a certain someone else."

There was a pause at that while Tommy thought about what had just been said.

"He's either really confused now or he's somehow plotting in that twisted mind of his, how to kill me and make it look like an accident for getting the better of him." Callum whispered to me, and I couldn't help but giggle. The excitement and adrenaline making me giddy.

"And there it is. The sweet little laughter of Isabella." Tommy called out and I could just imagine the smirk on his face. My heart raced even though my breath caught in my throat, and I looked at Callum wide eyed.

"We need to get out and run back to our flag." He hissed, poking his head up to look out the window.

"No, it'll be pointless going back because he will just follow. You go back and he will think I'm with you, then I can make a run for his flag."

He turned back round to eye me as he weighed the limited options we had. His phone buzzed in his pocket, and he pulled it out.

"Ricky's out. Let me distract them two and you run as fast as you can to their flag. They will have some others guarding it but from what I've seen, you can easily take them out."

I grinned at him, thrilled that he recognised my skill and was allowing me to go on ahead. "I'll go round, follow the path that Felix took."

Callum sat back up to see Tommy and Darren's position. "They're waiting for us to make a move. I'll fire some random shots. Hopefully they'll think it's both of us and it will distract them long enough for you to slip away unseen."

"Make sure you get Darren though." I shivered. "He

scares me."

"More than me and Tommy?" He grinned playfully.

"You'd never cause me pain Callum." Not now I was protected by them all. "And I'm kinda counting on Tommy to not do that either."

"He will cause you pain but not in the way you think."

I wanted him to elaborate but we didn't have time for this discussion. We had to get going with the half-arsed plan we had made.

I shifted to the opening, but Callum grabbed my arm. "Don't get shot. It fucking hurts."

"I'll be sure to avoid that then." I deadpanned and my eyes rolled as I started to descend back down the ladder with Callum's soft laughter following me.

Chapter 23

I could hear the shots being fired as I ran to the edge of the war zone. My heart beat rapidly, nervous but also excited. There was a certain thrill to being here, playing against dangerous people and trying to make it out alive.

Well of course I would make it out alive. It was paintballing. Not really a life-or-death situation. If it was, would I still be as excited?

Running a little further, the fake trees and foliage cleared, leaving just the grey stone walls for me to navigate my way through. Felix had eliminated Ricky so that meant I didn't have to worry about a sniper.

Hushed voices made me come to a halt behind a wall and I slowly peered around the corner to see who was there. The girl from my year group, the only one on Tommy's team and another from his year. They weren't exactly stationed, just strolling around with their guns at the ready. Well the boy was ready. The girl was nattering his ear off and by the exhausted look on his face, he had had enough.

I rounded the corner and fired at him first, taking him down with one shot. He groaned in pain as the pellet hit him in the stomach and lowered his weapon. The girl was next and as she lifted her gun, I shot her quickly in the chest.

"Owww." She pouted, rubbing the spot the pellet had hit.

"Sorry." I smiled softly at her and they both sauntered away.

My phone vibrated in one of the oversized pockets of my trousers.

Callum
Darren is out but I lost sight of Tommy.

Fuck. I needed to hurry and find that flag. Just as I was about to put my phone away again, it vibrated in my hand.

Callum
Felix's out. Tommy got him. He's coming for you.

My already racing heart started to beat harder as a feeling of emptiness settled in my stomach. Why did Callum have to make it sound scarier than what it was? Probably because it was scary as hell. Being hunted by Tommy.

Bella
Where are you?

Callum
Still in and trying to find him.

Bella
Well hurry the fuck up

I ran forward, being less careful as I raced towards where I thought the flag would be. Darren was out and Ricky. I had just got two out too so that left Tommy and three others. Was Felix the only one from our team out or were there more? There were two others with him, so I had to assume that they were out too. Tommy wouldn't have left them untouched.

Every corner I rounded; the opposite team was nowhere to be found. Which meant there was no signs to where the flag was. Without any guards, it hadn't been made obvious. It could be anywhere behind the walls or in the small buildings.

I cursed myself and Callum. I didn't know the layout like the other years did, whereas if I was still with one of the others, they would have been able to point out where exactly it was.

I kept going, my ears more sensitive to the quietness surrounding me. A cry came from the distance, towards my end of the field. I wasn't sure if it was my team or the others but from the shouts and the screams, shit was going down.

Stepping in to one of the makeshift builds, I took a breather, hiding myself from the outside. The flag had to be around here somewhere. A thought crossed my mind that they had maybe taken it with them but that would be cheating. It was also a good plan that we should have probably done. There were many things that we should have done differently now that I was playing it back in my mind.

The door creaked open, and my gun flew up ready to fire but my finger hesitated on the trigger.

The air was instantly sucked from the small space as Tommy entered and closed the door behind him again. I sucked in a breath, trying to release the tightening of my chest and backed up against the wall.

He took a step forward, only a small gun in his hand. His eyes burned into mine then wandered down to my breasts and I was certain he could see the flush around my cleavage, even in the dim lighting.

"I will shoot you." I breathed out the best I could, keeping my finger on the trigger and aiming for his heart.

He stopped with a wicked grin on his face and something flashed through his eyes. "I don't doubt it."

Slowly, he put his gun in the holster, distracting me for a moment then in one swift movement my gun was knocked to the ground. His body was pressed against mine, pushing me harder against the wall. His arm came up, beside my head, balancing himself as he eased the pressure, but it didn't help the fact I felt like I was suffocating.

"Why didn't you tell me you could shoot, Isabella?" He drawled, placing his other hand on my hip. The softest touch sent my heart pounding and my breath turned erratic.

His gaze flickered down again while the corners of his mouth tipped into a calculating smirk. "You know, I still haven't decided how I am going to punish you for last night."

My palms pressed against the cold wall behind me, grounding myself mentally while my body trembled at his words. His fingers pulled at the material of my top, releasing it from being tucked into my trousers.

"The way your body reacts to me," He lowered his lips to my ear, purring the words and tickling the delicate skin of my neck with his breath. "Not even your smart mouth can deny it."

I took a sharp intake of breath as the warm leather of his gloves made contact with my bare flesh, his fingers finally finding a gap between my top and trousers. He let out a muffled chuckle, burying his face into my neck and I loved the sound.

My head moved slightly, allowing him more access and he exploited my moment of weakness by grazing his lips across my already tingling skin, placing a gentle kiss on the throbbing pulse. I whimpered softly, making him do it again. Each tiny kiss sent a tingle down my spine and made my body crave more.

His hand glided further up my side, past my waist and stopped just under my bra. "You can't begin to imagine the things I'm going to do to you once you finally submit to me." He grasped my breast roughly through the thin lace bra making me inhale harshly.

The pad of his thumb swiped over my already pebbled nipple, sending all the nerves surrounding it wild. Heat pooled between my legs, and I knew the tiny lace thong that I wore was probably soaked from the provoking he was doing.

Tommy's teeth grazed my neck softly before sinking in. A very unflattering noise left my mouth, but it didn't deter him as he nibbled and sucked at the tender flesh.

Pinching my nipple hard between his index finger and thumb, I whimpered again, arching my back into him. He groaned and released his teeth as my stomach pressed into his erection. And fuck, what an erection. He was big. I didn't mean wow that's big. I meant fuck, that's going to destroy me big.

He pressed himself harder against me. His husky voice was nothing more than a whisper, yet it still vibrated through my body, right to my pulsing clit. "How wet will I find you if I put my hand down there right now? How easily will my fingers slip inside your tight cunt?"

He pinched my nipple again and I didn't think becoming wetter was possible, but it happened. Lifting his head to look at me, he had the same burning passion in his eyes that he had the previous night. Only this time, he seemed like he had more control.

"I asked you a question Isabella."

I panted out my answer before I could stop myself because at that point I didn't care anymore. I didn't care that he was a massive prick or that I was trying to deny myself of this obvious attraction I had for him. I wanted his hands all over my body. I wanted him to rip these suffocating clothes from me. I wanted him to release this built-up pressure that was aching inside me.

"Very."

A satisfied smirk tilted his lips as his eyes lit up. "Good girl."

His hand left my breast and slid back down towards my trousers. Would I regret this after? Yes. Did I care right now? No.

His hand left my hip for a second and the arm that

rested next to my head came down to grasp my chin and forced it up to meet his heated gaze. Running his tongue over his bottom lip, he grinned wickedly. "It's just a shame you were such a brat last night."

A sharp, sudden pain stabbed me in the stomach, and I automatically pushed him away. He willingly let me, stepping back with a treacherous smile. Looking down, I saw the red splodge of paint on my top. The sharpness of the pain had faded moments after it came but a dull ache was in its place.

Tommy had distracted me, and I had let him. My stupid feelings had kept me from being smart and I let my guard down.

"You're a fucking dick." I glowered, more pissed off with myself than at him but he was still enemy number one.

"See you at the end of the game, baby."

That fucking nickname again!

He walked out the door, not even giving me another glance and I stood there reeling, flustered and frustrated.

Walking back to where everyone had started didn't take too long when you were mumbling insanely under your breath all the ways that you planned on killing the man who gave you uncontrollable feelings.

Most of the class were already standing there, meaning there was only a few remaining on the field. Archie and Felix were deep in conversation but when I reached them, they stopped to check out the damage on me.

"Who shot you?" Felix frowned, reaching into a cooler beside him and passing me a bottle of water.

I took it from him and chugged half of it before answering, "Who do you think?"

Archie grinned, "That don't look like all he gave you."

Tilting my head, my brows creased together in confusion, and he pointed up to my neck. Reaching up, my fingers traced the curve until an acute but sharp pain stopped me. The bite. He had marked me.

"He's such a prick." I moaned, not admitting that I actually liked it.

Felix laughed but lifted my other hand with the cold bottle and pressed it against the marred skin. "It'll reduce the bruising."

"Thanks," I muttered. "What happened with you anyway. Last I heard, you had got Ricky out and then Callum texted to say Tommy had got you?"

"I got Rik easily, but I did sacrifice one of our own to do it."

"Harsh."

He shrugged, "That's life. But once he was out, I kept an eye out for you. Cal said you were on your way but while I was distracted by you running around like a fucking moron," - His lips tipped up in amusement and I scowled at him. - "Tommy found me and shot me and that other kid."

"In my defence, I didn't know where the flag was."

"You were close at one point, and it was me swearing when you walked right past it that alerted Tommy of my location."

"I want to know who the fuck shot me." Archie grumbled. "Cal int that fucking good."

"It was me."

Archie observed me for a few seconds then let out a gruff laugh. "You're quite funny sometimes, Russo."

Unbelievable. My eyes rolled in frustration but didn't bother to plead my case.

Laughter could be heard from behind us, and I spun round to see Tommy and Callum walking towards us. Both had paint on them, making it impossible to see who had got who first but by their smiles it looked like neither cared. And for a split second my heartbeat faltered, and flutters entered my stomach.

I didn't see this carefree side of Tommy often. Nudging

Callum with his elbow with a real smile on his face, lighting it up from the darkness or emotionless state I was used to. It was short lived though. As soon as his eyes met mine, the smile faded and when he glanced down at the bottle still pressed against my neck, the wicked grin came back making me pout my lips in annoyance.

"Please tell me you shot him first?" I glared at Callum, but he shook his head.

"No, I just shot him back."

"Suppose that's something." I muttered, glowering at the prick.

Callum threw his arm over my shoulder. "Is everyone back?"

"Yeah, everyone's dead." Ricky replied, walking over to us then stopped to frown at me. "What happened to you?"

"You talking about the red paint or the slag tag on my neck." I snapped, finally removing the bottle. Callum released me from under his arm to get a better look while Felix snorted a laugh but then turned away to try to hide it.

Ricky's eyes wandered from the bite back to my face, raising his brows then over to Tommy who was smirking in his arrogant way. "I'm gunna assume you did that seeing as no one else is dead already."

"From what I was told, she deserved it for something that happened last night." Archie grinned and I almost scoffed but caught myself before any sound came out.

Instead, I reached round, taking Callum's small gun from his holster and without hesitation, brought it forward and shot Archie in the head.

He staggered back, caught by surprise and swiped his hand over his forehead, smudging the paint. He could have been angry with me, and I think everyone was waiting for him to explode. That was the impression I got when Callum slowly snaked his hand around my waist, pulling me slightly behind him and even Tommy and Felix stepped forward.

"Well, fuck me. You were the one who shot me." He huffed, amusement lacing his tone. Callum's chest shook from his laughter while Felix covered his mouth with his fist to conceal his. Tommy rolled his eyes and walked away from us to meet Alfie who had just entered the room. They spoke for a little while before coming over to the rest of us.

"Well it's obvious who won that game," Alfie clapped Tommy on the back. "But I have seen some real skills from some of the newcomers. In the next few weeks we'll change things up slightly, use blanks and have you all against each other. Make it harder and more interesting. Now get out of my sight."

Everyone moved, picking up their gear and headed for the exit. "Miss Russo." I paused as I bent down to pick up my hoodie and turned to look at the teacher. "Can I have a quick word."

I nodded my head then continued to pick up my clothing and walked over to him. Tommy was standing with him, arms crossed with a look of indifference on his face.

"Where did you learn to shoot like that?" Alfie asked, his eyes soft and warm.

"A friend of my dad's thought it would be a good idea to learn before coming to this school."

"Jefferson." Tommy said, and I was a little taken aback by him remembering his name but nodded all the same.

"How old were you when you started practicing?"

"17 sir."

"You learn fast then."

"Thank you, sir."

"I'll be interested in what else you have to offer in coming lessons… But maybe be a bit more aware of other's intentions before allowing yourself to be shot." His eyes wandered from the paint on my top to the mark on my neck.

I felt my cheeks burn as I looked down at my feet. I knew he could see everything outside the buildings, but surely he didn't know what had happened inside one. Unless there were cameras. Fuck. I have no idea how I would have reacted knowing that if Tommy had actually gone further.

Alfie walked away from us both, but Tommy remained

standing a few feet in front of me.

"What other skills are you hiding from me?"

I glanced up and an involuntary tremor ran through my core at the heated look in his eyes. I hated the reactions my body had to him. Probably more than what I actually hated him. But I lifted my chin before I blessed him with an answer.

"It's funny you think I would tell you."

His jaw ticked in annoyance but then a slow, sinister smile crept up. "Hoping to use some against me Isabella?"

"There're quite a few skills I would like to use against you, but your sick and twisted mind would probably enjoy it." I huffed and pushed past him.

Before I could get far, he grabbed my elbow, pulling me back to him. I lost my footing, crashing my hand against his hard chest. His fingers lifted my chin, forcing me to gaze into the fire that ignited his eyes.

"I'm pretty sure you would enjoy how my sick and twisted mind works too."

Heat roared through every vein in my body, melting any icy feeling that I had towards him. But he was still a dick, and I wasn't going to let him get away with what he did.

"Maybe I would. Maybe I want you to show me how sick and twisted you can really be." I pressed myself up against him and rose onto my toes. Still shorter but the height made it a tad easier to get the desired effect I wanted. "Maybe I want you to do all the things you have dreamed of doing. Maybe I want to submit to you."

His fingers pinched as his grip tightened around my arm.

"That's what you want isn't it, Tommy. You want me to be your good girl."

His grin was wicked as his lips got closer to mine and we exchanged air. His was minty with the subtle hint of cigarettes that I didn't hate.

"But being good sounds so boring." I finished and he loosened his grip. I pushed myself off the floor, getting that extra height to place a delicate kiss to the tip of his nose. Planting my feet flat back down I smiled sweetly at him. "Bye."

Before he could respond, I walked out of the massive warehouse, not giving him another glance.

Chapter 24

I was laid on my bed with my legs resting on Jack while Daisy braided Maddy's hair into two long plaits. The four of us had planned to do homework together but not one of us had got our books out to start. Instead we were lazing about in our uniforms still, waiting for dinner time.

"What about this for Halloween?" Jack asked, flashing the picture on his phone to me. Dorothy, lion, scarecrow and the tin man.

"Yeh, but who will go as who?" Finding a foursome for the Halloween party was proving quite hard.

"You'll have to be Dorothy because of your long dark hair." He looked at his sister and Maddy. "She'll have to be the scarecrow and Madz can be the lion."

Daisy responded by giving him the middle finger, making Maddy and me chuckle.

"I don't mind being the scarecrow if you want to be Dorothy." I said to her.

"It's fine, if we can't find anything better, I'll be the tin man."

"Because you have no heart?"

"No, dickhead." She fired back at her brother. "Because

you'll be more realistic as the brainless oaf."

I laughed again and Jack slapped my legs lightly.

"What about the scooby gang?" He suggested.

My eyes lit up. "Oh my god, yes. Daisy can be Velma. Maddy can be Daphne and you can be Fred."

"I'm not ginger." Maddy pouted, crossing her arms.

"We'll dye it." I waved my hand in the air, dismissing her. "I can be Shaggy."

"Or the dog?" Jack fired back like it was meant to be a playful insult, but my eyes lit up again.

"Yes!" I ripped my legs off him and kneeled up. "I could get the blue dog collar and a lead."

All three broke down in hysterics.

"Only you would get excited about that." Daisy cried. "Who's going to be taking you for a walk and calling you a good girl though."

Tommy's words echoed in my mind. He liked me being his good girl. And I kind of liked the feeling I got when he called me it. As if the thought had summoned them, butterfly flutters tickled my stomach, and I felt my chest heat.

"I need a Shaggy." I sighed.

"Or just a shag." Jack piped up making Maddy cackle.

I punched his arm, glaring at him. "I do not need a shag. All this pent-up frustration can't just be released by a simple fuck with just anyone."

"Yeah," Maddy mocked, frowning at him. "The man she needs has to be over six foot with dark hair and blue eyes."

"And goes by the name Tommy." Daisy joined in, making kissy lips at me.

I chucked my pillow at her face, and it managed to bounce off and hit Maddy too, making it more satisfying. "I wouldn't fuck him even if it saved the world."

"What if it was to save your three best friends?" Maddy flashed me a sweet smile.

I looked between the three of them. Even though I had

only known them for a very short period of time, I felt closer to them than I had ever done with anyone else I had made friends within secondary school or college. And that was probably because we were all killers with nothing to hide.

But still…

"I will see you all in hell."

"Charming."

"You are not getting a Christmas card this year."

"I think she would," Jack smirked at me, and I narrowed my eyes. "Because that little mark on her neck tells me there is definitely something between them."

"How do you know it was from him." I countered, raising a brow.

"Because no one is dead." He basically repeated what Ricky had said, and I couldn't help but smile.

Even though I hated being marked like that usually, and I definitely hated him, something about others knowing he was the one to do it made me feel something that I hadn't before. Not even by my ex. I just couldn't explain the feeling because it was new and strange, and I never wanted it to go.

That brought me back to glancing at the unopened text on my phone though. It was from Tommy, and I had received it ten minutes ago. Part of me wanted to open it but I also didn't want to see what he had to say after the way we had left it earlier.

"What about you anyway? What happened between you and Archie?" Maddy asked Jack, distracting me once again.

"Ohh yeh, I want to know this too." I dropped my phone beside me and laid back down to put my legs on him again.

"A man doesn't kiss and tell ladies."

"Fuck off, I'm more of a man than you." Daisy scoffed, looking him up and down.

"We're not talking about your moustache right now, Magnum PI."

I snorted while Maddy looked confused at the reference

and Daisy threw my pillow back at us. Jack gave me a side-glance and grinned. "He's a good kisser."

"Aww." I cooed. "Have you spoke to him today?"

"He hasn't text me, but he did take my number so that's good right?"

"Yeah, that's a good sign Jack." Maddy smiled at him, and I nodded.

My phone vibrated beside me and another text from Tommy popped up. Taking in a deep breath, I tapped the conversation open, reading the message I had ignored first.

Tommy
Can you please come to my room. I need to talk to you.

I frowned at the message. Tommy didn't say please. He demanded what he wanted. There was no way he would have been so polite unless this was part of an act to get me to do what he wants.

Tommy
I'm not going to ask again.

That was more like it.

"I'll be back in a minute." Swinging my legs around, I pushed myself off the bed. I shouldn't be going as soon as he beckoned and technically, I wasn't because he had asked ten minutes ago. I should have just ignored the message but really, I wanted to hear what he had to say. I wanted to be near him. But I still hated him and going to him saved the agro of him coming to get me by force.

"Where you going?" Maddy asked, moving her head to watch me put my shoes on and causing Daisy to pull her back by her hair. That girl was rough.

"Tommy wants to talk to me about something."

"Ooohhh." Daisy and Jack sang in union. Both received an exasperated eye roll from me.

"Tell him to text me back. I've been messaging him all

day to ask about the plan for this weekend, but he is such an ignorant fuck sometimes."

I had almost forgot about having to go with them to visit their family this weekend. "I'll let him know, I might even keep in the ignorant fuck bit."

"Do it." Then she reconsidered. "Actually only say it if you haven't already put him in a foul mood."

"Then he will never know what you called him." I grinned and walked out the room.

Tommy's door was slightly ajar when I got to it, but I still tapped lightly to let him know I was there. He didn't answer though, and I pushed against it, opening it a bit further.

"Tommy?" I kept my voice soft but was unsure why. Still no answer from him so I pushed it open fully. The room was empty but the light from his bathroom was on even though the door was pulled to.

Shutting the door behind me, I sat down on the small sofa, crossed my legs and waited for him to come out. It didn't take long but as the door to the bathroom opened, the person who walked out wasn't the person I expected.

"Look at you, coming here like a lovesick puppy." Sindy smiled in a vile tone.

I didn't respond, only glared at her. What the hell was going on? Had Tommy just wanted me to come here to see her with him? Was this what my punishment was? Make me jealous with that bimbo.

"You really are that easy aren't you. Coming as soon as you get a message from him." She sneered, walking further into the room and holding up his phone. My brain worked fast as it clicked into place. She had sent the texts. She had taken his phone. That was why he hadn't messaged anyone back. If only I had known his phone was missing. "Do you know how desperate that makes you look. Tommy doesn't like desperate girls."

My brow rose as my lips tipped a little at the side. "No, he would prefer someone fake that would roll over and beg when told."

"You know nothing about what Tommy wants." Anger flashed through her dull eyes, making them look interesting for the first time.

"I know that he is getting bored with the usual girls that fall down at his feet and he's looking for more of a challenge." I didn't know this at all, but it sounded good in my mind. And Callum had mentioned it before.

"That's not what he was saying last night when he was balls deep in me from behind."

"Full of class aren't you." I smirked calmly when inside I wanted to thread my fingers through her overly bleached hair and rip it out. And not only did I want to hurt her, but Tommy was fast moving to the top of my list too.

"You're one to talk with that on your neck."

My smirk widened to a grin. "Tommy likes to mark things he likes to think are his. I notice you don't have any marks."

Her eyes widened, obviously unaware that Tommy had been the one to do it. "They might not be on show."

"Then he obviously doesn't want to show you off. Probably ashamed." I knew I was taunting her and by the way her cheeks flushed I was having the desired effect. But then I sighed, having enough of this little exchange. "Why have you got me here, Sindy?"

"Stay away from him."

"Gladly. Maybe tell him the same."

"I mean it. He doesn't need a girl like you. He needs someone that's going to help him when he takes over his father's business. Someone who is going to be the doting wife and give him what he needs when he gets home from work. Not someone who's going to make his life difficult."

"Didn't he call off your engagement?"

Anger turned to rage in her eyes, and she took a step

forward. "Little girl, you don't know what you are messing with. This isn't playground games anymore. You will get hurt if you don't fall in line and realise what's yours and what isn't." She reached behind her and thumbed for something in her back pocket. It would have been more menacing if she hadn't almost dropped what she was trying to get.

I rolled my eyes as she brandished a small pocketknife in front of me, flipping it open to reveal a five-inch blade. "Firstly, Tommy was the one who claimed me, I didn't want anything to do with him, but he obviously wanted something from me. Secondly, he ended your relationship and you showed up being the desperate one. If he fucked you after that but still doesn't want you, that's a pity fuck love."

She snarled, stepping forward to intimidate me but I didn't even flinch.

"Thirdly, I don't like being threatened. It's a coward's way out. If you want to stab me, do it now because I promise you, you won't get the chance again."

She launched herself at me, dropping Tommy's phone to the wooden floor and to be honest, I was quite surprised because I didn't think she had it in her. Slashing the knife around wildly, she caught my side, just under my ribs. I staggered back but not too far and the next time she sliced through the air, aiming for my face, I managed to block her. It did result in a small slice across my arm though. Bringing my other arm up, I pushed her back away from me.

Both wounds stung like fuck and blood was already saturating the cotton of my shirt, but I didn't have time to dwell on it. Sindy leapt forward again, knocking me to the floor.

This bitch was more psycho than half the girls in this school. There was no rhythm to her moves, she wasn't even aiming. She just wanted to cause me as much pain as she could before she killed me. Her eyes were erratic as she screamed incoherent words in my face.

I managed to get my feet under her while my hands

grabbed her wrists to stop her from slashing my face. Kicking forward with all my strength, I succeeded in getting her off me.

I only had a second to glance round the room for something I could use against her, but Tommy was such a neat freak, there were no weapons to be seen. Anything can be used as a weapon if you put your mind to it.

Sindy staggered to her feet, regrouping herself but I was already across the bed, reaching for the glass of water from the side table. I grasped it just in time and as I spun round, the glass tumbler smashed across her face, creating deep cuts through her cheek and above her eye. It also cut my own hand open, making a curse slip from my lips.

She fell onto the bed then bounced back onto the floor. Grabbing her hair in my uninjured hand, I stepped over her and dragged her back to the centre of the bedroom. My knee came up, colliding with her jaw and the sound of it cracking made my stomach turn but it also caused the biggest grin.

Coughing up blood, she had the audacity to glare up at me like she still had a chance. But I wasn't done. She had managed to piss me off enough for me to actually want to cause her pain and not just fight for survival.

Grabbing the knife she had dropped, I waited for her to struggle back to her feet. The cuts on my arm and side were now burning but that just made me want to hurt her that much more. She wanted me out the way so she could have Tommy and Tommy wanted to torment me while still fucking his ex.

Only one of us was going to walk out of this room alive and Tommy best hope it wasn't me.

Chapter 25

Every student that saw me either gawped at the sight or completely avoided my gaze. Not that I was concentrating on any of them. I walked through the entrance hall of the school towards the back door, passing them all without a word being exchanged between any of us but their whispers followed me on my search.

"Is that Isabella?"

"What the fuck happened?"

"Did she kill someone?"

"Does Tommy know?"

Does Tommy know? That was the question that probably pissed me off the most. The fact everyone assumed that Tommy had to know everything that I did. No, he didn't know but I was about to be the one that showed him.

Blood dripped from my fingers onto the flag stone floor. I was unsure if it was my own or Sindy's, but it left a clear path like a bread crumb trail to the evidence of what I had done.

Every step I took, my body groaned against it. Every muscle burned making me unsure if I had just the three cuts or possibly more. But I kept going because I wanted to face the reason for this all.

I stepped out the door, making another student gasp and back away from me in horror. Considering the type of school we attended, I should have been surprised by their reactions, but I wasn't. My shirt was drenched in blood, and I was sure there was some smeared across my face too, along with my legs and arms. I was covered in it. Fingers crossed budget Barbie didn't have any diseases because I could guarantee some of her blood was covering my wounds.

Tommy was standing at the far side of the courtyard, leaning against the wall, one hand in his pocket and the other with a cigarette between his fingers. The other three Krays were standing with him, laughing at something the other had said while Tommy stood, smirking at the ground.

Demonic little flutters rushed through me once again but the fury I felt was still greater.

Archie was the first to spot me. "What the fuck Russo?!"

The others looked my way as I raged over to them and when Tommy looked up, panic flashed through his blue eyes before it vanished and was replaced with a burning rage. He stepped forward, meeting me as I took my last step.

"Are you hurt?" The rage wasn't for me, but the panic had been.

"Works both ways Tommy." I smiled insanely at him, not breaking the intense eye contact between us. "If no one can touch me, I'm going to make it damn hard for someone to touch you."

"What did you do sweetheart?" Callum asked softly, coming to stand beside me.

Ignoring him, I held out my uninjured hand that had Tommy's phone in it. "You'll probably be needing this." He took it from me, looking at the cracked screen then back up.

"Where did you get this?"

"You really should take better care of your property." I

smiled sarcastically, "But then again, I'm your property aren't I so it's a good job I can look after myself."

His eyes flashed. "Whose blood is this Isabella?"

"I know you called off the engagement, but you weren't that attached to her were you?" Tilting my head, I smiled again. This time more sweetly.

"Shit." Felix breathed out, running his hand over his tight curls.

"Is she dead?"

"Yes." My eyes darkened and my smile vanished as I answered Tommy's question. "Your room's quite a mess."

His eyes bounced between mine and I didn't look away. There was something else between us and at first, I thought it was all the rage, but something was stronger. A dark desire that kept drawing us together.

"Clean it up." Even though he didn't acknowledge the other three, they knew it was them he was giving the order to.

They moved fast, walking away and towards the door I had come through. It was just Tommy and me. If any other students had been out here when I first arrived, they had soon left.

"Where are you hurt?" He asked, his eyes dragging along my body and leaving goosebumps scattering in their wake.

"Nowhere." I turned on my heel to leave. I didn't want to be near him. I was fuming with not only him but myself. What my feelings for him had made me do.

Grabbing hold of my arm, he spun me back around. "You need to talk to me."

I winced as his other hand clasped my other arm, right where one of the cuts had been made. He noticed, ripping his hand away again, only to grab my wrist and lift it to inspect the seeping wound.

I snatched it from his grip. "I don't need to talk to you at all. I don't owe you anything."

"Where else are you hurt?"

"Nowhere. Bye Tommy."

Just as I was about to leave again, he grabbed my uninjured arm. Not as roughly this time though, probably in case there was another cut that he couldn't see.

"Fuck sake Isabella, can't you just do as you are told for once without the constant battle."

I tore my arm away once more, wincing at the pain again but this time from my side. "You need to leave me alone."

"I'm trying to fucking help." He reached out for me, but I took a step back.

"Help?" I scoffed but a wetness pooled in my eyes, stinging worse than the opened wounds. "How can you possibly help when you're the cause of all this." He stopped searching my body for injuries to gaze up into my eyes. "I wanted to do my time in here Tommy and keep my head down. Maybe make a couple of friends like Maddy. I just wanted to get through the next three years undetected. But you put a target on my back as soon as you claimed me. You made it impossible for me to have a quiet life here."

He swallowed "Isabella —"

"It's because of you that Sindy tricked me into coming to your room and I was so stupid, so fucking stupid that I actually went." The first tear fell but it wasn't because I was upset. Well, maybe it was but it was also because I was frustrated, angry and tired. I was so fucking tired of it all.

"I thought I could play your games, but I can't. I really can't do this. I can't be whoever you want me to be."

More tears fell now, slipping warmly down my cheeks. Tommy raised his hand, wiping them away with his thumb. "I don't want you to be anyone else other than who you already are." A frown of worry creased his forehead. "Let me help you."

I let out a deep breath. He wasn't listening, not really. But my body ached. My wounds hurt and my head felt light. I didn't want to shout anymore, I wanted to sleep.

"I just want to go to bed. I'm tired and my head is starting to hurt."

"I need to clean those cuts before they get infected." His eyes were searching again, making me cross my arms over my stomach and grimacing at nudging the painful area.

"I'll get them looked at when I wake up." I tried to argue but he shook his head.

"I don't want to hurt you but if you don't let me help, I will carry you kicking and screaming."

I believed him but that wasn't the reason I agreed. "You might have to." I breathed out, stumbling forward as my head went heavy and my vision blurred.

"Shit." His strong arms caught me, supporting me. Gently, he scooped me up in his arms and walked back towards the school. I didn't argue, I didn't have the energy to. But I did close my eyes and let him take me to wherever he wanted.

I must have only been out for a couple of minutes but when I came too, I was still in Tommy's arms, and he was now standing still.

"Is she ok?" It was Callum. I recognised his voice.

"She will be." Tommy's gruff voice followed, vibrating against my cheek. "Is everything sorted?"

"Archie's with the others. They're digging the hole at the graveyard as we speak." Felix responded this time.

"And they weren't seen?"

"No." Felix paused for a moment. "Too many saw her covered in blood though and you must have walked past others too with her passed out. How are you going to swing that one?"

Tommy's hand that was gripping my thigh squeezed gently. "No one saw us come back. Everyone was at dinner, so we got lucky. The only people who saw her would have seen her angry and we can work with that. Say she was pranked or something. No one apart from the four of us, Darren and Ricky know that she killed someone and that's how it's going to stay."

"What about when Sindy doesn't go home. What will you say to her father?"

"That we haven't seen her for a few days. With any luck he'll think she's gone on one of those holidays she usually fucks off to when she doesn't get her own way. But if it comes to it, I'll take full responsibility for her death."

Would he really take the blame for me? I wanted to ask him, but I still felt groggy. Too groggy to even bring myself to move an inch.

"It was a mess, Tommy. When we got here, it was a complete fucking mess." Callum started, and I heard his footsteps on the wooden flooring as he walked around the room. "I think we managed to get it all but maybe get Tracy to do a deep clean to get rid of any other DNA or evidence."

I felt Tommy nod his head and he nudged me to move his arm. I flinched at the pain as my eyes scrunched together.

"You want me to send the nurse over?"

"No, I don't want anyone else knowing the extent of what has happened. The less witnesses the better. Callum has stitched us three up enough to know what he's doing."

"You want me to stay?"

"Give me about half an hour then check back in."

"I would say text me but one of them smashed your phone." Callum chuckled.

"Wouldn't shock me if it was that one." Felix said and I could even hear the amusement in his voice.

Tommy didn't reply though, and I listened to the footsteps of all three and then the door closed as Tommy went to lay me on the bed. As he did, I tried to sit up, wincing from the pain. I still felt a little lightheaded, but it wasn't half as bad as what it was in the courtyard.

"When I said I was tired, I was hoping you would take me back to my own room."

"I told you, those cuts need cleaning before they get infected." He didn't give me a chance to reply before he left my side and strolled into the bathroom.

The water from his shower started to run, causing me to frown slightly. Glancing down at my hands and every other part of my body, I was covered in dried blood. The cut from the glass on my hand had stopped bleeding but I wasn't sure about the others.

Tommy walked back into the room. "Are you going to willingly get into the shower or…"

Sighing heavily, I sluggishly moved my legs off the bed and rose to my feet. The room was spinning, like I had just drunk a bottle of cheap vodka and was already feeling the effects. Tommy was alert though and was at my side before I could fall back.

"Can I just sleep it off?" I moaned, wanting to put my head down on the fluffy pillow.

"No."

Before I could protest, he picked me back up and walked with me cradled in his arms again, to the shower.

The water should have been welcoming but as soon as it hit my still clothed body, I whimpered in pain. My injuries sparked back to life, stinging just as much as they had done after the adrenaline had faded.

The water ran red as it flowed down my aching body, washing away Sindy's and my own blood from my skin. I glanced up through heavy eyes to watch what Tommy was now doing. He had retrieved a small cloth and had placed it on the side. Removing his shoes and socks, he started to unbutton his shirt.

I watched, sucking in my bottom lip as he undone each button. He didn't look at me at all as he pulled it from him then chucked it to the floor. My eyes skimmed over his sculpted muscles and the black tattoos, but I adverted them as soon as he stepped into the shower.

His hands reached for me, and I unconsciously stepped back out of the shower stream, softly hitting the tiled wall behind me. Sighing with a pained look in his eyes, he attempted it again and with no space left behind me, he made contact with the first button of my shirt.

"Tommy." I murmured, watching the water fall from his head to his shoulders.

"I'm not going to touch you anywhere you don't want me to Isabella, but this shirt needs to come off so I can see how bad it is."

How bad it is? It probably felt worse than what it was. That's what my mum always used to say to me when I fell over and scraped my knee. The cut across my side was most likely just a scratch. I didn't stop him though as his fingers made quick work of the small buttons then pulled the shirt from my shoulders and down my arms.

His eyes momentarily lingered on the lace bra that cupped my breasts but as he looked lower, his lips thinned, and his jaw ticked.

"This is going to need stitches." His hand lightly cupped my waist as his thumb gently ran a line under the cut.

Flinching slightly, I grabbed his wrist in instinct then just as quickly, released it again. "It's fine. It's stopped bleeding."

"That's not the point. You will still need it closed up before it gets infected."

"I can't have stitches." I frowned, pouting out my bottom lip in protest. I wasn't saying it to be awkward and he was right, I probably did need them, but I couldn't have them.

"Trying to be cute won't work on me when your health is at risk." He didn't even meet my eyes as he said it, but something warmed inside of me. Did he actually care?

"I have cheerleading tomorrow; can I still do that?" I asked, some sort of hope lingering in my voice.

He glanced up from inspecting the wound with the tiniest bit of amusement in his eyes and the rest of his features softened a little. "I doubt you'll be taking part."

"But-"

"You're not doing it, end of."

Moving on to the next cut, he lifted my arm to get a better look, then my hand. "Is there anymore?" I shook my head. "These two are going to need dressing but won't need stitching."

"Tommy," I almost whispered. He looked up from my hand that was close to his face.

I should have just told him I was scared of needles, but I couldn't. It may not have seemed like a big deal to say it, to admit that I had a fear, but to someone like Tommy, it was a big deal. It was a weakness that he could use against me, and I didn't know if I trusted him with it.

His dark eyes studied me for a moment, completely unreadable and I swallowed feeling like I had made a mistake not finishing what I was going to say. But then he released my hand and ran his fingers across the waistband of my skirt.

"I'm going to take this off now." His thumb slotted between the fabric and my skin.

"Why?"

"It has her blood all over it. We need to burn it all."

I accepted his answer, understanding why it had to be done. He was covering up the murder I had committed. The words he had said to the others came back to me as he slid the skirt down my legs.

"I don't want you to take the blame for what I did." He let the skirt pool round my feet and then helped me step out before chucking it to the side with my discarded shirt.

Standing back up, he took my chin in his hand, making me meet his eyes. "I don't know what happened in my room, but I can paint a pretty good picture. You did what you needed to do."

I pictured Sindy's face in my mind as she begged me to stop. Every time I plunged the knife into her body and her screams. The sickening screams. My stomach turned as nausea started to make an appearance.

I didn't need to do all that to her. I just had to stop her from killing me. "I still don't want you taking the blame."

"I'm not going to let you take the fall for something I should have done the first day she turned up."

"What do you mean?"

"She was trying to cause trouble. Create drama by

feeding us false information about what her father has been up to behind our backs." He released my chin but only to run his fingers down the curve of my neck. "It nearly resulted in an unnecessary death."

I let out a tiny gasp that I hoped he had missed. "One of your own?"

"Her fathers." He answered bluntly.

"Why would she say something that would put her own father at risk?"

"I don't think she intended to when she first came here. She wanted to talk about why I had ended the engagement over a petty reason."

"Why did you end the engagement?"

He didn't answer straight away but his fingers glided lower, over the strap of my bra. I watched his eyes follow the movement of his own hand as his other brushed against my hip.

"I had something else that needed my attention more." His gaze flicked up to mine, searing into me with enough intensity to make my body flush in response.

"W-what made her do what she did?"

"You." I frowned but then closed my eyes and a whimper left my lips as the pad of his thumb swept across my already hard nipple on his way down to rest on the other side of my hip. "When she saw me with you."

Jealousy had made her like it. Jealousy had caused her to risk her father's life, had made her want to kill me. Even when she had first seen us together, it was clear we were in a physical lesson. The second time I had been heading to his room just as she was coming out but that was neither here nor there. Neither of us had been intentionally close in front of her.

But Tommy had made it worse by leading her on. Continuing to fuck her when he should have just sent her on her way. Keeping her hoping for something that he never really wanted.

I opened my eyes again, meeting his stare. "But you still

fucked her."

His jaw ticked. "Let's get you out and dried so I can dress your wounds."

He made to move away, releasing his hands from my body and the coldness he left behind was punishing. Without thinking it through, I reached out, grabbed his arm and tugged lightly to pull him back. We had never spoken like this before. Not where he had shared a conversation so openly. Or where he was so gentle. None of this was for show like it had been at the charity event. This was real and I didn't want it to end. But I didn't have much energy to make him stay either. I was exhausted and if he really wanted to, he could have just kept going but he didn't move away again.

"I'm sorry, I shouldn't have said it like that. It's none of my business what you did with her."

His eyes softened a little as his lip tilted up at the corner. "The pain must be messing with your head if you are apologising to me."

I slapped his chest lightly, leaving my hand on him. "Don't get used to it."

He chuckled darkly as he stepped further forward. His body brushed against mine, sending electricity through every nerve. Every part of me was responding to him, just like I always did.

As his fingers glided round my neck, his thumb brushed over my mouth. My lips parted, sucking in a breath that I desperately needed. Our breaths exchanged with each other as his lips hovered an inch from mine.

"I didn't fuck her Isabella." His heart thumped hard and fast against my hand, matching my own erratic beat. "I didn't touch her. Not the way I want to touch you anyway."

The air was sucked from my lungs at his words and my head began to feel light and dizzy again. This time it wasn't from the pain or the exhaustion. Tommy's hand slipped further around to the back of my neck as his lips ghosted mine. With one careless move, they would be touching.

But we were both hesitating. Neither of us wanted to be the first to take the next step.

"Fuck it."

Our lips collided as his fingers dug into the back of my neck, refusing to let me retreat from him. But escape wasn't on my mind. The only thing I wanted to do was kiss him back. Every part of my body screamed in delight at the contact it had yearned for.

My eyes closed as his lips pressed harder against mine and his fingers left my hip, snaking round to my lower back. His kiss was nothing like I could have imagined. Toxic enough to be deadly to my inhibitions yet there was still a restraint that made me ache for more.

His tongue ran over my bottom lip, begging for entrance. Opening slightly, we both fought for control resulting in him pulling on my hair lightly to gain it. A tiny whimper slipped out and he sucked in the sound like he owned it. And maybe he did because no other man had made me feel this way with just a kiss.

He was driving me crazy. Since being at this school, he was driving me insane, and I didn't care. All the doubt and regret that played in the back of my mind was being erased by the burning inferno igniting every inch of me.

Tommy pressed his body onto mine, forcing his erection to push against my stomach. Another whimper slipped out as I wished that there wasn't the barrier of his clothing between us. I wanted to feel him. I wanted to send him as wild as he was sending me.

My arms wrapped round his neck for support as my body shuddered at the thought of what could be happening and a hot wetness pooled between my legs, putting the warmth of the shower to shame.

A deep, uncontrolled growl rumbled from his throat when I pressed my breasts harder against his chest, forcing more pressure on his erection. The restraint he had was ebbing away. He wanted to lose control and I wanted him to.

But Tommy pulled away, panting lightly. His pupils almost took over the midnight blue as he stared down at me. Desire still glowing deep inside, but the control was back. My lips closed, missing the warmth of his. Slipping my hands back down his chest, I brought them down to my side. His own hands ran down my arms, grazing the cut on my forearm. My flinch managed to startle him out of whatever stupor he was in, and he looked down.

"Are you going to let me dress your wounds now?"

I nodded, somehow starting to feel nervous but also confused about what had just happened. Tommy seemed satisfied with my nonverbal answer though. Stepping back out of the stream of water, he exited the shower and grabbed a towel for himself then placed another on the side.

"Take off your wet underwear and come out when you're ready."

He walked out the room, not looking back. It was a good job as I could feel my cheeks burning. My underwear was wet, yes, but the cause wasn't just from the shower. Maybe he already knew that though.

Doing as I was told, I removed my bra and lace thong, then my long socks and heels. Dumping them on top of the rest of my uniform, I stepped out of the shower and wrapped the fluffy towel around my body. Thankfully the cuts were not bleeding enough to completely cover the white towel but there would still be some stains after I was finished with it.

Tommy had changed out of his wet trousers by the time I walked into the bedroom. He was now in a pair of grey sweats and to my subtle disappointment, a white crew cut top. He looked up as soon as I entered, expression blank like everything that had happened in the shower had either been erased or never happened.

Striding over to me in two wide steps, he shoved a black t-shirt against my chest, making me flinch from the pain as it jolted my side. "Put this on."

"I have my own clothes." I frowned, looking from the

264

top to him. His eyes were still on the top, refusing to make contact with mine.

"If you think I'm going to let you walk to your room in just a towel, you are clearly mistaken."

"And is just your top any better?"

His gaze flicked up to mine and I winced at the change of emotion. The desire and heat had been replaced with the cruel, unforgiving glare that he had given me the first night we met.

"Put the top on." He drawled, pressing the top harder against me.

Rolling my eyes, I snatched it from his grip. "Your bipolar arse is really starting to get boring."

Before I could see the reaction on his face, I gave him my back. Tommy marched past me quickly, straight into the bathroom.

Dropping the towel, I slipped the top on. It was obviously too big and hung to just above my knees making me more aware of how short I really was.

I looked at the bathroom door, waiting for Tommy to come back out. I wasn't sure what his problem was or how he could make a U-turn so quickly. One minute it's like he couldn't get enough of me. Like I was the only person he wanted and desired. But now it was like he saw me as a burden.

A new heat ran through me. Anger. How dare he do this. How dare he kiss me then act like this after. What the hell was his problem. His hot and cold act was wearing thin. He reels me in then pushes me back out again. Enough.

Walking towards the door, I reached out for the handle.

"Walk out that door and you won't be able to sit down for a month."

My heart completely skipped a beat as I choked back a gasp. Spinning around, strands of my damp hair whipped across my face.

"What do you want now? I've put the top on, I'm going back to my room."

"Drink this." He held up a small glass tumbler of what looked like water.

"What is it?" I frowned.

"It will ease the pain." He stepped forward; his voice softer as his temperament changed again. I was surprised the man didn't have whiplash from his rapidly changing emotions. "I need to dress your wounds and you need to relax."

"Maybe I would relax more if you weren't such a prick. Kissing me in there and then out here it's like it never happened."

"Did it distract you from the pain?" His lips curved up into a teasingly wicked smirk, not only making my lungs ache for the breath it had taken away but my stomach flutter. What the fuck was wrong with me.

Tommy stepped forward. "Drink."

I grabbed the glass from his hand. "Fuck, I hate you." Downing the water in one, my brows creased together. There was no taste of a painkiller in there, but I placed it on his dresser without another word.

Someone knocked on the door behind me and I moved out the way as Tommy walked around to open it.

"Need this?" The person on the other side asked and I knew at once it was Callum.

Tommy moved to the side, allowing for him to walk in. He took one look at me then back to Tommy.

"How bad is it?"

"Three. Her hand and arm don't need stitches but the one on her side does."

"I told you, I don't want stitches." I glared at him, but he ignored me and carried on talking to Callum like I wasn't there.

"The drug will kick in soon, then you can get to work."

"Drugs?" I uttered, looking between them both. As if I had summoned the effects on myself, my head started to feel lighter, like I was in a balloon. Or I was a balloon. I didn't know, I couldn't think straight. What had he put in that drink?

They both stared at me. Callum dragged his eyes up and down my body that I was certain was swaying on the spot. Although, it could have been them and the room swaying.

"She doesn't look as pale any more. Are her clothes ready to burn?"

"Yeah, take them to Archie after you've finished here." Tommy replied and Callum nodded.

My head started feeling heavier and I reached out to steady myself against the baseboard of the bed. Everything in front of me started blurring into one fuzzy image. Little black dots formed, getting larger the more I tried to concentrate on them.

One of them stepped forward to grab hold of me as I started to fall back. His arms were tight around my waist.

"Turn around." If Tommy was talking to me, I didn't know why. I couldn't turn my head. I couldn't get any part of my body to work with my brain.

"Why?" Callum asked.

"Because I need to cover her before you see something I might have to kill you for." Tommy growled, lifting my limp body onto the bed.

"What the fuck did you give me?" I mumbled but the words that came out was nothing like what I had tried to say.

As he gently lay my head back on his pillow, he moved my hair behind my ear. A sheet was placed over my lower half before he lifted the top to just under my breasts, revealing the injury. I tried to protest once again as the other blurred figure of Callum came to stand beside him.

"Why'd you give her something to knock her out completely? Why not just something to take the edge off?"

My eyes closed, unable to keep them open anymore no matter how hard I tried.

"She's afraid of needles."

Chapter 26

The sound of a lock clicking into place stirred me awake. I didn't want to open my eyes. Not when the autumn sun was already burning through them from the window, making my head feel unnaturally heavy. Rolling away from the light, I groaned at the dull pain in my side.

Shit.

My eyes opened; my vision blurred at first until it cleared. The room was spinning slowly but it was mine. Tommy had brought me back to my room. Looking down, I was still in his top. There was a small dressing across the cut on my arms and my hand had also been bandaged. Lifting his top high enough to see, the last of the wounds had been covered too.

Slowly, I peeled back the tape. Under it was clean of any blood and the cut had been neatly stitched. Even though I wasn't a fan of how they had accomplished it, I had to admire Callum's handywork. He had done a good job that would hopefully result in minimal scarring.

I replaced the dressing and reached for my phone. 12.15.

Double shit!

I had missed the first two lessons which was sure to mean another detention with Williams. And I had missed half of lunch. Not that I was hungry.

I had a few texts too. A couple from Maddy wondering what had happened seeing as people had seen me covered in blood. One actually asked if I had killed her cousin with the laughing emojis. The last message from her was telling me to stay in bed and she would come check on me at lunch time. That must have been what the noise was that woke me. Her locking the door again as she left.

The next message was from Callum. Just telling me that Williams and Bane were both sympathetic over my stomach bug and wished me well. I chuckled at that message. There was no way Williams would believe I had a stomach bug, let alone send well wishes too. Bane on the other hand was sweet enough to.

And the last was from Tommy on the group chat. He had obviously got a new phone already.

2Beauts and 4fucktards

(I really should think of something else to change that to)

Tommy
Meet out front after the third period. I've already informed those who need to know that we are leaving early.

Callum
Are we eating dinner at home?

Tommy
Obviously.

Felix
Better be nans home cooking instead of that shit your new cook tried

Callum
Yeh, that quinoa stuff. Wtf is that shit.

Maddy
I thought it was nice.

Callum
Fuck off Maddy, your lack of a mature pallet makes your
opinion irrelevant.

Maddy
And your lack of sex life makes your dick irrelevant, yet
you still act like one.

I snorted out a laugh then whimpered at the sharp pain
it caused my head.

Callum
Tramp

Maddy
Cockwomble

Archie
You riding with me and Felix?

Felix
I'm taking my bike home

Felix rides a motorbike. You learn something new every
day.

Callum
Want me to take yours home Tommy?

And so does Tommy. I'm partly impressed.

Tommy
You are not going anywhere near my bike after last time.

Callum
I honestly didn't see the wall

Archie
It was right in front of you

Tommy
My bike is staying here

Callum:
Fine, I'll ride with you and the girls

Callum
But I'm bringing my own car back

Maddy:
I'm riding with Archie. He has a bigger boot space and I'm taking a lot home.

Archie
Nice to be asked

Maddy
Can I ride with you

Archie
No

Maddy
Thank you

The last message was sent only an hour ago, while they were in lesson. Well Archie and Callum were meant to be in

AP Poisons. I had no idea where the others were.

I quickly fired a message across to them all.

Bella

I'll ride with Archie too. Maddy will want some female company.

Placing my phone on the side, I swung my legs around and stood up. The effects of whatever drug Tommy had given me still lingered and I staggered back, falling onto the mattress again. My head felt dizzy, but I pushed myself back up, fighting through the daze and the ache of every joint in my body.

Cheerleading was my next class, and I wasn't going to miss the first ever lesson, even if I wasn't able to perform at my best. Heading for the wardrobe, I stripped off Tommy's top and chucked it on the wash pile that Maddy and I had both vowed to do as soon as we got back from her family's.

Grabbing the cheerleading outfit that had been delivered just a couple of days ago, I started getting dressed. The black pleated skirt was short. Like extremely short but luckily, black Lycra hotpants were provided to wear underneath. The matching vest top left half of my stomach exposed but my injury was thankfully covered. The only ones exposed were the cut to my arm and my hand.

Looking down at my legs, a purple bruise from where Sindy had kicked out had appeared through the night, blemishing my calf. Pulling the socks on that came with the whole outfit, the bruise disappeared under them. I was lucky Sindy hadn't managed to strike my face at all. At least I knew that that didn't have a mark on it.

After having a quick wash and applying a light coating of mascara and red lipstick, I threw my hair up into a high, rather messy ponytail. I could have made it neater but what was the point when I was just about to mess it up again most probably. Wrapping the compulsory red ribbon around it, I tied it into a bow then looked back at my reflection.

The outfit wasn't too bad. All black with a red trim at all the edges. On the front of the top was the official school logo made up of small silver and ruby coloured diamantes. I slipped the black trainers on and sat back on my bed. It was too early to go to class yet and if I went down to grab some food I would no doubt see Tommy.

Not that I purposely wanted to avoid him because I didn't. He drugged me after kissing me. That boy had so much explaining to do. But I wasn't strong enough for the argument I knew was going to happen once he saw me in my cheerleading outfit after telling me that I won't be doing it today. Because that had just made me want to do it more.

Picking up my phone, I looked at the replies that had been sent to the group chat.

Callum
Afternoon sleeping beauty. How you feeling?

Archie
Not enough room in my car love, you'll have to put up with Tommy and Callum.

My eyebrows furrowed together as I glared at the message from Archie. There was only him and Maddy in the car.

Bella
Tommy get you to say that?

Felix
Haha

Archie
Of course not

Bella
Liar

Callum
You coming down for lunch?

Bella
No, I feel too ill after being drugged

Tommy
It was for your own good

I scoffed at the screen. For my own good! What was for my own good? Yeh, it calmed me enough that I didn't feel any pain while Callum had stitched me up. And I also didn't see the needle, saving myself from the embarrassment of a freakout. But that wasn't the point.

Bella
And it will be for your own good to let me travel with Maddy

Tommy
Fine. Maddy, you are coming in my car.

Maddy
WTF

Bella
I hate you

Tommy
So you keep telling me

I chucked my phone down on the bed, ignoring the next load of messages that came through. I would be early but fuck waiting around in my room, stewing in my own anger. I was going to the pitch where the first practice session was and give Tommy a massive fuck you with my middle finger while arse flipped through the air.

By the time I had found the pitch, Maddy and the rest of my team were already waiting for the captain to begin the try outs. About half were in the cheer uniform while the rest were in their normal combat gear.

I jogged over to Maddy, coming up behind her. "How come we have a uniform, and the others don't."

"Jesus Bella." She jumped, spinning round to face me. "What are you doing here?"

"Cheer practice." I smirked, then looked past her to the football team warming up across the field. Tommy was speaking to Alfie who looked like he was coaching the team while the others were doing push ups. He hadn't seen me yet, but I didn't anticipate it taking long.

"You aren't fit enough to do practice Bella. Your stitches." She glanced at my arm even though that wasn't the worst injury. The worry in her eyes though did make me feel a little guilty but I tried to give her a reassuring smile.

"I'm fine. I won't do anything over the top." I promised. "I just didn't want to be kicked from the team before we even made it. I wanted to have at least one extracurricular with you."

She gave me a sympathetic look then a small sigh. "We're on the team anyway."

"Huh?"

"That's why we have the uniform, and they don't." She nodded towards the others. "As soon as the coach saw our name on the list, he made sure we were on the team."

"Alfie?" I asked, confirming he was the coach.

"Yeh, he's a family friend and Tommy's godfather."

"Oh." Explained why they were always talking like they were close. I looked back over to him again. He was grinning down at the grass with his arms crossed. Whatever they were talking about was clearly entertaining him.

Alfie said something else to him and Tommy's

shoulders shook as he laughed lightly, still looking at the grass. I kind of felt warm and fuzzy watching Tommy like this. He was comfortable, at ease and it was almost perfect.

His head lifted as he said something back but then his calm face changed as he caught eyes with me. I swallowed hard and pressed my lips together as even with the distance between us, I could still feel the sting of his rage.

Alfie's head twisted round, trying to see what had changed Tommy's mood but before he could find the culprit, Tommy was already moving.

"You're in trouble." Maddy muttered beside me.

"Aren't I always." I grinned at her but even though I wanted to piss him off, he was suddenly making me nervous in the more exciting way.

"There's still time to run back to our room." She suggested, backing away from me as Tommy got closer. His teammates followed him with their eyes, but no one made any attempt to call him back.

"And where would the fun be in that." I looked back at Maddy and gave her a cheeky wink. She chuckled before her smile faded and she looked away.

I could feel him before I even turned back to face him. The heat of anger radiating from his tall, stone physique burned into me. I turned my head, giving him the sweet as honey smile I knew he hated.

"What the fuck do you think you are doing?" He growled and a shiver ran through my body that I hoped he hadn't noticed.

"Trying out for the team." I answered sweetly.

"You're on the team." He countered, eyes narrowing.

"But how will they know what skills I have if I don't show them."

"I told you you're not doing this."

"But I am."

He stepped closer, invading the safe distance between us. "I said no."

"I love how you think you can stop me." It was like I

had just set the ultimate challenge and his eyes flashed with a heat that melted the icy glare.

He lowered his head, "Why do you keep trying to piss me off?"

I shrugged, then leaned up on my toes so my nose was almost touching his. "Maybe I'm waiting for that punishment you keep promising but don't deliver."

Settling back down on my heels, I watched as his blue eyes turned molten. Something was going on inside his head and I had to fight to keep the smile on my face as a nervous tension fell over me. Saying something like that was an invitation for whatever he had to offer, and I wondered if I was ready for it.

To my surprise, he turned around and stormed back to his team. I let out a relieved breath, forgetting where I was for a moment and Maddy came to stand beside me again.

"I don't think I want to be in the car with you both now."

"Don't you dare leave me."

For forty-five minutes, I stood shivering in the cold autumn air, watching the try outs. To my displeasure, it had even started drizzling and I was pretty certain Maddy was going mental as she cursed the sky under her breath.

There was no need for me to be out here at all. We hadn't done any practice at all. Just stood about watching the other students try out to hopefully get a spot on the team. Our cheer captain, Courtney, had already selected who she wanted before any of them had made a move, but she let the others do their little routines for pure entertainment.

Occasionally, I'd glance over at the boys practice game. You could argue that it was a typical football match but the brutality of it made it anything but. Fouls and red cards were ignored. Punching and kicking was encouraged. And at one point, I could have sworn I saw Archie headbutt someone for trying to score a goal past him.

The good thing about them playing so roughly though was the fact that Tommy was releasing all the frustration and anger. Good for me but not good for the players that were trying to prove their skills to get on the team.

"Right ladies and gents." Courtney called, bringing everyone's attention to her after she dismissed the ones she deemed unworthy. "Our boys have their first friendly coming up soon against the school from up north. Their cheerleading squad will be coming down too." Some hisses sounded from the older members and Courtney gave them a knowing glance. "They play nasty but we're going to be vicious. I want to hear them begging for forgiveness for even trying to be better than us."

"We going to do a whole new routine?" One of the girls asked her.

"Betty, it's a new school year. Of course there is going to be a new routine." She exasperated. "I know that you are only scheduled in to have one class a week but last year we also worked Saturdays and Sundays plus a couple of evenings after dinner. Just while it's football season."

A few groaned but I honestly didn't mind. Maddy stuck her hand up though and Courtney gave her a nod to speak.

"Bella and I can't come to practice this weekend. We've got somewhere to be that we can't get out of."

Courtney looked across the field at the four Krays then back to us. "That's fine. We'll start Monday at 6pm. If it's raining, meet in the gym. Bella looks like she might pass out soon anyway."

I gave her a tight-lipped smile and stuck up my thumb because whether it was an insult or not, I did in fact, feel like I had been hit by a bus that had reversed and then ran over me again just to make sure the job was done properly. And if hurting everywhere wasn't enough, I also felt sick. I blamed that on the lack of food since lunch the day before. What I would give to have a burger right now.

A scream sounded from behind us, making half of the cheer squad turn towards it. Tommy was just starting to get back up from the grass. Mud smeared all over one side of him and a dark, malicious grin forming across his face. He walked away from the lad on the floor, not even second glancing to check if he was ok.

I couldn't see properly from where I was standing but the boy's leg looked bent in a vulgar way. Felix slid beside him, confirming what I already knew.

"It's broken." He called out to Alfie, who was now running over to the scene too.

"Tommy broke his leg?" I whispered to Maddy.

"Part of the game." She shrugged, rubbing her arms to warm herself up. "Albeit he isn't usually this bad with try outs and his own team. Must have a lot on his mind."

"Didn't someone actually die last year?" The girl from behind me asked.

"I'm not sure. I only went to a few of the matches and Callum never really told me much about them whenever he used to come home to visit."

"Someone did die." Courtney had now joined us too. "It was someone from another school though so not one of our own."

I frowned, tearing my eyes from the stretcher now being brought out to look at her. "What happened?"

"Tommy and Archie happened. Tackled him at the same time and somehow managed to snap his neck."

"Fuck."

"I know right." A slight hint of a smile lit up her face. "The game is brutal, but everyone signs that little bit of paper, letting them know exactly what they are getting themselves in to." Sighing she turned back to acknowledge the rest of the squad. "Remember, Monday, 6pm. Don't be late. We have a lot to get through before the friendly."

"Do we have to bring anything with us?" Someone asked.

Courtney shook her head. "Just yourselves. I have the

knifes and grenades we will be needing."

My eyes widened and Maddy laughed, linking her arm through my elbow. "I love cheerleading already."

"Same." I chuckled and we started our long walk back to our room to get changed for our little trip.

Chapter 27

After having a quick and very careful shower to wash away any lingering effects of the night before and eating a whole pack of cookies and two packets of crisps, I finally got dressed. Keeping it simple, I threw on a burgundy, corduroy skirt that came midway down my thighs. A thick knitted black jumper covered my injuries perfectly while also keeping me toasty and long black socks that were accompanied by black heeled ankle boots. Simple but cute.

I didn't bother with a coat but had packed one just in case I needed it over the course of the next couple of days. Maddy had also packed a load of other bits for me that I was sure I wouldn't need. Like cocktail dresses and underwear that really didn't leave much to the imagination.

By the time she had managed to close her own suitcases, (yes plural.) and we had dragged them down to the front of the school, our rides were already waiting. Callum was leaning against Tommy's car, checking his watch then tapping it as Maddy struggled to drag one suitcase across the gravel, leaving the other by the steps.

"Help would be nice."

"Of course." He smiled at her then walked over to my suitcase, picked it up, popped open the boot of Tommy's car and chucked it inside before closing it again.

"Thanks." I chuckled as Maddy glared at him, still struggling to pull hers along.

"You could have at least left it open you prick."

Archie sighed in aggravation. "Your bags are going in mine." Stalking over, he picked up her suitcase with ease then grabbed the one beside me and slung them both into the rear of his car.

My eyes darted from her to Archie's Range Rover. "You're still riding with me though, aren't you?"

She gave me a sympathetic smile. "Do you really want to argue against him after you saw the kind of mood he's in." I raised one brow and she chuckled. "Don't answer that."

"Is it too late to ask Felix for a lift on the back of his bike?"

"He's already gone." Callum laughed then opened the passenger seat for me to climb in.

"You can sit in the front if you want. I don't mind." He laughed again at the sweet tone of my voice and the hope that it was brimmed with.

"Just get in while we wait for Tommy."

Pouting out my bottom lip, I sat down in the seat, and he closed the door behind me. I had only been sitting there for a couple of minutes, listening to Archie and Callum rambling on about the football practice schedule, when I heard Tommy walking across the gravel.

"Where the fuck is she?"

I frowned as I leaned out the window to look at him. "Who?"

His eyes met mine looking just as confused. "You. What are you doing here?"

My gaze flicked between Callum and him, wondering if this was some kind of trick. "You messaged to tell us to meet here."

"After earlier, I thought I might have to..." He sighed heavily, not finishing what he was about to say but glared at me all the same.

"I can go again, and you can come take me by force if that's what you really want." I grinned, leaning my chin on my arm as it rested on the open window.

Releasing a low, vexed growl, he pointed his long finger at me. "Stay in the car."

Rolling my eyes but satisfied that I had annoyed him, I turned back to sit in my seat properly. Tommy climbed into the driver's side seconds later and started the ignition. I had expected him to wait for Callum to get in the back, but the car started moving without him.

"What about Callum?"

"He's riding with the others."

Fuck sake.

"How long does it take to get to yours?"

"Couple of hours."

Even better. Two hours alone with Tommy. My fingers fiddled with the hem of my skirt. Having the balls to taunt him was easy when I had the buffer of another person or the space to run. But on our own, trapped in a car, pushing him was a bigger risk.

We pulled away from the iron gates onto the tarmacked road and headed in the opposite direction to where the cabin was. Neither of us spoke to each other but instead of being a comfortable silence, it was excruciating.

"Can I-" I didn't even need to finish my question before Tommy handed me his new phone. Like the previous time, I brought up Spotify and selected a song. Don't Blame Me by Taylor Swift. Then I passed him the phone back and went back to staring out the window.

The silence between us was still there but with the music playing in the background it was more bearable. For over an hour we didn't say a word to each other. We didn't even look at each other. It was like he had forgotten I was in the car with him.

The sun was starting to set as we drove down a deserted road. I looked behind us and Archie was still following. I could just make out him and Callum laughing in the front seats and Maddy's little head poking up in the middle, grinning like a child at Christmas. At least they were having fun.

"How much longer?" I dared to ask and his hand gripped tighter on the steering wheel as his other changed gear. The car slowed down allowing for Archie to overtake and take off into the distance. "What's happening?"

He picked up speed again but instead of following Archie, he took a turn down a dirt road. Following it until he came to a woodland area, the car came to a standstill a couple of hundred yards up and Tommy took the keys from the ignition. Without answering me, he opened his door and stepped out. Slamming it shut, I jumped in my seat. Was he planning on killing me? Was that a punishment that I was about to receive for not doing as I was told.

I watched as he walked to the back of the car and opened the boot. Taking something out, he shut it then walked to my door. I was half tempted to lock it but that would just anger the beast more. The door opened and he stared down at me.

"Out."

Swallowing, I slowly stepped out, standing in front of him.

"Hands."

I hesitated, wondering if this was a good idea. He wouldn't kill me; it was silly that I even thought that. But just how far would he go. Curiosity got the better of me and I held up my hands. He lifted the rope that I hadn't noticed and wrapped it around my wrists, binding them together.

"What are you-"

"I suggest that you keep that mouth of yours shut."

"But-"

He pulled roughly on the rope, pinching my skin and making me gasp. "No one can hear you out here Isabella. If you speak without permission again, every scream that comes from your mouth will be for my purposes only."

Fear bled through every inch of my body, making it shake uncontrollably. Pulling me with him, Tommy opened the back door and pushed me down on the seat. I opened my mouth to say something. To ask if he was really going to hurt me but closed it again as he raised one eyebrow, daring me to give him a reason.

"Good girl."

Why the fuck did the praise feel so good? Maybe if I continued to be a good girl, I might actually come out of this unscathed.

"Move back."

It was easier said than done with your hands bound but I managed to shift myself to the far end seat. Tommy climbed into the car and shut the door behind him. Leaning over me, he grabbed the rope and secured it to the handle above my head.

I took a deep breath as his chest pressed against mine. His hands ran back down my arms, making me squirm. But instead of backing away, he quickly grabbed my legs, bringing one up on to the seat then slid himself between them.

"Do you enjoy provoking me, Isabella?"

His voice was nothing but a husky whisper. The sound vibrated through me, making my belly tense. What the fuck was he doing to me? His fingers dug into the flesh of my thigh, and I sucked in a breath.

"Answer me."

"Yes."

A growl left his throat as his hand wandered higher up my skirt. "Do you enjoy disobeying me."

I bit down on my bottom lip not wanting to answer. He would know if I lied but I didn't know how much trouble the truth would get me into.

"Isabella?" Grabbing firmly, he moved my legs further towards him and the ropes bit at my wrists as I jolted them.

"Yes." I managed to whimper.

His hand rose and he looped his thumb through my

thong. He pulled it down with no hesitation and freed them from my ankles.

"Tommy-"

He leaned forward, pressing himself against my centre and whatever I was going to say next was lodged in my throat forever. Pulling my jumper free from my skirt, he slowly lifted it.

"Do you know why I told you not to go to your cheerleading class?"

"Uhh-"

His lips pressed to my skin, next to the dressing of the worst cut. Gentle kisses circled the area and even though there was a very dull pain, it felt so good. He kissed higher then released my breast from the bra cup.

"Why did I tell you not to go Isabella?" His tongue teased a circle around my hard nipple, wetting it enough to send a tremor through my core when he blew gently on it. "Answer me."

"Because you didn't want me to hurt myself."

"Because I didn't want you to hurt yourself." He repeated venomously.

Taking my nipple into his mouth, he bit down roughly. I cried out, squirming under him but with my hands bound, I was at his mercy. Releasing me from his teeth, he ran his tongue over the area, soothing the pain. Although his breath was warm, mixing with the wetness was icy but it felt amazing.

"Why don't you do as you are told?"

One hand wandered back down my stomach, towards my inner thigh while the other still cupped my breast as his teeth latched onto my nipple again. An embarrassingly loud moan left my parted lips and I slammed them shut. Tommy's dark chuckle vibrated against me.

Prick.

"Why don't you do as you're told Isabella?"

"Because I don't like being controlled." I breathed out. My heart was racing so fast that if it was any other situation,

I would be worried.

Tommy lifted his head, his gaze burning into me. "Let's see how much you don't like being controlled now." I sucked in a breath as one finger ran across my slit. "Fuck baby, you're soaked"

A devilishly lustful grin curved onto his face, making my cheeks heat. As soon as he touched me there, there was no denying that what he was doing was turning me on. He lowered himself, placing his head in between my legs. I tried to close my thighs, blocking him from going any further, but his hands held them into place.

Before I could attempt to close them again, his mouth was on me. My eyes rolled back, and my back arched unwillingly at the sudden contact. His tongue ran a straight line from my hole to my clit, and a silent scream tried to escape my already parted lips. Each flick of his tongue was controlled and precise, just like everything else that Tommy did. And he did it so fucking well.

A sharpness hit the small bundle of nerves, making my eyes flash open. Never have I been bitten on my clit before. Hell, I'd never been licked like this before. But I didn't hate it. The heat of my arousal dripped out on to his waiting tongue, and he groaned in satisfaction, licking it up.

Sitting back up, he stared down at me. Running his tongue over his bottom lip, he smirked. "You taste better than I ever imagined."

Narrowing my eyes in annoyance, I squirmed under him. I wasn't sure what was frustrating me more. The fact that he was doing this, the fact that he had stopped or the fact that I actually liked it. I liked it so fucking much.

Tommy ran his fingers through my folds, coating them in my wetness. My back arched again as I pressed my lips together to not give him the satisfaction of hearing my enjoyment. He leaned down, almost pressing his lips to mine, but he didn't.

"Tell me Isabella. Is this what you wanted all along?" His finger teased my entrance as his nose ran up and down my cheek. My eyes closed as one finger slid in slowly. "Open your eyes. I want to see how much you desire this."

I obeyed his order as he pulled his finger out again. "You don't want to be controlled but here you are being so obedient and doing exactly what you are told."

He rewarded me by inserting two fingers and I almost choked on my gasp. His fingers where thick and long, stretching me in the most pleasurable way. Gently massaging my favourite spot, the pad of his thumb pressed against my clit. The slow steady build up was driving me insane. But my whole body wanted release.

Grinding down against his hand, he tsked and stopped moving his fingers. I groaned in disappointment, yearning for more.

"Desperate little thing, aren't you?"

I wanted to yell at him, to scream for him to get off. Anything to wipe that smug look from his annoyingly handsome face. But instead, I stilled my hips because he was right, I was now desperate.

"Do you want me to make you cum?"

I licked my bottom lip before trapping it between my teeth.

"Do you want my tongue back where it was until you are a withering mess beneath me."

I slowly nodded my head as my mouth opened, panting out each breath.

"Then tell me who you belong to."

Our eyes connected, his flared with heat and power, demanding my submission. But no matter how much I wanted him to touch me or how I now wanted to touch him. I wouldn't give in.

"Fuck you."

His dark chuckle nearly sent me straight to hell. "Who owns you, Isabella?"

I still didn't give him the answer he wanted. He kissed against my jaw, pulling his fingers from inside me. I inwardly groaned at the loss but still refused to answer.

"Who owns every pleasurable sound that comes from this mouth?" Tommy padded his thumb against my pulsing clit, creating the gasp he wanted to claim.

"Who owns this sweet cunt?" His fingers slid into me again. One, two.

I pulled on the rope, chafing my wrists painfully as the pressure in my belly built. He slipped in the third, drawing out a long unwanted whimper. His strokes were disciplined and painfully teasing. Each pump of his fingers and flick of his thumb over my clit bringing me closer to my imminent orgasm.

My body was on fire. I desperately wanted to rip these clothes off. Fuck, I even wanted his clothes off. I just needed to feel every inch of him on me and I wanted to touch him so badly.

I was getting so close, so damn close and he knew it. The way my body shook around him and the way my head lolled back, hitting the window gently. But then he slowed again, and the pressure eased, taking the pleasure with it.

"Who own's you Isabella?"

"Please Tommy." I hated myself for saying the words, but I needed it. I needed him.

"Say it."

Could I say it? Could I really give in, giving him what he wanted so I could get the release I wanted?

His lips grazed my jaw again. "Don't disappoint me baby."

I gasped in a ragged breath as he kissed down my body, his fingers still working slowly to keep me on the edge of my sanity.

Fuck it. Send me to hell because I was about to give in to the devil himself.

"You."

"I what, Isabella?"

"You own me."

"There's my good girl."

His eyes instantly flared with a blue fire as his face

lowered, and his mouth devoured me. He bit, licked and sucked my clit with such power as he fucked me hard and fast with his fingers. Each thrust in was as relentless as the last.

Peering down, I caught the desire staring back, watching me come apart before him. I panted, bucking my hips and he bit down harder. The pain mixed with the pleasure sent me over the edge and my eyes rolled to the back of my head as I screamed out. My walls closed around his fingers, and he groaned against the tender bundle of nerves, sending shock waves through my body.

Fucking me through my climax, Tommy didn't ease up. I clenched around his three fingers, coating them in my come and his tongue lapped it up. Drinking every last drop.

Never has anyone made me feel like this. My ex and I may have had sex, but I faked it with him. It wasn't his fault; I could just never reach the point of finishing and would have to do the job myself once he had gone home. But with Tommy, it was like he knew how to work me. What my body wanted.

He slowed his pace, letting me come down slowly before finally removing his fingers and mouth. I already ached. My clit throbbed. I was truly spent.

He lifted his head to gaze over me. I looked like a panting mess. My cheeks were flushed. My skin was damp with sweat from the heat between us. But he looked at me like I was the most beautiful thing he had ever seen. His lips glistened with my climax and his carnal eyes sparkled with a fulfilling satisfaction.

Leaning over me, his erection pressed against my now overly sensitive centre. A small moan escaped again making the corners of his lips tip up. He reached up and released my wrists from the bounds. I caressed the red welts that tarnished the skin. I didn't like them, but I wasn't sure if I hated them either.

"Get back in your seat."

He opened the door behind him and climbed out,

leaving it open for me to follow. So that was it. He was done with me. He didn't want anything more.

I pulled the cup of my bra back over my breast and readjusted my jumper. Before I climbed out, I smoothed my unruly curls back down, wishing I could get to my suitcase to get a brush. Tommy had already opened the passenger side door and was waiting for me to get back in. I did, without a word.

He shut both mine and the back door then walked round to get in his own. Starting up the engine, we continued on our journey to his family home.

"We'll be there in fifteen minutes."

I didn't say anything back. I just continued to stare out of the window in front of me. In fairness, I didn't know what to say. Like what the fuck just happened? Tommy had me begging. He had me surrendering to him. And I was partly disgusted with myself.

"Ignoring me now?" The amusement in his voice irritated me more.

"I want my underwear back."

A dark, malicious chuckle rumbled from him. "Oh no Isabella. You wanted a punishment. You're going to sit at the table while we all eat our dinner with your cunt still soaked from the pleasure that I gave you."

I could see my chest rising and falling as my lungs tried to grasp at the air that was knocked out of me. "That's my punishment. The first time I meet your family, I'm going to be naked down there."

"Pretty tame really."

"Tame?" I fired at him, turning in my seat. "What if someone see's something."

"Only I can see what you have to offer. If anyone else sees it, your next punishment won't be as forgiving."

I swallowed hard. If being so exposed in front of his family was a tame punishment, I didn't want to know what else he had planned.

"What about what happened back there. Wasn't that my

punishment?"

"You don't usually enjoy a punishment, Isabella. That back there, I know you did."

My cheeks flushed and I sucked in my lip. I did enjoy it, but I wouldn't tell him that even if he did already know.

We drove in silence once again. I was nibbling my lip, nervously anticipating our dinner, while Tommy wore a smug smirk like he had just won something. And again, he had.

Chapter 28

We pulled up outside the large country manor. Tommy's family home wasn't what I expected at all. After being at his place of business, the glass palace, I had imagined his home to be of the same structure. Modern, cold and untouched. The manor in front of me, although it was large, seemed cosy and lived in. The orangey glow of light in the windows gave of a warm and welcoming aesthetic. Even though I knew that the home housed psycho killers, it looked inviting.

Tommy stopped just behind Archie's Range Rover. Parked beside that was a motorbike that I assumed was Felix's. Stepping out, he walked round to open the door for me and held out his hand. Completely ignoring the gesture, I climbed out myself.

He rolled his eyes then slammed the door shut again. "Going back to being bratty now?"

My eyes flashed with anger, but I smiled sweetly at him. "I'm going to make you wish you hadn't brought me here."

His finger ran across his lips as he smirked down at me. My clit twitched at the thought of him kissing at it again and I inwardly cringed. Fuck he had some sort of hold on me, and I hated it. Sort of.

Turning on my heel, I walked towards the large front door. Before I got to it, it swung open. Maddy came rushing out, flinging her arms around me with the biggest grin on her face.

"Finally. What the hell happened?" She scanned my body and I instinctively pulled at my sleeves to cover the red welts on my wrists and crossed my legs. "What did you do to her?" She looked over my shoulder at Tommy.

He walked towards us with my suitcase in his hand. "Nothing she didn't like Madeline."

I glared at him as he strode past into the manor. Maddy linked her arm through mine and dragged me to follow him.

"As your friend, I want to know all the details. But as his cousin, I really don't."

"If I could get away with it, I would poison him." I muttered, letting her lead me into the hallway. She chuckled and said something else, but I was too distracted to listen.

The room we had just entered looked magnificent and it was only the entrance. Although the outside of the manor looked older, the inside had undergone major updating. Oak double doors led to another room on the left of me and on the other side were three more. In the centre was a large circular table with a tall vase filled with an arrangement of autumn flowers.

The stairs led to a galleried landing where two women were standing and talking. Tommy had set my suitcase down at the foot of the staircase and had then disappeared, but Maddy was beaming as she waved towards the two women.

"Mum, Nan. This is Bella."

Both turned to look down at us as Maddy dragged me forward. The younger of the two looked like an older version of Maddy. The same milky skin and the same grey eyes. Her blonde hair was pinned back without a strand out of place and her pencil skirt and blouse looked tailored to her exact size.

The other lady was obviously older but looked just as

stunning. Her blue eyes were more like Tommy's than Maddy's and her grey hair still had flecks of dark strands. Each one wore a warm smile on their face though, much unlike the four males in their family.

Both came to the bottom of the staircase and before I could protest, her mum grabbed me from Maddy's arms and into her own embrace.

"Bella, I'm so glad that you wanted to come here." She beamed, just the way her daughter had, and I smiled back.

"Wanted? She was forced, the poor girl." Her nan laughed, taking me for her own loving hug. As she released me, I frowned slightly. "I know how my grandson can be. He's just like his father and late grandfather."

"They're all the same." Maddy's mum sighed and rolled her eyes. "Your father used to –"

"Mum, I do not need to know about your intimate details."

I smiled, feeling a little more at ease even though I was completely naked under my skirt.

"Dinner is nearly ready. Let's get to the table ready before my grandsons leave us with nothing to eat at all." The elderly lady moved towards one of the doors, but I didn't move.

"Umm Mrs Kray, where would you like me to put my suitcase?"

"Someone will take it to your room soon enough." She flicked her hand, dismissing my question. "And please, call me Thelma."

"Oh yes, I didn't think. Please call me Lizzy. It's Elizabeth but I prefer Lizzy."

I nodded at them both then followed them into the dining room. The others were already sitting at the table. A man with dark hair sat at the head at the far end with Tommy beside him. Beside Tommy was Callum then another man. An empty space followed him that Lizzy filled then another empty space that was maybe for Maddy. Thelma sat in her seat, opposite the man taking the head and Felix and Archie sat on the other side.

"Isabella." The dark-haired man drawled out my name the way Tommy had the first time he said it. This was his father. "Come take this seat." He signalled to the empty one beside him and I followed his instruction.

Maddy took the seat next to me instead of next to her mum, and then everyone fell into a conversation as they helped themselves to the food on the table.

I soon learnt who was who. The man beside Callum was his father, John. John was the second oldest of Thelmas' four sons but instead of taking his place as second in line to the Kray throne, he had passed it straight down to Callum. Felix and Archie's parents weren't here. Both their fathers were away on business but were planning on attending the friendly football match.

The man at the head of the table was, in fact, Tommy's dad. Thomas Kray. but his mum wasn't here. She was gone. Maddy had managed to whisper that no one had sat in this seat since his mum's passing. I felt some sadness towards Tommy then. He had listened to me talking about my own mother's death while still dealing with the loss of his own.

The sadness was soon eradicated when I glanced across at him to find my thong scrunched discreetly in his hand, pressing it against his nose with a wicked smirk on his face. Fuck, I wanted to punch him so hard. Luckily, no one else was paying him any attention and hadn't seen what he was doing to me. Giving me a taunting wink, he placed them back in his pocket. My thighs clenched together as heat pooled between them. Why the fuck was this turning me on?

My cheeks heated as my pulse rate started to pick up. Tommy grinned again but turned to speak to Callum.

"So Isabella," Thomas was like Tommy, he would only use my given name. Not the name others called me. "How are you liking school so far?"

"It's very different to what I'm used to sir but I'm enjoying it more every day."

"Sir?" He turned to Tommy, amusement lacing his tone. "She speaks to me with more respect than you do."

"Shame she can't be as respectful to me."

My mouth dropped but I quickly picked up my glass of wine to stop something rude slipping out.

"Do you like your teacher's dear?" Thelma asked

"I like Dr Bane. She's nice."

"That's because you are a teacher's pet with her." Archie grumbled then took a swig from his beer.

"Just because I'm smarter than you with poisons doesn't mean I'm a teacher's pet." I deadpanned then caught myself before anymore attitude came out. Callum laughed but Archie gave me his middle finger before downing the rest of his drink.

"Sorry, that was rude."

"Fucking hell, who are you and what have you done with our Bella?" Callum scoffed.

Lizzy smacked him round the back of the head, knocking her husband at the same time. "Language at the dinner table."

"Isabella." I faced the head of the family. "Madeline has told us plenty enough stories for me to know that you have some spunk in you." Felix snorted, then bowed his head after receiving a scowl from his nan. "Please don't be anyone other than yourself while you are in my home. I will be more appreciative if you treat my son and nephews how you would at school."

Tommy let out a heavy sigh. "You have basically given her permission to try to kill me."

"She did mention wanting to poison you when we came in." Maddy grassed on me, and I pressed my lips in a thin line to stop my smile.

Tommy's eyes narrowed but under the table his foot kicked playfully against mine. "Should I be checking my drinks all weekend?"

"No, I don't have the supplies I need here." I pursed my lips, feigning my disappointment and a dark mischief filled his eyes.

To my surprise, Thomas laughed heartedly, inviting everyone else to do the same. Everyone but Tommy, who just smiled tauntingly at me. His foot ran up my calf and I waited for him to kick me again, but he didn't. Thomas wanted me to be myself. Tommy wanted to play. It was like he was daring me to be a brat. Taking my thong, teasing me with it.

I was ready to play back.

"Anymore news about the Italians?" He asked his father as the others got back into their conversations with each other again.

"No, they still haven't replied since we sent our condolences for Carlo's death."

"They've left England again?"

"Yes, as far as we know." Thomas nodded. "But they didn't leave with anyone else so the person they were looking for, they didn't find."

"They did but didn't they realise." Tommy muttered and Thomas nodded again.

"We'll discuss this more later."

Maddy drew my attention to her, talking through what she had planned for us over the weekend. I managed to slip my foot free from my ankle boot without much difficulty or bringing attention to myself. Maddy's list wasn't too extensive. Tomorrow, she planned for us to spend the morning and afternoon just chilling and waiting for company to arrive.

My foot slid up Tommy's leg. Although my legs were short, I was able to get my foot high enough to do what I had intended.

Tomorrow evening, once everyone had left, Maddy wanted to have a really girly sleep over of makeup and hair dressing. Something that kids would do but I loved the idea. I let Maddy rabbit on about all the plans, nodding and smiling in all the right places but my attention was really on the man opposite.

Tommy cleared his throat as my foot rose higher, momentarily interrupting the conversation with his father but then carried on like nothing had happened. I had reached his cock and teasingly ran my toes up and down through the fabric of his trousers. He was already hard, forcing me to hide my grin behind another sip of wine.

He moved in his seat, adjusting himself but that only gave me better access. I pressed harder against him, running my toes up and down. I couldn't quite reach with my whole foot but I didn't need to. The feeling of him growing harder was just making me wetter. It was a price I was willing to pay to score one up.

I dared to give him a side glance and it was worth it. His jaw was set as he rested it against his clenched fist. The veins were almost popping in his hand as he fought to keep control. He refused to look at me, but I was pretty sure the murderous look in his gaze wasn't meant for his dad.

I pressed harder and he almost groaned but covered it with another cough. His head spun in my direction, and I met his heated glare with my own. He was livid. I could have done anything else to be my usual self. I could have given him the attitude that he was used to, but this was new to him, and I loved it. I had the same control that he did in the car and that feeling of power was magical. No wonder he enjoyed it so much.

I watched as he tried his hardest not to come undone just by the movement of my toes against his cock. The only downside was that more I watched the control ebb from his face, the more I became wet. I wouldn't have been surprised if my arousal hadn't formed a puddle on the seat.

I pressed harder again making him jolt and bang his leg on the underside of the table.

"Everything ok?" Thomas asked his son.

"It will be." The chair scraped from under him, and he stood up. No one would be able to tell that he was sporting a massive erection. Not with his trousers being so tight.

Quickly, I pushed my foot back into my boot and acted

like nothing was happening. He stalked round the table and grabbed my arm lifting me from my seat. Not saying another word he pulled me away from the others.

"What happened?" Lizzy asked the table.

Through the three boys' laughter, Maddy answered. "Bella has a certain skill. She can piss Tommy off without trying."

"Oh this brings back so many memories." Thelma sighed but I didn't get the chance to hear anything more before I was dragged from the room and across the hall.

Shoved into a small bathroom, Tommy locked the door.

"Did you think that was funny?" He glared at me with such burning intensity that I nearly withdrew my satisfied grin.

"I thought it was hilarious."

His hand flew up, wrapping around my throat and I gasped at the sudden contact. Forcing me back against the cabinet he applied more pressure, cutting off my airways.

"Did you really think I would let you get away with it? That, because we were in front of everyone, I wouldn't react?"

I couldn't answer, the pressure on my throat was taking away my ability to talk back to him. He watched me for a moment, unable to breath but not struggling. He could kill me there and then and I wouldn't be able to stop him. Rage but also desire was etched over his perfect face, and it was all for me.

Just when black spots started to cloud my vision and I thought I might pass out, his grip loosened, and I sucked in a much wanted breath only to have it taken away again by his mouth covering my own. His lips bruised mine, domineering every part of our kiss. But it was fleeting.

Once he pulled back, I was panting. His eyes glowed, sparking electricity throughout my body.

"Get on your knees."

I gulped at the darkness in his order, but did I was told. I kneeled on the cold tiled floor, waiting for his next instruction.

"Take out my cock."

I reached up and undid the zip. He was still hard from my teasing. I pulled him free from the confines of his boxers. He was a lot bigger than I thought and my eyes bulged at the sight before me. He could truly tear me apart if he wanted to and I would let him. My stomach clenched at the thought as my clit pulsated.

But this wasn't about me right now. This was about him, and I was going to enjoy showing him what I had to offer. I licked my lips in anticipation as saliva built in my mouth.

Without the need of any prompting or instruction, I grasped the base of his shaft and brought it to my lips. My tongue ran over the thick vein right to his tip, eliciting a hiss of approval. Gazing up at him through my lashes, his face was a picture. His jaw was clenched, trying to keep the control I wanted to destroy but his eyes burned with want and need.

I ran the point of my tongue over the tiny slit, tasting the salty precum. Popping him into my mouth, I sucked hard at just the tip as my hand pumped the shaft. All the time, our eyes stayed connected.

I released him and he let out a frustrated growl. "Stop teasing me, Isabella."

Grinning up at him, I did exactly what he wanted. I took him in my mouth, letting him fill the space as far as I could while I pumped the base. Each stroke of my hand and mouth was bringing him closer to his climax and I went faster, sucking as hard as I could to get him there.

"Fuck baby."

His hand fisted the back of my hair, tangling it between his fingers as once again he took control. Thrusting forward, I let him take what he needed. Fucking my mouth with a force I could only imagine feeling so good somewhere else.

Tears streamed down my cheeks as he repeatedly hit the back of my throat and drool dribbled down my chin, but I remained being his fuck toy while he lost himself in me. And it was fucking amazing.

His eyes closed and his thrusts became more erratic. The grip on my hair tightened, pinching at my scalp. All of a sudden, his hips bucked forward one last time, forcing his cock to the back of my throat and that was where it stayed. His head fell back, and he let out a deep grunt. His cock twitched against my tongue as his hot come filled my mouth. Panting heavily, he opened his eyes and looked back down at me.

Tommy pulled out and I swallowed but not before a dribble of his climax fell over my lip. Bringing up my finger, I swiped it away then sucked it back off. His eyes lit up with approval and something else that I couldn't quite place. Adoration maybe? I had never seen it before.

Placing his hand on my cheek, he wiped away the tears with his thumb. "You're perfect." He shook his head like he couldn't believe it. "So fucking perfect."

Pulling me to my feet, he turned me around to face the mirror. Mascara streaked my cheeks, and my lips were swollen. My throat also hurt but I would happily go through it all again to have him.

"Look how beautiful you are after taking my cock like a good little whore."

I grinned as I looked into the reflection of his eyes. He gave me a sexy smile then shook his head again.

"Clean your face before anyone else sees you."

What would the others think? Did they assume we was arguing, or did they know what sort of sordid thing we were doing?

I ripped two tissues from the box and dampened them with water. Tommy put himself back into his trousers while I wiped the evidence from my face. Placing his hand gently on my hips, he placed gentle kisses to my neck. Each one sent a tingle through my centre. But his fiery gaze remained fixed on mine in the mirror.

"Soon, I'm going to fill every one of your holes with my cock."

I pushed my arse back, pressing it into his groin. His cock twitched against me, already prepared for more.

"I bet your wet right now aren't you, Isabella?"

I sucked in my bottom lip and twisted myself around in his arms. Not saying a word, I took his hand and guided it up my skirt. Letting his two fingers feel just how wet I really was, I fought to keep control. With his hand there, I wanted nothing more than for him to release the pressure. Once I was happy that he got the picture, I pulled them back out and popped them in my mouth, sucking off my arousal.

His pupils almost swallowed the blue I loved so much. Before he could stop me, I dropped his hand, opened the door and wiggled my fingers in farewell. He stood there speechless for all of three seconds but that gave me enough time to cross the floor and meet with Maddy who had just walked out the dining room. .

Grabbing her hand, I pulled her towards the stairs. "Show me where my room is please."

She frowned at me but when she looked over my shoulder her confused expression turned to an understanding grin. I followed her gaze to see Tommy leaning against the doorframe, arms crossed with a dark but amused smirk on his face. His hair was slightly mused like he had just ran his fingers through it and my heart skipped several beats. He was so fucking hot.

"Maddy's sleeping in my room tonight. So I don't feel so lonely in this big house."

He raised a brow but didn't argue. Not giving him a second to rethink, I tugged Maddy, urging her to take me to my room and hopefully stay with me. I wanted him. Fuck, I wanted every part of him. And I desperately wanted him to fuck me but not tonight. Not while I was still confused about what was going on between us. Not while I still hated him.

Chapter 21

5.45 am and I had been awake for too long. Maddy was breathing heavily beside me, but she wasn't the reason I was awake. I had woken up from a nightmare. One I hadn't had for a very long time.

I'm fighting the men that killed my brother and mother but as I'm stabbing them, they become people I know. Tommy, my father and my brother. Before it would be my mother too but now it was Tommy. After waking up in a cold sweat, I wasn't able to get back to sleep but laid there trying in vain.

Creeping from out of the thick cover, I tiptoed across the plush carpet to the door. I wasn't about to snoop around their home, but I was desperate for a drink. Opening the door, I went to step out but something on the floor caught my eye. A single burgundy rose. Picking it up, I closed the door softly behind me.

The kitchen light was on when I arrived, and I heard the gentle noise of tins hitting against each other before I stepped in. Thelma was standing by the countertop with her back towards me. She was spooning batter into a muffin tin. At the sound of my bare feet padding on the tiled floor, she turned her head.

"Sorry," I whispered, walking further into the room so it didn't seem like I was spying. "I didn't mean to disturb you. I just wanted a glass of water."

"Don't be silly. You're not disturbing me. I haven't seen anyone up this early in a long time." She smiled warmly then gestured for me to come closer. "Blueberry muffins. They are my grandson's favourite."

"Callum's?"

"All four."

I had never seen Tommy eat anything sweet like that before and somehow that gave me a bit of joy. Thelma's eyes squinted at the rose that was still in my hand.

"Burgundy." She smiled, then moved across the room with a speed that shocked me for an elderly lady. I watched her disappear for a second and when she returned, she had a small thin vase in her hand. The perfect size for my rose. Filling it with a bit of water, she passed it to me.

"Thank you."

"Is this your first rose?"

"Third."

"Really." She raised a brow, but her thin lips gave me the same amused smirk her grandson did. "Is it always just the one?"

"Yes, but the other two were different colours. Blue and orange."

"Roses mean a great deal." She touched the delicate petals as I put it down between us. "Each colour has a different meaning."

"Maddy did tell me. Blue means unattainable and orange means fascination." I wasn't sure what burgundy meant.

"And my grandson gave you them." It wasn't a question, more of a conformation for herself and she seemed happy about it.

"I'm not sure. I thought the first two were from Callum but now I don't know."

Thelma smiled like she already knew then returned to

spooning the batter. "I'm not going to bore you with every meaning of every colour but what you have there is something deeper than fascination. Tommy is very much like my late husband. Frankie courted me with roses. Each colour was a step closer to telling me his true feelings when he couldn't say the words himself."

She moved the tray to the oven, taking out another filled with cupcakes.

"So Tommy is trying to tell me that I'm fascinating but also unattainable because he has claimed me?" I asked, helping her move the small cakes onto a cooling rack.

"You're forgetting the burgundy rose."

"What does that one mean?"

"A deep, longing passion." My cheeks burned as soon as she said it and she laughed. "Passion doesn't just mean sex Isabella."

"Oh god." I could feel the heat radiating off me with the embarrassment of having Tommy's grandmother talking about sex with me.

Thelma laughed again as she reached into the cupboard to get the ingredients she needed for the frosting. "The number of roses you receive also have a certain meaning."

"The number? Surely this all gets confusing."

"Of course it does. Frankie had a truly evil side of him, but he was also a hopeless romantic that couldn't express the way he felt. I was left to decipher each rose, each meaning. But it was something so special to us that it was passed down to our four sons and now our grandchildren."

"Maddy mentioned something about a black rose. That one doesn't sound too romantic?" The thought of her husband sending her one of them seemed strange, but I still had to ask.

"Ah yes. The dreaded black rose." She rolled her eyes then started work on mixing the butter with the icing sugar. I waited patiently for her to continue. "Pink or lavender?"

"Huh?"

"The frosting colour, dear."

"Oh." The question took me by surprise. "Uhm, lavender?"

"Perfect. With a white viola decoration." Pointing at one of the cupboards, she wiggled her finger for me to get the items.

I quickly rummaged around while she finally continued. "My boy Thomas was the one to start the black rose. After my darling daughter in law passed away, my son lost a little part of his soul. The person who had been responsible was dealt with soon after and then laid on a bed of black roses. Now if Thomas wants someone dead, he will send them a single black rose to let them know he is coming. Fear makes someone act erratically and that is what the rose causes. He had lost his soulmate and part of his world. Tommy had lost his mother. And because of that, people fear just how far they will both go once they see the flower of death. "

"I'm sorry he had to go through that." I put the items she wanted in front of her. "I'm sorry you all had to go through that."

Thelma graced me with a sad smile, telling me she knew I meant it and it wasn't just a throw away statement.

"Did you know that Tommy's mother was claimed?"

"I did. Tommy told me while trying to explain the stupid rules to me."

Thelma laughed. "Yes, the rules are pretty silly when it comes to claiming something you want and not just need." I frowned at that. Something you want and not just need. "I was the first claimed one."

My mouth hung open as I took in what she said then quickly closed it again. "I thought Tommy's mum was. I didn't realise that you all attended the school."

"No. Frankie went to Ravenwood Academy, but I didn't. I lived in the town close by. I had a part time job working behind the bar of his favourite pub. At the time, I didn't know who he was related to. He came in with his friends every night I was at work, trying to establish a name for himself. I knew he attended a different school to me, and I knew he was dangerous, but just between us girls, that's what made me want him more."

She gave me a little wink and I chuckled. "His courtship started with roses. Every evening after I finished my shift, there would be a rose waiting for me. A single rose. And each night would be a different colour. I didn't understand what any of them meant and he didn't tell me. So I went to the library and found a book that explained it all.

I was floored by the very thought that the man who carried a gun in his coat pocket had such a softer side. But only for me. It was only ever for me."

Her sad smile formed a lump in my throat. They must have loved each other so much.

"But I was afraid. I had heard rumours of the school he attended. I had heard stories of the kind of man he was. I rejected every advancement that he made. And then instead of giving up, he made it known to everyone that he had claimed me as his."

"I bet that made it difficult for you to have any other relationships?"

"It made me angry but in truth, I didn't want anyone else." Just like I didn't want anyone else. I just wanted the freedom to make my own choice. "Frankie was the one I had fallen for and he had fallen for me. We had each other's heart."

I sighed softly. "That sounds perfect"

"We had our ups and downs. There were the rules he expected me to follow as a claimed one."

"And did you?"

"My Frankie was the first one to come up with the rules for a girl. Obviously because I was the first. They were simple. I had to marry him. I had to provide him with an heir, and I had to play the doting wife." My face must have said it all because she chuckled and nudged my arm. "Times were different back then dear. And our world is completely different to the one you have been brought up in. He looked after me. I was untouchable. And he taught me many things.

I learnt my love for poisons from him."

Her wicked grin reminded me of Tommy's, and I chuckled. "Romance at its finest." I joked and she laughed too.

"When he proposed to me, he did it with 108 red roses. All laid around our home. Our house was a lot smaller than this one at the time so I could hardly move in our little living area."

"That's really cute." I smiled

"One day, after around 7 months of being together, I came home from my first midwife appointment to 365 red, pink and orange roses. One for every day he had loved me. When I argued that we had not been together that long he simply said that he loved me the moment he saw me and that was a year ago to that day."

My smile was bittersweet while my heart tightened with a pain I hadn't felt for a long time. A feeling of loss. The romance she had experienced was something I would never have.

"I don't think Tommy has claimed me for the same reasons Frankie claimed you. His rules are quite…" I paused, thinking of a way to say exactly how he had told me the rules without actually saying it. "…unnecessary."

Thelma gave a little laugh and started filling two piping bags with the thick lavender frosting. "Tommy claimed you because of the fight you have in you, dear. He likes that you bite back even if doesn't show it at times. Just like his mother did with his father."

"He has no interest in being with me though. He told me that he didn't want me."

She stopped what she was doing to look at me. "Would you have fell into his arms if he told you he wanted you from the start?"

"No."

"Men say things they don't mean to protect themselves from rejection."

I rolled my eyes. Tommy wasn't afraid of being rejected

by me. Apart from how physical we had been the last couple of days, he had given me no other reason to believe that he wanted me in any other way than to control me for his own fun. There was no love or romance there like there had been for Thelma and Frankie. Possibly even his mum and dad. The roses were an insult to the memory of his grandfather.

Anger and misery swam in the pit of my stomach as tears pricked the back of my eyes. Without looking at Thelma in the fear the dam would break, I brushed the petals of the rose.

"Do these really mean something to Tommy?"

"They mean more than you realise."

I felt the silkiness of the burgundy petal between my thumb and index finger. A single rose, like the others. This one meaning a deep passion.

"What does a single rose mean?"

Thelma smiled caringly as she took my hand from the rose and covered it with hers. "I think you might find out for yourself soon enough."

"Find out what?"

My head whipped around just in time to see Tommy walking through the open door. His hair was dishevelled like he had come down straight from waking up. Grey sweatpants hung on his hips and the sleeves of his black hoody were pushed up to his elbows. My stomach flipped at how hot he looked but I quickly faced Thelma again who was grinning now.

"Girl talk." She simply said.

Tommy wrapped his arm around his nan's shoulder and kissed the top of her head. "It's 6.30. Why are you baking?"

"Blueberry muffins for my boys."

He raised his brows and removed his arm from her shoulder. "Where?"

I chuckled at the eagerness in his voice as he searched the counter tops for the sweet treat.

"Always so impatient." Pushing him out of her way she reached for the oven gloves.

He backed away giving her the space she needed to get the tray from the oven. "When it comes to your muffins nan, I don't have time for patience."

The delicious smell filled the kitchen as she pulled the tray out, making my mouth salivate. Tommy reached out straight away to grab one, but Thelma swatted his hand away.

"Silly boy. Do you want to burn yourself?"

I snorted softly, covering my mouth with my hand. Tommy threw me a side-glance and smirked.

Moving across the room, he flicked the kettle on. "What's with the other cakes."

"My book club has a meeting this evening and I wanted to bring something." She reached into another cupboard and pulled out a small jar of pink dried flowers. I recognised them instantly. Oleander.

"Aren't you putting violas on the cakes?"

"Oh yes dear," She smiled sweetly. "These are for the sweet tea I plan on serving."

I had so many questions but kept my mouth shut. Was she really going to poison her book club group?

"Who's pissed you off this time?"

"Sharron. That woman is such a slow reader and I want to move on to the next book."

My mouth dropped open. What a reason to kill someone.

Tommy moved back over to us, passing me a cup of tea and probably causing me just as much surprise as his nan had done. "Thank you."

He smiled, taking a sip from his freshly made coffee. "You're not going to be here tonight when the others arrive then nan?"

"No, and I actually have an appointment in a couple of hours. Bella dear, would you mind decorating these cupcakes for me?"

I spluttered slightly at my sip of tea then set it down on the side. "Oh sure."

"I'm sure Tommy won't mind helping."

Before he could protest, she had left the room, leaving us both alone. I picked up the cup again and cradled it in my hands like it was some sort of barrier between us. Why was I suddenly nervous? Probably because he was being nice. I could handle his possessiveness and his anger but Tommy being nice always threw me.

He set his drink down and picked up a piping bag. "I thought you didn't know how to cook?"

"This isn't cooking. It's baking." I followed his lead, picking up the other bag. "And I didn't bake them, your nan did." Swirling the frosting over the first little cake in perfect formation, I smiled to myself.

"Impressive." Swirling the icing on his own, it flopped to the side a little.

I cocked my head, trying not to laugh at his attempt. "Umm did you want to give it another go?"

"There's nothing wrong with it." He scoffed, shoving me slightly.

"Tommy, it's falling off the side." I watched as his mounting of frosting fell, hitting the marble counter.

Reaching across to scoop it off and start again, he caught my wrist.

He grabbed the cake with his other hand and held it up high. "It's fine."

"Tommy." I flicked some of the excess icing sugar at him and he chuckled, bringing it back down. Scooping off the access, I made him try again. "Go slowly and don't squeeze the bag too hard."

I placed my hand over his, attempting to guide him but the touch was too much. Still, as my heart thudded painfully in my chest, I moved his hand around, creating the perfect peak.

"Perfect." I breathed out, repeating the word he had called me the previous night.

Just as I was about to take my hand away, his fingers interlaced with my own, keeping them in place. "Do another with me."

I sighed, mainly annoyed that my breathing was becoming unsteady. He looped his arm over my head and came to stand behind me, giving him a better position to do the task. But even I knew there was an ulterior motive. With this position we were closer. Intimately closer doing something so innocent.

His body pressed harder against mine, but I ignored it and took another cake. "Something that Tommy isn't good at. Never thought I would see the day." I teased because it was easier than being nice or being silent.

"Even my skills have limits baby."

That fucking nickname. It was meant to be a joke to start with but every time he called me it, it made me want things that only he could give me.

With his hands covering mine, we decorated three more cakes. I took another but he moved his hand to my hips then wound it around my stomach, pulling me closer to his body. The embrace was different, more tender than what he usually dealt.

And it was probably the shock of it that made me spin around and squirt the frosting across his chest. He jumped back, looking down at the mess on his hoodie. I sucked in my breath, trying not to laugh but it was too late. He looked back up and saw the wide hilarity of my eyes.

"Oops" I choked out, still trying to stop my laughter.

"Ooh you're dead." If he had said it without the mischievous glint in his grin, I might have believed him. Not needing anymore encouragement, I ran around the kitchen island, trying to create a distance. Only then did I realise that he was on the side of the exit.

Laughing, I tried to run around again but he moved the same way. Picking up a decorated cupcake, he chucked it in my direction. I ducked down just in time for it to hit the wall behind me and watched it slowly slide to the floor.

"Your nan's going to kill you." I grinned, looking from the smeared frosting to his playful smile.

He shrugged, pulling a less than caring face. "I'll just blame you."

"Me." I threw my hand over my heart in mock disbelief. "She would never believe it was sweet, innocent me."

"Then she obviously doesn't know you that well." He launched himself over the island, taking me by surprise. I was too busy laughing to react, and he grabbed me, coating my t-shirt with the frosting on his hoodie.

"Ow, ow, oww." I cried out, clutching my side.

"Shit." Tommy hissed, loosening his grip around my waist. His eyes filled with panic as they scanned my body to where the cut was under my top.

I backed away shaking from silent laughter while he still stared at the area. His eyes rose, probably to judge how much pain I was in by the look on my face but on seeing my wide smile his eyes narrowed.

"You manipulative little-" Cutting himself off, he grabbed me again but gentler this time. "Does it even hurt?"

I shook my head, biting my lip to stop myself from laughing out loud. His grip was softened even more just like the mischievous look in his eyes. All the playfulness had melted away along with the worry for hurting me. Something else had replaced it. Something I wasn't used to seeing. A warmth. A protection. A lust.

His eyes glistened like all the darkness had faded as they gazed into mine. Raising his hand, he stroked across my cheek and ran his fingers through my hair until he rested it at the back of my head. His lips came closer and mine parted, ready to accept him.

"Why are you my only fear?" His husky voice was a whisper, ghosting my lips with every word.

"I didn't know you were scared of me." I breathed out, a little teasing to my voice but really my head was spinning. None of my thoughts were clear anymore. I wished I could still hate him, but he was making it very hard. Every little thing he was doing was leaving me confused. My body was trembling, and I knew that he felt it too.

He chuckled deeply, resting his forehead against my own. "Maybe I should start being clearer."

The door opened behind him, forcing him to turn to see who it was. I pushed myself back, creating a much needed space. The air was stifling between us, and I needed the room to breathe.

"What happened in here?" I peered round Tommy's sturdy frame to look at Callum who was still rubbing sleep from his eyes. When he lowered his hand, his eyes focused on me. "Didn't see you there, Bella."

"Nan made some muffins and there's fresh coffee in the pot." Tommy informed, ignoring his question.

"Blueberry?" Though he didn't need to ask as he was straight on them and taking a bite.

Making a move past Tommy, he grabbed my wrist, stopping me. "I'm going to get showered and see if Maddy's awake yet."

His eyes were fixed on mine. He wanted to say something, and he held on to my wrist while he found the words he needed. Callum had his back to us, still munching on the muffin in his hand while he poured himself some coffee.

"Stay with me tonight."

It wasn't a question but there was also a softness to the demand. I swallowed. "Ok."

He let go and I walked out of the room. What the hell did I just agree to? And what the hell was going on between us? We seemed to be slipping further and further from the enemy zone and I wasn't sure how that made me feel.

Chapter 30

Maddy and I looked at our reflections in her full-length mirrored wardrobe. She was right, she really did have the most spectacular bedroom. All the pastel colours and green foliage made the room appear fresh and light. We came up with a plan to decorate our room as soon as we got back to the school. Just so it represented us more.

We were both wearing dresses, and both were white. Mine was a lace, off the shoulder little number. My arms were covered by the lace sleeves, concealing the small cut that Callum had removed the dressing from earlier that day. You could see a tiny amount of cleavage, but it really wasn't too revealing. The A-line skirt hovered just above my knees, making it appear even more modest. A perfect dress to appear sweet and innocent because we didn't want the rival firm to know what a psycho bitch I really was. Those were Maddy's exact words when she picked it out for me. She also added that Tommy would probably want to tear it off the moment he saw it. Like a wolf devouring its lamb.

Her dress was much less modest. It had a metallic sheen that almost made the white appear silver. It hugged her figure perfectly, accentuating all her curves and rested mid-thigh.

There was a knock at the door but the person on the other side didn't wait for us to answer before they came walking in.

"Stunning." Callum proclaimed, eyeing me as he walked over to where we were standing.

Maddy pouted out her bottom lip. "What about me?"

"You look alright."

She rolled her eyes and hit his chest.

Tommy leant against the door frame, arms and ankles crossed. "You both look beautiful."

I felt the blood rush to my cheeks and quickly looked back at my refection to run my fingers through the coils of my hair.

"Thank you, cousin who I wished was my brother." Maddy smiled at him before shooting Callum a death stare. "So what's the plan?"

Tommy pushed himself to stand straight then walked further into the room. "Scott and Tyson will be here in roughly 20 minutes. The guest room has already been set up for them. Kane will be with them too." His eyes lingered on Callum for a second before resting on me.

I had no idea who these men were and no interest in them either.

"Why's Kane coming?" Maddy asked, a sudden wariness to her voice.

"I'm not sure." He answered, scratching the back of his neck making his bicep bulge in his white shirt. "But…"

"Don't you dare Tommy." She pointed her perfectly manicured finger at him, and he generally looked sorry with what he was about to ask. "Don't you dare."

"Maddy, you know we wouldn't ask if it wasn't important." Callum said.

"Fuck sake." She turned her back to him to look at Tommy again. "Kane isn't going to be distracted easily."

"We just need him out of the office while we talk. With him in there he will try his hardest to cause a scene and we can't afford a fight between us all. Not when we have other issues that we are dealing with."

"What issues?"

"The least you know the better Madz." Her brother interrupted.

Maddy scoffed. "Fine but you both owe me some answers."

"I'd like some too. Who is Kane and why is Maddy so against us distracting him?" I asked, frowning between the three of them.

"Kane is Scott's older brother." She started to explain. "Scott took over the firm from up north when his dad was killed in a drive by shooting. Kane has always blamed Tommy for it but there was no proof."

"Was it you?" My eyes fell on Tommy, and he shook his head. If he said it wasn't him then it wasn't. I believed him. "Why did Scott take over and not Kane?"

"Because Kane's too irrational. It was in their fathers will that Scott would inherit everything, but Kane wasn't too bothered anyway. He was more interested in the drugs and killing side of working this type of business, not the actual work part of it." I nodded at Callum's explanation like I understood. "Scott provides all the killing and drugs he needs to keep him in line."

"So our job is to distract a bigger psycho than you two?" I asked, grinning.

"Should the fact you are smiling about this worry me?" Tommy came to stand in front of me. I could still see the wariness in his eyes, but his smile was soft as he lifted my chin to study the emotions on my face. But I wasn't worried.

"I'm pretty sure between the two of us, Maddy and I can handle him. I've managed to handle you pretty well."

A dark playfulness flashed across his face before it blanked again. "He's dangerous and unpredictable."

"Sounds like fun." I grinned again, showing I really wasn't afraid.

Tommy clicked the fingers of his other hand. "Out."

"This is my room." Maddy argued but Tommy shut her down with one look. She followed Callum out silently, closing the door behind her.

"Isabella-"

"Tommy, I'm a distraction." Stepping back, his hand fell from my chin back to his side. I turned to face the mirror again. "Maddy and I will talk to him, take him for a walk around the grounds. We'll keep him away from you all while you speak to the other two."

He watched in silence as I ran my hands down my dress, smoothing out imaginary creases. Then I pulled on the soft material, revealing a little more cleavage.

"I'm pretty sure a little flirting will keep him distracted enough." I smiled a little slyly at him in the reflection.

His face instantly darkened, and I had to avert my gaze to stop it from burning me. "You are not to seduce him in any way, shape or form." His hand went into the pocket of his navy slacks and brought out a small box. "You so much as bat an eyelash at him and there will be consequences Isabella."

Tommy opened the box, but I couldn't see what was inside. He came to stand directly behind me, the heat of his body warming my back. Moving my hair to the side, he placed something around my neck, and I flinched slightly at the coldness of it. My hand reached up to touch the delicate necklace. The white gold chain was thin and light. A heart pendant rested just above my breasts. In the centre was a rose gold rose. There was nothing over the top, it was small, understated, yet the most beautiful and dare I say romantic thing I had ever been given. The simple necklace was exactly what I liked.

After he did up the clasp, he let my hair fall down my back again. I touched the dainty heart as his hands ran down my shoulders. "What's this for?"

"Do I need a reason?"

"Thank you."

Even though I loved it and coming from anyone else it

would have been a loving gesture, coming from Tommy I couldn't help but feel there was an alternative motive. I turned slowly and looked at him through my long, dark lashes. Parting my lips slightly to say something, he caught my chin again and pressed his thumb against them to stop me.

"You are mine Isabella. No one is ever going to get the pleasure your mouth brings again so do not flirt with him."

My eyes narrowed at the passion in his. "I had a moment of weakness when I agreed to be yours yesterday. And I feel disappointed that you thought I was going to bow to you so easily."

"You didn't have a problem getting to your knees last night."

"And I look forward to you being on yours." I smiled sweetly at him. A challenge flashed in those midnight blue eyes.

"Don't flirt with him to get a reaction out of me because you won't like what you see."

It's like he knew me too well. And I wanted to, just to see how he would react, but I also didn't. Kane was dangerous so they said and so was Tommy. To flirt with him wasn't going to be like playground games. I was playing with the big boys now and there were certain things that even I knew not to push to its limits.

"I promise to behave and be your good girl for just tonight."

Tommy tipped my chin back and softly kissed my lips, stealing the gasp that he had caused by the tender act. "Does that promise extend to when we are alone."

Regaining myself quickly, I took a step away to create a distance. "Don't get your hopes up."

I walked from the room, fiddling with the small pendant around my neck. My hands were clammy, and my heart was banging against my ribs. I hated this. I hated him. I just had to keep reminding myself. All his tender moments, the roses, the necklace. It wasn't real, just another part of his game to keep me in line.

I could give him the attitude; I could also give as good as he gave with the toying, but it was all starting to feel like it wasn't fake. The jealousy I felt when he was with Sindy wasn't fake. The feelings I got when he touched me weren't fake. Because the longer this was going on, the less I hated him and that was more dangerous. Loving him was going to be more dangerous than anything I had ever done. Him loving me was going to end up killing us both.

But this wasn't real. He didn't love me, and I didn't love him. We had fallen in love with the challenge of each other.

I walked along the path with my arm linked through Kane's. Maddy was on his other side, chatting back and forth with him about the current issue of women not bowing to the superiority of men anymore. We both wanted to argue back but after seeing he was packing two guns; we kept our mouths shut.

Not that I actually had any right to argue when the man who was trying to control me was the only man I actually wanted. Something about Tommy's control was different though. Or maybe that's what I just kept telling myself to now justify it. I needed a good slap. One fucking orgasm from him and he was starting to change me. Every time I thought about him, I was contradicting myself. I hated it. I hated him. Prick.

Yet my fingers played with the small chain around my neck and a smile crept to my lips.

"So Kane, I feel like it's been way too long since your last visit." Maddy flirted, leading us both towards the fountain in a smaller rose garden.

"Would have been longer but when we heard about Charlie, Scott wanted to pay a little visit."

I had learnt from Maddy that Charlie was an errand boy. He wasn't much older than us when he had been shot. He had been shot on their turf. Because of this Scott had felt the need to reassure Thomas that it wasn't their firm that had done it. Kane was already mad at Thomas for trying to sell in their city and on top of the pointing the finger at Tommy for his father's death, if he was the boss, tonight's meeting would have been a blood bath. But Scott was the boss, and he didn't want any confrontation between them all.

"That was very kind of you for coming all this way when a condolence card would have sufficed." I heard the groan from Maddy, but I hadn't meant it in a sarcastic way. Maybe the annoyance of my mixed feelings towards Tommy were coming out in my attitude.

Kane let out a low dark chuckle that would rival Tommy's. "But being here in person is much more personal."

"Well we appreciate that you have made the journey." Maddy smiled at him.

"And I appreciate the company of two lovely ladies." He pulled his arms from ours and faced us both with a crooked smile. He wasn't bad looking. Around the same hight as Tommy. Strawberry blonde hair and dark eyes. Where Tommy had a controlled look about him, Kane looked unhinged. "Even if you both are meant to be a distraction."

"We-, W- What?" Maddy stuttered looking between us both with sheer horror on her face.

I merely smiled at the man in front of me. He wasn't dumb. "How did we do?" There was no point in pretending.

"Even if I didn't already know Tommy's game, I wouldn't have been impressed. Agreeing with everything I said about women being lesser than a male just to appease me. I expected more from the Kray women."

Maddy shuffled on her feet, her nerves getting the better of her. She opened her mouth muttering softly. "Tommy isn't playing any game"

"Then why are you both here." Neither of us had an

answer for that. "I'm actually more interested why Tommy's new plaything is allowed to be out here on her own."

"Plaything?"

"Are you not his new toy?"

My eyes blazed as I narrowed them at him. "I'm not his toy."

Another dark chuckle followed my protest and he reached forward to move the curls from my chest and sweep them behind me. Maddy grabbed my wrist, but I stood my ground. He may have two guns, but I wasn't afraid. If anything, I could feel the anger igniting the confidence I needed.

Kane's fingers glided down my collar bone before picking up the small heart and grinning down at it. "This tells me a different story to what you are denying. Does he share you with everyone, or am I just that lucky?"

I stepped back, making the necklace fall back against my skin. "Tommy doesn't have a say who touches me and who doesn't because I don't mean anything to him." Lies. I hated to admit it, but Tommy had a say in everything, and he would never let anyone else touch me. But I didn't want Kane knowing this. He could use that knowledge against Tommy. "I'm a friend of Maddy's and that is the only reason why I was invited here. The necklace was a gift from her."

Maddy was nodding beside me but a little too enthusiastically, a sure sign that everything I had said had been utter bullshit.

Kane pulled out his gun, pointing it at my forehead. Blood rushed through my ears and my stomach knotted completely but my face remained hard. I hid my fear and anger from him, not giving him what he wanted.

Maddy squeaked beside me but didn't move. Any rash decision could see me dead, and we knew better to not make that mistake.

"I'm feeling a little parched Madeline. Can you go get Isabella and I a drink?" Maddy still didn't move. I could see the panic in her eyes as she looked between us both. Kane's lips curled back, and he flashed her a sinister smile while pressing the barrel of the gun harder against me. "If you don't go back to the house and leave Isabella and me alone, I will put a bullet in her head. It would be a shame to ruin this lovely white dress."

She looked at me again and I finally tore my glare away from him to nod my head at her. She gulped back any words she wanted to say and made to run back to the manor.

"Oh, and Maddy." The tapping of her heels against the stone path stopped. "Not a word to Tommy. If I see him at all, I will shoot her." Her fast steps continued.

Once he was sure that she couldn't see us any longer, Kane lowered his gun. "It's all fun and games until someone gets hurt." He placed it back in the waistband of his suit trousers. "Isn't that how the saying goes?"

"We have a very different view of what fun and games are." I breathed out slowly, relieved that the gun was now gone but equally still pissed off and terrified that I was now alone with this maniac. Give me Darren Biggs any day over this mess.

"Do you think she will tell Tommy that I just stuck a gun to his girl's head?" He chuckled like it was some big joke to him.

I shook my head. "No, she won't say anything."

"Shame. I would have liked to see his face." He stepped into my space. "There is no point lying to me. I know you're his." Running his finger along my cheek, he stopped at my jaw. "I could kill you right now for what he did to my father."

My body was trembling. I tried not to show fear, but he could probably already smell it. Even if Maddy was going to tell Tommy, he wouldn't get here in time and Kane was probably quicker. All he had to do was reach behind him for his gun as soon as he saw Tommy and I would be dead.

There was nothing I could do right now. Kane had the upper hand. I had no weapon, nowhere to run and no one to help. So much for the fucking training at that school. Shit load of good it was doing me right now.

"I'm only playing with you love." He tilted my chin up. "I don't have to kill you to ruin Tommy's life." His mouth invaded mine so quickly that I stood in shock for a couple of seconds, letting him kiss me.

Recovering from the shock, I pushed him with as much force as I could. All contact left me as he stumbled back. Losing his footing, he tripped on the low wall of the fountain, falling back into the water. He was going to kill me for this, there was no doubt that the lunatic wouldn't let me get away with that. And if he didn't kill me, Tommy definitely would before I would get the chance to explain.

To my surprise, Kane laughed. Not a low dark chuckle that sent unnerving chills through me but a full bellied laugh.

"You have guts. I like that." He held out his hand for me to help him out. I drowned at it, he smiled. "Truce."

Sighing, I reached out to pull him back up. He could have easily shot me, but he didn't. And if I turned to leave, he could still shoot me.

Before I could pull him to his feet though, he took hold of my hand with his other too and pulled me on to him. I hit into him then the icy water, soaking myself. My only saving grace was that although all my body was soaked, my face was dry.

"The fuck Kane." I screamed out and hit him in the chest without thinking.

"You're fun. I might keep you for myself."

I huffed an insult at him, making him laugh louder as I pulled myself from the fountain and started walking back towards the manor. He followed me, shoes squelching under him.

Ignoring his attempts at conversation, I threw open the front door. Cursing at who was already in the entrance hall, I stilled myself in the hopes that they wouldn't see me. Tommy was already there with Callum, Archie, Felix and his father. Maddy was in front of Tommy and by the way she was deathly pale, and Tommy was looking like he might slice someone's throat, the conversation that I had just walked in to wasn't good.

Scott and Tyson were also standing with them. Scott was considerably smaller than Kane, which surprised me as they were brothers, but they had the same strawberry blonde hair. Tyson was taller and stockier. He looked as mean as Kane but when he had spoken to me earlier, his voice and smile were a lot softer. He had the same strawberry blonde hair but his was because of a very bad bleach job.

I turned back round to push Kane out of view, but it was too late. Tommy cleared his throat and I stopped what I was doing. Turning slowly to face him, he stuck up two fingers and signalled for me to come forward. Sighing out a heavy breath, I did as he expected and walked to the centre of the room. Kane followed me with a shit eating grin plastered across his smug face.

I caught eyes with Maddy. For a second, she looked relieved but then dread replaced that feeling. She slowly backed away from Tommy and I couldn't say I blamed her. I wanted to back away from the murderous glare in his eyes too.

"What happened?" His voice was eerily calm. The voice that made the tiny hairs on the back of my neck stand in fear.

I opened my mouth to answer but Kane spoke over me. "We were just having a bit of fun, wasn't we darlin. She's a firecracker this one."

His arm landed over my shoulder, and I stiffened. My eyes didn't leave Tommy's and I watched as what little patience he had evaporated in the heat of his fury.

"What happened?" He gritted out through his clenched teeth.

"She wanted to see how wet I would get her." Kane laughed, "I don't think I disappointed did I."

I tore myself away from him, "Seriously?!?" He wanted

to make it look like I wanted this, that I was playing with him.

"She threw herself at me." His wicked grin made his face uglier. "We both fell into the fountain because she couldn't keep her hands off me."

"I'm not going to be able to keep my hands off your throat in a minute."

Everyone else around us was quiet, listening and watching what was being said between us both.

"You might want to keep your bitch on a leash Tommy. Throwing herself at men just makes her appear desperate."

If I didn't know he had two guns behind him, I would have launched myself at the bastard. But I didn't want a shootout, I didn't want any of my own getting hurt. Instead I said something that I should have known would cause trouble.

"Throwing myself at you? You held a gun to my head then you kissed me."

A single shot was fired. Ringing filled my ears and a warm wetness sprayed across my face and dress. Kane's cocky smile slowly dropped as his eyes glazed over before he dropped to the floor.

Chapter 31

Everything else after that happened so fast. I was wretched back out of the way and shoved behind Archie. Callum had put himself in front of his little sister, shielding her from danger. Everyone had pulled out their weapons apart from Tommy whose gun was already out and was now pointed at Scott. Scott's gun wasn't on Tommy though. It was pointed at Archie. And that's when I understood what was happening. Archie was putting himself between me and the bullet.

When Tommy spoke, there was a smoothness to his voice but the iciness in his dark eyes showed the danger that Scott and Tyson were now in. "Your brother made a mistake of underestimating me. Do not make that same mistake."

"You killed him." Scott's glare bounced between me and Tommy. "All because this whore couldn't keep her legs closed."

I would have said something, but I was smart enough not to open my mouth at that point. I didn't open my legs; I didn't even kiss him back. Idiot.

Tommy's eyes flared and his fingers twitched on the

trigger, but it was Felix who spoke, and his gun switched from Tyson to Scott. "Be very careful how you speak about our Isabella. She's a lot of things but a whore she isn't."

Scott scanned the room. He wasn't stupid. He was outnumbered and his gun was pointing at the wrong person. Even if he shot Archie to get to me, Tommy would kill him in seconds.

"You're not the boss here Tommy. You deserve a bullet between the eyes for what you just did." Scott snarled, but still slowly lowered his gun.

Thomas stepped forward. "He may not be the boss but I am. And your brother crossed the line by assaulting my son's lady. You know we wouldn't have let that lie once we found out. And we would have found out. You can either walk out of here alive or you can try your luck with a shot at her."

Scott's hand was now completely parallel with his side. Tyson had dropped his too, making the others lower theirs. Without another word, Scott stormed out the front door, leaving Tyson to drag Kane's body behind him, streaking his blood across the tiled flooring. We all watched, not saying a word until the door had closed.

I tried to meet Tommy's eye, but he was glaring at the pool of blood where the body had been. His jaw was clenched and lips tight. A crazed rage danced about his irises, scaring me enough to not say a word.

"Isabella." Archie moved to the side, and I looked at Thomas. "I suggest you go to your room and clean yourself up." The order was soft and soothing considering everything that had just happened.

I nodded, rushing past my human shield and to the stairs. Without turning to see what the others were doing; I ran to my room. I needed to wash Kane's blood from me, and I needed to wrap my head around what had just happened.

Slamming the door shut behind me, I turned when I didn't hear the bang. Tommy was in the doorway. I hadn't even heard him following me.

Smashing the door shut, he stalked towards me menacingly. "I told you not to flirt with him."

"Are you serious right now?" He stopped inches away from my face. He didn't let up. He was angry and in his mind, it was my fault.

"You did something to make him kiss you. You did it to piss me off."

"Why the fuck would I do that Tommy?" I was almost shouting. Tears were pricking the backs of my eyes, making them sting but I didn't allow for them to fall. He really thought that I had just done this to get one over on him. After everything.

"You like to do it don't you, you like to test my patience. It's what you fucking do. You can't just do as you are told. You always have to fight what I say." His hand flew up to my neck, squeezing tightly. Spinning me around, he thrust me against the door. "Why?"

"I didn't do anything Tommy. He held a gun to my head and made Maddy leave us. If not, he was going to shoot me."

He pulled me away from the door then hit me against it again, his eyes still burned into mine. I gasped as my head hit the wood. "What happened when she left?"

"He told me there were more ways to hurt you other than killing me and that's when he kissed me." His grip loosened and I glared at him. Bringing my hands up, I pushed him away just like I had done Kane. "So once again, I'm dealing with shit because of you."

Tommy growled in frustration as he took a step back, releasing me. "But you both decided to have a little swim." His hand gestured to my white lace dress, still soaked and splattered with blood.

"He tripped and fell." I shrugged. "Then he dragged me in with him."

"You're lying."

"I've never lied to you." His words hurt because after

everything that had happened between us, apart from keeping certain feelings for him secret, I hadn't lied to him. "Why the fuck am I explaining myself to you anyway. I've told you the truth. He kissed me to piss you off. When I pushed him, he fell into the fountain. I tried to help him back out thinking you would be mad even though I was actually defending myself and he pulled me down with him." My hand ran over where Tommy's hand had been around my throat, where I could still feel the ghost of his fingers. "That is the truth. Whatever other thoughts you have running through your head are wrong. I wouldn't flirt with him to piss you off, not now. And I definitely wouldn't allow for him to touch me when there is only one person I want to do that."

His eyes snapped back to mine, and I quickly shut my mouth at my confession.

Turning his back to me, he ran his fingers through his dark hair. "Bringing you here was a mistake. I made a mistake."

My heart dropped. He turned to look at me again, face completely blank of all emotion.

"Pack your shit up. You're going back to Ravenwood."

"Fine." I pushed past him and grabbed my suitcase under the bed. "I didn't want to come here anyway." Flinging it open, I reached into the bedside drawer, chucking my underwear into it. "Or are you forgetting, I didn't have a choice."

He didn't answer me, he just watched what I was doing.

"Fuck I hate you. I hate you so much."

Still no reaction as he stood there, arms crossed, no emotion at all.

I slammed the suitcase shut even though I hadn't finished packing. "What do you want from me Tommy?"

We stared at each other. My breathing ragged through all the mixed emotions I was feeling and his, as stoic as ever.

"I want you to wash his blood of your body before we leave."

He opened the door and walked out, slamming it behind him. I let out a shaky breath as the tears fell down my face. I wasn't angry or upset about going back to the school. That didn't bother me, and I wanted to be with Jack and Daisy. They made me happy.

What did upset me was Tommy's blame. It was like what I was saying didn't register in his head. He was the one that wanted Maddy and me to keep Kane busy and then when he overreacted by shooting him, (and yes, it was an overreaction.) Tommy was angry at me for it.

Screaming in frustration, I emptied the closet, chucking everything haphazardly into the case and just leaving out a silk night dress that I would wear in the car. Inappropriate for the journey back? Of course. But by the time we get back to the school, it would be late, and I could go straight to bed. And maybe a part of me wanted some sort of reaction from the prick.

I stood in the shower, washing away the blood and the tears that continued to fall. What did he want from me? One minute he wanted me and the next he's dismissing me like I can just be tossed away. I shouldn't care. I didn't want this life any way. I wanted an easy one. But he drew me in. I needed to admit to myself that he made me fall.

But fuck him, I was ready to leave. I was ready to go back to the school and completely ignore them and get on with my life. Whatever was going on between us both was over.

I finished showering and dried myself quickly. Slipping on the night gown and underwear, I threw Tommy's navy hoodie over top that I still had from the meeting where he had declared this little visit. I ran the brush through my towel dried hair then left the room, looking for the idiot.

"He's in the office." I spun round. Callum was leaning against his bedroom door. His eyes wondered up my bare legs to the hoodie. "He's also not in the best of moods."

"When is he ever?" I rolled my eyes and turned back in the direction I was going to find this office.

"Bella, bringing you here wasn't a mistake. He didn't mean that."

I stopped again. "You heard it all?"

His footsteps sounded down the hall and stopped just behind me. "The only thing he regrets is putting you in danger." Placing his hands on the tops of my arms, he slowly rubbed them, trying to comfort me. "Speak to him." I moved out of his grip and carried on walking. "Downstairs. The room next to the living room."

I followed his directions, leading me to the room I needed. Hearing voices from inside though, I didn't go in. I also didn't want to eavesdrop, but I couldn't exactly turn back around. There were two people in there. Tommy was one of them and the other I was sure was his father.

"You made a reckless decision son. You retaliated without thinking because of a girl that you barely know."

"I know."

"You are meant to be taking over this firm but how do I know you are ready when you do things like this."

There was silence between them. Tommy sounded a lot calmer than what he had been in the bedroom even though it was clear that the conversation between them both was heated.

"You've started a civil war, Tommy. They are not going to let this lie even though he was in the wrong. They are going to retaliate and you have to be prepared for that."

"Would you have done the same if it was mum?"

There was another long silence filled by the sound of glass clinking against each other.

"Yes." The glass was placed back on a surface. "But I also wouldn't have allowed for your mother to leave my side."

"And that was another mistake I made."

A gruff grunt of agreement was the last thing I heard before the door opened and Thomas walked out. His eyes instantly fell on me and apart from the initial shock of me being there, he gave me a sad smile then walked on by, giving my shoulder a comforting squeeze on the way.

I tapped lightly on the door, even though it was already open, and I could see inside. Tommy was seated in the large, backed leather chair behind the mahogany desk. One hand was clutching a crystal glass filled with bourbon, the bottle on a small tray behind him. The other was wiping the tiredness from his face as I stepped into the room.

"I'm ready to leave." My voice was almost a whisper as saying it hurt more than I realised it would.

Tommy looked up. Closing his eyes, he sighed heavily. "Close the door."

I did as he told me.

Opening his eyes again, he pointed to the two chairs in front of the desk. "Take a seat."

So this was how it was going to be. I was going to receive a formal lecture in the seats that were used for business. Completely ignoring where he had told me to sit, I walked round the desk and pushed myself up on it, crossing my legs and folding my arms.

Tommy's lips tipped up slightly as he watched every move I made then gave a little shake of his head. Standing up, he reached for another glass from the tray. "Drink?"

"No, thank you."

As if ignoring each other was a thing, he poured out two knuckles worth then handed me the glass anyway. I took it and brought it to my lips, letting the rich alcohol wet them. It wasn't bad tasting, but I wasn't used to it. Licking the substance from my lips, I placed the glass back down.

Tommy sat back down in his seat, not taking his eyes off me. I wanted to see what he was feeling but I couldn't read him at all. He had masked his emotions so well.

"I'm sorry."

I was glad I had put the glass down because I was pretty sure I would have dropped it after hearing him say that. The worse bit, I wasn't even sure what he was apologising for. I wanted to ask but I couldn't quite find the words.

"I did make a mistake, but it wasn't bringing you here.

Fuck, I've made loads of mistakes these past couple of weeks." He looked away, running his fingers through his hair. His mask was starting to slip.

"Tommy?" I wanted him to continue after going quiet.

"Have you figured it out yet?" I frowned and he placed his glass beside mine. As he pulled his hand back, he rested it on my knee. "Why we took you that first night?"

"Because you were a bunch of pricks." I smiled lightly and a soft chuckle from him followed.

"That and because I wanted you." My heart thumped against my chest. "From the moment I saw you standing by my car I knew I wanted to play with you. Have you as my new little toy. I wasn't going to hurt you that night. The others didn't know it at the time, they knew I didn't want to hurt you, but they didn't know that I was going to claim you."

"But you let me go. You could have kept me there, but you moved out the way and let me run."

"I wanted to see if you would come back."

I arched a brow "And if I didn't?"

"I would have found you." A cocky smile tilted on his face, and I believed him.

Rolling my eyes, I asked another question, taking full advantage of his sudden honesty. "So why be a jerk the whole time. Why not just tell me that you wanted to use me?"

He frowned and I understood my mistake. What girl would agree to being someone's who they had just met.

"Would you really have given me the time of day, after what we did? Would you really have come to me willingly?" He paused but even though I didn't answer, he already knew. "Claiming you ensured that you were mine and it also got your attention again. Even if it did piss you off more, you were always going to be mine while at that school and it gave me time to actually get to know you better."

"You barely know me, Tommy." I sighed and his hand pulled on my knee, uncrossing my legs.

"I know that you secretly like my cousins, but you won't admit it because you're too proud after what we did to you."

That was true. I did like them. Being claimed had forced me to get to know them and even though they still had their moments, I liked certain things about each one.

"I know that one of your favourite smells is fresh coffee, but you hate the taste."

I smiled, sucking in my bottom lip and trapping it between my teeth. His hands ran further up my thighs.

"When you're sad or nervous, your heart races, your eyes sparkle and you voice goes quiet enough that I have to lean in to hear you."

"That happens to a lot of people."

"But it's only you that I see."

He stood up, pushing himself between my legs. Feeling for the hem of his hoodie, he pulled it up, over my body. I raised my arms making it easier for him and he dropped it to the floor.

Placing a warm kiss to the curve of my neck, flutters caressed my stomach. "The biggest mistake I made was not telling you how much I wanted you from the start. Not telling you that the moment I saw you, I lied to myself. Telling myself you were going to be a nice new plaything. Because I don't want that. I never truly wanted that." Another kiss placed, directly over the last. "I want you and I want everything that comes with you. I want your attitude. I want your smiles. I want your laughter. I want every sound that comes from your mouth. That was why I claimed you, because I want everything. My mistake was not admitting it to myself and waiting too long to admit it to you."

He looked up, his dark eyes finding mine.

"My mistake was not telling you that I fell the moment I saw you and I keep falling deeper and deeper the more you reveal yourself to me."

Chapter 32

My eyes searched his looking for the lie. There was nothing but truth in them. A warmth that was so rare, I wanted to pinch myself to make sure I was awake. Everything he was telling me was so unlike him. But he had never given me a chance to actually get to know who he really was. Was this a taste of what was possible? This was him? And if it was, I could bask in this feeling he was giving me for the rest of my life. I had been ready to leave, but he was pulling me back. Making me feel things that I didn't know was possible and I was loving it.

My throat grew thick and the drink beside me was looking really good. Heat was radiating throughout me, and I was thankful that he had already taken the hoodie off because I would have been sweating.

"I thought you hated me." He was right, when I was nervous my voice was nothing but a whisper.

"I've never hated you." He smirked, leaning his face into my neck again as one hand curved around my hip, pulling me closer to him and the other played with the spaghetti strap of my nightgown. "I hated the way you purposely tried to get a reaction out of me."

"You deserved all that." He bit down lightly, and I chuckled.

Kissing the same spot, I felt his smile against me. "You definitely impressed me. Not many would dare push me as far as you would."

"Don't think I will stop now." I teased as his hand ran up my thigh again.

"If you did, you wouldn't be the girl I fell for." More words that were just driving me over the edge. He bit down on my neck again and a tiny moan slipped from my lips. "I love that fucking sound."

His lips were on mine, taking what little breath I had left. Reaching between my arse and the desk, Tommy grabbed a good handful of flesh and roughly pulled me to the edge. I gasped into his mouth, feeling his hard cock straining against his slacks. He looped the thin fabric of my thong around his thumbs, pulling it down. I tried to adjust myself to help him, but he moved so quickly, my attempt wasn't needed.

"You lied to me earlier."

"What?" I pulled away, looking at him confused.

He grinned at me wickedly. "You told me you had never lied to me, but you have. A few times."

My head tilted to the side as I frowned at him. Just as I was about to ask what he meant, his fingers ran through my folds, grazing my already pulsing clit. My head lolled back with another moan exiting my mouth.

"You told me you hated me, but you lied."

"At one point I was telling you the truth." I lied more to myself than to him, and one finger slipped inside my entrance as his breathy laugh shivered through my core.

"The way your body reacts to me tells me different." He pulled out then pushed two fingers in. My eyes closed and I pressed my lips together, suppressing the whimper that was trying to escape.

Tommy pulled his hand away and my eyes snapped open. Glaring at him, he stood grinning playfully at me.

"Admit it."

"You're such an arsehole."

"But you don't hate me."

"But I should."

His eyes sparkled at my indirect confession. "You're right, you should."

Gripping hold of his tie, I pulled him closer and locked my lips with his. His hands gripped my hips as I made quick work of the buttons on his shirt then started on his belt.

Releasing him completely, he groaned against my mouth at my touch. The sound alone made my body ignite. Having his own body react the same way mine did was like a reward for every shitty thing we had tried to do to each other.

My hand circled around him, stroking back and forwards a couple of times. His lips left mine and he looked down at my racing heart. Moving my hands away from him, I placed them on the desk, steadying myself. He grabbed the base of his cock and pulled my arse further off the desk. Running the tip up and down my slit, he coated himself with my wetness.

"I've always used a condom, but I don't want to with you. I want to feel you."

I gulped back a cry as he slid the tip in. "I have the implant." I couldn't get pregnant, and I had only been with one other boy who I had been safe with the whole relationship.

"I wasn't asking." His wicked grin sent goosebumps down my spine and my body trembled in anticipation.

He eased in further, stretching me to the point of pain but the pleasure made it much more satisfying. He pulled out then pushed back in further as his hand came to the back of my head. Tangling his fingers in my hair, he ripped it back, giving him the access he wanted to my neck.

Crying out, I tensed around him, and he hissed in a breath. "Shit."

I let out a shaky breath. He pushed in, fully filling me then stilled for a moment, letting me adjust to the size of him. I moved my hips, urging him to move. I didn't care if I seemed impatient. I wanted him. I needed him.

"You feel so fucking good Isabella." Satisfied that I was ready, he started rolling his hips, slowly at first and I hummed in appreciation. "You need to be quiet, baby. As much as I want to hear your screams, I don't think my father would be too happy to hear what we are doing on his desk."

I chuckled lightly only to be cut off by a merciless thrust forward making me suck in a cry. Glaring up at him, he gave me his most handsome smile and repeated the motion. And again, and again. My eyes closed, trying my hardest not to make a sound as Tommy pounded into me hard and fast. With each unyielding thrust, he placed a delicate kiss to my neck as if it made up for the beating he was giving me. I wouldn't have cared either way. He had me and he could do whatever he wanted because my body was always going to want him.

I reached out to hold on to him for support, digging my nails into his shoulder. His feral growl against my neck only made my body tremble around him more. Placing his thumb on my already swollen clit, he began circling it, teasing it. Even the slightest touch was provoking my impending high and he felt it too. My body tensed and my back arched into him.

"Fuck, Tommy." I needed the release. I needed him to push my body harder. "Please."

He pressed his thumb against that sensitive spot firmer and every part of me came undone around him. My name slipped from his lips as I clenched down around him, pulsing involuntarily around his cock. He jerked his hips into me, shooting his load deep inside.

Tommy pulled out, leaving behind a feeling of emptiness and just as breathless as I was. There wasn't a smile on his face, or any joy at all at what we had just done. Instead there was something that I hadn't expected to see after just having sex. Panic. There was panic and uncertainty in his eyes that made my chest tighten with unease.

"Tell me you want me too."

"Tommy, I-" I stopped whatever I was going to say. His eyes searched my own and I realised it was the reassurance he needed. A vulnerability I had never seen before.

"I want you too."

Grabbing my face with both hands, he smashed his mouth onto mine. Whatever had just happened between us had crossed the line of what we were before. He had admitted what he felt and even though I hadn't said it when he did, I wanted him too. I wanted to get lost in this world that he lived in as long as he was with me because after the torment that we had put each other through, it was him I wanted more than anything.

"So needy." I joked once he finally released me.

"Only for you."

My heart skipped a beat again. "Am I going to see this side of you more often now?"

A deadly grin corrupted his face. "Depends how good you have been."

I swallowed. "Are you taking me back to the school now."

"No." His grin widened. "That was just the warmup Isabella. You told me you would stay with me tonight and I intend to make use of that time."

I breathed in deeply then jumped down from the desk. "Can I have my underwear." I held out my hand, not seeing them on the floor so guessed he must have put them somewhere else.

He let out a low, cruel chuckle. The kind I loved and made my clit pulse for attention. "You're going to walk to my room with my come dripping down your leg."

I looked at him horrified. "What if someone sees me."

"Then you better run." He sat back down in his seat, looking down at my legs and ran his finger over his savage smirk.

If looks could kill, I was pretty sure he would be dead by now. How could someone be so loving and tender moments before turning back to the complete arse they were best known for.

Cursing under my breath, I ran from the room and straight to his. I didn't pass anyone on the way, which was a huge relief seeing as his come, was in fact, running down my leg. Getting a cloth from his bathroom, I started to remove the evidence while looking around the room.

Tommy's room was like him. Dark but alluring. Three walls were a soft grey, each with different black framed arts. Double French doors led to a small balcony and just in front of that was a two-seater leather sofa. The back wall was painted black with the bed against it. It was of course bigger than the one I had been flung on a few times at the school.

I had just finished cleaning up when the door opened and closed again. "Did I give you permission to clean yourself?"

His shirt was buttoned up again, but his tie was off now. "Did I give you permission to take your tie off?"

He crossed the room, taking me in his arms then dropped me on his bed. Sliding himself between my legs, I giggled as he kissed my jaw. "You mean this tie?" Pulling it out of his pocket, he dangled it in front of my face.

Taking my hands, he held them above my head and slowly started to wrap his tie around my wrists. I bit my lip in excitement when he secured them to the headboard. He pulled on the restraints, testing the strength and I sucked in a breath as it pinched my skin in the best way possible. Once he was happy that I wasn't able to go anywhere, he climbed back off.

"What are you doing?"

Ignoring me, he walked across the room and opened up a drawer. From the position I was in, I couldn't see what he was doing but as he walked back over to the bed, he had another tie in one hand and a knife in the other. His beautiful yet sinful smile looked down at me as he moved on top of me again.

Wrapping the tie over my eyes, my vision was

completely taken away. "Tommy?"

"Do you trust me?" Something cold ran over my cheek making me flinch.

Chills ran across my body as he glided the knife over my jaw and down the curve of my neck. I arched my back, pushing my chest out towards him. He took the blade away.

"Listen to me carefully. If you move even in the slightest, this knife will cut you. I won't be moving it away again. Do you understand me?"

I nodded my head slowly, licking my dry lips.

"Do you trust me?" He asked again and I nodded. Maybe I shouldn't trust him, but I couldn't help it.

"Yes."

"Good, because this is going to hurt."

My chest rose and fell heavily against the cold metal as he slid it further down over the satin of my gown. I tried to focus so much on not moving but as his warm breath followed the blade, my body was shaking more and more.

"Do you know why I killed him?" His hand pushed up the fabric, revealing my stomach.

"Because you're a psycho."

His deep chuckle vibrated against my navel, making me tense under him. "Yes, but that's not why." Placing a soft kiss on my skin, he dragged the blade lower. "I killed him because he disrespected you. Because he threatened your life. Because he touched what was mine."

The flat side of the blade pressed against my clit, and I hissed in a breath. Not being able to see what he was doing was driving me insane. Mixed with the desire to have whatever he offered and the fear of what he was actually capable off, I was fast losing control.

"Tommy-" He removed the blade and replaced it with his tongue, cutting off whatever I was about to say and instead a strained whimper came out.

"No one will survive if anyone touches you again. I will take everything he holds dear and destroy it. I will destroy his world just because he laid one finger on mine."

I believed him. Tommy was proving to me just how crazy he was, and I loved it. I loved every deranged thing he could throw at me.

The point of the knife pressed into the soft flesh of my inner thigh. The sharp shock of pain made my leg jolt. Tommy's hand came down, pressing it down with enough force to stop me from moving again.

"I said keep still baby."

He ran the tip down, creating a small, precise cut then changed direction. Tears soaked into the tie as the severe stinging was close to becoming unbearable.

"Tommy." I whimpered again, almost begging him to stop. But even if I begged, I wasn't sure he would. And I wasn't sure I even wanted him too.

"Shh." He soothed, kissing around where he had just carved my flesh. He started again, just beside it. The blade dragged down, and I released a cry as more tears fell. This time though, Tommy did something else. The fingers of his other hand slid over my clit, massaging the sensitive area.

I bit down on my lip to stop another cry. The pain mixed with the pleasure was something I never knew my body craved. Pressure started to build as he continued working on both overly sensitive spots.

Moving the knife away, he removed his other hand too. I groaned in disappointment as the pressure eased.

"If I find out anyone else has seen this Isabella, I won't be responsible for my actions." Something wet touched the space he had cut, making it sting even more. He licked at the wound then placed a delicate kiss over it. My legs shook under him, but he kissed back up my body making me breathless.

The fabric of his slacks suddenly felt rough as he pressed his hard cock against me, and his thigh rubbed against the fresh cut. I opened my mouth to catch my breath, but he captured mine with his own, invading it with his tongue. I tasted my coppery blood on the tip and groaned.

Pulling away, Tommy removed the tie from my eyes. His were on fire as he gazed down at me. A burning desire that seemed to be stronger now that he knew he had me. Another tear fell down the side of my face and disappeared into my hair.

His tongue ran over the tear track, "You belong to me."

"Tommy please." I didn't care how desperate I sounded. I needed him inside me again. I needed the distraction from the stinging on my thigh.

Moving his hand in between my legs, his fingers pushed into me, finding that I was already soaking. He released a growl of approval. "Let's see if you can last the night."

Chapter 33

The bed dipped beside me and even though I was awake I still refused to open my eyes.

"Are you going to get up at some point today?" The amusement in his husky voice made my belly summersault.

I opened one blurry eye to look at Tommy grinning down at me. "No."

He laughed and pulled back the sheet to uncover my naked body. At some point, my gown had been sliced off by the same knife that he had used to carve his initials into my thigh. After the shock that he had physically branded me, I actually admired his handy work. Clean cuts that would eventually scar as long as I kept picking off the scab. And I wanted to. Having that permanent mark from Tommy made me smile even though it probably shouldn't. If that made me just as fucked up then send me to the asylum because I didn't care.

I stretched out my body, scrunching my eyes shut and groaning as every muscle ached. "I hurt everywhere."

He had definitely tested how long I could last before passing out. Eight orgasms he had got out of me before my body finally gave up. Each time I begged for more until after the very last one where I had to beg him to stop, much to the psycho's enjoyment.

"Don't want to go for another round then?"

I pointed a finger at him. "Touch me and I will stab you."

"The only reason I'm not, is because I believe you will try."

He leaned over to kiss me, and I finally opened my eyes properly, squinting in the natural light. I felt like I was suffering from a hangover but without the headache. The only good thing was that after Tommy had finished with me last night, he insisted that we wash off the blood that had smeared all over our bodies. Once he had helped me into the shower, that I swear I had fallen asleep in at one point, he then went on to dressing the newest addition to my cuts. The dressing that covered my stitches had already been removed and that wound was healing nicely, along with all the others.

Tommy's gaze wondered down my body to my latest addition. "I'm going to take that off, let some air get to it."

Frowning, I pushed myself up to be seated. "How is it going to get air? It's on my inner thigh. I'm not going to walk around like I'm straddling a horse all day."

He blinked at me twice before shaking his head and standing back up. "Get up."

I watched as he moved across the room. He was in dark jeans and a long-sleeved white top. The sleeves were pushed up to his elbows showing off his tattoos and the veins in his forearms. If I wasn't hurting so much already, I would have made him come back to bed.

"What time are we going back to school?"

He walked into his closet. "2.30"

"What's the time now?"

"10.30" He walked back out, holding one of his white shirts.

"Then I still have four hours to stay in bed and recover."

He chucked the shirt at the end of the bed and crossed

his arms. "Get. Up."

Although his voice was stern, the heat in his eyes told me different. "Make me."

Arching a brow, his lips tipped up on one side. My thighs clenched together, and heat pooled between them. I wanted to keep pushing him, but my body wouldn't be thanking me after.

One step from him was all it took to have my feet out of the bed. "I'm up."

Chuckling, he picked the shirt back up and handed it to me. Slipping it on, I did up the buttons. It was miles too big, skimming my lower thighs and I unfastened the button round the cuffs to roll them up.

"Fuck, you should wear my shirts more often."

Looking up at him through my lashes, I licked my bottom lip then let my teeth scrape over it while my fingers teased the fabric near my breasts.

Stepping forward, his hand flew to the back of my head, gripping my hair and ripping it back so my eyes met his. I gasped at the pain, enjoying the electricity it sent through me.

"Keep going Isabella, and I won't care how much your body aches. I'll bend you over this bed and fuck the brat out of you." His menacing snarl only made me want it more.

Fuck it, my body could take it. Recovery was overrated anyway.

Reaching for him, I felt how hard he already was through his jeans, and I smiled deviously as I squeezed. Letting out a deep growl, Tommy spun me around and forced my face into the mattress by the back of my neck. Chills of excitement rippled through my core as a small smile of triumph tilted my lips.

Pushing up the shirt, his hand ran over my arse cheek. He slapped my bare skin, hard enough to sting and my back arched, forcing my arse further into the air. Running his hand over my centre, he chuckled darkly. "Always ready for me, aren't you baby?"

I whimpered, pushing myself against his hand for the pressure that I needed. He responded by pushing two fingers inside me. Satisfied with how ready I actually was, he removed them again and I heard his belt and jeans come undone.

Pushing the tip of his hard cock into me, I held my breath. "Is this what you wanted Isabella?" He pushed in further, stretching my already tender pussy. "You wanted to feel me inside you again."

I gasped as he sank deep into me, hitting the exact spot I needed him to. Without wasting a second, he fucked me hard and fast. My face rubbed against his sheets as his hand stayed at the back of my neck. Every stroke was eliciting my impending orgasm.

His fingers twisted through my hair, ripping my head back. Pinpricks stung my scalp, but it was only making my clit throb more. My back hit against his chest and his other hand curled around my throat.

"You're so fucking beautiful when you're being fucked. It makes me want to chain you up and watch you come all day."

Chain me up? Fuck yes. "Do it."

He licked my earlobe before biting it and I moaned out loudly. "Not today brat." His hand released my hair and snaked round my waist to cup my breast. "As much as I would love to torture your body to the brink of exhaustion, we don't have time for that." He pinched my nipple through the fabric hard enough that I hissed in a breath. My walls clenched around his hard cock as he rolled his hips slowly into me still.

Running his thumb over my bottom lip, my mouth parted enough for him to slide it in. "Lick it." I ran my tongue around it, sucking at it also. "Make it nice and wet baby."

I gasped again as he pinched my nipple harder, and he pulled his thumb back out freshly coated in my spit. Releasing my breast, he thrust my head back down, roughly into the sheets.

"Has anyone ever touched you here Isabella?" His wet thumb ran over a hole that had never been touched and it instinctively clenched. My body tried to jerk forward but his grip on my neck stopped me from going far. "By that, I'm guessing no."

I whimpered as he circled his thumb, slowly applying more pressure. "I look forward to being your first. But we'll start off small."

Pushing harder, his thumb slipped in, and he started moving his hips again. I panted out quick breaths, adjusting to the new foreign feeling. It didn't hurt like I thought it would but then again, it was his thumb. Not his cock.

"Touch yourself. I want to feel you come around me."

I slid my hand down, placing my fingers on my clit and did exactly what he said. Tommy started thrusting faster. Pounding against me ruthlessly as I rubbed my own clit, and his thumb filled my arse. My body was burning from the heat of the climax that was coming.

Letting go of the back of my neck, he gripped my hip, using it to drive into me harder than before. I screamed out as my orgasm ripped through me and I came hard. But Tommy didn't slow. He fucked me through it, grunting as he finished deep inside.

Once he was done, he gently pulled out and my body collapsed onto the bed. Used, worn out and aching more than when I had first awoken. Did I care about the trauma my body was facing? No I didn't.

I rolled back over, looking at the man that had given me more from sex in one weekend than my ex had given me in the year we were together. He was putting himself back into his jeans when his dark eyes looked over at me through his lashes. My clit instantly throbbed again just from that one look.

Climbing onto the bed, he crawled between my legs and leant himself over me. As he kissed me, I wrapped my arms around his neck. "I'm tempted to just take you away somewhere and never come back."

"That wouldn't be the worst decision you've ever made." I giggled as his breath tickled my neck and he kissed the same spot.

"Maybe I will one day." Kneeling back up, he pulled me with him then climbed off the bed. "I'll meet you downstairs." Pouting that he really wouldn't just let me stay in bed, he laughed and slapped his hand against my arse, making me jump closer to him. "Unless you want another go. This time I might fuck this right here."

Running his finger over my lip, I quickly dodged his kiss. "Nope. My body may want you and welcome the torture, but I do not."

"That makes no sense."

"Nor does your whole new personality, but I'm accepting it."

My sweet as pie smile had him rolling his eyes but his dark smile remained, and I felt him watching me as I left the room.

Quickly running to my room, I changed into a pair of leggings and cropped white top after having a quick wash. I was sore after the pounding I just got but I never wanted this feeling to subside, I wanted to feel Tommy on me for ever.

Smiling to myself, I walked into the kitchen. Callum was sitting at the island, sipping coffee and eating a grilled cheese. I walked over and sat in the seat beside him.

"Where's Maddy?"

"Popped out with mum to get some bits to take back to school. Apparently, you both need chocolate and crisps for all the gossip you have to tell those other two."

By other two I assumed he meant Daisy and Jack and grinned, looking forward to seeing them again. Archie walked into the room, grabbed the coffee from Callum's hand and downed it in one mouthful. Slamming it down on the counter, he sat down in the seat opposite me. Callum looked daggers at him but got up to refill his cup.

Yawning, Archie stretched out his arms. "Pour me one too."

"Want a tea sweetheart?" Callum asked, ignoring his cousin but he had already retrieved two more cups from the cupboard.

"Please." I looked over to Archie. "Didn't get much sleep?"

"No," He grumbled and reached across the island for Callum's food. "You might want to remind your new fuck toy that my room is right next to his and the walls int that fucking thick."

My cheeks instantly flushed, and Callum snorted a laugh.

"Fuck toy?" Tommy walked up behind me, wrapping his arms around my waist and kissing the top of my head. "I think she is more my toy than anything."

I groaned, throwing my head into my arms to hide the embarrassment. "Can we change the subject please?"

"Some of the things I heard last night should be illegal." Archie continued.

"Some of them probably were."

"Oh my god." I sat back up properly and elbowed Tommy lightly in the stomach. "I think I preferred when you were a brooding arsehole."

He laughed, nuzzling his face into the crook of my neck and I couldn't help but melt. This Tommy was quickly becoming my favourite.

Callum came back over and passed us both a cup as he sat back down. Soon after Maddy returned, and we headed back to the school a little earlier. The rest of the day and evening was spent eating and having a laugh with my three best friends. Tommy was a little disappointed that I wasn't spending the night with him but what can I say. This was new. And I didn't want to ditch my friends just because I had got the hottest guy in the school. He was still a jerk though.

Chapter 34

I walked into the food hall, smelling already what was on the menu and cringed. Curry. It wasn't that I didn't like curry, but the smell of the school's version was overpowering. Jack was moaning about his poisons class with Maddy and Daisy. Apparently, there was an incident involving extracting poison from a tarantula and whoever he was partnered with was an incompetent oaf. His exact words. Maddy and Daisy were nodding in agreement, but my mind was elsewhere.

Tommy hadn't been in school all day. Callum had told me during AP Art of Killing that he had some things that he needed to sort out and I never questioned him. After what happened over the weekend, I assumed it was to do with that.

But there he was. Sitting at the table with the other three boys, smiling at something one of them had said. My stomach was suddenly in knots. How did I act with him? We had no label for what was going on between us and no one else knew that we had got closer over the weekend. For all I knew, Tommy wanted it to go back to how it was. Hardly talking to each other than at each other's throats, but now with the occasional fuck. Was that how it was going to be from now on?

I didn't need to worry about how to act though. Tommy had made that decision for me. As soon as I got to the table, he pulled me on to his lap and kissed me deeply. A few gasps sounded behind him as everyone else in the hall fell silent.

Pulling away, my face remained close to his, but my eyes roamed around to see other students watching us.

"People are staring." I whispered, licking my lips nervously.

Tommy smiled then kissed me again. "Good. I may have claimed you but now they know you are truly mine."

Rolling my eyes, I slid off his lap and into the seat beside him. The others had already taken their seats. There were no questions about Daisy and Jack joining us. It was just something that was now going to happen and even if the boys did have something to say, I'm sure Maddy would have protested.

"How did the zoom meeting go?" Felix asked, looking at Tommy.

"Didn't find out much. But they are secretive fuckers. When they are ready to share what I already know then we will act. Until then, we prepare for the worst."

"The worst?" I asked, my brows furrowing together.

He leant over to kiss the crease on my forehead. "Nothing for you to worry about."

Looking at the others, all three boys avoided my gaze, but Maddy shrugged. If she wasn't worried, then I shouldn't be. And I wouldn't have been before anyway. Or maybe I would have been but not have shown it.

"Why are you not eating anyway?" He asked, forking some of his own food in his mouth.

"We ate before we came down."

"A packet of biscuits isn't a substantial meal." Callum argued.

"Sorry dad." I deadpanned and Daisy snorted beside me. "We had cold pizza too that we had left over from last night."

He looked at me disgusted then to Maddy. "What the fuck's wrong with you both?"

Rolling her eyes, she stood back up. "We might as well go to the field now, get changed into our outfits."

"Yeah ok." I quickly planted a kiss on Tommy's cheek. "See you on the field."

The four boys were already in their football kits ready for their training session, but Maddy and I still had to get changed into our cheerleading uniform.

Tommy narrowed his eyes at me. He wasn't happy that I was still determined to go to training while I was still healing. We had a discussion about it on the journey back in the car and he had argued that he was only looking out for my best interests. My argument was that even though he was now giving me a good dicking, I wasn't about to let him have full control over me without a fight. That seemed to settle the argument because he couldn't get over the fact I had called it a good dicking and the rest of the way back he just kept grinning and shaking his head occasionally.

Once we got to the changing rooms with the other girls from the squad, Courtney went through what we would be doing as we changed.

"I want to do a whole new routine for the friendly."

"What about if they attack us again?" One of the other girls asked.

"Then we'll kill them." Another answered sweetly.

"This time I'm bringing knives into it." Our captain grinned devilishly. "They will be going first so if any of them try anything, when it's our turn, we will return the favour."

A few of the older girls grinned at this while some of the newer ones exchanged worried looks.

"Who here is good with a knife. Not close range but more like throwing." She got out a little note pad from her bag and started jotting down the names of the girls who rose their hands. I put my hand up to.

"You need to have good aim too." She added and a

couple of them put their hands back down and I rolled my eyes. "You three," her pen pointed between me and two others. "When we get out, I want to see your aim. The rest of you, warm up. The boys should be out there already, and we will be practicing lifts today."

Without any other instruction, she walked out the room. I tied my black ribbon round my hair and followed the others. When we got to the field, the boys were there waiting, chatting to two people that shouldn't have been there.

"What are you doing here?" I asked Daisy as Jack laughed at something one of the boys had said, pushing him gently. What a flirt.

"Thought we would come and show you both support on your first lesson." She smirked but her eyes wandered to across the field.

"Really?" I laughed and followed her gaze to the football team doing their warmup. There was something about seeing Tommy passing the ball back and forth with Archie that was just thigh clenching.

"Perving over my brother again Daisy?" Maddy smirked, joining us.

"Actually no, this time I have my eye on a certain cousin." She was still watching them, a glint of heat in her eyes.

"Felix." It wasn't a question. She nodded her head to confirm my assumption and both Maddy and I grinned like a couple of young teenagers.

"Girls!" Courtney shouted over, looking slightly annoyed that we weren't already doing what she had instructed.

"This conversation isn't over. You need to tell us everything tonight." Maddy demanded but Daisy shook her head.

"There isn't anything to tell you."

"Not yet." I grinned slyly at her. I had a feeling that Felix might like her a tiny bit too but there was no way to prove

I was right.

I came to stand beside the other two girls that were about to show their knife throwing skills to Courtney. One was already chucking her chosen daggers at the target. Her aim wasn't too bad. Out of the five daggers she had thrown, four of them had hit the bullseye while one was just a little too far to the left.

I picked out the knives, letting the next girl take her turn. She was just as good, only missing one because of hitting the handle of the knife before it.

"Good, good." Courtney praised absentmindedly, marking off something in her notepad.

I stood up next and chucked my five knives. All five struck the board, all five hit the target.

"Excellent." Courtney smiled. "Now all three of you do it again but while you are doing a forward handspring."

The two girls glanced at each other while I stood in a stupor. What the fuck was a handspring? Stepping back, I watched one of the others get into position then flip forward. The move was literally in the name. She sprung forward onto her hands then flipped herself over. The only issue was that using both hands, even with her dagger in one of them, she wasn't able to get enough force or accuracy to hit the target.

The next girl stepped up but made the same mistake as the first and her knife landed in the grass. It needed to be done one handed and the knife needed to be released at the right time. I wasn't an expert nor would I pretend to be, but I did know how to do flips even if I didn't know the fancy names they were given.

Holding my knife in my healing but weaker hand, I ran forward and flipped using the other one. As I landed back on my feet, I released the knife and let it fly through the air. It was off centre but hit the target circle.

Smiling in triumph, I turned back to Courtney who was clapping along with a few others that were watching also. "That was a good idea going one handed. You think you will be able to do that on the day?"

"Work it into the routine and tell me who the target is, and I won't miss." I grinned at her and she grinned evilly back.

The next half hour of the training session was filled with practicing lifts and other stunts then including the new knife manoeuvre into it. Courtney had refused to let me do any of the lifts, saying that she didn't want to take the risk of one of the boys ripping out the stitches. I knew that the real reason was because Tommy had probably forbidden it though when she glanced nervously across to him. But she did make the promise that I would be practicing them next week as being one of the smallest in the class, it was a great advantage.

By the time we had finished, Tommy was already walking towards us, covered in mud and what looked like blood too, but by the corrupt grin on his face, it wasn't his own. I ran over, not caring about what anyone else thought. They all knew there was something definitely going on between us now, so why not be hands on.

As if he already knew what I was about to do, Tommy held out his arms and I leaped into them, wrapping my legs around his waist. Instant regret filled me, and I winced at the stinging in my thigh as they hit against him.

"Did that hurt?" His breathy chuckle almost made it worth it.

"Uh huh." I nodded, scrunching my eyes tightly shut as if it would shut out the sharpness of the pain.

Grabbing my arse, he pulled me further up his body to get a better grip and started walking back to the cheer squad. "Do you regret it?"

"Nope."

"Good, because I'm about to make it hurt more."

He walked straight past the others and to the boys' changing rooms. Locking the door, he set me down on the bench and started to peel off my cheer uniform. Not a word was said as he pulled off each item, kissing every part that he revealed. The only sound was my panting as my body flushed. The heat between us could have sent the locker room on fire.

Once he had succeeded in stripping me bare, he stepped back to admire what was his. I stood up and walked the two steps to being right in front of him. Playing with the hem off his shirt, he helped me pull it off, along with his shorts and everything else that I needed to get rid of, so he was in the same state as me.

Lifting me again, he took us both to the shower room, still kissing my neck as his erection pressed against my centre. Banging from the door could be heard with raised voices following, calling for the door to be unlocked, but Tommy ignored his fellow teammates and continued to press me up against the cold tiles.

He turned the water on, letting the warm stream wash over us. His dark hair stuck messily to his forehead, and I ran my fingers through it, pushing the dripping strands back. Reaching between us, he felt how wet I already was, and it wasn't from the shower. I hummed out my pleasure, making his face light up with satisfaction.

"Tommy, come on mate." Someone called out but they still hadn't managed to get into the changing room.

"You've got to be quick." I breathed out as his fingers slid inside me. "Before they get in."

His eyes darkened at the challenge, and he removed his fingers. He replaced it quickly with something so much larger and I cried out.

"Fuck, Tommy." Burying my face into his neck, I tried to drown out another cry as he thrust into me again deeper.

"Don't worry about them hearing baby. I want them to know exactly what I have." His hips moved, pounding me into the tiled wall and I did exactly what he wanted me too. My moans drowned out the cheers and wolf whistles and I became more turned on knowing that they could hear every single thing that we were doing.

Tommy's head lowered to my breast, capturing my

nipple between his teeth painfully. My muscles clenched around him, and he bit down harder. Running my fingers through his hair, I ripped his head back, causing me more pain but also receiving a groan of desire from him.

His eyes met mine again and he slowed his pace as we gazed at each other. We were both panting. The water from the shower ran down our bodies, making Tommy grip on tighter while his body rolled against mine. I refused to close my eyes and give in to the pleasure. I wanted to watch him as he watched me. Something was going unsaid between us but whatever it was, neither of us wanted to say it.

Instead, I gave in and broke the eye contact to kiss him. He groaned in my mouth, accepting it like he had been waiting patiently. His tongue swiped across my lips, demanding access and I let him take it. Just like everything else I was willing to let him take. Thrusting forward again, he picked up his speed. With one arm wrapped around his neck and my other hand still tangled in his hair, I clung on to him tightly as he fucked me into complete euphoria.

I didn't care about the boys still trying to get in or the fact that we were in the changing room showers. I just cared that I was lost in Tommy once again and he was lost in me. Exactly where we both wanted to be

Chapter 35

Gangsta by Kehlani was playing softly in the background. I was laid on my front between Tommy's legs, with one hand rested on his stomach and my chin upon that. His head was propped up by his pillows with his arms behind him as he watched my fingers trace the black ink that decorated his torso.

"I'm still finding this a little strange." I admitted without looking up at him.

"What?"

"You and me."

His hand came out from under his head, and he cupped my chin forcing me to look into his eyes. "And what's so strange about it."

"We've done a complete U-turn in the space of a few days. I was ready to plan to make your death look like a suicide not so long ago and now I can't get enough of you."

His lips twisted into an amused smirk. "You were really planning that?"

"I was ready to." I deadpanned and swatted his hand out the way. "But you understand what I mean right? We've gone from one extreme to the other."

"Do you want it to go back to the way it was?"

"Of course not."

Sighing heavily, he wrapped his arms around my body and pulled me up further then on to the side, so I was on the bed. Tucking my hair behind my ear, his fingers brushed across my jaw.

"I've wanted you since the moment I saw you and I'm pretty sure you wanted me too even if you did hate me."

"I didn't hate you." I finally admit, smiling. "I just wish I knew you more."

"Ask me anything."

"Anything at all?"

"Anything at all." He repeated, kissing my lips.

"And you'll answer honestly. No redirecting."

He grinned mischievously and my stomach flipped. "Truth for a truth? I'll tell you a truth and you tell me one."

I pushed myself up to be seated and crossed my legs with the biggest smile on my face. Something about him willing to be so open with me had suddenly made me feel as excited as a child would be at Christmas.

Turning to his side, he propped himself up on his elbow. "What's your first question then Isabella?"

"Favourite colour?"

"Red."

"The colour of blood"

"And many other things." His hand reached up and he ran the pad of his thumb over my painted red lips. Thank God for lip stain. "My turn. Your favourite song?"

"Song. Oh well I like loads, but my all-time favourite has to be Always by Bon Jovi."

"You like older music, don't you?"

"That's two questions."

"That was an observation."

Shaking my head, I chuckled softly. "Yes, I do like the older music. You can thank my dad for that. He always had music on and used to sing and dance around the house with my mum. I know a lot of Elvis music too."

"Elvis did have some good songs. Your dad has good taste." He nodded.

"What's your favourite food?"

"Lasagne." A straight up answer with no hesitation or thinking.

I grinned, remembering that I told him that was all I could cook. "Convenient."

"How did you get that scar?"

His eyes wandered to my forehead, and I frowned. "What scar?"

Placing a finger to my eyebrow, he stroked across the tiny gap in the hair. "That one."

I had completely forgot about it. "Oh, it's kinda a long story but it also isn't. Like I could tell you how I did it but there is a story leading up to it."

"Just tell me." Tommy smiled.

"While my mum was pregnant with me, she, my dad and brother moved here from Italy." I paused waiting to see his reaction to the fact I was actually Italian, but he didn't falter from the warm smile as he listened to every word I had to say. "They came here with nothing but the clothes on their back. That's what my mum told me anyway. Dad worked hard for everything we had and that meant he worked a lot of hours. For the early years of my life, dad was always working. He had set up his business from the ground but being the boss and trying to get established, it meant that he wasn't really around a lot and had to do a lot of traveling."

I paused again thinking about the time he had sacrificed away from his wife and kids so we could all have a better life, only to have them taken from him anyway. Ironic really.

Tommy nudged my hand. "How did you get the scar then?"

Letting out a soft laugh, I started to explain. "Whenever dad was away and the phone rang, I would race my brother to it. Both of us always wanted to be the first to speak to him. When I was six, I was still quite small. One night when the phone rang, we both ran but I hit the handle of the door. It got me good, and I needed butterfly stitches. After that, Antonio would always let me get to the phone first. He used to say he didn't want me to get another boo boo. He also gave me the nickname Boo too and that kind of stuck. No one calls me it now though. "

He gave a soft smile, understanding why they didn't. "Any other scars?"

"That's another question. It's my turn."

"I'll give you a free one."

Rolling my eyes, I adjusted myself to bring up my foot. There was a tiny white scar at the heel. "When I was nine, my brother and I were building a tree house. Mum had told us to wait until the weekend for when dad was home, but it was the summer holidays, and we were bored so we didn't listen. Antonio left me for five minutes to get us both a drink and by the time he had come back I had managed to hammer most of the first wall together and also step on a plank of wood with a nail sticking out. Mum wasn't happy at all with either of us, but Tony and I thought it was hilarious. Bloody hurt though."

"So you were the kind of kid that was more into getting dirty than playing with dolls and makeup?"

"All these questions are going to cost ya." I winked at him, and he pulled me back down on top of him.

Kissing my neck, I giggled as his lips tickled. "I want to know everything about you Isabella. You have bewitched me from the moment I saw you. I'm willing to pay whatever price I need to, to learn all I can."

I sighed deeply at his words. "I liked makeup and dolls and everything else considered girly, but I also liked climbing trees, making mud pies and doing that sort of thing with Antonio."

I was smiling but Tommy could tell it was a bittersweet one. Memories with my brother were always sad but I never wanted to forget them. They were happy but just brought sadness with them.

Holding me a little closer, he kissed the top of my head. Wiggling myself off him and to his side again, I thought of my next question.

"Who did you first kill?" Tommy frowned so I elaborated. "Callum said that before you came to this school, your dads made you kill someone to prepare you for what was about to come. He told me who he killed but he said that yours was your own story to tell."

He turned his head away and looked at the ceiling. His eyes were pained, and I regretted my question. I thought it would have been some pervert like Callum's but now I knew it was something more personal. "I'm sorry. You don't have to tell me."

"No, I want to." He sighed and I waited for him to continue. "My brother."

My heart crashed against my ribs, and I was glad he wasn't facing me because the pure horror and shock that was on my face was something that I didn't want him to see. His brother? I didn't even know he had a brother. There was no evidence of him at his family home and no one had ever mentioned him.

And to kill him. How could you kill your brother? I had lost mine in a most brutal way, I would have done anything to bring him back but the man that laid on the bed, staring up at the ceiling with a tortured glint in his dark eyes had killed his own brother.

"Why?" I whispered.

"Because it was either I do it or my father. By me doing it, he was shown mercy. But he didn't deserve it."

"Tommy-"

"He was older than me. The next in line to take over the family business." He finally turned his head to look at me. "He didn't agree with the way my father was doing certain things and there were loads of arguments between the two of them all the time. Richie wanted to take over sooner. He came up with a plan that fucked up from the moment he walked into my parents' room."

"Instead of killing our father like he had planned to do. He killed our mother. Shot her when she put herself between father and the gun."

My hand came to my mouth to block the tiny gasp that came from it, making my words sound slightly muffled. "I'm sorry Tommy."

He frowned but smiled softly. "You have no reason to be sorry."

"I know, sorry."

He rolled his eyes and chuckled at my second apology. Running his fingers through my hair to the back of my head, he pulled it towards him and kissed my forehead. "Richie never meant to kill our mother so when he did, he was in shock. It gave father the chance to disarm him and take him down. He was going to leave the others to deal with Richie and my uncles would have made his death a lot more painful. But I said I would do it. He deserved the torture but I…"

"He was still your brother at the end of the day. Even though what he did was unforgivable, you still loved him."

Tommy nodded and I completely understood. Richie was going to die anyway. Tommy gave him the easy way out with a single shot.

Cupping his cheek, I gently stroked him with my thumb. "I'm sorry that you had to go through that."

"We've all gone through shit Isabella. It's how we come out the other end that makes us who we are." He took my hand from his cheek and pressed his lips against my palm. "I owe you another truth."

"You've just given me a big one. You don't have to tell me anything else." I smiled softly at him, but he disregarded what I said and rolled over so he was on top.

I opened my legs, making it easier for him to get closer. "I lied when I told you I didn't want you."

"I figured that one out." I giggled as his fingers intertwined with my own and he started planting little kisses across my jaw.

"I also lied when I said I had no intentions of marrying you."

"Tommy." I gasped out, unsure if it was because of what he had just said or the sudden scrape of his teeth against my neck.

"Oh not yet Isabella. I want you to love me first."

Love him. After two weeks of knowing each other, how could someone fall in love that quick? I cared about him. I cared about him more than I had cared about anyone else. But love was a big step.

I had never been in love. Even with my ex-boyfriend. I had loved him but more in a best friend kind of way because that's what I guess we were. Best friends. We had lost our virginities to each other, and we were like a normal couple but when it came to saying goodbye, it was more like saying goodbye to a friend than it was to someone I loved.

Tommy was different to him. He had consumed everything that I was feeling. From not liking him to craving him then to right now when I…

I didn't love him. Not yet. It was too soon.

Tommy didn't give me chance to give him my reaction to what he had said though. He kissed down my clothed body, distracting me from thinking about it anymore and distracting himself from the memories I had reminded him of.

"I can't get enough of you." He breathed, taking his hands from mine to lift my top and place soft kisses over my stomach. "You're everything I never knew I needed."

He pulled down my shorts, revealing my naked pussy. "You're the perfect distraction from everything that is dark."

Kissing his way back up, he dragged my top with him, and I lifted my arms, helping him to remove it.

As soon as it was off, his blue eyes connected with mine. "I can't lose you Isabella."

I swallowed. I didn't love him, but he was making it so hard for me to keep telling myself that lie and believe it.

Pushing him back, I moved in a way to spin myself around and straddle him. He fell back onto the pillow, letting me take control.

"You won't lose me Tommy. Not now that I know who you truly are. You're stuck with me."

He leaned up, grabbing my face to kiss my lips. I let him for a few seconds before pushing him back down. My eyes flicked to the knife on his nightstand and his gaze followed, clocking it too.

He reached across and as if reading my mind, handed it to me. "Wherever you want."

The pad of my finger pressed against the point but before it could break the skin, I stopped. "Is it ready?"

He knew what I meant by the question and nodded.

Holding the knife over his right pec, I slowly pressed it into his flesh. A bead of blood formed around the point and I carefully sliced the blade down, creating a clean cut. He didn't flinch or make a single sound. All his concentration was on me, watching every single move my face made while I did exactly what he had done to me. I ran my thumb over the blood, clearing it away to start again.

Tommy's hands moved underneath me and I pulled the blade away quickly.

"Don't stop." His voice was low and husky. He pulled down his sweats and released his hard cock. I lifted my arse, not wanting the distraction but he roughly pulled me back down. My wetness spread, coating him in a slippery slickness.

"Don't stop." He repeated and I lowered the knife again. This time my hand shook with nerves from the distraction he was providing. Pressing it in, I created another incision.

He lifted my hips then brought me back down hard, filling my fully. I gasped out, accidently pushing the knife in deeper as he did the same to me. I tore it away as quickly as I had done it. His deep laugh made me clench around him, and he groaned in his throat.

"Fucking psycho." I moaned before he brought my hips up again and thrust in as deep as he could fill me from that angle. I cried out, throwing my head back.

"I – I can't concentrate."

His dark chuckle set me on fire as he carried on, each thrust harder than the last.

"Oh shit."

He didn't let up.

"Fuck, Tommy. Stop!"

He slowed, grinning up at me in the most mischievous way. Glaring down, I waited before starting my work again, not trusting him to behave. Creating the last line I needed to finish the letter I was easier without him moving but as soon as I brought the blade away again, he started rolling his hips gently.

"Stop moving."

"It's too hard."

"I can feel that."

He laughed again and I grinned. "I mean it's too hard not to move when my cocks in its favourite place."

"Shouldn't have put it there then."

Smiling, he took his hands away from my hips and rested them behind his head again.

"Good boy."

Tommy's brow rose as my words ignited something primal inside of him. I felt his cock throb inside of me and almost moaned out in pleasure. Looking away from the burning passion in his eyes, I concentrated once again on the cuts. I just had to add my last initial. There was an issue though. I had two birth certificates. Two last names. Russo and Moretti. What letter did I put?

I smiled to myself and started to carve the letter I knew he would appreciate the most. The letter that sealed my fate with a promise.

Setting the knife down, I smeared the blood away with my hand, revealing the fresh wound. Tommy looked down at his latest piece of art then back up to me with such a multitude of emotions filling his face that I giggled nervously.

As he sat up, he adjusted my arse so he could stay inside me, right where I wanted him. "You're just full of surprises."

I ran my fingers over the red markings, tracing each letter and spreading more of his blood.

I.K

"I may belong to you, but this means that you belong to me too."

"Since the very first day I've been yours."

Kissing me deeply, I ground my centre against him. He groaned into my mouth as I lifted my hips and sank back down onto his hard cock and repeated doing so continuously.

"Fuck."

His head fell back and I pushed him down on to the bed. Watching him come undone by my hands was just what I needed to tip me over the point of oblivion. I moved my hips, riding him to near completion before he had to get back the control he wanted so badly.

Lifting my hips, he thrust into me ruthlessly. My nails dug into his chest, marking him even more as he fucked me hard and fast until I was screaming out his name and coming hard around him. His hips jolted up, filling me with his hot come and I collapsed on top of him.

One thing was for sure. Things were never going to be the same again.

Chapter 36

Maddy passed me her kitten heel brown boots, smiling at my outfit of choice. Skinny denim jeans with a cream oversized knitted jumper and a thick woollen scarf. Perfect for an autumn date night.

"So what's he doing? Taking you to the glass palace then out again?"

"Yeh, he's got to pop in to sort out some business then he's got the rest of the night planned with something else but nothing flashy."

"I take it you're not staying here again tonight?" Maddy pouted out her bottom lip, but her eyes told me she wasn't really that bothered and only teasing.

I hadn't stayed in my own bed all week. Every night I had ended up in Tommy's and it was now becoming a norm. Half of my clothes were already in his room along with most of my other bits, such as schoolbooks and toiletries. I did feel guilty that I kept leaving Maddy, but she was just so happy that we were finally together that she didn't mind. I had promised that I would be staying with her the next night though so we could have a proper girly night.

"After practice tomorrow, shall we go out and get some

supplies?" I asked, zipping up the last boot.

"Yeh, I'll get the keys to Callum's car. He won't mind. Get some face packs too."

"Yeh Ok then."

"I would ask Daisy and Jack if they want to join us but I kinda want it to be just me and you. Do you mind?" She asked, looking slightly guilty but I completely understood.

Giving her a nudge with my shoulder, I gave her a smile. "Of course not. It'll be nice."

Someone's knuckles rapped loudly against the door, and I knew instantly who it was. Grinning at Maddy, she rolled her eyes and sat down on her bed. I opened the door and Tommy was standing there smirking with a single red rose in his hand.

"You were taking too long." He held out the rose to me and I took it. Bringing it to my nose, I let the silk petals softly brush against my skin.

"So impatient." I teased, but walked out of the door, giving Maddy a little wave before shutting it behind me. He took my free hand then led me down the corridor and down the stairs. He was dressed casual like me. Dark jeans and a simple light blue polo top.

As I got into the car, he passed me his phone. Swiping to the playlist I wanted, music filled the car. Tommy got in and we set off down the drive and away from the school.

"Where are we going?"

He grinned, glancing over. "And you say I'm impatient." When I rolled my eyes, he laughed. "I thought we would go to the beach, get some chips."

My eyes lit up with delight. He already knew exactly what I liked and it warmed my heart to the point it could burst.

"So what does red mean?" I asked, twirling the rose between my fingers.

He took my hand with his, while his other gripped the steering wheel. "A red rose means desire, passion."

Similar to burgundy. "What does a single rose mean?"

"Devotion."

"So you're devoted to me?" I grinned while I looked from the rose to him.

Bringing my hand up to his mouth, he kissed the back of it. "Always." Placing it back down, he let go and ran his hand over my thigh instead, giving it a light squeeze. "It also means love at first sight."

My breath caught in my throat, and I gawped at him as a slow sexy smile lifted his lips while he still looked at the road ahead. I opened my mouth to say something back that I was sure I was ready to admit to, but his smile faded in a blink.

Slamming his foot on the brakes, we both lurched forward. Luckily the seatbelt had stopped me from hitting the dash, but it had also dug painfully into my chest, making me wince. It didn't help that Tommy's hand had smacked across it too, trying to stop me from flying forward.

"Fuck. Are you ok?" I could see the panic in his eyes as well as hear it in his voice as he looked over every inch of my body.

"I'm fine." I breathed out, unclipping the seatbelt, hoping to relieve the pressure on my chest. "What the fuck happened?"

Tommy didn't answer. His eyes were fixed in a murderous glare at whatever was in front of us. I turned to see what had changed his mood so quickly. Standing in the wake of the headlights was a silhouette of a man. Taking slow steps, he walked closer to the car, making it easier for me to see him. Dark hair, equally as dark beard and thick bushy brows. He was tall but lanky. And smartly dressed in a tailored suit.

"Petrov." Tommy muttered to himself, and I frowned still looking at the man. I had heard that name before. Or at least seen it somewhere.

Petrov moved his jacket to the side, showing Tommy the weapon he was holding.

Tommy shifted slightly in his seat, slowly lifting the

centre console to get his own gun out. "Stay in the car."

"Tommy-"

"Stay in the fucking car Isabella." His voice was deadly as he gritted the words out and I shut my mouth.

Opening the door, he slipped out and slammed it shut again. I watched as he walked around to the front, standing before the other man. They started talking but I couldn't hear what was being said and I had never been good at lip reading. A couple of times Petrov glanced over at me, grinning like a cat that had just got the cream but Tommy didn't take his eyes off him. I couldn't do anything but watch.

And subtly open the glovebox to see if Tommy had another weapon in there. There was only a pocket knife and I inwardly groaned.

The door ripped open beside me and before I had chance to even stick my hand in, I was wrenched out of the car with the barrel of a gun pressed against the side of my head.

The brute's fingers dug fiercely into my skin as he dragged me to Petrov. Tommy instantly pulled out his gun, aiming it at the guy with his hands on me.

"Get your fucking hands off her."

"Now, now. Zis doesn't need to be bloody" Petrov grinned, slowly taking out his own gun like he had no care in the world.

"Zis her boss?" The man behind me gruffed, pushing me forward roughly and making me trip on my own feet. With his hand still having a strong grip on my arm though, I didn't go far.

"Izabella Moretti." My brows pinched together, and I looked at Tommy, but his anger clouded any confusion he had over my name. "Ve have been looking for you for a vhile." Taking a step forward, he ran the barrel of his gun down my cheek.

"Petrov, I swear to god-"

Petrov snapped his head back to him, a sinister gleam

to his dark brown eyes. "Vhat Tommy. Vhat are you going to do?"

Tommy's eyes flicked between me and the gun to my head and face. I was completely fucked.

"I should have fucking hit you with the car." He growled out and Petrov gave a dark laugh before stepping away from me again.

"You know, Ve only came for ze girl but you," He pointed a finger at Tommy. "You vill be like added bonus."

"Leave her here and I will come without a fight."

"You vill come villingly. If not, I vill shoot her now." He walked away just as another car pulled up. Stepping out were two other men in dark suits. One walked over to Tommy, holding out his hand and without a word, Tommy placed his gun in it.

"Tommy, don't-"

"Shh." The brute behind me whispered, running his gun down my cheek to my neck. His slimy tongue licked at my ear lobe, making me shudder in the most disgusted way. "You're too pretty to kill yet milaya."

I gritted my teeth together as I pulled my head away from his mouth. "I'm going to kill you. You know that right?"

Releasing a deep laugh, he stuck something sharp into my neck. I hissed in a breath as he let go of me. I could have run to Tommy, and I probably should have but instead I spun around, slapping the man round the face. He staggered back slightly.

Someone else grabbed hold of me from behind but I wasn't too bothered who it was. I was too busy grinning at the handprint that was already forming.

The brute stepped forward, clenching his fists around the gun and the other around the syringe that he had injected me with.

"She'll be out soon; you can have your fun then Igor." The man who now had hold of me said and I could hear the sleazy amusement in his voice.

Sounds of a struggle came from behind me and by the way Tommy was now shouting at them all, I was guessing he had changed his mind about coming willingly. But whatever he was doing behind me, I wasn't going to be much help. My body had already started to sag in this new man's arms and my vision was already blurring. My name was being called by someone, but all the voices and shouting was muddled along with the laughter.

I felt like I was floating but that was impossible. Instead I was being carried. Then chucked down with no care. But I was fine. I didn't feel anything because I was already gone.

Chapter 37

I opened my eyes to complete darkness. The temple in the side of my head, throbbed against the material that was wrapped around my eyes. I ached all over but to my relief there was no other pain to signify that I had been hurt in any way and as I shifted on the seat, I felt the denim of my jeans rub against my legs. Again, a little bit of relief ran through me that I was still clothed.

Pulling on my hands, the sound of metal against metal rang through my ears. I had been handcuffed to a metal chair.

"Ahh, she avakes."

My heart stopped. I wasn't alone. Licking my lips, I flexed my fingers and gripped the arms of the chair.

"How long do you think it vill be till she breaks Tommy."

Tommy was with me. Another wave of relief. He was quiet though. Was he gagged? Or was he hurt so much he couldn't speak.

The blindfold was ripped from my face and my eyes squinted, adjusting to the bright light of the small white room.

I was seated at a table, and I was right, both wrists were cuffed to a metal chair. Opposite me was Tommy. He wasn't gagged or blindfolded but he was cuffed to his own chair. His lip was split and there was a very light bruise forming on his left cheek, probably the result of the struggle I had heard, but there was no other mark on him. He just remained cold as he glared across the table at me.

My gaze left his to look at the other two men in the room with us. Petrov was sporting an already black eye and a cut just below the other. Igor still had my hand imprint on his cheek with the beginnings of a purple bruise forming under it.

A smile twisted at my lips before I could stop it and Igor's eyes narrowed on me.

"Something funny, milaya?"

I pressed my lips, refusing to answer but I knew he could see my struggle at hiding my amusement and it seemed to irritate him more. As he stepped forward, Petrov put out his hand to stop any more advancement from Igor.

"I like zat you can still smile vhen you are staring death in ze face Izabella."

I looked back at Tommy. His cold eyes remained fixed on me, and his jaw ticked. He was thinking of something, and I really hoped it was a plan to get us out of here because right now it looked like we were fucked.

Petrov moved to my side of the table and rested his hand on my shoulder. "Ve vere meant to deliver you to someone but that vas years ago." His hand stroked the back of my neck, coming to rest on my other shoulder as he leant down to speak directly to my ear. "Zat vas before you killed my brozer."

Ripping my hair back, my head went with it, and I ground my teeth together to stop myself from crying out.

"You killed him, and his friends didn't you, little girl." Pushing my head forward again, he let go of my hair and walked round to the side of the table again.

I looked up at Tommy. He was no longer looking at me,

his eyes were on Petrov and even I flinched at the satanic glare in them. His chest rose and fell rapidly as his fury rose, but his mouth remained shut, like he was waiting for something before he said anything.

"Ve vere meant to hand you over but ve vill have more fun on our own."

"Err boss, zey have been called. Zey know she iz here."

"Zen ring zem back. Tell zem ve vere mistaken. She iz not ze one zey are looking for." Petrov snapped at Igor, who just nodded and exited the small room we were in, in a hurry.

"Who is looking for me?" I dared to ask and Petrov grinned.

"Little girl, you vill never know." Pulling out a small revolver from his back pocket, he set it on the table, central between Tommy and me. "Ve play game in Russia."

Tommy's brows creased and it was the first sign of worry I had seen since the blindfold had been ripped away. But it was so fleeting that I wondered if I had imagined it and it was only my own panic that I was projecting.

Petrov went on to pull out a single bullet. Picking up the gun again, he added it to the chamber and spun it round, losing the position he had placed it in. "Russian roulette." He mused, setting it back down again.

Fishing in his pocket the last time, he pulled out a set of keys. Releasing me from the cuffs first, he went to Tommy's side and paused. Taking out another gun from the belt of his jeans, he pointed it at me. "Any funny moves and she vill die."

Tommy nodded once and Petrov with one hand, released one cuff off his wrist then dropped the keys to the table for Tommy to do the other.

"You know ze rules?"

I nodded. Who didn't? Take it in turns to pull the trigger until one of you dies. It was as simple as that, yet it was probably the most horrifying game there was.

"You," He grinned. "You vill go first."

"Why are you doing this?" I breathed out, shaking my head as I looked from Tommy to the gun.

"Because vhy should I hand you over to zem ven it is me you have wronged."

"Your brother killed my mum and my brother. They were going to kill me."

"Oh, you don't know do you?" His smile turned spiteful, and he looked at Tommy, shaking his head. "Tsk, tsk ,tsk. Tommy, Tommy, Tommy. Zat is selfish. Keeping her for yourself."

Tommy growled at him, but my head tilted to the side, confused by what he was saying.

"What are you going on about?"

"Ve iz done talking. Now ve play." He slid the gun closer to me. "And if you don't take ze first shot Izabella, I vill shoot him." Petrov held up the gun pointing it towards Tommy.

Tommy seemed unfazed by that but there was fear in his eyes as he watched me pick up the revolver and place the barrel to the side of my head. My heart was beating the fastest it ever had, and I was certain both men could see it through my chest.

My hand was shaking, pushing the barrel harder against my temple to try to steady it. There was one thing thinking you were about to die but having no control over killing yourself was a whole different experience. The choice was being taken from you like all murders, but you were doing it yourself.

"Close your eyes." Tommy finally spoke. The softness in his voice only made it worse. The sound was calm, controlled. A complete contrast to the burning rage in his eyes.

I closed my eyes, picturing everything that I was saying goodbye to. It wasn't helping.

"Take a breath."

I breathed in deeply and released it slowly.

"Come on. Ve haven't got all night."

I pulled the trigger.

Nothing.

Just the click of an empty chamber.

My eyes flew open, and Tommy closed his, releasing a breath of relief that he had been holding in. Sliding it across the table, he picked it up and without hesitation, pointed it to his head and pulled the trigger.

A tiny scream of panic left my mouth even though there was no need to. The bullet was still in one of the chambers. He dropped the gun to the table, looking at it intently.

As I moved to take it again, Tommy spoke. "This is boring. Have you not got another way to have your fun that will make it less mind numbingly dull?"

I gawped at his words, looking from him to the Russian and back again. Was he seriously trying to make it worse for us? Petrov considered what he had said though and scratched his temple with the end of the gun in his hand.

"And vot vould you suggest."

"Personally if I was using this form of torture, I would have her shoot at me. And vice versa. Think of how much more painful that would be. Killing the one you care about the most." Tommy smiled maliciously.

Again, my mouth fell open as I tried my hardest for him to see my 'What the fuck are you doing?' face. He merely smirked, looking down at the table like he knew something that I didn't.

A grotesque smile spread across Petrov's face, and he scraped the gun across the table. "Pick it up."

I picked it up, placing the barrel to my temple once again. Tommy's eyes narrowed as his fingers flexed on the table and he moved as if he was about to stand. But Petrov spoke, making him remain seated.

"Oh no, no, no Izabella." Petrov came to stand behind Tommy, positioning his own gun to the back of his head. "You vill have new target zis time."

My eyes widened as my stomach plummeted. He was deranged enough to go with Tommy's suggestion. Tommy had got exactly what he wanted. Petrov wanted to play by different rules. To have the gun pointed at my own head was one thing but to turn it around on Tommy was completely different. The probability of killing myself was nothing compared to possibly killing the man I was falling in love with. Because I was. I was falling in love with the fucking idiot, if I wasn't already completely there. And he had just signed his own death certificate if the bullet was in the right position.

Tears stung my eyes, blurring my vision. "I can't."

Petrov dug the gun harder into Tommy's head, making him lean forward slightly. "You do it, or I vill."

"Please." Shaking my head, tears started falling down my cheek. "Please don't make me do this. I will do it to myself but not him."

Tommy's smirk died as he saw the torment slowly running down my face.

"I like it ven zey cry." Petrov chuckled. "But I iz losing patience. Take your turn Izabella"

Sniffing, I took the gun from my own head and took aim between Tommy's eyes.

"I'm sorry." Cocking the revolver, my hands trembled, matching my voice.

Slowly Tommy nodded his head. It was barely noticeable, but he was telling me it was ok. That everything would be ok. But it wasn't. Nothing was ok with what I was about to do.

Taking one more look into his eyes, I breathed in deeply and held it.

I was ready.

The sound of the gun fire rang through my ears and specs of red glistened on the metal table in front of me.

He was dead.

Chapter 38

Tommy's blue eyes were still fixed on mine. The man behind him stared too. Mouth open and eyes lifeless. A second later his body fell to the floor with a thud and Tommy was up from his seat and across the table.

Snatching the gun from my hand, he slammed it on the table and took me in his arms, bringing me to the floor with him. I sobbed into his chest, clutching on to his top like it had been him I had just killed.

"W- Why did you do that? Why did you get him to change the rules?" I choked out but my words were muffled by his chest.

"I'm sorry baby." He stroked my hair, holding me tighter with his other hand. "I'm so sorry. But you did brilliantly. You did so fucking well."

"How did you know?" I lifted my head to look at him.

Wiping the tears from my cheeks, he cupped both sides of my face. "I saw the bullet. When I put it back on the table, I saw the bullet in the chamber. I knew it would be the next shot."

I hiccupped another sniffle. "But what if I didn't shoot him instead. What if I didn't chance it?"

"Then I would be dead."

He would have been, and I would have been next because there was no way Petrov would have let me live still. I took a risk aiming for him instead. If there was no bullet in the chamber, I could have possibly passed it off as my trembling hands forced my aim to falter but that was a long shot.

But there was a bullet and it very nearly had Tommy's name on it.

Throwing my arms around his neck, I crashed my lips into his. This fucking man was going to kill me one day and it was going to be from a broken heart. Kissing me back roughly, he held me as tight as he possibly could until I had to break away to gasp for air.

Slapping my hand across his chest, I glared up at him then climbed off his lap. "Don't ever do that to me again. Do you understand?" I stood up and he followed with a typical mischievous grin. "I mean it Tommy. That fucking hurt. I would have rather taken that bullet than go through the thought that I might be killing you."

Before I could move away, his arm wrapped round my waist, and he pulled me back to him. "Careful, one would think that you are already falling in love with me."

"Wishful fucking thinking, arsehole." I huffed and pushed myself away again, swiping away the last of the tears.

Tommy smiled to himself then walked over to Petrov's body. Taking the gun he checked the clip to see how many bullets there was. "We've got to get moving. That big fucker will probably be back soon, and we don't know how many more there are out there."

He nodded towards the door then moved Petrov's jacket to the side to check if there were any other weapons. Huffing in disappointment, he stood back up and held the gun out to me.

"I don't need it." I frowned, refusing to take it.

"Just take the gun Isabella."

Ignoring his order completely, I crossed the room to the

door and looked out through the tiny window. There was no one outside but that was obvious. If there had have been, they would have come in as soon as the shot was fired. But it didn't explain why Igor hadn't returned yet.

Tommy came up beside me, pressing the gun against my hand. "I'm better at fighting than you so just take the gun."

"You're also better with a gun."

"Fuck sake." He rolled his eyes, exasperated at my continued refusal and opened the door. "Stay behind me then."

Smiling at my little victory I followed him into the hallway. "Do you know how many there are?"

"No, even though they didn't drug me, they did blindfold me. I think I know where we are though."

He stopped, slapping his hand across my chest and pushed me against the wall. As he peered round the corner, I heard what had made him stop. Voices. Two different voices. Both were Russian. Before I could register what he was about to do, he whipped out, shooting both men. As soon as I heard their bodies fall to the floor, I poked my head round to see.

Seeing Igor on the floor, I groaned. "I wanted to kill him." Pouting, I walked over and kicked him in the side.

"I'll let you take the next one." Bending down, Tommy started searching the two men. "Here." Tossing me a hunter's knife, I caught the handle rather impressively. Then he started rummaging in his pockets for something else and pulled out a set of car keys.

"Robbing them now?"

"They're mine."

They had brought his car here. That was definitely a good thing.

Shouting came from behind the double doors at the end of the hall and Tommy ran forward, he crouched, hidden so they couldn't see through the window. I kneeled down beside him, watching him check again how many bullets he had left.

Rising slowly, I looked through the small pane of glass. Seven men were cautiously stepping towards us, checking every room that they passed.

"How many are there?"

"About four or five." I lied, shrugging like it was nothing.

He stood up to check himself. "There's fucking seven Isabella."

"Yeh but only four have guns." I defended my answer and he kneeled back down. "How many bullets have you got."

"Four."

"You can take them." Giving him a smile of confidence, he rolled his eyes.

"You severely overestimate my skills."

"Can you not take them?"

Flashing me a wicked grin with eyes shining with pleasure, he gave me a little wink. "Of course baby."

Standing back up, he kicked the doors open. Four shots sounded and four bodies fell. Just as shots fired back, Tommy slammed his back against the wall, protecting himself against them.

"You could have shot the ones with the guns." I shouted over the noise.

Snarling at my attitude, he looked at the knife in my hand. "Pass me that."

"No." frowning at him, I held it closer to my chest. " I want to use it."

"You can't fight."

"No, I can't fight you." Grinning I slowly pushed myself away from the wall. "I can fight them."

Standing in the line of fire, I flung the hunters knife through the air, hitting the one that was waving the gun about erratically. It struck him in the skull, and I smiled as he stood for a second then fell back. The other man with the gun was momentarily distracted at what had just happened, giving me enough time to run at him.

Just as I reached him, he regained his concentration and fired in my direction. The bullet flew past, narrowly missing. Launching my tiny body at his stocky frame, I didn't so much as nudge him. But I did manage to grab the arm that held on to his weapon. Clinging on to him, he spun me around, trying to shake me off but I grabbed his hand and bit down.

Crying out, he dropped it and I fell to the floor too. I reached for the gun just as he landed on top of me, clasping his hand around mine. My finger slipped on the trigger and a shot fired. Tommy swore and I looked up to see him glaring down at me, another guy's head gripped in his arm, smacking out at him to let go. On his other arm, red was dribbling down from a graze that could have only been done by the bullet.

Bringing the gun back round, I shot the guy on top of me in the neck, spraying myself in thick, warm gore. He staggered back off me, grasping at the wound as the blood pissed out of it. I stood back up, panting.

The sound of bones cracking came from behind me and then Tommy was by my side again.

"How's your arm?" I asked, still looking at the bloke writhing about on the floor.

"It's a graze." Turning me round to face him, he took my chin in his hand. "If it was any other situation, I would accuse you of doing it on purpose."

"Maybe I did." I smiled mischievously. Stepping up on my tip toes, I flung my hand to the back of his neck and pulled him down to my level to kiss him hard. He returned the favour, wrapping his arms around my waist and groaning into my mouth.

"When we've killed everyone in this place, I'm going to fuck you before we leave."

Giggling, I slapped my hand across his chest and pulled away. "The fact that all this killing is getting you going should be worrying."

"No," He roughly pulled me back. "Seeing blood

dripping down your body and watching you unmercifully kill men is what is making me hard." Chewing on my lip, I looked up at him through my lashes. "You are a beautifully violent woman Isabella, and you are exactly what I want and need."

His next kiss was brutal, engulfing me in his heat that rippled through my body. Gasping for the air that he had sucked out, I withdrew from him. He pushed my hair behind my ears, searching my eyes for something as his mouth opened to say something else but then closed again.

In the distance, more voices could be heard. Tommy grabbed the gun from one of the fallen bodies and aimed it at the door that the voices were coming from. At first, I couldn't place the language. It wasn't Russian but it was familiar. It was too quiet and fast for me to make sense of though.

Tommy took a step forward, getting ready to fire and then it hit me.

"Tommy, wait." I pulled on his arm, just as the door opened.

Matteo strolled into the room, gun in hand. Nico was with him and the other guy from the game's night, but I couldn't remember his name.

"Fuck." Tommy lowered his weapon but didn't look any more pleased to see them than what Matteo looked.

His eyes wandered around the room, grazing over the dead men then fixed on me with a hint of a smirk. "Isabella Moretti."

"Matteo." It was said in warning as Tommy stepped in front of me protectively.

Matteo's eyes switched from me to him, the smirk falling as his lip quivered into a snarl. "You tried to keep her from me. Yet dangled her right before my eyes."

"I didn't know you were looking for someone until your sister shared that information."

"You knew she was someone of importance?"

"I couldn't be certain."

"But you had some idea. That is why you said she was your wife. Threw me off for a while."

Tommy grabbed my arm, pulling me further behind him. "You're not taking her Matteo. She's mine and she always will be."

"But she's not truly yours is she." His dark grin matched the darkness of his eyes. "Not when she's been promised to another. Not when she's been promised to me."

"What?" I choked out, coming out from behind Tommy. I looked between the two men. "What is he going on about?"

Tommy was glaring at Matteo, like he wanted him to spontaneously combust. His jaw twitched as he was thinking about what to do but I wanted answers and I wasn't prepared to be ignored.

"What the fuck is he going on about Tommy?"

I looked back at Matteo, not getting any words from the man that I was meant to trust. He held out his hand for me to take. "Come principessa. Let me take you home."

"No," I scoffed, refusing his hand. "I'm not going anywhere with you." Tommy's lips twitched in satisfaction. "And I'm not going anywhere with you either until you give me some answers."

"What about me Bella?" That voice. A ghost from the past. "Will you come with me?"

The Italians parted, leaving enough room for another man to step forward. My throat began to close up as tears welled in my eyes. My chest tightened painfully as the air seemed too thin around me.

Nothing made sense. Nothing at all. But I still managed to say his name weakly.

"Antonio."

"Hello little sister."

Chapter 39

Tommy

The first time I saw her, when she turned around and looked up at me with those big fucking green eyes, I knew I had to have her, even if it was just to play with. Isabella was beautiful. And not in a try hard way. She was natural. I still remember how she looked that night.

Her dark curls fell down her back and all I could think about was of how good it would feel to tangle my fingers through it. She had very little make up on, if any. But her warm sun kissed skin was radiant, a natural glow to her cheeks as well as the glow from the fire. She wore ripped jeans and a man's hoodie that was miles too big, covering up the curves I later found out she had.

She looked too sweet, too innocent to go to a school like this. Even the way she spoke to us that night, there was a corruptible softness to her voice. I wanted to see what she was capable of. I wanted to test her, see if the boys and I could break her. Having her cry and begging us to stop would have been music to my ears but she, of course, surprised me.

The first night when we took her, I had every intention of making her break and then taking her back to Maddy a complete mess. Then fix her, mould her into my perfect toy. We weren't going to kill her, not like the others. Their death certificates were already signed. But Isabella? Isabella was going to be some fun.

That was until she showed us how strong she really was. Freeing herself in a smart way, unlike that pathetic military lad had done. He was meant to be trained for that type of situation, but he failed and that cost him his life. As for the girl. I don't usually like killing women, but she had sold out Charlie, getting him killed at an exchange. She got what she deserved too.

But Isabella, she had freed herself and managed to find a weapon. Then she had managed to defy my three cousins and escape. Granted I had let her run out but what can I say. The little maniac had impressed me. And continued to do so by stealing Archie's motor and giving me the finger.

But it was the moment Callum told me that she had come back. That was the moment I realised I had to make her mine and that no one else could have her. Because that girl was going to be the challenge I needed in my life. She was the girl I was already falling for and hearing that she had come back erased the disappointment that I didn't realise I was feeling at the thought she was gone for good. Not that she would have been gone for long. I would have found her again.

Of course, I was engaged. I still had stuff I needed to sort out with getting rid of that slut and I still wanted to find out more about my Isabella. As every day passed, she intrigued me more. Her refusal to bow down to me like everyone else at the school only made my want for her escalate. Her blatant disregard for my orders made the blood rush to my cock and my fingers itch to be wrapped round her neck. Her attitude, her funny little remarks, the way she made my blood boil with pent up rage. Every little thing made me fall that much harder.

And her smiles. The ones she shared with her friends and occasionally my cousins. The way her eyes sparkled like fucking emeralds when she laughed. Fuck I wanted it all. And not just the good bits. I wanted her anger, her frustration, her stubbornness, her jealousy. I wanted everything she had, and I wanted it all for myself.

And I finally had it all. I had her.

Now, I watched as she slipped away from me. Her green eyes shimmered with the tears that filled them, gazing at the brother she thought was dead. And I knew he wasn't. I had found out the truth over the past couple of weeks. Ever since she told me that it was the Russians that had come after her family, I had been searching for answers.

They looked like each other. Same eyes, same hair, same plump lips. His nose was crooked though. Probably having been broken a few times and not set back into place before healing. He was also taller than her but not by much, making him shorter than me.

Antonio held out his arms to her and she slowly collapsed into them, sobbing enough that we could all hear her. Her body shook against his, but he held onto her tightly, gripping her blood-stained clothes in his hands and nuzzling his nose into her hair.

"Shh boo." Boo, a nickname he had called her when they were kids. "I'm here now. I'm going to look after you."

He was her older brother; it was his obligatory right to protect his little sister, but that didn't stop the jealousy that was pooling in the pit of my stomach.

She lifted her head off his chest, the blood that had speckled her face was now smeared across his white shirt. "How? I don't understand."

"I'll explain everything soon Bella. But first, I'm going to take you home."

"Back to the school?" She asked, stepping back away from him and back to my side, nudging against my arm. Pride swelled in my bitter heart.

"No. Home." He repeated.

Isabella shook her head, and I slowly snaked my hand around her waist, still gripping the gun tightly in my other hand. Matteo glanced down at the weapon then back up to Isabella. I knew what he was thinking, and it was the exact same thing as I was. He wanted to protect what he had been promised and I wanted her safe with me and away from them all.

"Principessa." Even I knew enough Italian to know he was calling her princess. "Come home with us and we will start again."

"Don't call me that. I'm not your princess. And I'm not going anywhere with any of you." I could hear the wariness in her voice. Her hand reached to my hand that was gripping her waist and she intertwined her fingers through mine as she leant further into me. Her sudden vulnerability only heightened my need to guard her.

"We're going back to the school. You can follow us in the car. Then you can discuss things when Isabella has rested." It was the only bargain I could think of to get her away from here safely.

"My sister will be coming with me, Tommy, isn't it?"

I glared at her brother. There was no way I was letting her out of my sight. "You're on my turf now Antonio. Isabella is a part of my family. I'm not going to let her go easily."

Matteo stepped forward and I felt Isabella tense. Antonio held up his hand though, stopping him.

"Do you love her?"

I frowned and Matteo even gave him a puzzled look.

"I do." It was an easy answer, but I hadn't actually told her yet. I was going to, several times, but every time something stopped me. I knew she felt the same way, even if she hadn't admitted it to herself. I knew the moment she came back into my arms and away from her brother's. I could feel her eyes on me, but I didn't look at her, I stayed focused on him.

A cruel grin twisted on his face. The same one Isabella

sometimes wore but while on her it was alluring, on him it looked ugly.

"Why didn't you tell her I was still alive then."

Fuck.

Before I could answer, Isabella backed out of my arms. She frowned as she stepped further back, and the warmth of her body ebbed away. "You knew?"

Of course I knew. I found out everything. Petrov didn't just go after people without a reason. I just had to find out that particular reason. Finding out that she spoke Italian wasn't really a big giveaway, but it soon made sense. The Italians being in town looking for someone also didn't seem relevant at the time. It wasn't until my father and I did some research and found out that the new boss was called Antonio. It seemed like a coincidence at first, but Callum helped me confirm my suspicions.

The night Isabella was in Williams's office. Callum had gone there to find what I needed. Granted he had got a little closer to my girl than I would have liked but when she left to fight with me, he got the information he needed. Her birth certificate. Isabella Sofia Moretti.

After some more asking around I found out it was in fact her they had been looking for and the new boss was her brother. He hadn't died. I wasn't sure how it all happened or how he had managed to survive but he did.

"Isabella-"

"You knew and you didn't tell me."

I was going to tell her. I was going to tell her tonight while we walked down the pier at the beach. That was my plan before it all went tits up. Would she believe me though if I tried to explain that now?

"I'll tell you everything I know, just come back with me." I held out my hand to her, but she shook her head, betrayal in her eyes. After having her walls come down for me finally, I watched as they slowly reformed before my eyes, brick by brick. I hated the sight and that I had caused it.

My heart thudded against my ribs as I silently prayed to a god that I didn't believe in that she would just take my still outstretched hand. She didn't. She just backed away further to her brother's side.

Matteo smirked in satisfaction, making the pain of seeing her choose her side turn to rage. I lifted the gun and pointed it towards his head. While his smirk faded, I wasn't that surprised that one formed on my face. His glare pinned on me, but he didn't raise his own weapon.

Nico and Enzo unholstered their guns, both directing them at me. I wasn't thinking rationally and that tiny voice that was telling me to lower my weapon was disregarded. The gun was loaded, I was a quick shot. But was I quicker than them? It didn't matter. I would shoot him. Just him.

Isabella ran forward, placing herself between the gun and Matteo. "Tommy, don't do this."

I glanced down at her, taking my eyes off my target just for a second. "You're not going with him Isabella."

"They will shoot you."

That was true. I could see it in Matteo's grin. Even if she wanted to come with me, they wouldn't allow it. I would just have to kill them all. Including her brother.

"I'm not coming with you Tommy. You can either accept that now or die trying to get me to."

"Isabella."

She reached for the gun, lowering it and I let her. I couldn't force her, not yet. Not while I was out manned. Even if I did grab her and run, I didn't know where my car was. She would probably fight against me and there was a risk that she would get hurt in the crossfire.

So I let her lower my gun. Nico and Enzo kept theirs raised.

"We should just kill him now, save the trouble of him being a pain later."

Isabella's deathly glare hit Enzo before I could even raise the gun again. "Hurt him at all and I will snap your neck."

He looked like he wanted to laugh at her threat and looked at Antonio for his order. Little did they know what a sweet, little psycho my girl was, and she would do what she promised. With his arms crossed, Antonio shook his head and both guard dogs lowered their weapons.

Isabella stepped closer; her voice was low so only I could hear. "I'm going with them. You will not follow me, and you will not look for me. I'm not your little claimed one anymore. Whatever this was is over now."

"This is only over Isabella when I say it is." I grinned, tilting her chin up and running my thumb over her bottom lip.

She glanced down at my hand then back up, meeting my gaze. "Goodbye Tommy."

All I could do was watch her as she walked away with the men I was going to kill.

Because I was going to get her back.

This wasn't goodbye Isabella. This was see you soon.

ABOUT THE AUTHOR

Nicole Dennis is a mother to three children and a wife.
She lives in a small town in England.
From an early age she used to write fictional stories and
then revisited this passion again once her children had
grown a little to give her the time to.

Printed in Great Britain
by Amazon

18451989R00235